I HATE SUMMER
HT PANTU

Dreamspinner Press

Published by
DREAMSPINNER PRESS

5032 Capital Circle SW, Suite 2, PMB# 279, Tallahassee, FL 32305-7886 USA
http://www.dreamspinnerpress.com/

This is a work of fiction. Names, characters, places, and incidents either are the product of author imagination or are used fictitiously, and any resemblance to actual persons, living or dead, business establishments, events, or locales is entirely coincidental.

ISBN: 978-1-62798-867-4
Digital ISBN: 978-1-62798-868-1
Library of Congress Control Number: 2014943211
First Edition August 2014

Printed in the United States of America
∞
This paper meets the requirements of
ANSI/NISO Z39.48-1992 (Permanence of Paper).

1—DOG

THE DAY was a beautiful one: the sky was that intense shade of blue that was almost painful to look at, there were a pair of white clouds idling their way across the expanse, and the sun was a hazy corn-yellow circle. I was driving through the Peak District, and under my control, the car wound through the narrow lanes. The landscape that slipped past was stunning: all shades of red and brown and ochre even at this time of the year. The few hints of green were rare and those that there were, were the deepest jade of wet moss.

"I hate summer," I complained to no one but myself, my thick Yorkshire accent matching the scenery perfectly as I drove through the rolling hills with my window down. Those words were my mantra for the four months that seem to send everyone else into a state of permanent bliss and happiness. It's beautiful, I get it, but last summer, when it didn't stop raining, was probably the best summer of my life.

There are several reasons for this, and my skin is one of them. My English-Rose skin is a bloody nightmare. Pale and interesting it may be, but I am one of those "lucky" people that can burn come rain or shine. Even though I didn't plan to spend more than five minutes outside of the car for the bulk of the day I was already wearing factor fifty, and just to prove my point, my arm was starting to pick up a hint of red where the sun was streaming through the open window. I can tell you that as an outdoors kind of guy it is an actual pain in the arse to put suncream on every fricking morning.

There were other reasons, too, mostly stupid leftovers from when I was a kid. Things like: having my birthday during the summer holidays was enough to make me hate them and living on a farm completely isolated from everything except the next-door farm—ten miles away—and a local pub—only six miles, but who cares about that when you're a kid.

I had got back from Canada yesterday, and this year I spent my birthday in the middle of nowhere with a few friends from uni—which was great. Plus, clearly I could drive, and these days I live in York for university. So usually when I headed home, it was with that warm glow that came from knowing I was going to see my family and was shortly about to eat my own body weight in meat products and roast dinner.

As I turned my car into the driveway of my parents' farm sometime before midday, there was no warm glow, and there was no anticipation of meat and delicious roast dinners. It wasn't because I was jet-lagged as hell—which I was—and it wasn't because I was exhausted from staying up until three this morning fucking Ashlie—which I had done; fricking hell, that boy was insatiable. I had no warm glow, because the reason I was heading home this time was the main reason I hated summer: family holidays.

The last time I'd gone I'd been sixteen. I'd got out of it for four summers, carefully avoiding being free for the customary ten days at the start of August by getting jobs with arsehole bosses and rubbish hours, getting jobs abroad, and just generally getting jobs. I'm twenty-one now and this was probably my last summer as a student, so I'd taken a flexible job, organized to go on holiday with my friends, and foolishly assumed I was old enough not to be forced into a family holiday. Especially one they all knew I despised. Clearly that had been a mistake.

When my parents found out I'd been given time off to go to Canada, they had assumed I could get time off to go to Scotland. I'd told them I couldn't get more holiday so close to returning from Canada, and they had called my boss to check. So I'd told them outright that I didn't want to go. I could still hear my mum's feigned smile down the phone when she had gently suggested, "Well, love, if ye dun fancy coming to Scotland, then maybe I dun fancy cooking ye any roast dinners for a while." Seriously, she makes the absolute best roast dinner you have ever tasted.

As I pulled to a stop in the farmyard, I reminded myself that it would be worth it. But part of me was starting to wish I'd just taken the hit.

In the middle of the yard, my parents' 4x4 was currently overflowing with supplies. The trailer was already hitched to the back and piled high with bikes. I didn't have time to switch off the ignition before my door was tugged open. Two balls of fur launched themselves onto my knee, followed by a much bigger one, and then a pair of arms was thrown around my neck. Jorja ignored the dog and cats that had already attacked me and proceeded to try her best to throttle me affectionately.

"Idrys!" my sister squeaked into my ear.

"Hey, Jorja," I returned her greeting, my voice strained as I struggled to breathe properly under her hug.

She eventually pulled away, but not far. She took my hair in her hands, squealing once again, this time in jealousy. She tugged a handful in affection, but still caused me to wince.

"I want yer hair!" she lamented as she hauled my locks toward her and pressed her head in against mine to cover her dusky blonde hair with the shimmering strands that adorned my head. "Cut it off and give it to me right now."

I chuckled. "Sorry, need it for work."

My hair was also blond, in the same way that you could call gold— yellow or silver—gray. My sister's hair was a lovely natural ashen blonde color inherited from our Swedish father. Whereas mine looked like it'd been bleached and then washed through with a strawberry toner like some mutated combination of my dad's Scandinavian roots and my mum's beautiful fiery ginger. I generally kept it short because being almost six three with ivory skin and eyes the color of the inside of a glacier makes me stand out enough without adding my weird-ass hair to the mix. But my well-paying and flexible summer job required it to stay at the highly androgynous shoulder-length mess it currently was.

I reminded myself how much the job paid as I pressed Jorja gently out of my way and tied my hair back off my face. I let the cats and the dog sort themselves out as I unpacked myself from my little three-door car. Jorja launched herself at me again, and she had to stand on her tiptoes to hang herself round my neck.

"Still growing I see," a gruff voice mocked from the other side of the yard. I gave Theo a wave as I unlatched Jorja's hands from my neck, only to have her tuck herself under my arm instead. Theo lived "next door" and had been my best friend since we'd been old enough to make the ten-mile journey between our homes on bikes. The dog was a collie called Tess, it was his, and she'd returned to his side and was now lying with her tongue lolling out like she hadn't just been part of the greeting party that had left my skinny denim shorts and white T-shirt covered in fur.

"Can't stop me these days," I mocked myself as my accent lengthened the vowels and wove them through the sweaty midday air that hung with the faint aromas of home that were so familiar: animals, shit, dust, mud, heather, and wind.

My height was a long-standing joke, although prior to my sixteenth Christmas it had been because I was short. Then I grew a foot in six months and eventually settled at my current height. I detached myself from Jorja and went to give Theo a brief man hug/slap.

"How's things?" I asked. "Ye need me t' stay? I don't mind if ye need a hand. It's a big farm for ye by yerself?" While we were away, Theo was going to be looking after my parents' farm on top of helping at his mum and dad's place. He'd done it before, but I really hoped that he'd take pity on me this time.

Theo just laughed at me. He knew why I didn't want to go.

"I dun think ye'd even know how t' help these days, city boy." He gave me another clap round the arm as my dad came out of the house.

"I was starting to wonder." My dad eyed me disapprovingly. He was Swedish, and his English accent was still the almost perfect Queen's English he'd learned as a child, despite living surrounded by thick northern accents for the last thirty years.

I shot him a wave and a smile.

"Sorry, Dad, traffic." Which was half the truth. The other half was that I'd woken up late and then Ashlie had looked too gorgeous to leave without a parting gift. I tried not to smile at the memory of him moaning beneath me and begging me not to go. I'd been in Canada for two weeks, and now I was going to be in Scotland for ten days with a family of beautiful yet massively homophobic people, and I'd only had one night to make up for almost a month away from my "friends."

Dad grumbled something under his breath as he proceeded to strap down another plastic box in the trailer with the bikes.

"Put your stuff in the boot and take a piss, we're off in ten minutes," my dad added at a more audible level. I rolled my eyes at my dad and looked back round at Theo, pleading with him, but he just shook his head.

"Ye *like* camping, Ide," he said, then dropped his voice. "And it's been what? Four? Five years? Yer adults now, t'will be fine." I grimaced at him and pressed my fingers into my eye sockets before wiping them back over my head and through my messy hair.

Theo plonked his hand onto the top of my head. "And if there's nae else, these days yer probably big enough to just twat him one." He dropped his hand and squeezed my upper arm. "Look, muscle and everything," he mocked lightly.

Theo had a point. Last time I'd been on one of these family camping trips I was dead-on five foot, and my arms were the size of an average person's wrist. I'd always been stronger than I looked and I'd usually return a few bruises, but inevitably, it had been me that came off worse. These days I was tall, and while I wouldn't exactly call me anything other than lanky, the little muscle I did have was toned and as strong as I could get it.

"Seven minutes, Idrys!" my dad called from inside the house.

"Ye gonna be around for a couple o' days when ye all get back?" asked Theo.

"Yeah, I'll text ye, let ye know I'm still alive."

I waved Theo a temporary good-bye and turned back to my car; Jorja had already unloaded my tent and rucksack and was fixing the front tire back on my bike so it could be loaded into the trailer. I held the frame still and she squatted to tighten up the bolts.

"Ye still stringing that poor guy along?" I said quietly to her. My best friend had been in love with my sister for as long as I could remember, and I had absolutely no issues with it; in fact, I thought it would be about damn time. Jorja, on the other hand, had an endless list of reasons why they shouldn't date, the latest being because she was away at uni. The only reason I *hadn't* heard was that she didn't like him back, which was also the only part that Theo paid any attention to. Jorja's lack of commitment either way meant that his dating record was almost as bad as mine—okay, it was much better than mine, but by normal standards it was low.

"That ain't none of yer business, Idrys."

"Yeah it is: he's my best friend, I like him more than ye, so I want ye to stop being such a tease."

"Oi!" She straightened and slapped me lightly over the arm. "That hurts 'cause I know yer not lying." She stuck her bottom lip out momentarily, then lifted the bike easily and dropped it into the back of the trailer. "And just cause I'm not a whore like ye does not make me a tease," she mocked lightly.

"Three minutes."

"*Shutup*, Dad!" Jorja shouted right back with a roll of her eyes as she helped me secure the bike. "Come on, then, best use the bathroom or he'll leave us behind."

"Maybe I'll dawdle, then," I mused absently but followed her anyway. My sister shot me an arch look over her shoulder.

"Stop being such a pansy. It's been ages since ye saw them and they're really not that bad these days." She had a funny smirk on her face that said she knew something and was purposefully keeping it from me. I didn't give her the satisfaction of asking. Jorja and Theo were probably right: it had been five years, and I was sure as hell different so there was no reason that the holiday wouldn't be.

"Idrys, love," my mum cooed as we came into the kitchen. She was hastily packing a cool box with driving supplies. My dad was standing behind her, and I was sure my mum found the way he tapped his foot really helpful. She gave me an absent one-armed hug—her fiery head just about reached my shoulders—as she used her other hand to fish something out of the fridge. "How was yer drive, love?"

"Hey, Mam. It were fine. I got stuck behind a couple o' tourists who slowed to twenty for every goddamn bend." There were a lot of bends on the roads around here.

"Oh goodness," Mum said sympathetically and paused for a moment to tighten her hug.

"Grace!" my dad barked, causing my mum to jump. "We are now late leaving. Can't you ask him this in the car?"

"Oh yes, love, sorry." She grinned absently and let me go to finish the last of our packing. I went to the bathroom and then sat in the back of the car where Jorja was already waiting.

I feel I should clarify. My dad isn't some kind of monster; he just stresses about traveling, he likes punctuality, and in case you don't know, the Swedish aren't renowned for their affectionate personalities.

As soon as Mum pulled her door shut, my dad's shoulders relaxed and a smile slipped across his lips. "Let's have a great holiday, everyone," he said, and he caught my eye in the rearview mirror, finally shooting me a smile. "It's nice to have the whole family together again."

PEOPLE THINK that bleak and beautiful are two mutually exclusive things. They're wrong, or at least they are in my opinion. I grew up with bleak. Believe me when I tell you that the UK doesn't get much bleaker than the Peak District on a wet winter's day; it doesn't get much more beautiful either. You just have to know what you're looking for. The place me and my family were going to spend the next ten days in was one of those bleak, beautiful places in the depths of Scotland.

The campsite we pulled into sometime around seven that evening was tiny. We'd dropped off what was described as the "main road" in the directions—read: single-lane tarmac track with passing places—into a valley that we drove up until even the gravel gave way and turned into a grass track. Dad stopped to unlock the gate slung across the way with two half-tumbled stonewalls on either side. We locked it behind us and drove the last ten minutes up to the campsite bouncing in our seats while Jorja and me kept an eye on the trailer.

The campsite was half-full, but this shouldn't give you the wrong idea: there were two tents up. The sight of them made my heart sink just that little bit further.

"Oh, Jerry and Samantha are already here." My mum beamed.

"Cheer up, sunshine," my sister whispered. "Yer the one that *likes* camping, remember?" I nodded and tried to drag the scowl from my face as we were jostled for the final hundred yards of the track.

The campsite was sheltered on one side by a sparse selection of struggling trees that looked like they'd been planted with good intention but little hope. A couple of them were doing okay in the harsh surrounds that were otherwise only covered with heather and low-lying willow. There was a pipe sticking up randomly through the ground with a tap on the end, so there was "running water." I've been to places like this many a time. In fact, I've spent a few summers working in places like this, and I knew that the water was probably from a pipe buried into the side of a nearby stream.

The car stopped. I sighed again, gave myself a mental shake, and opened the door. I instantly regretted dressing for the "balmy" southern climate of home. I had on skinny knee-length shorts and a fitted tee, which had been fine in the air-conditioned car and might plausibly have been fine at midday here. The sun was still up, but it was definitely evening, and a bitter wind cut through my cotton top. I'm not a heat person, but that doesn't mean I like windburn any better. I tugged my windbreaker from the back as I slid out of the car. Then I groaned as I sank up to my ankles in a puddle that immersed my canvas Toms completely in sludgy brown mud.

"Fricking hell." I'd packed those shoes for the sole purpose of driving home—I hadn't intended to even wear them again until we were safely back in relative civilization. My much more practical waterproof/mudproof/great-for-everything-except-driving trainers were right next to me, and I'd just forgotten to change them over.

I heard someone snigger and my heart actually sank into my stomach.

Great, just fricking great. That was exactly the first impression that I wanted to make. After five years, I really wanted the Jackson family's first sight of me to be cursing about standing in a damned puddle. I'd probably waded through more shit and mud and spent more nights in a tent in the past five years than they had cumulatively. I didn't care about mud; I just didn't want my one good pair of shoes to look like the rest of my pairs.

With another groan, I jumped back into the car and chucked yet another pair of ruined shoes into the footwell as I changed into my more suitable footwear. Mum, Dad, and Jorja had all got out and hurried across to the waiting Jacksons. I watched for a moment from the safety of the car.

We'd been going on our summer holidays with Samantha and Jerry Jackson since I could remember. Apparently they met my parents in a campsite when I was three, they'd hit it off, and since their—then only, now eldest—children were the same age they'd agreed to go together the next year for moral support. That had turned into every summer since. Samantha and Jerry had three sons: Josh was fifteen, Vince was seventeen, and Trystan was six months older than me, six precious months he had lorded over me for thirteen agonizing summer holidays. This family was the reason I hated summer, and in particular, this man, Trystan-bloody-Jackson. The golden boy who had started growing when he was fourteen, he was always faster, stronger, taller, smarter, braver. I cannot explain to you the number of times that I have wanted to throttle that boy/man.

I slid out of the car with yet another weary sigh. I knew putting it off was not going to make it go away or go any easier. I let my head drop to one side and gave a wary smile as I jogged over through the mud.

"Hey, guys."

"Oh, Idrys? *Look—at—you*," Samantha cooed as she wrapped her hands around my upper arms, examining me for a moment with a look of startled awe, which is not an unusual reaction from people who haven't seen me for a while. I am, after all, over a foot taller than the last time she saw me. I've always had a unique kind of look, but I'm aware it's more noticeable now that I'm an adult, and that it is not at all diminished by my currently too-long hair. Someone asked me if I was albino once.

Samantha was dark haired like her children. She had a warm smile and dark sparkling eyes and had always been my favorite Jackson—mostly because she broke up rather than encouraged fights. "You look so well and so *tall*. I can't believe it's you."

"Yeah, I finally got my growth spurt." I laughed lightly and turned to shake Jerry Jackson's hand. He was just the same: tall, stern, and faintly disapproving. He was also dressed entirely in this season's most hyped outdoor gear. I stifled a sigh because I knew what he was wearing was worth at least a grand and there would be numerous outfits like that waiting to be worn.

"Aren't you cold, lad?" He glanced down at my bare legs, and I shrugged. Jerry was a homophobe, and he generally spoke to me as little as possible. When he did, it was always with belittling comments like that one or to justify why his children's *playing* had left bruises on me.

"Not really," I answered with a shrug. My lightweight jacket kept off the wind and that did me just fine.

"*Eeeed* doesn't feel the cold, remember, Dad?" the youngest Jackson chimed in, stretching out the start of my name comically as he'd done when he'd been a kid and couldn't say it properly. Josh shot me a grin and held his hand out. Last time I'd seen Josh, I'd been sixteen and he'd been ten, and we'd been about the same height. Now he was about five nine and at that odd point where he didn't quite look like a man or a child. We shared a mutual grimace as I was obliged to give the standard comments on his height.

"Well, it can snow up here even in summer. You better have something other than jeans and cotton T-shirts. Cotton kills, you know," Jerry said, pulling my attention back round to him and away from the unashamed appraisal in Josh's chocolate-brown eyes—which was definitely unexpected.

"Yeah, I know," I said to Jerry. I resisted the urge to roll my eyes and tell him exactly how much more I knew about what he was talking about than he did, but I was almost glad for the distraction and a reason to look away from Jerry's rather too-gorgeous-for-his-own-good youngest son.

"How you doing, Idrys?" Vince asked. I shook the middle Jackson's hand and managed to smile back. Vince was about six foot and handsome enough, but there a was gleam of distaste in the brown eyes he shared with his brother—he was asking out of ingrained politeness rather than interest.

"Just got back from Canada yesterday, so I'm a bit jet-lagged, t'be honest," I answered, hoping it would give me an excuse to put my tent up and retire early.

"What were you up to there?" the eldest son asked.

I didn't let myself sigh as I turned to face the final Jackson. Have I mentioned how bloody good-looking he is? No? Well that's because it pisses me off. I could deal with everything else, but fricking hell, why did he have to look like that?

"Trys," I said by way of a greeting and shook his hand briefly. "Camping, walking, biking, ye know?"

"Doesn't that mess up your shoes?" he mocked.

I ground my teeth, flicked him the finger, and ignored my mum's outraged bleating as I headed back to the car to get my tent.

"*Idrys*," my sister called as she hurried to catch up with me.

"He fricking started it," I muttered through gritted teeth. I was irritated at him and at myself for getting so pissed so quickly.

"It was a joke, Ide. And yer *did* sound like a pansy when yer got out of the car."

I chucked my head back and stared up into the cloudless blue sky. "Yeah, well, maybe I did, but I've not had enough sleep t' deal wi' this shit. Maybe if I put my six-hundred-pound tent up they'll give it a rest, eh?"

"Or they'll think yer a poser like Jerry. Look, Ide, just chill. I know yer tired, but we're stuck here for now; at least try to give them a chance. They're really not that bad these days."

I leaned back against the boot of the car with my tent bag hooked under my elbow and pressed my fingers into my temples to squeeze them together. While I had been spending my summer desperately avoiding these holidays, Jorja had been too young to escape. By the time she was old enough to get out of going, she admitted to me that she kind of liked it—even more surprising, as she wasn't always a fan of camping—and that she got on with the Jackson brothers okay. But that was probably because she was a girl, and a pretty one, as opposed to definitely gay me.

I'm not camp by any stretch of the imagination; I've always made sure of that. But when I first came out, I'd naively made the mistake of not keeping it a secret. I'd assumed that everyone would take it as easily as my family and closest friend. And so, instead of just being picked on for being short, skinny, and odd looking, I'd been ostracized and beaten up for being gay.

With a sigh, I straightened and shot my sister a grim smile. "Yeah, yer right o' course."

I returned to the main group, and my apology was met with a ripple of understanding that I'm sure was helped by the fact that I'd already told them I was jet-lagged. Then I was finally allowed to put up my tent. I found a nice patch of ground a good way from where the Jacksons' tents were already up, and I unpacked the structure that would be my home and sanctuary for the next ten days.

I loved that thing: it had been my eighteenth birthday present, and thanks to many trips and a couple of summers living out of it, to me it was more than just a tent. I loved everything about it: from the slightly mossy smell, to the color it turned the light, and the tenderly patched up scars left by one hell of a storm. I gave it an affectionate pat as I drove in the final peg and was squatted in the entrance to lay out my Therm-A-Rest when I heard footsteps behind me.

"Buy that specially?" Trystan was southern born and bred. To give you an idea of how he sounds, it's a lot like the new James Bond—yeah, Daniel Craig. He's a twat, right…. I'm talking about Trystan obviously; I don't know Daniel Craig, though I'd probably like to.

I smirked to myself at my internal commentary. Without saying anything, I pointed to where the carefully applied patch was.

"So you got it secondhand?" he mocked lightly.

I stood slowly, uncurling to my full height, which nine times out of ten allowed me to look down on people that are pissing me off. Unfortunately Trystan was more or less the same height as me, possibly half an inch shorter—not enough to make a difference.

"Really, Trys? Ye going to do it this way?" I kept my voice low as I stared into his smirking face.

I ran through things that irritated me to distract myself from the fact that Trystan Jackson was infuriatingly good-looking. I think I'm a masochist or something, because when I first realized I was gay, it was mostly thanks to the face currently smirking at me and the body it's attached to.

It had happened over a couple of summers. Looking back, I'd always preferred guys, but it was when I was twelve that it finally hit me that liking other guys wasn't normal. I was being beaten up for something—God knows what, maybe daring to win a bike race—but I remember eight-year-old Jorja rugby tackling Trystan off me. Then I'd dropped on top of him to hit him back, only I'd stopped, because everything had felt weird.

The next year Trystan had started to grow, and by then I'd more or less worked it out—which made trying to wrestle him off me very distracting. When I was fourteen, I came out to my family, and it hadn't even crossed my mind that I should hide it from other people. The Jackson brothers—mostly Trystan and Vince—made damn sure I knew that was a mistake.

I'm not bothered anymore, not since I've been at uni. But that didn't change the fact that Trystan was still gorgeous, and I disliked him intensely for it. He was your stereotypical tall, dark, and handsome—*What*? I'm easy to please—he had wayward dark-chocolate hair, matching eyes, smooth skin, a nice jaw dusted with a fashionable amount of stubble. He wasn't super ripped, but as a gym goer I could recognize another one. I'd guess he climbed and/or biked, because his arms and shoulders were covered in well-defined cords of muscle, not like body-builder ripped, but just "hey, I look after myself" toned. He'd had a six-pack when he was sixteen, so I doubted he didn't have one now, his hips were neat, and I would have put money on his legs having the same nice balance of definition as his arms. Unfortunately, personality-wise he left a lot to be desired.

"Just concerned that this isn't really the type of place a *model* would be used to?" he scorned with a smirk on his face.

I sighed and wondered who had told him. Probably my dad with his bizarre misplaced pride. I think he *likes* that I'm gay—go figure.

I cannot count the number of times I've been randomly scouted since I reached my current height. Despite my looks and sexual preference, modeling had never really appealed to me. However, this summer the flexible hours and the fat paycheck had been just too good to pass up.

"Yeah?" I cut back archly. "So if I'd not taken the two-hundred-and-fifty-quid-a-day job, then ye would've had no trouble accepting the fact that I enjoy being outdoors? I'll be sure t' bear yer feelings in mind next time I'm searching for employment."

He sniggered. "Two-fifty a day? Reckon they need someone to wear the man's clothes?"

I sighed, twisted round, and dropped back into a squat. "Ye don't really have the face for modeling," I said with my back to him as I released my sleeping bag from its tight confines—I wasn't quite as attached to the bag as my tent, but it was a close call. "Ye have t' be good-looking."

"Ooh, burn," he replied, and his voice was rich with sarcasm. There was a moment of silence and I thought that he was going to leave me alone. "It's so weird: you're exactly the same except for the fact that you're a foot and a half taller."

I craned my head over my shoulder and looked up at him with a condescending smile.

"Hardly exactly the same."

"Exactly the same: you're still prickly and rude and take offense too easily." He grinned. "That glare is the same too, I'm getting all nostalgic looking down on it."

"Ha-*fricking*-ha." I ran a hand through my hair and plucked the tie off my wrist to keep it from my face.

"So, do you still like boys?" he asked me.

I groaned and looked back round into my tent. I tried to keep my voice level and hoped the familiarity would ground me. "Aye, Trystan, I still like boys. Ye still a fricking homophobe?"

"Nah, my next-door neighbor in freshers was a fag. Listening to him bang his boyfriend every night for a year rid me of that."

"Wonderful." I didn't sound very convincing.

"Indeed, 'cause I need to share your tent."

2—SNAIL

"WHAT!" I had spun round and I stood so I could glare at him from an even height. I realized I'd shouted and I waved a concerned-looking Jorja away.

I had never let anyone share my tent. It was a two-man, but it was like a home to me. Even in Canada, I'd preferred to carry the whole kit while we trekked than split it between the others and have to desecrate the haven that was my personal snail home.

"Why the hell would ye want t' share a tent with me? Why the hell should I let ye? Where's yers?"

Trystan gave a small shrug as if it was no big deal. "Our three-man finally bit the dust; Vince put his hand right through the outer when we checked them over last night. Our spare was only a two-man. Dad spoke to your dad. He said you had a two-man and I could share."

"Yer fricking kidding me?" I could have bloody strangled my father right then—how the hell had he neglected to mention this? More to the point: why the hell hadn't he offered our spare one instead?

"Why's it such a big deal?" he asked.

Why was it such a big deal? Because this was *my* tent, only mine. Even if I hadn't been so protective over it, there was no way in hell I was ever going to be happy about sharing a tent with Trystan-fricking-Jackson.

"Jorja, did ye know about this?" I called over to where my sister had just finished putting up her tent. She had clearly heard everything that we'd said because she looked back over with a pained expression and shook her head.

Her face brightened slightly as she had an idea. "Ye can have my one-man if ye like, Trys, I'll kip wi' Ide."

That was not ideal, yet it was significantly better than the other option and still completely implausible.

"No way he'll fit, Jorja." I sighed. "Thanks, though." My sister was tall, but she wasn't that tall, and there was no way Trystan was fitting in the diddy coffin tent she insisted on using.

"Seriously, why's it such a big deal?" cut in Trystan. His smirk had disappeared and a thin irritated crease had formed down the middle of his forehead.

"Why's it such a big deal?" I chipped back. "Because I love this fricking tent, I've got a load of great memories in it, and I didn't intend on adding sharing it wi' the guy who spent thirteen years bullying me to the list."

Trystan snorted. "You still got your pants in a twist? We were kids. I'm sorry all right, but I need somewhere to stay and your dad said it wouldn't be a problem or we would have stopped and bought a new one on the way up." Suddenly he sounded exhausted, and I wondered what time they'd left home that morning to make it all the way up here from Kent.

I was being a dick and I knew it. But seriously, no amount of mental preparation could have got me ready for this. The old Trystan Jackson had been the biggest homophobe I knew, and I've come across a lot of homophobes. When he found out I was gay, he'd had a problem swimming in the same lake as me, never mind sharing a tent. However you look at it, a tent is an intimate space if it's shared.

"Shit, fine, ye can stay in ma tent." I ran a hand back over my skull.

"Awesome, don't rape me, yeah? I know I'm irresistible, but I know self-defense."

A strained laugh gurgled up from my throat as he turned and jogged away to get his backpack.

"Ye gonna be okay, Ide?" Jorja had arrived silently by my side; she had a pained expression on her face.

I nodded slowly; really, how bad could it be? It wasn't like I was a middle-aged pervert unable to control myself. Despite my comments about being a masochist, being treated badly was more than enough to counteract whatever physical attraction I had to Trystan. Then again, given that he was sharing my tent, there was a slim chance he might not be a complete arse for the whole ten days.

"Ye really didn't know?" I asked her again softly as we stood side by side and watched Trystan collect his holdall, roll mat, and sleeping bag before pausing to chat with our dad for a few minutes.

"Honestly. I know how ye feel about the guy; I wouldn't o' let Dad do that to ye." Jorja was talking about the fact that I hated his guts, not that I fancied him something rotten. "On the plus side, he's hot, right?" My sister smirked up at me and I rolled my eyes at her. So this was what that secret look had been for earlier. I resisted the temptation to tell her I'd already known he looked like something carved by a famous Italian.

"If I were shorter, I would honestly switch tents wi' ye." Because it really didn't matter how closely he resembled an Italian statue, he was still Trystan Jackson. The man who was probably number one on the list of people I would least like to share a confined space with, never mind my precious tent.

"Seriously? That bad?" My sister also knew how I felt about my tent.

I glanced back at the soon-to-be defiled nylon structure; it wasn't going to be the same after this either way.

"Aye, that *fricking* bad," I murmured as Trystan ceased his chat with my dad.

"Cheer up, it's only ten nights," Trystan said as he stopped in front of me with his smirk firmly back in place. "You going to let me get in?"

"Give me a sec," I said as I dropped back onto my knees and into the tent. Everything was organized and had its place, and now everything was going to have to be moved. Two-man tents *sleep* two men. I'm not trying to be funny. It's just sleeping is all you can do with two full-grown guys in one of those tents; there's no room for anything else. Which meant it was going to be a mess. I moved my belongings onto my roll mat.

"Pass me yer...." I stuttered to a stop as I twisted round and found my face very close to Trystan's. He had dropped to a squat in the entrance, and he balanced on one hand as he leaned forward with his stuff clutched under his free arm.

He grinned, as if he knew that having his face so close to mine was the reason I'd stopped talking.

"... roll mat," I finished in a deadpan.

"You kind of look like a girl when you're flustered."

"Wow, I've never heard that one before, Trys." My voice was withering with sarcasm. "Or are ye saying it's me that should be worried if ye think I look like a girl?"

"Ha, I never said you looked like a pretty girl."

I sighed at that one.

A low chuckle rumbled through his chest. "Chill, Ide. This is a nice tent. How long have you had it?"

"Mam and Dad bought it for me for my eighteenth." I took his roll mat from him and laid it out next to mine.

"So you camp lots?"

I nodded.

"So my dad making those comments about cotton?" He passed me his sleeping bag.

"Very unnecessary," I confirmed.

"He's a twat, but to be fair, you don't really look like you know what you're doing, turning up in skinny jeans and Toms."

"I'll remember t' wear all Gore-Tex tomorrow, see if that impresses him, eh?"

"It would probably help."

"That all ye got?" I asked as he passed his rucksack through.

"Yeah, I've got a few extra bits in the car, but I packed light," Trystan said as he ducked back out of the tent. I watched as he pushed his hands into the small of his back and stretched like a cat. "How long until tea, Mum?" His deep voice cut through the desolate silence of the landscape.

"An hour, darling," Samantha called back. Now that we were all old enough, we took it in turn for cooking duty each evening, but it was an unspoken rule that it was always the mums' turn on the first evening.

"Sweet." He ducked and caught my eye again. "There's a lake round the corner; want to come for a swim? That hair of yours must need a lot of work."

I clambered out of my tent and looked up at the sky. It was nearly eight p.m. The sun still had another three hours in it yet, and the wind had died down, but it wasn't exactly balmy. Trystan didn't wait for my answer; he jogged off and rounded up his brothers and Jorja, and somehow I found myself heading "round the corner" to the lake.

The lake was a fifteen-minute walk up the valley. It was roundish, and gravel ringed the shore that was dotted with coarse grasses and a few shrubby herbs. We dumped our bags by a pile of boulders and everyone but Trystan eyed the lake with a certain amount of trepidation.

"Ye sure this is a good idea?" asked Jorja.

The wind had died down but it was still cold.

"Don't be such a pussy. I thought you northerners were supposed to be hard or something?" Trystan said. This had little effect on Jorja and me, but it certainly spurred his brothers on to prove that they were harder than us "northerners."

Jorja and I watched with matching arched looks as Josh and Vince stripped to their underwear and raced down toward the edge of the water. Trystan laughed but started to toe his shoes off; he stripped quickly and ran to the water's edge in just his boxers. Jorja whistled lightly through her teeth.

"Phew, I'm really wishing ye were still a short arse right about now," my sister said under her breath as we watched Trystan join his brothers in the water.

"Aye, I'm feeling pretty similar right now." My assumption about his six-pack and legs had been right.

"Yer kidding me? Ye get to sleep wi' *that*! Maybe ye can work some o' that infamous charm I've heard rumors of and convert him or something."

"Yer joking, right?" I looked down at my sister, letting her know I thought her suggestion was ridiculous.

"Why?" She looked genuinely puzzled.

"For starters, I've never seen a finer example o' a straight man. Secondly, yer do remember how he tormented me for thirteen years, right?"

"How could yer hold a little bit of torment against… *that*?" I laughed at her lightly. She had a point, Trystan was a fine example of male beauty, but I had absolutely no intention of making my life or this holiday any worse than it already was.

"Maybe yer'll understand when yer older, eh, baby sister?" I pulled her into a rough one-armed embrace. "Right, let's show these soft southern puftas how to enter a lake, eh?"

She giggled and peeled off her jumper as I followed suit and tried not to think about how effing freezing it was.

We sprinted in, splashing and screaming as we launched ourselves headfirst into the bitterly cold lake.

"For God's sake, why the hell are yer still in this hellhole?" Jorja came up spluttering with her lips already turning blue.

"Eh? Surely ye and yer sister need to wash yer pretty hair?" Trystan mocked in his best northern accent. Jorja and I glared at him: her for implying she cared about her hair that much, and me for implying I was a girl—*again.*

"Yer seem surprisingly fascinated wi' ma hair, Trys? No copping a feel while we're sleeping, eh?" I returned his smirk. "This shit is grown out for ma job, nae for a pervy southern boy t' croon over."

I flinched as someone touched me. Trystan was two meters away, looking faintly amused as his youngest brother pressed a hand against my side.

"How come you have a waist, Ide?" Josh asked as he ran his hands over my already goose-bumped skin. I didn't have a waist exactly, but I was narrow.

I looked down and round at the youngest Jackson, an eyebrow cocked. He was staring at my skin beneath his palm, and in the depth of those delicious chocolate brown eyes all the Jacksons shared, there was the kindling of something deeper than simple curiosity. I could see his elder brothers looked horrified and fascinated in equal measure and I really didn't want to upset the boy—but *seriously?*

"Josh, ye know I'm gay, right? Would ye do that to a girl?" I asked gently. Although the way he was looking at my body and the way his breathing changed slightly as he turned his gaze up to my face made me wonder if he was actually interested in girls.

His eyes widened and a blush spread across his pale cheeks. "But I'm... you're not."

"I know. And I don't know why I look like I do any more than ye know why ye look how ye look. And I dun really mind but, yer should be careful." I hitched a thumb in the direction of his brothers. "Some people are prissy about shit like yer touching another guy, eh?"

Josh looked round at his elder brothers, and they considered him with weary looks. Trystan gave a shake of his head, as if it was something he was used to dealing with.

"You can't just touch whoever you like and ask whatever pops into your head, Josh," Trystan said.

"I was just curious," Josh replied innocently, and I noticed that his hand was still pressed against my side. I stepped out of his reach.

"Well, Ide might still be bothered, and what he was trying to say—though he was implying wrongly in mine and Vince's case—is that if you go around touching up gay guys, people might get the wrong idea. Not that it's wrong to be gay, just don't hit on guys in front of your brothers. It's weird, yeah?"

"What do you mean, 'mine and Vince's case'? I can think for myself you know." Vince shot Trystan a hateful look, then turned his attention to me and his brother. "And if you're a fag, that's disgusting."

"Gee, nice t' see homophobia's an adolescent trait in the Jackson family," I muttered, but a smile quirked the edge of my lips as Trystan cuffed Vince round the side of the head.

I ducked back under the water, ran my hands quickly over my firm skin to loosen the worst of the sweat and dirt, and then I emerged spluttering and gave a brief shiver.

"Right, that's about enough for me," I said, mostly to Jorja, who was shivering with her arms wrapped over her chest as she watched Trystan and Vince argue with just a bit too much enthusiasm. "Come on, ye little perv." I wrapped my hand around my sister's upper arm and tugged her out of the lake.

"So this is why ye always seemed so keen to come on these holidays," I commented dryly as I held a towel up for her to hide behind while she stripped out of her wet underwear and pulled on full thermals, a fleece, and jacket.

She giggled as she hurried into her clothes.

"Remind me why I did that again?" my sister slurred through chattering teeth as I got dressed.

"T' perv on Trystan, as far as I'm aware," I whispered back.

A dreamy look passed across her face as she stared over my shoulder. "Mmm…. I hope we can swim every day."

I gave her a light clip round the ear as I shrugged my jacket on. "He's too old for ye anyway. If yer gonna perv, at least do it on Vince; he's not too bad for a kid."

"Meh," my sister grumbled as she tucked herself under my arm. We turned to watch the Jackson brothers continue messing about in the water. Vince Jackson was a good-looking boy and the family resemblance didn't end there, but Jorja didn't look impressed. "I canna stand homophobes, bro, I just wanna hit him now after what he said in the lake. Josh is cute though, right?" Her gaze turned mischievous and I knew exactly what she was getting at.

"Not going there, Jorja," I said beneath my breath.

"Since when did ye have morals?" she chimed right back. I glanced over my shoulder to see the three Jacksons hurrying out of the lake to change back into their clothes. Josh was turned our way and he grinned at me as I looked over.

"Since I started being eyed up by a fifteen-year-old." I couldn't help but wonder if Trystan was going to be the least of my troubles.

I WASN'T prepared for sharing a tent at all. I mean physically, and no, I don't mean I wouldn't be able to control myself because I hadn't jacked off. My tent was designed to keep two people warm in the depths of winter somewhere north of the Arctic Circle. So why did I have it in Scotland? Because two-man tents don't work the same way if there is only one body inside. By myself, with my nice three-season sleeping bag I would have been the perfect temperature—maybe I would have had to stick a leg out if I couldn't get a pitch where I'd be in the shade when the sun rose, but that would hardly have been a problem by myself. If I'd known I was sharing, I would have brought my old shitty tent, and not just because I'm super protective. But because it was going to be way, *way* too hot.

I sighed and slipped into my sleeping bag in just my boxers. We'd eaten and both families had sat around chatting for the few hours before night finally fell. I tucked my hands behind my head and stared at the roof of my tent. This was it; these were the last uncontaminated moments. Although in truth, my snail home had been destroyed the moment I'd laid Trystan's roll mat down next to mine. Outside I heard the soft sound of footfalls on the mossy grass outside the tent.

"Knock, knock," Trystan's low voice sounded and he crawled in without waiting for an answer. "Wow, I thought I was joking when I warned you to stay away, but you're actually not wearing any clothes."

"Yeah, well." I didn't bother looking round at him. "If I'd known I was sharing I would've brought ma shitty tent. We're going to boil, so unless yer sleeping bag is a piece o' shit I wouldn't leave those sexy jim-jams o' yers on."

"This your way of perving on me?"

"I got ma fill at the lake, ta."

"So you're admitting that you were looking?"

"No, I'm saying that if I'd wanted to, I could've." He quirked an eyebrow and held my gaze in his as he hunched over and tugged his T-shirt off over his head. I determinedly kept my eyes on his face and away from the rippling muscles of his torso as he made an exhibition of himself.

"Are ye for real?" I asked with a scowl, as with a fixed grin he slipped into his sleeping bag beside mine.

"How'd you mean?" he asked.

"I mean, ye, Trystan Jackson, the boy wi' the worst case o' self-centered homophobia I've ever met—and I've met a lotta homophobes—agreeing to sleep in ma tent, spouting that shit to yer brother up at the lake, and now yer *flirting* wi' me? So I'm asking: are ye for real?"

A faint frown lowered his brow. "It's been a while, Ide."

"Ye made us all have our own plates and cups and cutlery so ye didn't have t' accidentally use something I'd used and get contaminated by ma 'condition.'"

"What're you talking about? We've always done that—to save on washing up."

I shook my head slowly. An electric lamp hung above the door, it filled the tent with muted light, and for a moment it was just the two of us contained in a world of nylon. His obliviousness was pretty damn convincing, but surely no one could be that ignorant? "No, Trys, we started it when ye found out I was gay. The washing-up reason doesn't even make sense."

"Huh?" He cocked his head to one side and for a moment looked genuinely puzzled, before he dismissed the whole thing with a hitch of one shoulder. "I guess so. But still, it's been a while. Like I said, I lived with a fag for twelve months. And anyway, I wasn't flirting, I was teasing. Your frustrated face amuses me."

"Ye know there ain't a lotta difference, between flirting and teasing?" I pressed with a condescending grimace.

"Yeah, there is. One I'm amused by pissing you off, and the other I want to get into your pants. I *don't* want to get into your pants."

I rolled my eyes at him. I could already smell the faint salty sweetness of his sweat mixed in with the freshness of the lake and his deodorant. It was filling the small space; it was pressing into the nylon walls; it was contaminating my tent second by second.

"Yeah, well, I wouldn't let ye anyway. I have some standards, ye know." I was pretty certain that was the truth. It wasn't as if I was some ugly closet case. I didn't do boyfriends, but if I was inclined toward some company getting, it wasn't exactly a challenge. I didn't have to resort to seducing straight guys.

"So you don't fancy me?"

I turned my head and fixed him with my most derisive stare. "Trystan, yer a smug egotistical bastard, ye have a pretty face, and ye have a fine body. And I think these things in exactly the same way ye think about a page-three girl: nice t' look at, not t' take home."

"I'm not sure anyone's ever called me pretty before."

I opened my mouth, shut it again, and turned my gaze back up to the roof of the tent.

"Are ye going t' be like this all week?" I said eventually.

"I'm just curious."

"I thought ye said ye lived next door to a gay guy; didn't ye get these questions out o' yer system wi' him?"

"Not really, I wasn't interested in him. He looked like a regular fag."

I rolled my eyes, wondering if he was even listening to what he was saying.

"But yer 'interested' in me?" I asked archly.

"Sure, apart from sometimes when you look like a girl—usually when you're pissed—you seem like a regular guy, but you're also pretty flagrant about it, like what you said to Josh."

"Well I'm not embarrassed o' the fact I like guys, and besides, ye all know, so what would be the point in dancing around the subject?"

"Huh, I guess," he said absently as if the thought genuinely hadn't occurred to him. The sound of his muffled yawn cut through the rustling silence that engulfed the tent. He gave a muted good night, and with nothing more he turned over and went to sleep.

I turned off the small lamp that had been valiantly holding back the falling dusk. The summer sun had finally lost its sway and returned the countryside to darkness. I'm not sure how long I lay there staring up at the black that obscured the space above me. It wasn't the lucid gray-and-yellow-tinged darkness I'd grown accustomed to in the city. This was the utter darkness that was removed from civilization. Only the rustling of the wind against my tent, the steady breaths of the sleeping man next to me, and the creak and cricketing of the wildlife beyond our cocoon could be heard; the silence was deafening.

When I woke up, I was too hot. I'd managed to work myself half free of my sleeping bag and my legs were sticking out the side of it, but I was still too hot because Trystan had decided to join me on my half of the tent.

"Yer fricking kidding me…," I grumbled, my voice still low and gruff with sleep.

You read about people getting enjoyment from waking up entangled with an attractive person. Well, that's a load of rubbish. Attractive or ugly did not change the fact that Trystan's breath was hot and his skin was sweaty.

Trystan had discarded his sleeping bag completely. He was curled on his side with that fine ass of his pointed away from me. His face was tucked in against my neck, and he was breathing hot, musty morning breath into my ear. And his legs—those toned and tanned legs—were wrapped through mine, clammy and slightly hot where our skin was touching.

I detached myself and he garbled some half-asleep complaint into my ear as he pressed his face in closer.

I really could not get my head around this man, this version of Trystan Jackson that was so okay with gay men he didn't even stir in his sleep. It seemed implausible to me that this could be reality. I'd spent four years avoiding a holiday I should have loved because I'd been fed up of dealing with a frankly extreme level of homophobia from the same man who was now trying to snuggle back in closer to me. I hadn't been making that stuff up about the bowls. He really had insisted. I remembered because even though Trystan had always been a bit of a bastard, the extreme level he'd achieved when he found out I was gay had been a real shock to the system. Yet here he was breathing into my ear, a funny little smile quirking the edge of his lips as some dream kept him amused.

With a roll of my eyes, I got up quietly and escaped into the blissful cool of the early morning.

I had always been an early riser, and I stretched and enjoyed the dew-covered dawn. I pulled deep breaths of cold, crisp air into my lungs as I tugged some clothes on—ones Jerry Jackson would find acceptable, I hoped.

It was going to be a scorching hot day if the cloudless blue sky had anything to say about it, so I made the most of the blissful cool as I made a flask of tea. Jorja was the first to join me. She shot me a mute nod as she wordlessly took the cup I offered. She didn't speak until it was mostly empty.

"So, how was it?" she asked in a low voice, since our camp was beginning to stir.

"Hot," I answered bluntly, and the look she gave me let me know that she expected more details. "Ye would o' *loved* it, sis: he's a snuggler."

Her pale eyebrows skyrocketed up her forehead and disappeared into the blonde sweeping fringe that was tucked behind her ear.

"Yer fricking kidding me?" she exclaimed in a stage whisper. I responded with an exaggerated shake of my head. "Did ye snuggle him back?"

"What d'ye think?" I asked, knowing full well that she knew the answer to that question, but it didn't make her look any happier.

"Yer a crazy, crazy man, Ide."

"Having a little bit of self-respect and restraint do not make me crazy."

Jorja spluttered, "Right now I'm honestly doubting whether ye are actually gay? Have ye been lying to me this whole time?" She dropped her face into a look of mock outrage. "Ye just said it so ye could see ma friends' boobs, didn't ye?"

I stuck my tongue out at her, but the rest of our conversation was cut short as we were joined round the little stove. I handed out more tea and conversation turned toward planning our first walk of the week.

3—CHICKEN

BY THE third morning of waking up with Trystan's face pressed into my neck and his legs entwined with mine, I was resigned to my fate. The hand that slipped passively across my torso was new, but really, sleeping Trystan was kind of sexy. And I didn't particularly mind the opportunity to wake up to a bit of gratuitous perving each morning. I was an early riser, and it seemed like he was a heavy sleeper and he never did more than grumble when I rolled out from underneath him.

It may have only been the start of day three, and I didn't want to jinx anything, but so far I was enjoying the family holiday. It shouldn't have been that surprising; the kind of stuff we were doing—hiking and mountain biking—was what I did in my spare time anyway. Which was part of the reason I'd always resented the Jackson brothers; they had made me dread and hate a holiday that I should have loved. It wasn't that Trystan was suddenly being nice to me or anything. He still had a sharp tongue, but his comments were in jest and lacked the downright nastiness that I had learned to expect from him when we'd been younger.

I laughed at him as he mumbled something incomprehensible in my ear in his sleep. I carefully untangled myself and got up.

This morning I wasn't the first up, and I gave my dad and Jerry an absent wave as I dressed and went over to join them by the stove. They were discussing today's activities and they greeted me absently with a mug of tea and a bottle of suncream. So far I'd avoided burning by wearing long sleeves and full trousers, while everyone else wore as little as possible against the baking sun. Today was a biking day, and once I was suitably protected from the sun, I dropped into a squat next to the dads to add my opinion on the route they were planning.

We ended up doing about thirty miles, and the back of my neck burnt despite the frequent reapplications of suncream. It was the two youngest Jacksons' turn to cook, and despite their protestations, Jorja, Trystan, and I left them behind and hiked back up to the lake to wash up and cool off before dinner. We were flushed from the exercise, but it was a much more respectable temperature this time round and we lounged in the edge of the water. It was still warm and the sun was still up, but it was harmless even for me and it was a nice change to feel the sun on my skin.

I splashed water on my flushed neck as I watched Jorja flirt shamelessly with Trystan. He certainly seemed to notice, and he was strutting around like a bloody cat preening under her unsubtle gazes.

"So have you always been an early riser or have you just been sorting out your morning wood thanks to sleeping with such a hot guy," Trystan said with a smug grin as he lay himself out in the edge of the water next to me.

Jorja giggled as she settled on my other side.

"What? It happens, babe. Nothing we can do about it," Trystan said.

Jorja sniggered again and splashed water in his general direction as she turned a wry look my way.

"One, I'm not yer 'babe'; two, that wasn't what I was laughing at. You still haven't told him?" she asked me.

"Huh? Told me what?" Trystan cut in before I could answer.

"Ide's been leaving to be nice," Jorja said with a smug grin.

I rolled my eyes and lifted another cup of water to my neck. "Yer a clingy sleeper, Trys."

A look of realization slipped over Trystan's face. "No shit? I know I am with girls… shit, sorry, Idrys."

He looked genuinely concerned, which surprised me.

"No worries, I've been taking pictures of yer drooling face as blackmailing material."

"I don't drool," he countered.

"Tell that to ma shoulder."

"Huh, well I'll try and stay on my side tonight if I can."

It wasn't like him curling up to me had woken me up or anything. On the contrary, I fell asleep in my bag by myself and I slept through 'til morning. And when I did wake up entwined with a straight guy like it was the most natural thing in the world, it was around the time I usually woke up, so I really had nothing to complain about. I hadn't mentioned it because regardless of how cool this new Trystan seemed to be, I did not want to risk any of the old hostility returning.

Yet he stared at me now and seemed genuinely more bothered about pissing me off than getting cozy with a gay guy.

"Can I get a copy of those pictures, Ide?" Jorja quirked up from beside me as we all clambered out of the water to dress and head back to camp. Trystan shot her the finger. He did it again when he caught her blatantly staring at his arse as he pulled his jeans on. But nothing changed. He ribbed my sunburn with everyone else. Sat next to me at dinner, stole my toothpaste, and fell asleep next to me with a last moan at the heat.

"IDE, IT'S too bloody hot," someone was muttering in my ear. Their actions were completely contradicting their complaints as they pressed their face in closer to my neck and slipped the firm sweaty leg that was between my calves higher up above my knees—so much for trying to stay on his own side.

"Open the door then, idiot." I was still half-asleep as I tried to extract myself from the claustrophobic heat of the embrace.

An unintelligible curse filled my ear and then the heat peeled away. I reveled in the cool and the breeze that washed through as the sound of a zipper filled the night.

"Mmm, sorry," Trystan murmured as he settled back on his side of the tent. He turned himself over and was breathing deeply again in moments. I wondered if he noticed his feet slide straight over and find mine. I let them be; the contrast of warm skin against the breeze wasn't too bad.

"SO," THE single syllable hissed into my ear was full of silken promise. "This was why you didn't say anything, eh?" I could feel the lips that formed the words were only millimeters from my skin. A shudder wracked my half-asleep body as my senses were suddenly flooded with too much information.

It was still early, judging from the gray light working its way through the walls of the tent. Clearly it had gotten cold again at some point, because for the first time all week, my sleeping bag was actually over me. I was huddled on my side and although my nose was chilly and my sleeping bag wasn't really doing all that much, I wasn't particularly cold. Probably because of the body that was spooned tightly against my spine. Our legs were entwined as usual, but there was a hand tucked around my torso. Unbelievably—even for my sleep-addled head—the fingers of that hand were teasing ever so lightly against the faint definition of muscle that was the closest to a six-pack I could manage.

The fingers were nice. But that only registered somewhere deep in my brain because all my consciousness was able to do was try to compute the unmistakable mass that was pressed against my ass.

"It wasn't this bad." I concentrated on holding myself very still because I was almost certain that Trystan had just rolled his hips against mine, pressing his erection into my arse—which was far too suggestive and my brain was having trouble keeping up with the fact I wasn't supposed to be getting turned on.

"Must have gotten cold; shut the door and go back to sleep," I said, and I was glad that the faint notes of appreciation for his actions were hidden in my sleep-gruff voice.

But he *definitely* rolled his hips that time, and in response, my body released a delicious—and thoroughly inappropriate—wave of heat.

"I'm not really in the mood for sleeping," he whispered against my ear. His words were slow and sultry as he continued to toy with my chest. It was *almost* enough to make me forget that it was Trystan whispering honey-laden seductions into my ear.

"Go back to sleep, Trys," I grumbled and wished that his teasing wasn't quite so convincing.

"Come on, you're gay, right? You said I was hot; well, now's your chance to blow me."

I rolled over in the cocoon of his arms and fixed him with a cold stare that let him know what I thought of that suggestion.

"Ye think 'cause I'm gay I'll fall at yer feet at the chance of a taste o' yer cock?"

He grinned. "It tastes good; girls have told me before." The light was flat and gray but it was enough to see the taunting twinkle in his eyes. This was just another game.

An irritated murmur escaped from my chest, and with a growl I grabbed his shoulders and rolled him down onto his back. I let a smirk tighten my lips as I slipped myself between his legs and pressed my hips down against his. I held his gaze as I rolled slightly against the pressure there and fully expected my presence to rid him of his excess blood problem.

It didn't. He grinned up at me with those irritatingly sexy lips and those sultry brown eyes—half-closed with sleep still and looking far too much like postcoital enjoyment for my sleep-addled brain—and he fricking pressed up to meet me back.

The guy was playing gay chicken—with a gay guy.

So he really must be an idiot.

I resisted the urge to shake my head and laugh at him.

"So, ye want me to blow ye?" I dropped my head to whisper the words along his neck as I let my hands skim along the surface of his enviable torso. "Aren't ye worried that'll make ye gay?"

"I don't want you to, I'm *letting* you," he chuckled as my fingers caught on the waistband of his boxers.

I watched his face as I dropped my weight swiftly back over my ankles and tugged his boxers out of the way in one swift downward movement. A very satisfying—if faint—look of surprise flickered across his dark eyes as I dropped my head into the well between his hip and thighs. Beneath my ear, I could hear the thick beat of blood as it surged beneath his skin.

"Hmm?" I let the low rumble resonate out of me and watched a ripple of tension wash up his body in response. "Still not lost it?" It was pretty surprising that his erection remained firm against his stomach. If I shuffled my head forward a little, I'd be able to reach it with my mouth. I knew he'd be able to feel the faint pressure of my words as I spoke. It wasn't like he was even screwing his eyes shut to block me out: he was staring down at me, and I could see his need to win battling against his surprise at what I'd done and where I'd put myself.

"It's easy to pretend you're a girl, especially in this light and with all the pansy teasing you're doing."

"Hoh?" Well, that I hadn't expected. I chuckled darkly and enjoyed the ripple of tension the vibrations of my amusement caused. I let my tongue slide out to moisten my lips. "Well, ye let me know after if ye still think I'm like a girl, eh?"

"Ide…. Idrys, what are you… ah fuck—" Trystan's words petered out into a spluttered gasp as I lifted myself up, pressed a hand against his hip to hold him still, and reached forward to wrap my lips around the head of his penis.

"Ide, fucking…. Nnn," he gasped as I circled his head with my tongue and slipped my lips down lower onto his shaft. A strangled groan shuddered from his chest as he hit the back of my throat and continued. I sucked gently as my tongue danced up and down his flesh.

He clamped one of his hands over his mouth to muffle the worst of his moans.

"Oh God, you really need to stop," he whined again, but despite his protests, his other hand was working its way into my hair. I gave my own little moan of pleasure as that hand pressed my head farther down. At the same time, his hips jacked up into my mouth, thrusting his erection way past my nonexistent gag reflex.

I'm good at blow jobs. I mean, you always hear that guys give better head because they know what they're doing, and it's true to an extent. But unfortunately—or fortunately depending on which way you look at it—for Trystan he chose the wrong gay guy to tempt with a blow job, because I like giving head. And I like it for all the reasons the beautiful man below me was suddenly exhibiting. I loved the slight thrill of being dominated; I loved a hand tugging almost uncomfortably at my hair, and I loved the buzz of knowing the way the body below me was jacking up into my mouth was because of what I was doing. I could feel my blood thickening with desire and lust as it curled round my body to pool between my legs. The knowledge that this was a onetime thing and that it was utterly one-sided actually made things worse, and I groaned into Trystan's erection as my cock completely solidified.

I found a rhythm that he liked and I used it to my advantage; I pulled off as far as his hand would let me and drove back down until the crisp mat of dark hairs that framed him was pressed against my pale stubble. All the while my tongue danced over his flesh, one of my hands still pressed against his hip—though I wasn't bothering to try to hold him down—the other one I'd dropped to play lightly with his balls. He was putty in my hands. His head was thrown back, exposing his throat, and his eyes fluttered open and closed in lustful bliss. His grip was tightening in my hair and I could feel his cock swelling between my lips before suddenly he was jamming his length as far inside the heat of my mouth as it would go and was shuddering as he pumped his release against the back of my tongue.

Trystan was wrong. His cock didn't taste any better than any other cock I'd tasted—flesh is flesh, after all. But his cum was up there with my favorites. It was rich but not too sickly; a hint of bitterness—like dark chocolate—lingered against my lips as I cleaned him up and sat back on my haunches.

"Can't believe you did that, you whore," Trystan panted with his eyes half-closed. His face was a mixture of bliss and irritation, and I shot him a grin in return as I licked my lips suggestively.

"Yeah, well." I lay back down on my roll mat and tugged my sleeping bag back over my shoulders. "Ye just remember I'm not a girl from now on, eh?"

"Fucking faggot," he muttered. He rolled over onto his side to face the opposite wall of the tent.

I didn't let my sigh slip from between my lips. Between my legs, my cock was still hard, but my erection wouldn't last long now that the heat of the moment had passed. It wasn't as if I hadn't known what would happen, but I couldn't help but feel a bit irritated with myself when I was half asleep and my legs unconsciously reached out to find the absent heat they had grown used to.

Well, at least the first three days had been fun.

I woke up the only inhabitant of my side of the tent, which shouldn't have been surprising; after all, it had only been three mornings, and I had screwed up so perfectly last night. Still, I stifled a groan as I army-crawled out of my sleeping bag and into the blissfully overcast morning. My eyes drifted over to Trystan's sleeping form of their own accord as I leaned down to zip the tent back up. Trystan was curled up almost against the wall of the tent. I wanted to tell him off because he was making the inner lining touch the waterproof outer and it would get damp, but I was silent as I zipped my tent up and hid the sleeping Trystan from my sight.

I had fallen asleep justifying what I had done. Not that I was bothered by giving a blow job. The facts were that Trystan had woken up with a hard-on and he had come on to me—but I still should have said no. Instead I'd let myself be baited like an idiot, and then I had done something that was going to make the rest of the week awkward. We were both adults, and it wasn't as if I'd raped him, but he had still told me to stop and I hadn't. Yeah he'd come and yeah he'd got into it in the end, but he'd still asked me to stop and the smug satisfaction of calling his bluff had faded to a throbbing background sense of guilt.

"What's the drooling sleeping beauty done this time?" It was a testament to how out of it I was that I hadn't heard Jorja arrive and I hadn't even managed to make tea. I'd just been staring at the gray horizon.

"Huh?"

"Ye look worse than the time ye realized ye couldn't marry Theo," Jorja said with a smirk, and I gave her a playful whack across the arm.

"I was eight; he's all yers these days."

"I know. That wasn't what I meant. So? What's up?"

I shook my head absently as she took the initiative to make the morning brew. Jorja and I were close despite the age difference, and it wasn't as if I'd never talked to her about guys. Hell, when she decided to have sex for the first time, it was me she asked. Apparently, she figured anything that happened to her couldn't possibly be more difficult than my first time—she was almost certainly right, but that's a story for some other day. Still, this felt a little different. Trystan was straight, and even though he'd been fine with me up until last night, I couldn't quite get over the boy he had been.

"I'm fine, just didn't sleep very well. Too hot, then too cold." It was the truth in both senses of the interpretation—but Jorja did not look convinced and her blue eyes darted over to where my tent was pitched.

"Ye sure? 'Cause I spoke to Josh, and he said he'd swap with Trys." My eyebrows flickered up my forehead as I recalled the youngest Jackson.

"That boy is a little too curious for me to be sharing a tent with him—he has 'jailbait' written in those chocolate truffle eyes of his," I said quietly.

Jorja's spluttered laughter almost caused her to miss the flask and pour the just-boiled water all over the grass.

"Ye sure Josh is gay?" she hissed when she had stopped laughing. No one else was up, but tents didn't exactly make for private conversations.

I shrugged. "Maybe not, but he's certainly curious." I thought of the way he'd touched me back on that first evening by the lake. Often when he was talking to me, he had a puzzled frown on his face. "But he can go find someone else to be curious with." I had enough problems with one inappropriate Jackson, and I was certain Jerry wouldn't take a son of his being interested in guys as easily as my dad did. I did not want to be the cause of some family rift.

"Hmm, he did seem oddly keen…. Aw." Mischief danced through her eyes as she grinned at me. "Ye should be nice t' him, Ide."

"Oh yeah? I should be nice to the underage boy, should I? Yer a pervert, Jorja."

She whacked me affectionately. "I don't mean like that. But if he is gay, it must be hard in a family like theirs. There isn't a lot of estrogen."

"Yeah well, if he wants to talk to me, that's fine. But there's no way in hell I'm getting in a tent with him. His brother is bad enough and he definitely likes girls."

Her smile faded a little as she was reminded of our original topic. "So then, *I* can swap with Josh, he can have my tent, Trys can share with Vince, and I'll come in with ye?"

"What's this? Palming me off, Idrys? And I thought we had a connection." I grunted and almost spilled boiling tea over my lap as Trystan's words were accompanied by a heavy chest draping itself over my shoulders.

Jorja looked genuinely confused as I blushed—I honestly don't remember the last time I blushed. Trystan chuckled and straightened up to get himself some tea.

"Thank God it's finally cooled down, eh? I thought I was going to boil last night. And there is no way in hell I'm sharing with Vince; that boy farts so bad I'd rather sleep in your coffin tent." He sat down cross-legged on the ground next to me and brushed sleep from his eyes. "Seriously, how do you sleep in that thing, Jorja? I borrowed one from a friend once and I woke up thinking I was buried alive, and it wasn't even half as hot as it was last night."

Jorja gave me a puzzled look and turned back to Trystan to answer his question, leaving me to watch and feel slightly bewildered.

"You spacing out again, faggot? Didn't get your fill of me last night?"

I jumped as I realized I'd been staring at him with the same bewildered frown on my face for the past five minutes. Jorja had gone to brush her teeth and the rest of our families were stirring but out of hearing distance.

"Ye for real?" I asked quietly.

He rolled his eyes and looked slightly pissed off. "You asked me that before. What's your problem? Fair enough I didn't expect you to actually go through with it, but I did ask you, so why would I be bothered?"

"Because yer straight?"

"Yeah, and I still am. A mouth is a mouth, idiot, and now that I've apparently tried both I can tell you that there isn't that much difference."

I spluttered a little at that. I was offended and my indignation was overriding my uncertainty.

"Isn't much difference?" I asked archly. He shrugged but the reluctant irritation that passed across his face gave me a warm glow of satisfaction.

"Top three. Happy?" he grumbled beneath his breath.

"Ha, yer kidding me?" There was no way in hell that there were two random girls who were better at head than me.

"I didn't say which position."

My smug smile was wiped away by the sudden realization that we were having this conversation at all—never mind the fact we were having it within speaking distance of our families. Not that mine mattered, but his did.

"Anyway, I can't switch with Josh," Trystan started again after a moment, returning to his usual unfazed attitude. "That boy has an unnatural interest in you that I don't think should get the opportunity to develop while Jerry is in shouting distance."

"D'ye think I'm an idiot? And never mind yer dad, has it slipped yer mind he's only fifteen?"

"Josh isn't a virgin; he's slept with girls before. I'm just starting to think maybe he's not that interested in them."

"That doesn't change the fact it's still *illegal*. What kind of brother are ye?"

"The kind that thinks that if my brother is gay it would be better for him to find out with a friend who I trust than getting his ass ripped open by a random guy in a club."

I blanched at that because of how close to my own first time experience it was. I ran a hand through my tousled hair and downed the last of my now lukewarm tea in a gulp. I was a morning person, but really, this was too much for so early in the day. And had Trystan just implied I was his friend?

"Look, ye can tell Josh he can talk to me, but I'm not going t' sleep with the boy now or when he's actually legal."

"Don't swing that way?" He smirked.

"I do both, depends on my mood," I cut back and kept my tone deadpan. "Would ye sleep with Jorja?"

"Different."

"Nope, it isn't," I replied firmly. "I'll talk to him, I'll introduce him t' some nice guys if ye want me to, but that's it." I wondered what had happened to my life that a guy I'd just blown was trying to get me in bed with his brother. It was going to be a long rest of the week if shit like this didn't settle down.

"Give me your number, then," Trystan said.

"Why?" I asked, genuinely puzzled.

"Because you're probably not going to be able to talk to him this week with Dad and Vince around, so I'll give him your number when we're home and he can call you if he wants to."

I considered him in silence for a moment.

"That is *honestly*"—I shook my head as I tugged my shatterproof/waterproof/lifeproof phone from my pocket and dropped it in Trystan's lap—"the lamest excuse to get my number I have *ever* heard— and I've heard a lot of shitty excuses."

"Huh?" He looked up blankly from my phone, and it was my turn to smirk as I dropped my head in close to his.

"If ye wanted me to blow ye again, ye just had to ask," I whispered then stood up and left.

"I wasn't—" Trystan shouted after me, only to cut off just as abruptly. Ahead of me Josh was just emerging from the tent he shared with Vince. Josh offered me a smile, but Vince was looking beyond me; he stared at Trystan, a sour expression painted across the features he shared with his brothers.

4—WOLF

IT WAS kind of amusing now that I had gotten used to it. Trystan was a cocky and egotistical jock, and he was almost impossible to faze except for every now and again. Over the next couple of days, those few and far between moments brought me a sense of smug satisfaction.

"So?" My sister's tone was pointed.

I looked up from the pot I was stirring and met Jorja's curious and frustrated stare. It was our turn to cook and we were on our own around the stove. Our parents were chatting with Jerry and Samantha on the other side of the camp where the sun still lingered. The Jackson boys were playing football, and the last time I'd looked up she'd been stealing envious glances in their direction.

"So what?" I asked.

"So when did ye and Trys sort yer shit out? Did ye chat or something? And why didn't ye tell me ye were going to? I thought ye were waiting until we were alone, but well, we're alone and yer irritatingly schtum."

"Huh?" I said absently as I turned to follow Jorja's gaze to the topless football players.

"Oi! Don't burn the food, you two pervs!" Trystan called over when he turned and caught us both staring. Jorja and I stuck our fingers up at him in return. Our respective parents called some admonishment, but it was halfhearted as tonight was a wine/beer night in recognition of the lazy day we had planned tomorrow that always came halfway through our holidays.

"That's 'cause we haven't," I said as I turned my attention back to the pot. After yesterday morning's incident in the tent, we'd just returned to normal—or what I'd thought was normal. This morning, I'd once again woken with my personal space invaded and carried on as usual. Trystan didn't seem bothered, so I'd decided to chalk it up to an odd game gone wrong, and I'd spent the last two days as I'd spent the first couple: enjoying the countryside while being the brunt of jokes and trying not to get sunburned. That had been it.

"Seriously?" she pressed.

I gave a small shrug. "Yeah, we chatted about Josh, but I guess it just took me this long to get used to the new Trys." Although if I was honest, I wasn't at all used to him. The only inappropriate thing he'd done so far was proposition me—oh, and try and set me up with his brother—yet despite the evidence that he really wasn't bothered, I sometimes had to resist the temptation to flinch and hurry away when I caught him looking in my direction.

"Ye chatted about Josh?" Either my sister missed the undertones of puzzlement in my voice, or she was resigned to my reluctance where the eldest Jackson brother was concerned.

"Well, yeah." I chuckled as I looked round at her. "He wanted me to sleep with him, I think."

"He *what*?" she shrieked.

"Shh," I hissed, but I couldn't help but laugh at the outrage on her face. Despite her perving, my sister was a bit old-fashioned where sex was concerned. She tolerated my less than wholesome attitude toward it, but she would never be happy with the idea of a one-night stand, never mind that Josh was almost six years younger than me and still a minor. "Weird, right? And if *I* think it's wrong, that's saying something."

My sister spluttered and she was looking at me with a mixture of amusement and condescension, which I thought was a bit unfair—even I drew the line at sleeping with anyone underage, at least knowingly.

"Well, yeah." She had clearly decided that she was going to have to spell out for me whatever was going on in that "only have sex with someone you love" head of hers. "But it's weirder because Trys has been flirting with ye."

I considered her across the camping stove.

"Ye got some vodka in that wine o' yers?" I asked archly as I eventually leaned over to see how much my sister had drunk. The cup was still half-full, and as I reached over and gave it a mocking sniff, I confirmed that it was indeed just wine. She snatched it back.

"Are ye blind or just stupid?" She cocked her head to one side, looking genuinely puzzled.

"Neither, as far as I'm aware. I don't tend t' pay much attention to straight men, t' be honest, and Trystan is just a tease."

"Well I'm not denying he's that. But he's hardly had his eyes off ye for the past two days straight. Honestly, it's enough to break ma heart." I raised my eyebrows at her and she rolled her eyes. "Not like that; just on behalf of the female population in general." Her gaze drifted back over my shoulder, and she dropped her voice again. "Right, there he's doing it now! He's staring over here with a weird look on his face."

"He's probably wondering why yer staring at him, idiot." I kept my voice droll.

"Or he's looking at ye to try and work out why he suddenly finds ye so dashingly attractive; ooh, it's like a manga."

"Except shouldn't one of us look like a kid, then?" I commented dryly as I thought of the yaoi Jorja had showed me—specifically the doe-eyed jailbait that usually ended up being half raped by a straight guy who suddenly found himself unable to control his suppressed gay impulses any longer. Trystan and I were both a similar height—if anything I was taller—and while I wasn't as ripped as him by any means, I was not stick thin, either. Plus, I generally liked to top.

"Not in all of them," my sister replied, completely unfazed. "There's this one called—"

I interrupted her. "I don't need to know, Jorja, real-life gay guy, remember?" She pouted but stopped elaborating and continued to look at me as if I was a bit simple.

"Fine, let's *assume* yer right." I made sure she knew I thought it highly unlikely. "Now can ye please explain to me why was he trying to get me to sleep with his brother?"

She flicked her gaze over my shoulder with a little frown on her face. If anything, Josh fit the manga profile much better: he was shorter than both his brothers but still shared their pleasant coloring and good looks. Each time I caught him staring at me, I swear there was more and more being said by those gorgeous eyes of his. It was as if each morning he woke up a little more certain, a little more interested, and a little more dangerous. If we were anywhere else, if I didn't know how old he was, I would definitely go there. Without a doubt, without hesitation, I would enjoy devouring him, taking his first time for myself, making it amazing for both of us. I shivered slightly at the thought. But we weren't anywhere else, we were here, he was still fifteen, and there was no way I was going there.

"I dunno, maybe he's in denial," my sister said eventually, and I could tell I'd won because even she didn't sound very convinced by that explanation.

"Trystan Jackson doesn't really strike me as the kind of guy who's second-guessed himself a day in his life."

Jorja gave a bemused shrug. "Ye have a point, but seriously, he's still snuggling ye, right?"

I nodded.

"So just try something out." A wicked smile curled against the edges of her lips and she fixed her blue eyes on me in a way I knew meant trouble. "I bet ye my Yorkshire next time yer home."

"A Yorkshire pudding bet?" I mocked with a grin. "Yer really serious. But for something like this, surely it should be the next *two* Sundays?"

"Hmm." She paused to consider.

I feel I should explain: our mum made the best Yorkshire puddings, but she only ever made enough for one each. The chance for two was a rare treat, and Yorkshire pudding bets were reserved for only the most serious of all situations: Jorja's date to her first school dance; me coming out to my parents. I was hoping the threat of potentially being Yorkshire pudding-less for two weeks in a row would be enough to put Jorja off the bet. Because not telling my sister was one thing, but lying to her was something else completely. If she made the bet, she would ask me if anything had happened. It already had, and I knew I wouldn't be able to keep it from her.

"Deal. Ye try something, and if he goes along, I get yer Yorkshire for two Sundays." I gave an internal groan as my plan backfired. "If he doesn't, ye get mine."

I reluctantly held out my hand; there was still a way out. I could tell her I hadn't tried anything, which technically wouldn't be a lie—Trystan had started it, after all.

A hint of a smile plucked at one side of her face and she wrapped her fingers around mine before I could pull away. "If ye chicken out, I get yers anyway."

I tried to pull my hand out of her grip, but she held firm, giggling wolfishly as I tried to struggle. But I knew it was too late.

"That's cheating," I grumbled.

"We shook on it. Those're the rules!" she chimed as she stuck her tongue out at me.

"Seriously?" I groaned as she dropped my hand, but I knew that no amount of arguing in the world would change her mind now. It was my fault for letting my guard down and for upping the bet in the first place.

Yeah, I know we're both adults. You telling me you never revert to being a kid with your family?

"What do you look so happy about?" Vince asked Jorja as he and his brothers came over to join us around the stove.

"Nothing." Jorja's grin betrayed her guilt as she poked the food and shouted over for the parents to join us.

"You look like someone just told you Santa isn't real." Trystan chuckled as he sat down next to me. Josh sat on my other side, and I met Jorja's smirk with an unamused look. I think I'd had less attention in gay bars.

"Ye guys finish making a spectacle of yerselves?" I shot back as I let my gaze drop pointedly to Trystan's bare chest. "Yer audience must o' already left."

"Just keeping the ladies amused while they cook," Trystan said.

"Don't include me in your perverted faggot tendencies!" Vince muttered from the other side of the stove. He shot Jorja a quick sideways glance and pulled his shirt back on.

The rest of us rolled our eyes at him, and Josh shifted slightly uncomfortably on my other side. He'd already put his top back on.

THE FOOD wasn't amazing, but then we weren't out here for five-star cuisine. When we'd all finished, we moved over to a stone-lined area set aside for fires. Jerry lit it tonight, and we all dropped to the grass in a big circle to admire the flames as they licked up the wood we'd brought out here especially. Around us, the blue and yellow evening was falling to twilight as we chatted and drank the beer and wine we'd brought out just for this evening. The parents gravitated to one side and us five "children" to the other. Although technically it was only Vince and Josh who fell in that category now, and even they were allowed a couple of bottles of beer each.

I lay out on my back as I stared up into the steadily deepening blue of the sky above us. The first stars would be out soon, and the air was chilly but the fire kept back the worst of it. I kicked off my shoes and socks and ran my toes through the cool grass. Vince and Trystan lounged out on the other side of my legs, and they were chatting with Jorja who was lying across me with her head on my stomach. The three of them were talking about which university Vince was going to apply for. Just behind me, Josh was nursing his second beer and had fallen oddly silent. I craned round to get a better look at the youngest Jackson.

"Ye know where ye wanna go?" He shrugged and although I was the elder of Jorja and me and had never had to follow in anyone's footsteps, I could guess the pressure was frustrating. "Well, there are plenty of other options too," I added, trying to sound understanding but probably still sounding like every other know-it-all adult.

"What's it like kissing a guy?" His voice was low. His brothers were by my feet, lain out with their legs toward me, probably eight feet away, his mum and dad the same distance on the other side of the fire. The chatter was loud enough, and the crackling of the flames filled the background. Still, it must have taken a lot to get those words out even at that volume.

I stared at him over my shoulder in slightly stunned silence. It was with some relief that I heard the parents announce they were turning in for the night. I waved an absent good-night with everyone else. Then I shifted round, rolling onto my front and ignoring Jorja's protest as I forced her to rest her head on my back instead. I was on my fourth beer, and I had a nice warm glow that fuzzed the edges.

Josh was staring down at me, his gaze fixed on my mouth. His tongue darted out to moisten his lips. Despite my earlier protests, I had an urge to run my fingers where his tongue had just been, then possibly my own lips, to show him firsthand—oh, the joys of alcohol.

"Kissing is kissing, Josh," I answered somewhat unhelpfully. "We all have the same parts up here."

A faint blush colored his cheeks.

"So you don't mind kissing girls?" he asked despite his apparent discomfort.

"No, I like men." I'd used the word "men" on purpose, but the flicker of sadness that darkened his eyes made me feel like a complete twat. I wanted to hug him, to press a kiss to his cheek and tell him he was gorgeous. That would definitely give the wrong impression. And my slightly tipsy brain was all too aware of how close his lips were to his flushed cheeks.

"Sorry, yer right, it's not really the same. But the only girl I've kissed was when I was about fourteen. So I'm not really the right person t' ask." I hesitated as I saw the frustration flash over his face. I didn't need to deal with this. It was obvious that he wasn't out yet, which meant this was probably just a teenage infatuation and was all the more reason to steer well clear. But as I stared up into his downcast eyes—turned gold by the flickering flames of the fire beside us—I couldn't shake the feeling of guilt that he had dared to ask and I was being massively unhelpful.

I'd never had someone around to ask these questions to when I was coming out. Then again, my problems hadn't started until later.

I'd realized pretty early on that I wasn't really interested in girls, I think I was about thirteen, and I'd kept it a secret from everyone but Jorja and Theo—but obviously they couldn't help much. Theo had suggested I kiss a girl to see whether I liked it; he'd also offered to let me kiss him afterward to compare. I'd declined because I knew Theo wasn't gay and was only offering as a friend—a decision I am eternally grateful for making.

I'd kissed a guy for the first time two months later. I can't remember what he looked like or how it felt, I just knew I liked it much better. I preferred his smell, the feel of his body, the taste of his lips, everything. When I'd told my parents, they had chuckled and told me they'd already guessed. At the time I hadn't thought much about it, but I now know that I had been very, *very* lucky to have such an understanding family and open-minded best friend. I thought about Josh's family: Jerry and Vince were clearly homophobic, Trystan was reformed at best, but his attitude still clung to the edges of what he had grown up around.

"What I've heard from my friends who came out later than me is that kissing guys is a bit more… aggressive." I felt kind of weary, because I was possibly the most inappropriate person to be having this conversation with someone who was just coming out. Of all the gay guys I knew, only Ashlie was probably worse than I was, and it was still a fine line.

"Can you show me?" He spoke quickly, and his voice was low and breathless.

I hissed lightly. Because as I stared at those lips of his, I knew that I really wouldn't mind that at all. I knew that it was a result of the beer and probably getting so worked up with Trystan two nights ago, but suddenly I really wished that I wasn't seven hours away from an easy lay. In fact, Ashlie would definitely make a suitable replacement—albeit a considerably looser one.

I flinched as a hand slid against the inside of my ankle.

"Jorja," I snapped as I looked round at her. I was having enough trouble controlling myself as it was, and I really didn't need my sister's misplaced affection confusing my senses right now.

"Sorry." She shifted her head to a different spot against my spine. I realized with a start that her hands were draped across herself: one on her chest, the other on her stomach. The hand on me slid up a little higher on my calf, and then the fingers slid over the small soft hairless places on my ankle as it slipped back down into the arch of my foot.

I craned my head the rest of the way around and saw Trystan had shifted positions. He was sitting perpendicular to me now, leaning back casually against his arms outstretched behind him. Except only one of them was taking his weight, the other one was what I could feel on the inside of my ankle. He wasn't looking at me; he was staring at Jorja and his brother as he continued with his conversation. The only indication of what he was doing was the smirk on his face. But he was always smirking, and it was dark enough that they didn't seem to have noticed his hands.

I turned back to Josh, and I'm sure something in my face must have changed because he actually gasped a little bit, his pupils dilated, and his lips parted as a flush spread across his cheeks. Then my head decided to gift me with a vivid image of this boy gasping again, this time while he was beneath me and I was making him pant and moan and cling to me. Yet as soon as the thought flicked through my head, it was replaced by an equally vivid image, this time of his elder brother doing something very similar, except to me. Both of which were wrong on so many levels. I swallowed as I felt myself swelling uncomfortably against the grass.

"Sorry, Josh, I don't think that would be a good idea." My voice was a little hoarse, and I'm certain I didn't sound at all convincing.

"Please," he whispered. He leaned almost imperceptibly down and toward me as his tongue flicked out along his lips again.

"Nnnn," I garbled as Trystan's thumb pressed into the tender flesh in the arch of my foot, making me think of something completely different. I didn't get it. This was what he'd wanted me to do, right? So why was he distracting me?

"In front of yer brothers?" I tried to sound disapproving and to remind myself that I did actually want distracting, even if it wasn't in quite the way Trystan was choosing to go about it.

"Want some more beers?" Trystan piped up from behind me. There was a murmur of assent. Then he was getting to his feet, leaning over me as he did so, sliding his hand straight up the inside of my leg. I scowled over my shoulder, meeting his dark brown eyes in the ever-increasing darkness.

"Help me carry." He didn't wait for an answer, just wrapped his hand around my upper arm and tugged me to my feet. He dislodged Jorja, who grumbled before twisting around to settle her head in Vince's lap—who suddenly looked very happy.

"What's going on, Trys?" I complained as I followed him to my parents' car and the travel fridge that was in the boot. He pulled out the last of the beers and handed them to me one by one as he popped the caps off.

"I had a change of heart," he muttered as he leaned back against the boot. He took a swig from one of the beers in his hand and finally looked me in the eye.

"About Josh?" I shook my head. "I'm not going to do anything." I was more or less certain that was the truth. I mean, there was a difference between being tempted and actually acting on anything—even for me.

"You looked like you were about to push him down and take him in the grass."

"Well, that was because someone was confusing my senses, ye idiot. Having a reaction to a grown man and acting upon it wi' a kid are different, ye know."

"You reacted to me?" His smug smile pissed me off.

"Wasn't that kind of the point?"

"Mmm, but it's interesting to know it worked." He hesitated, and I watched as my and Jorja's assessment of this man was crushed by a look of indecision flashing over his dark eyes. Then his tongue darted out along the line of his lips, a gesture so similar to his brother's that suddenly my anger and frustration was replaced by a flash of rekindled lust.

"Ye Jackson brothers will be the death o' me by the end of this week," I said with a grimace, as suddenly I wanted the holiday to go quickly for completely different reasons.

"What did he say?"

"Josh? I'm not telling ye." And with that I turned and headed back to the warmth of the fire.

I sat down cross-legged in front of Josh, mirroring his position with our knees almost touching. When his eldest brother hovered by my back, I pointed in the opposite direction without looking around. He grumbled something but obliged and went to sit nearer to Jorja and Vince, leaving me and Josh slightly removed.

"Look, Josh." I tried not to look at his lips or his flushed cheeks or to think about the fact that it was the sight of me doing that to him. "I get that yer curious, and I'm happy to talk to ye about these things. But I'm too old for ye."

Not to mention that I'd apparently added "pervert" to my already impressive list of sins—which if we're making a list, probably had "excessively promiscuous" written in big red letters at the top, and that was only if the list maker was being polite.

"Five years is less than between my mum and dad."

"Yeah, except it's more like six, and they're both adults; yer still a kid, and I could get in trouble."

"Only if I told someone, and I wouldn't, and I'm sixteen in a month. And you don't have to have sex with me, just a kiss, to see if I like it."

"Hmm, yer brother said ye weren't a virgin. So ye already know whether ye like kissing or not, surely?"

Josh swallowed and his gaze darted over my shoulder toward Trystan. "You talked to Trys about me?"

I shrugged. "Sure, when ye offered to switch tents, he suggested ye might have an ulterior motive."

"Oh right, yeah," he practically whispered.

"And that he was fine with it, just not here," I clarified, just in case.

Josh nodded slowly and turned those eyes back to me. Then I wished he was still worrying over his brother. "So, you're saying you'd kiss me if we weren't here and I was sixteen?"

I grimaced, more for myself than Josh. "I would be more likely to *consider* it, yeah." Sober I was still more than likely to say no—I think—but with a drink in me, I couldn't deny that Josh was appealing.

His shoulders lifted on a sigh, and he released a long, slow breath as he looked up at me. His face still clung to the last edges of youth, but the way he held me in those eyes said he knew what his body wanted. And that right now it was me.

"*Jailbait*: that's what ye are, Josh Jackson," I whispered, but my voice was lower and more sultry than I had intended it to be.

He gasped again, sucking in breath between those lips of his.

"You want to fuck me?" he whispered as he leaned in toward me. His voice was so low it was almost not there and yet it overflowed with promise, whispering to me that he would let me do exactly that. I pressed my eyes shut to block out the image. They flashed open again as I felt a hand slide over my knee. Josh was staring at my crotch and was inching his hand slowly up my thigh. I grabbed his wrist.

"I said no," I grumbled. My body was betraying me, and for the third time in less than an hour, blood made its merry way into my groin. I wasn't completely hard, but it was enough.

"But I... I'd like to try."

"Shitting hell," I hissed as my patience and control were seriously tested. I was actually starting to wonder if I should escape for an hour in the night and find somewhere to pull myself off, because if things like this were going to continue, I was going to need the stress relief.

"Please don't put me in this situation, Josh. Yer a sweet boy, and yer cute, but I am *not* going to do anything with ye, understand?"

He considered me through hooded eyes. His breathing was shallow now, and despite myself I found my gaze drifting down and alighting on the bulge between his legs.

"I think it's safe to assume ye like boys, by the way," I grumbled— try it out, my ass.

"Yeah." He licked his lips again, and he glanced over my shoulder. His gaze darkened and I wondered what he'd seen. But when I looked back, none of our siblings were looking our way. "I won't try anything this week—I promise. If you promise to kiss me when I'm sixteen."

So he wasn't checking his brother's reaction so much as taking a leaf from his book. It should have hardly surprised me.

"Fine," I agreed easily because I wouldn't see Josh for another year—by which time he'd probably have gotten over his crush on me, and if he hadn't, a kiss wasn't a big deal, especially given he hadn't specified what kind of kiss. He opened his mouth to say something else, but I cut him off. "Don't push yer luck. A kiss is all yer getting."

"Fine," he huffed. I smiled at him and his slightly peeved look evaporated instantly into a glazed look of lust. Which was very flattering, but not what my body needed right now.

"I'm going to bed." I gave a weary shake of my head as I took myself and the rest of my beer to the blissfully uncomplicated isolation of my tent.

Of course, that didn't last long. I was wrapped up in my sleeping bag, staring at the ceiling with my hard-on just about gone, when the sound of Trystan unzipping the tent broke my bliss. I didn't pretend to be asleep; I just continued to stare straight up with my hands behind my head while he clambered in beside me.

I silently groaned in frustration and wished I had refused beer as the sight of Trystan's back twisting as he settled into place left a tingling sensation in my hips. What the hell was wrong with me? Fair enough, I usually had sex more often than this, but it wasn't as if I was incapable of going for a week—or at least it shouldn't have been.

I tried to think of other things.

That became increasingly impossible as a hand slid between the open sides of my sleeping bag and pulled me across the tent and against a hot and solid body.

"At least pretend to be asleep first, idiot," I muttered and realized my lack of struggle made my words very unconvincing.

"I'm drunk, no need." He pressed the hot words into my neck as his feet found mine, his toes slipping along the arch where his hand had been earlier.

"Ye had five beers. Yer not drunk, yer bloody shameless." They hadn't even been pint bottles.

"You're the shameless one; I thought you were going to fuck my brother right there next to the fire."

"Hmm, it was tempting."

Next to my ear I heard a growl, and it made me chuckle. "Ye have a brother complex or something?"

"No. Blow me again," he whispered in my ear.

"Huh? Why?" I garbled, because honestly I had not expected that.

"Because it was the best bloody blow job I've ever had, and every time I think about it or look at you I think I'm going to get hard; so do it again to say sorry." His voice was low and his teeth were slightly bared as he grinned down at me.

"Yer reasoning is twisted." I pulled myself together, but that was the only thing I could think to say—not the best comeback. His grin was feral. His hands came round my shoulders, and with startling ease, he rolled me on top of him. He pressed his groin up into mine, and I fought to keep my body in check as his growing erection pressed into me.

"You said I just had to ask. I'm asking," he said as he rolled his hips. I fought the urge to groan—between him and his brother I was going to end up with a serious case of blue balls.

"That was before yer brother spent an hour taunting me with sultry looks," I replied as I stared down at him. I was slightly satisfied by the look of irritation that flashed through his brown eyes.

"An hour? You've been killing me for two fucking days."

A smug smile slipped onto my lips. But even that wasn't enough to sway him from his course.

"What's in it for me?" I asked archly. "I mean, last time I was satisfied with knowing I'd won. This time ye want it, so…." I tried not to smile too disdainfully as an idea occurred to me. I grasped his shoulders and rolled us both over so I was on my back. I watched as his pupils dilated and he thrust his hips down into me.

"You want me to fuck you? You little fag whore?" he cursed in my ear, but his insults were softened slightly by the obvious arousal between his legs.

"Hell no." Which was a lie. And therefore surprising enough in itself, because I didn't do being fucked. There were only two guys I trusted to fuck me—and they were definitely not some straight, inexperienced idiots. Yet as I stared up into Trystan's hungry, lust-glazed face and felt his cock pressed into the well of my hips, I realized I very, *very* much wanted to be fucked by the man on top of me right now. I wanted to be brought to the edge and then to be fucked so hard I would have trouble walking. But Trystan *was* straight and therefore almost certainly clueless, and if that wasn't reason enough, we were in a tent with the rest of my family sleeping twenty meters away.

"Kiss me, then I'll make ye come," I said with a smirk, because if nothing else I was going to make this difficult for him.

5—LADYBIRD

TRYSTAN SCOWLED and stopped his thrusting. "I'm not kissing you; you're a man."

"I know, and yet ye just asked me to blow ye; kissing me doesn't make ye anymore gay than being blown by me."

"I'm not gay."

"I don't care, those are the terms: kiss me and I'll make ye come, kiss me good and I'll make it better than last time."

"Better?"

I smiled up at him because I was almost certainly not going to get off, but I was still going to enjoy messing with the guy.

"Mmm, I wasn't actually trying that hard, ye know…," I reached up to whisper softly against his ear.

I leaned back and watched the idea take root in his brain and work its way through his body. His tongue darted out across his lips—so like his brother's. I smiled at the irony that the one I was able to kiss was the one that didn't want to be kissed. I could see him considering it as he looked down at me, the lust fighting with the arbitrarily drawn lines he had set out for himself as he considered my lips.

He was actually going to say no. Part of me was a little impressed, and part of me was sad I wouldn't get to tease him. So I wasn't expecting the lips that were pressed down over mine. I was even less expecting the muted groan that slipped between the contact or the hand that came up to cup the back of my head.

"Fucking hell, this better be good," he muttered as he momentarily broke the kiss. He took my bottom lip between his to break my startled mouth open slightly so he could slip his tongue inside. He was working his hand through my hair, but as his tongue quested inside my mouth, he dropped it down to run surprisingly soft fingers down the sensitive flesh of my neck.

That wasn't at all what I had anticipated, and I quickly found myself getting carried away. I was breathing too heavily. My intention had been just to tease a little and force the guy out of his comfort zone, but my body was starting to expect more as that tongue dove into the cavern of my mouth. With one hand I was clinging onto his arms as he covered me; the other one had slipped down to his ass and was pressing his hips down into mine as I ground up into him.

"Mmm, shit, ye need to stop, Trys," I panted as his lips left mine to work down my jaw.

"Huh? This was your idea." He didn't stop his kisses, and his words had regained his smug tone as my rather obvious arousal returned the control to him. "You sure you don't just want me to fuck you? I mean, I've gone way further than I expected, and that way we could both get off."

I was pretty taken aback by the fact that he was even thinking about me, but I tried not to let it show.

"Not going to happen, Trys."

"Why not?"

I shuddered in surprise as his *fricking* hand actually dropped between our crotches. What kind of straight guy was he?

"You're not going to get off else, and you seem to be enjoying yourself."

Holy crap, he was so arrogant it was ridiculous.

"Why not?" I snapped. My frustration was turning to irritation as his fingers exerted gentle pressure against my groin, separated from my cock by only the thin fabric of my boxers. "Because ma family are sleeping out there, because I don't have a condom, because I don't have any lube, because I don't have anywhere to clean up afterwards and—most importantly—because the chances o' yer straight anal-virgin ass getting me off are slim to none."

"You saying I couldn't do it?" He sounded like he didn't believe me, which made me all the more certain that he didn't know what he was doing. And while I could deal with a hard-on from a little light petting and a grope, there was no way I was going to be able to keep my cool if I let him top me and he didn't get me off.

"Yes—that's what I'm saying," I growled, getting a little pissy because, through some fault of my own and some fault of this man and his irritatingly cute and underage brother, I was actually really, *really* horny, and the fact was all those reasons were perfectly valid. He shrugged and pressed a last kiss down over my lips.

"Ah, well, I was just trying to be nice. Your turn, Ide."

He went to roll off me and with a snarl I clamped my hands on either side of his waist, holding him in place where he was. I hooked my fingers into his boxers and tugged them down his thighs with more force than was probably necessary. Trystan's smirk was not lost on me, but I shot him one back as I wriggled down beneath him until he was straddling my shoulders.

He smelt stronger this time as I stared up at him. Less of the lake, more musty, and more of sex, thanks to our antics and apparently his overactive imagination. He groaned as I got to work, dropping his hips naturally so he could drive into my mouth. Which was exactly what I wanted. I tried not to think about the pressure in my groin; I was definitely going to have to go on a dawn trip up to the lake and sort myself out. My body arched up in anticipation of pleasure as I imagined fingering myself; it would do until I got back to civilization—and Dan; I was *definitely* going to need Dan.

Trystan was plunging into me, groaning and panting above me as I toyed with his balls and ran my tongue against his shaft as he fucked my mouth. Collecting a little moisture that had escaped from my lips, I let my fingers slip back along the smooth stretch of flesh behind his ball sac.

"What are you doing?" Trystan mumbled between panting breaths as he stilled his thrusting. I kept up things on my end and managed to pull a groan from him as my finger reached its destination and applied gentle pressure.

"Ide… fucking stop that right now." But he didn't pull away from me and I smiled around his erection.

"Don't you fucking da…. Ah." His words trailed off as the tip of my finger slid past the thick ring of his entrance.

"Shh, relax." I pulled my lips from around him and firmly replaced them with my free hand so I could talk him through it. "I'm not going to fuck ye. It'll just be this one finger, 'kay?" I felt him stiffen as I moved my digit subtly inside of him, working it in farther.

"Why?" he grunted as I continued to work his cock with my hand, distracting him from what I knew was probably not painful but at least uncomfortable and more than slightly embarrassing.

"My part of the deal: I said I'd get ye off, I said it would be better than last time…." A languid smile slid over my lips as my finger completed its journey. I gave it an experimental twist and watched tension ripple through Trystan as I got used to the angle. He wasn't relaxed, which meant what I needed was… there.

Trystan dropped his head onto the roll mat as his arms gave way.

"Yer going to need to be quiet, Trys" were my parting words as I wrapped my mouth back around his cock and worked his prostate in time with my ministrations.

His cum still tasted like chocolate.

It was a good job everyone had been drinking and were therefore soundly sleeping, because Trystan was not very good at being quiet. I didn't make it easy for him. That was kind of the point.

When my alarm went off at 4:00 a.m., I extracted myself from the source of my frustrations and headed up to the lake for a bit of alone time. I was fully sober again by then, but I let my imagination take free rein as I recalled Trystan's desperate moans and applied them to a new fantasy: one where we were in a room with thick walls and a bed and an endless supply of condoms and lube. At some point my head switched it all around so it was no longer Trystan pounding into my ass like he'd done my mouth, but me thrusting into a much smaller and cuter Jackson. I had three fingers inside myself as I ground to a halt and got a little closer to nature.

"Urgh, you're cold" was the grouchy greeting I got when, slightly dew-damp, I crawled back into my tent.

"Then stay on yer side," I replied and was completely ignored as Trystan draped an arm and a leg over me.

"Where've you been?" he asked against my neck.

"Wanking," I replied honestly as I snuggled into my sleeping bag and adjusted to the pressure of the arm over me.

"Did you think of me?" he asked dozily.

"Yer brother" was my arched reply, and I got a smug sense of satisfaction from the ripple of tension that affected my straight guy's chest.

"Pervert," Trystan shot back, and he actually sounded a little angry.

"Why would I think of a straight guy when there is a willing cute gay kid to perv over?" I mocked lightly. I'd been going to add that I'd been thinking about him too, but his flash of irritation made me decide against it.

"'Cause that's my brother you're talking about."

"Mmm, I know: a cute gay version of ye." I chuckled because Trystan was glaring at me, fully awake. I rolled my eyes at him. "Seriously—even though ye were the one trying to get me to fuck him not two days ago—I'm not going to touch yer brother, so chill out." I ruffled his hair affectionately and turned onto my side to go back to sleep.

"SO *HERE* ye are." Jorja's voice joined the soft shuffle of her footsteps through the undergrowth. I cracked an eye open and stared up at her—letting her know I was not happy about being found. Not that I'd particularly been trying to hide, but I had thought that me disappearing before everyone got up would have indicated I wanted to relax on my own for the day. So the fact she had been looking for me was kind of frustrating.

She dropped cross-legged on the sunny side of the patch of shade I'd been snoozing in. She was wearing a vest top and tiny shorts with walking boots. Her eyes were hidden behind a pair of sunglasses, but her curiosity was evident enough.

"Here I am; what d'ye want, Jorja?" I replied.

"Ooh, someone woke up on the wrong side of the tent this morning?"

I gave a weary sigh and pushed myself into a sitting position. I considered Jorja as I lay back against the boulder I had been resting in the shade of.

When I had woken for the second time this morning, my side of the tent had been lacking in clingy guys of the straight or curious persuasion. Which should have been fine because it had been muggy and hot again. But I'd stared at Trystan's back and it had occurred to me that it was not fine; I'd gotten used to waking up with him tucked up next to me, and worse, I liked it. Add that to the fact that last night I had seriously considered letting myself be topped by the guy and I realized I had a problem.

"I didn't sleep very well," I said as I watched a ladybird balance precariously on a blade of grass that really didn't look like it should take its weight.

"Drunk Trys by any chance? That man has a surprisingly low tolerance."

"Hmm" was my muted response. We hadn't drunk that much, but really he had seemed surprisingly tipsy for such a big guy.

"So do ye owe me something tasty by any chance?" A grin split my sister's face, and for a moment I had an awful feeling that she might have heard something. We were close, but I really didn't want her to hear me blowing some guy.

"Yeah," I said through clenched teeth.

"For trying and succeeding or for chickening out?" she asked. My shoulders drooped in relief as I realized she must not have heard.

"Does it matter?"

"Just wondering if I need to start counseling baby Josh for a broken heart. For someone who was so adamant about him being underage, ye were leading him on something rotten."

"Ye noticed?"

She pouted. "Ide... I had to practically hold him down to stop him from following ye into yer tent."

I blanched a little at that and flopped onto my back. "Shit. I really didn't mean to, but those fricking brothers. I could swear they were doing it on purpose."

"*They?*"

I offered her a pained smile at my mistake. "Argh, Jorja... don't be mad, 'kay...? Trys came on to me days ago; I upped the bet to try to get ye to pull out o' it without ye finding out. He was stroking my foot while I was talking to Josh. I was tipsy and it confused me and poor Josh got the brunt of that confusion."

"Sorry, what?" she spluttered and then exploded. "How *dare* ye not tell me about that!" Then she actually cackled. "Oh, *this—is—brilliant*, Trystan is *gay*?"

"Meh, not really."

"Tell me what happened. I'll decide for myself." She shuffled forward, clasping her hands in glee.

"I'm *not* giving ye details. But he's not gay, not really, just open-minded and horny."

"Did ye have sex? Who was the bottom?"

"Jorja!" I snapped. "We were in a tent with ye guys sleeping twenty meters away. There was no sex."

"Hmm, no mess, and yer unusually grouchy... so ye just got him off; blow job, then."

I shot her a droll look and her face curled around her grin—the girl had clearly been reading too much manga.

"Poor Ide," she lamented. "I do actually feel for ye, honestly. But ye said he came onto ye, right? So he could be interested?"

I didn't want to think about that at all; I had a bad history with straight guys.

"I wouldn't get yer hopes up, Jorja."

"Oh well, at least once this week of torture is over, ye get to know that ye are that god of a man's only gay experience. Ye have taken one for the team... although not literally...." She giggled and trailed off, having the good sense to look a little sheepish.

"I suppose all things considered, this holiday could have gone worse," I said, only a little sarcastically. "Ye know Josh made me promise t' kiss him when he's sixteen."

"Aw, bless. But yer so mean, Ide, it's not like it's illegal to kiss him, ye know."

"Hmm, but I don't trust him not t' try and push things further." And after last night I didn't trust myself not to get carried away.

"Yeah, they are a pushy trio, aren't they? But at least ye have something t' look forward to next summer."

I thought of Trystan's flash of irritation whenever Josh had come up in the conversation last night, and I wondered if that wasn't just going to make next year even more of a debacle.

What was I even thinking about? By next year Josh was going to have found someone suitable to experiment with, Trystan would have gotten over the blow jobs I'd given him, and I was going to ensure I was as far away from this ridiculous situation as was physically possible. New Zealand suddenly sounded very appealing.

"What's everyone else up to?" I asked just to distract myself from my own thoughts.

"Just relaxing: the boys are up by the lake, Mum, Dad, Samantha, and Jerry are reading and planning routes for the last half of the week."

"Ye came looking for me over going to the lake for yer favorite holiday activity?"

Jorja blushed a little. "They took lunch, so I thought I'd catch up with them once I'd routed ye out. Ye going to come?" I sighed at the thought, but I'd caught up on my lost sleep already, and moping by myself all day was already losing its appeal.

"Sure." I pushed myself to my feet, collected my rucksack, and followed Jorja to the lake.

It took about half an hour from the spot I'd chosen to relax in. Jorja made a small bleat of appreciation as we rounded the corner and were met with quite a sight. They'd brought a cricket bat up with them and they were playing in the sunshine: one bowling, one catching, one hitting.

Jorja's happiness was because they were playing in just their swimming trunks; all three of them were still damp from often running into the water, and they gleamed in the midday sunshine. I wondered if I'd done something wrong in a past life to be tortured so thoroughly. All three of them had lovely toned torsos and all three of them had gorgeous chocolate-brown eyes that were laughing as Trystan purposely hit the ball into the lake, forcing Josh to dive in after it.

"I think I might go back to camp," I muttered when we were still far enough away that we hadn't been noticed.

Jorja gave me a look that implied she thought I must be mad—there was a part of me that tended to agree with her. But staring at Trystan in all his shirtless glory was not going to help me rid myself of the stupid feelings I'd woken up with. Then there was Josh, who was in another league all together—a league of totally inappropriate. I watched with a mixture of self-pity and reluctant appreciation as he sprinted out of the edge of the water and lobbed the ball back toward the makeshift wickets they'd erected. He leapt up and punched the air as his throw sent the base tumbling and forced a change of batsman.

My ego completely ignored my conscience and took that chance to remind me of the way he'd looked at me last night. None of that frustrating indecision and arrogant mocking of his elder brother. It had just been lust in those silken eyes of his, and if I'd agreed he would have followed me into my tent and let me ravage that lovely young body of his. Unlike Trystan, *I* knew exactly what I was doing, and I would've enjoyed preparing him almost as much as I would have enjoyed taking his virginity. I already knew what I would have done to him, because I'd imagined it in great detail when I'd come to the lake by myself earlier that morning.

I cringed at myself as I turned my eyes upward, as if by not looking I could make all this shit go away. At least thanks to my nighttime escapades nothing responded that shouldn't.

"Ide!" Josh spotted us, and I wasn't alone in noticing how excited he sounded when he called my name. Jorja cocked a wry eyebrow in my direction as we both gave the brothers an absent wave and crossed the last fifty meters to where they had set up the makeshift cricket pitch.

I didn't make it all the way before a very wet fifteen-year-old launched himself around my neck, pressing himself up against me. I suppressed a groan as I peeled his arms from around my neck.

"Josh," I admonished, "didn't we have a deal?"

Josh grinned up at me as he let his hands slide from my shoulders and linger unnecessarily on my arms.

Don't think about it… don't even think about it, I chanted mentally.

"I know, but this is just a hug, see?" He turned to Jorja, who shrieked as he wrapped his cold body around hers.

"That is definitely cheating." I went to find a patch of shade to reapply some suncream. Trystan was definitely scowling at me as I sat down, and I didn't really know how to respond, because that was a pretty bizarre response for someone who'd had to psych himself up to kiss me.

"Want a hand?"

I looked over my shoulder at Josh. I'd heard him offer his turn batting to Jorja, and she was just lining up to take her first pitch from Trystan—i.e. there was no chance she was going to come and help. I looked back up at the youngest brother and didn't bother to hide my weary sigh. His grin didn't waver; it wasn't smug and arrogant. He just looked thrilled and a little nervous.

It wasn't hard to work out why the sudden change in attitude: thanks to my little slip of the tongue, he now knew I was interested in him. And I'd definitely lied to Jorja when I'd implied my reaction to Josh had only been because of what Trystan had been doing to me at the time; the boy was cute, and despite the continued protests of my conscience, my ego was loving the slightly lustful fawning in the eyes he fixed on me.

With a last shake of my head, I held out the suncream and turned around so he could do my back.

"Fine," I said in a monotone. The fact was Jorja wasn't going to stop and help, and struggling with it by myself was stupid when I was certain Josh was just going to stand there and watch either way.

I stiffened as he squeezed out three spots of bitterly cold cream on either side of my ribs. A pair of not-that-warm hands followed them.

I'm not sure I've ever been so self-conscious of a suncream application in my life. I was obscenely aware of Josh's breathing behind me—the way it seemed to get shallower and shallower as his hands worked my skin—and of the way his fingers seemed to linger in every nook and cranny of my ribs and spine. His hands pressed down over my kidneys and then his deft fingers made sure that my skin was protected well below the waistband of my shorts.

"A year is a really long time," he said from behind me. His breathing hitched as he finally stilled his hands against me after drawing it out as long as he could.

"Mmm." I let my head drop forward on my chest and didn't look round at him.

"Come on, Ide," he pleaded gently as he leaned forward so his chest was against my spine. His hands were still pressed into my shoulder blades, and his fingers curled slightly in my skin. "I don't think I've ever been this turned on in my life."

I felt his erection—clothed in his wet trunks—brush against the small of my back. I reminded myself that his sexual life had probably only been two years—*at most*—and that the comment definitely wasn't a big deal.

"I really can't, Josh. It's not that I don't think yer...." I hesitated because telling him what I thought probably wasn't going to help. "I just can't," I finished instead.

"Is it because of my brother?" he asked. "I know you used to have a thing for him, and now he's been acting kind of weird, but he's straight. He's just messing with you: I heard him joking with Vince about it."

"Huh?" I turned around, met big brown eyes, and instantly regretted it. Shit, the boy was sin. Instead, I focused on what he'd said. I knew Trystan was straight, and I knew he was just messing with me. But joking with Vince about it? Vince was a fricking homophobe to rival how Trystan had used to be.

With one last rueful look, I scooped my hand over Josh's ear, let my fingers slide through his damp and slightly-too-long dark hair, and pulled his lips against mine.

I felt more than heard the muted gasp that struggled from the back of his throat as I kissed him, gently at first. I let my lips slide and suckle over his and then I pressed my tongue forward, let it slip over his flesh and then inside his mouth as he granted me entry. We were still positioned awkwardly, and it was probably a good thing. He mewed softly and pressed himself desperately up against my spine. His chest was still damp, his shorts were still soaked; I could feel his arousal as he rubbed himself against me.

Don'teventhinkaboutit....

I balled my free hand in a fist against my knee to stop myself from reaching round and pulling him in front of me and pressing him down against the grass and.... Oh my God, the noises he was making—just from a kiss—were far too similar to my fantasy of last night. I concentrated on the crick in my neck as I strained round to reach him and the ache in my knees as both our weights pressed down through me.

I pulled away. Josh's lips followed mine, and I brought my hand round to his cheek to hold him where he was.

"Happy now?" I whispered. I didn't need his erection pressed into me to know that he wasn't; the desperation in his kiss told me all I needed to know.

"No," he bleated as he gasped for breath.

"Yeah, well, that's why I said ye needed to wait, 'cause I'm not having sex with an underage kid."

"You're a tease." It was his turn to chide.

"Well right back at ye," I chuckled lightly, and then scowled as my attention was caught by the cricket players who were not playing, but staring, all three of them, at me and Josh. Vince looked disgusted, Jorja looked aghast, and Trystan looked furious.

"Shit," I said. Josh looked puzzled as he turned to see what I was looking at. He looked back around at me very quickly, his eyes wide and his face suddenly bright red, and not from lust this time.

"Oh my God, why did you kiss me in front of them?"

"Sorry, heat of the moment thing. And anyway, ye were the one wi' yer hands all over me back and arse in front of them a second ago."

The truth was I didn't know exactly why I'd kissed him. He'd been cute and sexy, but I'd resisted that last night and I'd been tipsy then. Maybe it had been to prove a point, to show him that I was right and it was more than kisses he was after. On the other hand, it could have been because of the flash of anger that had stirred in my stomach at the thought of Trystan laughing with Vince at my expense. But he laughed at me all the time, so that didn't make sense.

"Get yer hands off my brother, fag!"

I sighed as I dropped my hand from Josh's cheek and looked up at Vince. The warm kindling of lust and amusement I'd experienced a moment ago was gone, extinguished by my mounting irritation as I met Vince's gaze dead on.

"I will if ye stop staring at my sister's tits." I kept my voice deceptively low.

I watched the middle Jackson bristle. Behind him Trystan and Jorja were keeping their distance, and both of them looked thoroughly pissed off. Josh remained kneeling by my back, but there was a little distance between us. I didn't move because I didn't want Vince to catch a glimpse of his younger brother's rapidly dwindling erection.

"That's different; Jorja's a whore."

I snorted at that because Jorja was nothing like me. She had only slept with one guy, and she only did that when they'd been dating for several months. Yet at fifteen, Josh was apparently already banging girls and had spent the last few days attempting to throw himself at me. I didn't mind, and technically, I almost certainly deserved the label of whore. My sister did not. Nor was she the type of girl to stand and take shit from a gobby seventeen-year-old.

Her balled fist connected with the back of his head.

"I am *not* a whore!" Not the most original comeback by my sister, but I think along with the punch it got her point across.

"Ye good?" I said in an undertone as I caught Josh's gaze in mine and dropped my eyes surreptitiously to his crotch. Wide-eyed, he nodded and I jumped to my feet, crossing quickly to Jorja's side. I stood squarely in front of her as Vince regained his footing and whirled around to face her. He hesitated when he saw me looking down on him with cold eyes.

"Touch my sister, and I'll knock yer teeth out, understand?"

Vince was shorter than I was, but he was still around six foot and he was stockier and undoubtedly stronger. But I've always been stronger than I look, and the three Jackson brothers—especially Vince and Trystan—knew this better than most; they grew up sporting the bruises from picking on me. Jorja, too, could defend herself, but after sixteen years of her standing in front of me, I liked the chance to repay the favor. Still.... I flicked my blue eyes up toward Trystan. Growing up being bullied for how I look, then who I like, meant I was pretty used to being beaten up; I had a high pain threshold. So I could probably hurt Vince more than he hurt me, but if Trystan helped, I was going to get my ass kicked and I would just have to hope that they wouldn't turn on Jorja as well.

"Vince, apologize to Josh and Jorja, then go cool your head." Trystan's voice was full of cold fury.

I wasn't alone in looking slightly startled.

"No way, Trys. Did you not see what the fag was—" Vince cut off as Trystan's hand twisted in around the bones of his shoulder.

"*Yes*, I saw. *Yes*, I think it's disgusting. And *yes*—I'm *fucking furious*." Trystan's voice was low and somehow, even though his dark eyes were fixed on Vince, I felt like everything he said was directed at me.

"But did it look to you like Josh couldn't have run away? No! So before you go around throwing insults at people, why don't you think about what that makes our brother and whether you're going to disown or belittle him for who he likes?"

He didn't give Vince a chance to argue or even to give the apology he had demanded, he just tossed him to one side as if his brother was a ragdoll. Then he turned to me.

"*You*," he hissed, "are the *whore* in this situation."

I shrugged. "Yeah, *and*? I don't deny it."

"You *said* you weren't going to do anything."

"I didn't. It was a kiss, Trystan. I didn't touch him."

"It was my fault, Trys, I just wanted to see. Ide didn't force me or anything," Josh cut in, his voice surprisingly strong as he took half a step toward his eldest brother.

"Shut up, Josh. The difference is Idrys is old enough to know better, and besides"—he turned that hateful gaze back to me—"he probably used some faggy mind tricks on you to confuse you."

"Hmm, hypocrite much?"

Trystan ground his teeth, he visibly tried to temper his annoyance as he turned to Josh.

"Sorry, Josh, it's fine if you're gay. I'm just pissed at this dickhead."

I felt a hand on my shoulder and twisted round to see Jorja glaring up at me. She leaned forward to hiss angrily in my ear so only I would hear. "Yer an idiot! Just in case yer stupid enough not t' realize; Trys is pissed."

"No shit," I interrupted and went to turn back. She grabbed my shoulder and whirled me around to face her. She stared up into my eyes, searching for something she didn't find.

"Oh my God, Ide; yer such a bloody head case. He's *fricking* jealous!"

That got my attention. My face crumpled into a scowl, and I pulled her slightly away from the other two. "Are ye crazy? What're ye talking about?"

"Are ye a moron or an *actual* dickhead?" She looked genuinely annoyed at me. "Ye said something happened, right? And now ye kiss his brother right there *in front* of him? That's a pretty low blow."

I craned my head over my shoulder to stare at Trystan, who was talking to his youngest brother in hushed tones. He shot me the finger without looking up.

"Trys is straight, Jorja," I said as I turned back to my sister. "He had trouble *kissing* me, for God's sake."

"Meh, maybe he is; doesn't change the fact that he *did* kiss ye, and it doesn't change the fact that he is currently livid and probably embarrassed. I know *I* would be." I looked down at my sister and realized I believed everything that she was saying. It didn't really make sense, but I did believe it.

"Fricking hell," I cursed and marched over to where Trystan and Josh were. "Josh, I need t' speak to yer brother," I said gently and shot him an apologetic smile. He looked sad but he nodded and I watched in silence as he headed over to where Vince was lobbing stones into the lake.

"Look, Trys." I only dragged my eyes back to Trystan because watching Josh was not helping. "I'm sorry if there was some kind of misunderstanding. Yer right, I am a whore, and I was playing along with ye because it was fun. Because I knew ye were straight and it amused me to tempt ye to do gay stuff with me. I didn't think for a second that ye might get confused by what we were doing, because ye always seem so fricking arrogant. Still, it's not really an excuse, I know, and I'm sorry for leading ye on and then kissing yer brother," I said, even though I definitely recalled Trystan asking me to do exactly that and probably more and even though I knew that I believed what Josh had said about Trystan mocking me with Vince.

Trystan stared at me, and then he shrugged. "Whatever; why would I care?"

Needless to say, the rest of the holiday was not as much fun as the first half, and not just because it rained every day.

6—SPIDER

MY PHONE started ringing as I was just reaching the outskirts of York.

"*Oi, dickhead, ye were supposed t' stick around fer a couple o' days, eh?*" was the eloquent greeting I got as I answered the call. I'd put it on handsfree so I could drive, and Theo's heavy accent over the background of his Jeep's engine made the speakers complain briefly.

"Aye, sorry, Theo." I stifled a yawn as I drew up to a set of traffic lights. It was still light but it was gone nine and I figured Theo had probably just called in after finishing up his evening duties, expecting to go for a beer. I hadn't slept well for the last couple of nights, half because it hadn't let up raining and the sound had been amplified by the tent, and half because of the person I'd still had to share a tent with.

Theo grunted something and was quiet for a moment. "*So what happened? Yer sister had a face on her worse than the time ye kissed that boy she was dating.*"

I chuckled at the memory. "He kissed me, and ye know it. But that's an improvement on the last time *I* saw her. She's been looking at me worse than that time ye pushed her in the lake and ruined those ridiculous pink trainers she insisted on wearing all the fricking time."

"*That bad, eh?*" Theo let out a loud chortle, and there was a pause as we both remembered simpler times. Back when Trystan Jackson was nothing but a bully and my sister would take my side even when I'd been a dick.

Honestly, the end of the holiday had turned out worse than even *I* had imagined, and we all know how much I was looking forward to it. Trystan didn't have a nice word to say to me and had reverted to more or less how he'd been five years ago, admittedly with less physical abuse. Josh wasn't allowed anywhere near me, and well, Vince never spoke to me out of choice anyway. Jorja was pissed with me, my dad was furious because he just went ahead and assumed it was my fault everyone had fallen out, and Mum was just sad, which was worse than her being annoyed with me.

The cherry on the metaphorical camping cake was that it hadn't stopped raining.

When we pulled up in the farmyard earlier, I had unpacked my stuff from the 4x4 straight into my car and driven off. I didn't even stay for the roast dinner I had technically earned by going in the first place. But no one tried to stop me.

"*Go on, what did ye do?*" I could basically hear Theo shaking his head at me.

I smiled even though there was nobody to see the melancholy it was tinged with. "Ye know, I know gay men that don't like t' gossip as much as ye do?"

"*Yeah? Well there has t' be some benefits t' having a gay best friend, eh? I'm in touch with my feminine side, the girls dig it. What do ye city kids call it? Metro?*"

Theo was the same age as me and the least "metro" person I could think of; he drove a mud colored jeep so that he didn't have to clean it, wore jumpers his Gran knitted, and dressed mostly for his job—which as a farmer required him to wear things he didn't mind getting covered in shit. With the exception of his love of gossip, cheesy pop music and tendency to turn into a mother-hen where I was concerned, he was the straightest person I knew in personality and appearance. But still, it made me laugh for the first time in a few days.

"Sorry for bailing on ye, man. But ye know what she's like when she's got one on her. Best t' give her some space and let her chill out." Actually I was giving her space because I was pissed with her almost as much she was pissed with me. I don't care what she thought had gone on, we were supposed to stick together, but she abandoned me and sided with Trystan-*fricking*-Jackson, of all people. It made my blood boil and I needed the alone time to chill out as much as she did.

"*Aye, that I do. Well drive safe, and ye owe me a beer next time yer back.*"

"Sure thing, Theo. See ye."

I was almost home when I hung up with a lingering half-smile. I kind of wished that I'd just taken the five minute drive to Theo's instead of the two hour trip to York. He would have let me crash there, and I could have caught up with him and probably got the clearance I needed to sort out this shit with Jorja. But I had wanted to come back to York, I wanted what only the city could offer me.

Ten minutes later I parallel parked into the only free space on my street, loaded my shoulders with my bag and tent and headed to the beaten up town house that was my student home. I didn't bother calling out a hello because it was really only me and Jason that stuck around over the summer and he was probably at work. Plus, I was kind of disgusting because bathing in the lake had been less fun in the rain, not to mention surrounded by people that didn't like me very much.

I gave Carmella's still empty room a rueful glance as I headed upstairs. Penny, Jason, Matt, Carmella and me had lived together since first year, and I'd thought I knew all of them pretty well. Obviously I hadn't known Carmella as well as I'd thought, because while I was in Canada she'd dropped out of uni with no explanation. I'd come back to find her room deserted and Jason panicking about how the hell we were going to pay her part of the rent.

But that was a problem for next week; in fact, it was a problem for any time other than right now.

At the top of the house I unlocked my attic-room, chucked my bags against one of the other assorted piles of camping, biking and climbing equipment, and dropped onto my bed like I hadn't slept in it for a month—oh wait, I hadn't.

Right then I had a whole list of things that needed doing. I needed to dry out my tent because it had rained constantly for the last four days. I needed to unpack my sleeping bag from its stuff sack to air. I needed to do some washing, I needed a shower, and I needed some food. Instead, I sat on the end of my bed and made a call.

"Dan?" I said as the guy on the other end picked up.

"*Ide, you're back in civilization? I missed your sexy ass.*" His voice was sultry and low, and then he switched back to his usual drawl. "*So was it as bad as expected?*"

"Fricking shit. Seriously, what is it wi' me and straight men?" I lamented as I lay back and stared at the brown stain that marbled the ceiling of my attic room. Honestly, the way things had turned out was probably worse than if everything had just been how it had used to be.

Dan chuckled. "*You confuse them.*"

"Meh, no shit, are ye free?" *What?* I already told you I was a whore. If Dan wasn't free I had other guys I would try, but Dan was my preference because he was one of the two guys I didn't mind going bottom for, and unlike Echo, Dan didn't mind switching—I wasn't entirely sure what I was in the mood for.

His tone dropped a note as he realized this wasn't just a social call and he chuckled again. *"I just got in from a run, give me forty minutes."*

"Sure, I need t' shower anyway." I ran a hand through my caked hair.

"Cool, see you in a bit, then, Ide," Dan said as he hung up, and his tone held all the promise and anticipation that I wanted to hear right now.

This was my life, my phone contacts full of fuck buddies from whom I could pick and choose whatever took my fancy, all of them more than happy to accommodate me. I didn't need to worry about some inexperienced teenager coming out of the closet, and I certainly didn't need to concern myself with some bi-curious/in-denial straight guy. In a few months, I'd have forgotten all about the stupid Jackson brothers once again. And next year I'd be making damn sure I was somewhere else.

At least that was the plan.

IT WAS eleven thirty and dark when I let myself in the house with a stifled yawn. I'd left at eight this morning for what was supposed to be an easy two hours at the gym, followed by ten 'til four of lectures and "no longer than two hours" of work—I should have known better. Next time Meredith begged me for a midweek work gig I was going to tell her no. Mind you, I distinctly remembered trying to tell her no this time.

I headed straight for the kitchen, because I was starving and exhausted and all I wanted was a bowl of cereal and my bed. But of course, every bowl in the house was dirty. I suppressed a shudder as I poured away the solid brown mass that may or may not have been the once chocolaty remains of Coco Pops.

"Aw, princess going to be sick?"

I stilled for just a moment, because James was exactly what I *didn't* want to deal with right now. James was the guy we'd found to fill Carmella's room. We'd had interviews back in August, and I had wanted the quiet girl, but I had been outvoted and we'd ended up with James, with his nasty little brown eyes and boring brown hair and a bit of belly. Who, incidentally, had also neglected to mention in his interview that he was a homophobic prick, despite the fact that I let him know I was gay. I mean, can you get any clearer than "Hey, I'm Idrys, and just so ye know, I'm gay"? I think not. Penny said that he was only mean because I confused him.

Oh wait, where have I heard that before?

"Give it a rest, James, I'm tired."

He snorted as he hovered at my back. "Aw, you get mobbed by your little fag friends? How many of them were there this time?"

"I've been at work."

I had no idea why James couldn't just ignore me, but I did my best to blank him, distracting myself with the spider that was crawling up the side of the window as I washed up the bowl and poured myself some cereal. I had to steal Penny's milk because miraculously mine had disappeared—*again*, also miraculously my fruit and veg had been shoved to the rear of the fridge and was frozen against the back wall—*again*.

I stepped around him, met his small smirking eyes with a blank glare and went up to my room, where I planned to eat my highly unbalanced meal and fall unconscious as quickly as possible.

I forgot to close the curtains, and I chucked an arm over my face as I woke up wondering when I had accidentally changed the alarm tone on my phone. Through one cracked eyelid I caught sight of the shimmery shit that they'd used on me last night, which was now all over my sheets. I pulled an irritated face at the poor decision not to shower, and grabbed for my phone because *what-do-you-know*, I hadn't changed the tone, I was getting a call.

"Y'ello," I croaked.

"*So yer alive are ye? I was about t' call Dan and see if he was asking for a ransom or something.*"

"Ha-ha, yer hysterical. What fricking time is it?" I pulled the phone away from my ear and grimaced as I saw the time. "Have I mentioned that yer a twat, Theo? Some o' us dun have to be up for another two hours."

"*Yeah, well if ye answered yer goddamn phone at any other time o' the day, then I'd call ye then. 'Til then, I'll call ye when I know ye'll answer.*"

I grimaced at him down the phone and swung my legs round so I was sitting over the side of the bed. A swig of stale water from two days ago took away the worst of my tacky morning mouth, and I liked to think I sounded considerably more human as I spoke again.

"So, how ye doing?" I asked pleasantly enough. It had been a couple of weeks since I'd last heard from Theo and more than two months since I'd seen him.

"*Nae too bad, just winding everything down after the summer, ye know how it is.*" I did indeed know how it was, and as much as I loved my home, I didn't miss the work at all. "*I've ordered some new front shock absorbers and I was just wondering if ye were going t' show yer face around here any time before the new year so I could get a hand putting them on."*

"Shock absorbers?" I pulled a face down the phone. "Theo, yer last ones were sweet, I've told ye, ye need t' get some new bloody disk brakes." We got sidetracked arguing the merits of his new piece of kit, and really I don't know why I was complaining when it meant I could have his old gear. It was more habit than anything else and I was grinning down the phone as we chatted.

"Anyway, the point is, it's been like two months, Idrys. Did ye guys go back in time ten years and nae bring me with ye? 'Cause yer acting like yer eleven and eight instead o' twenty-one and eighteen."

I contained a sigh as Theo got to the point of his call. Not shock absorbers or disk brakes, but me and my sister, who was still ignoring me two months after Scotland.

"Jorja was home last weekend," he carried on, and the mention of my sister's name was enough to sober the smile right off my face. *"When I brought yer name up I thought she was going t' scratch ma eyes out. It's been two fricking months, Ide. Ye guys never fall out fer this long, not even when we were kids. So can ye just hurry up and apologize already?"*

I didn't know what was more frustrating, the fact that my sister wasn't talking to me over something that had nothing to do with her, or that despite the fact that I was still annoyed with her, I would have apologized weeks ago if she'd answered my calls. But she wouldn't pick up the phone, so I'd stopped trying.

"I've nothing t' apologize for. She's the one that wouldn't answer my calls." I sounded like the child Theo was accusing me of being. But seriously, Jorja had no reason to be mad with me still. In fact, it was me that should be mad at her after she basically betrayed me by siding with Trystan. I mean, we always had each other's backs—or we were supposed to.

Theo sighed. *"I seriously doubt that ye aren't at least mostly in the wrong. But listen,"* he continued before I could complain. *"This is how girls work; ye fall out, and then ye apologize even if ye think yer in the right. It makes life easier for everyone involved, trust me."*

"Oh yeah, yer an expert are ye? Ye get yerself a girlfriend while I've been away?"

I could practically hear him rolling his eyes at me. *"At least I've had more than two relationships in ma life. Learn t' take some advice, yer twat."*

"Fine, fine. Don't get yer knickers in a fricking twist. I'll call her again, but I bet she won't answer." I realized I was pouting at the phone and let out an irritated huff. There was a reason I preferred men over women, and yet here I was taking advice on females so I could make up with my damned sister; the irony was painful. "Ye know yer as bad as she is sometimes. God save me if ye two ever get yer asses into gear and become a couple."

Theo grunted. *"Yeah? Maybe we'd be able t' drag ye into something like a reasonable person, eh?"*

"Ha-fricking-ha." I *was* a reasonable person, I just liked sex and didn't want to be tied down in a relationship that was going to end predictably. This way I could do what the hell I liked, as could everyone else, and we could all be happy.

"Speaking o' dragging ye into a reasonable person, how's Dan? He got fed up of ye yet? Or vice versa."

I chuckled because the idea was faintly ridiculous; mine and Dan's little arrangement kept us both happy and out of trouble, and Dan was about as likely to suddenly settle down as I was. "He's fine, pulling double shifts at the bar. I'm supposed to be seeing him tomorrow, I'll give him a kiss from ye."

Theo snorted and was distracted by a commotion on his end of the phone. Despite both of them being friends with me, Dan and Theo didn't get on all that well. Theo tolerated Dan as the lesser of two evils, and Dan thought Theo was just another in-denial straight guy and got pissed off when Theo didn't get wound up by his antics. It wasn't generally too much of an issue because it wasn't that often that Theo could get the time off from the farm to come to York, and I certainly wasn't about to take Dan home.

"And how's that dickhead downstairs?" Tess's barking had ceased in the background and Theo returned his attention to the call with a full dose of un-tempered disdain.

"Same-same," I lied.

I hadn't even meant to mention James to Theo because the guy worried too fricking much. But the last time Theo had called bugging me to come home for the weekend for some form of mountain biking related activities, I'd been up early and making breakfast. I'd cursed when I'd found my previously unopened yoghurt lounging in the top of the bin, opened, crushed and mixing with someone's leftover bolognese. In a fit of irrational irritation I'd ended up telling Theo what was going on.

It wasn't like I'd never dealt with homophobia; rightly or wrongly it was just an unfortunate side effect of being gay. Even if I couldn't deal, it didn't matter anyway, because we needed someone to pay the rent.

"I can't believe ye don't just kick him out. The shit he's pulling is abuse." If the whole thing hadn't actually been getting kind of serious I would have thought it was fricking hilarious that he was talking about us like we were some kind of married couple.

"Oh, well we're sorted, then, I'll just file for divorce, eh?" I rolled my eyes before sucking a long breath through my nose, because I definitely didn't need to be taking this out on Theo. I took a moment to pull a T-shirt on so I could go downstairs and make myself a morning brew—it wasn't like I'd be going back to sleep after this conversation. "Unfortunately it's not that simple. We're all in third year; none o' us have time t' waste searching for new people. Besides, anyone who needs a room a month into the semester is likely t' be a dick in one way or another."

"Well I think ye should make time, an' I know Jorja would say the same."

Exasperatingly, I thought Theo was probably right. It was for precisely this reason that I was so pissed off that she was ignoring me. Jorja was some kind of saint where homophobic idiots were concerned, she always knew what to do. Except she wouldn't talk to me, and every time I thought about it, it made me angry about Scotland all over again.

"So are ye going t' stop pansying about an' get yer ass over here? The forest track is just about looking nice again after the last load o' rain." Theo continued in my ear as I got downstairs and started searching for a clean mug. I'd put four to soak last night when I got in, and all but the foulest of them had magically disappeared again. Last night's spider scuttled across the windowsill as I snagged the washing-up liquid.

"Sure, sure. I'll try and call Jorja this evening, and I'll coordinate—" I was cut off by my own bleat of surprise as I turned to find James standing over me like some kind of creeper.

"Ide?"

"Shit. Sorry, Theo. Just a spider made me jump."

James laughed at me as I sidestepped around him to reach the kettle.

"Anyway, I'll call ye at the weekend. See ye." I eyed James warily as I finished up my conversation with Theo and was left alone with the guy that was giving Trystan Jackson a run for his money as my currently most disliked person. He seemed like he was just here for the same reason as me, though, and I turned my back on him as he silently started to make himself some toast.

The peace was nice for the thirty seconds it lasted. "Another whore you call a friend? He coming to stay?"

I pressed my eyes shut for half a second and swallowed down a loud "hell no." Instead I just shook my head and kept my back to him as I sat down to eat my breakfast. Even if Theo had been one of my hookups, I usually went to their houses anyway, and these days anyone coming here was completely off the books.

My phone rang and I answered it without looking, just glad for someone to distract me from James.

"Hello?"

"*Idrys Bjornson?*" the man on the other end of the phone asked.

"Yeah, speaking," I answered with my mouth full and hoped James would get bored soon.

"*Good morning Mr. Bjornson, I'm Mathius from W-publishing.*" I groaned as I realized my mistake and checked the number.

"Yes, look," I interrupted before he could go any further. When the summer holidays had finished I'd told my modeling agency that I wasn't going to take any more shoots for a while. That had lasted all of a week before they came back and told me someone had offered an extra hundred a shoot. And well, I really wanted a new tent. Now I mostly took work for a designer called Meredith who, although irritating, thought I was worth awkward hours and a lot of money. However, some companies just wouldn't take no for an answer.

"I don't know how ye got my number or how many times I have to explain to ye guys that I only work through my agency. I'm a busy guy; if they say it won't fit in my schedule, then it just won't. And if they say I won't do it, it's because I won't." And honestly, did these guys think I was an idiot? That I was just going to say yes to some random on the phone and turn up to have my kidneys taken or end up in a gay porno at gunpoint?

"*But I think you'll find the pay is very reasonable.*"

I exhaled obviously, because I'd momentarily forgotten about James and he was sniggering.

"I'm sure it is, but it doesn't change my answer. Bye."

I hung up.

"How much does a whore like you go for?" I winced as James's hand snarled through my hair. He yanked my head over the back of the chair, binding me in place and forcing me to stare up at his sneering face.

This was getting ridiculous. The guy had been here for six weeks and he was only getting worse. He'd started just slinking around in corners and making snide comments, but now he was basically assaulting me.

"Let me go, James," I said softly. To begin with I'd tried to meet his spiteful comments with my own. But that only made it worse so now I just ignored him and tried to be calm. Really, all I wanted to do was drive my fist into his face. But I had a job this weekend, and if I turned up with a black eye, I had a funny feeling that not only would I not get paid, but I'd also probably never hear the end of it from Meredith. I reached round and grabbed his wrist, extracting his hand from my hair and standing so I could look down on him.

"If ye touch me again…," I let my hand tighten on his wrist until I could see him wince. I kept my voice low and furious because shouting didn't work, sneering didn't work, nothing worked. But I was starting to get really, *really* pissed off. "I'll bend ye over the table and fuck ye like a girl, then we'll see how cocky ye are."

A mixture of fear and anger battled across his face as he tried to tug his hand away. I let him go, grabbed my half-finished tea and cereal bowl in one hand, and went back upstairs to my room. At least James was on the ground floor and I was in the attic, so he had no excuse to follow me upstairs. But I wasn't really hungry anymore as I leaned back on my bedroom door and turned the lock. I ate anyway and got ready for another long day.

I was definitely going to call Jorja this evening.

DESPITE BEING woken up two hours earlier than intended, I somehow managed to end up running late for my first lecture. I was almost jogging to campus when my phone rang again. It was another unsaved number so I sent it straight to voice mail.

"Suze, Patrick," I called as spotted the people I usually hung out with on my course. I hurried through the packs of people that were heading into the recently vacated lecture hall. They paused by the door and smiled warmly at me as I finally reached them.

"Late night?" Suze said as she tucked her arm into mine to walk into the massive lecture theatre.

"Not in an exciting way," I answered honestly. We found three seats and I rummaged round in the bottom of my bag before pulling out a small pot of makeup. "Was this the stuff ye were after?" I offered it to the small Asian girl and she shrieked and threw her hands around my neck.

"Oh my God, Ide. I can't believe you actually got it. This color is limited edition." Over her head I met Patrick's eye and gave a small shrug. I may have been gay, but I'd had to ask the makeup artist last night to find it for me. She'd been new and she had handed it over with a suggestion that I might go for drinks with her—when I told her I was gay, she said she would bring her boyfriend.

"How'm I supposed to compete against that?" Patrick complained as he took the small pot of eye shadow from Suze's hand to examine. He gave a puzzled smile as he passed it back.

"Sorry, mate, I'll give it to ye to hand over next time," I said with a wink and then the lecturer was arriving. I gave an irritated huff as my phone vibrated silently in my pocket.

My exasperation melted into a warm pool of relief as I saw it was Jorja. I gave silent thanks to Theo and a curse at the bad timing as the lecturer called for quiet.

"Go ahead, guys, I'm going to try and call my sister," I said to Suze and Patrick as the first of our lectures came to an end. It was a five-minute walk to the next one so I hoped I could call Jorja quickly, tell her how much I loved her and wasn't ignoring her, and that I would call her back properly as soon as I finished for the day. In case you're wondering—Jorja hates texts. Suze and Patrick nodded and waved as they hurried off with the rest of our class.

"Ide!"

I wanted to groan as I dropped the phone away from my ear as my name was uttered by a slightly too high and overly camp lisp. A small gay guy appeared in front of me, the kind you can tell is gay just by looking, with big eyes that were framed with suspiciously black and full eyelashes, an affectedly high voice, and feminine clothing. "Have you been avoiding me, Idrys?"

I sighed and slipped my phone back into my pocket.

"Of course not, Ashlie." I leaned down and pressed a kiss onto his forehead. Ashlie was one of my fuck buddies, but in all truth he'd been low down on my list of late because I was going through a phase of liking to bottom—which kind of limited my options to either Dan or Echo. "I told ye about my new housemate, and ye know I don't fit on yer bed." Which, while not the main reason, was a bloody good one because I could hardly stand in the small guy's room.

"Good." His mock scowl slid instantly into a grin and he clung to my arm. "A few of us are going out tomorrow night, you going to come?"

"A few of us are going out" was Ashlie's code for a gang bang, which I wasn't really in the mood for at the moment and definitely didn't have the energy for. Plus I'd already arranged to meet Dan, and I had to work on Saturday. The latter was the excuse I gave him as I slipped away. In the end I had no time to call Jorja and I had to run across campus to get in before the lecture started.

I then had a two-hour lecture followed by a one-hour lecture, and I had to eat in the short break in between. Leaving four and a half hours before returning a call from my sister was always a bad idea, and I was hardly surprised when it went through to voice mail.

"Boy trouble?" said Patrick. He had an understanding smile on his face; he had clearly clocked my frustrated sigh as I dropped my phone from my head for the third time on our walk home.

Suze giggled. "Ide would have to have a *boyfriend* to get trouble from."

I ran a hand through my unruly hair, then remembered it was long enough to tie back and tugged a hair tie from a packet I had stuffed into the bottom of my bag.

"Sister trouble." The irony that I refused to settle down so I didn't have to deal with this kind of stuff was not lost on me. "Seriously, I'm gay for a reason: girls are a nightmare. I don't even know why she's pissed at me; well, I do: she's pissed right now because I didn't call her back, but I mean why she was pissed before she called."

"Well," Suze paused to laugh, and ruffle a hand through my already messy hair. "That wasn't convoluted at all. The easiest way to work out what's wrong is to remember the last time she wasn't annoyed with you."

"Meh, I know *when* she got pissed off; I just don't know why *she's* pissed. I didn't do anything to *her*. Plenty o' other people, but not her."

"You stole a boy from her again, Ide?" Suze said with a smile because I'd told her a few of the more entertaining and E-rated stories of my childhood.

"Well, it did include boys, but not ones she was interested in; she was encouraging me."

"Boys—plural?" Trust Patrick to pick up on that. I shot him a grim smile; he knew what I was like, but he didn't necessarily approve.

"Yeah, well, it was an eventful holiday." Which was an understatement and a half.

"I thought you went to Scotland with that family you hate? Weren't you complaining about it for the whole of July?" Patrick asked. He was likely to know because he'd been in Canada with me and I'd sat next to him on the plane home and drowned my sorrows at having to go.

"Yeah, I did." His eyebrows flicked up his forehead, and I could tell even he was a little curious. But at that moment my phone rang again. My jubilation was cut short when I realized it wasn't Jorja's name flashing across my screen but yet another unrecognized number.

"Look," I snapped as I answered the call, my tone low and dangerous. "I don't know how many times I have to explain to ye that I'm not fricking interested in the damn job. No matter how much ye pay me or who it's for or how many new kidneys ye'll be able to buy yer dying daughter wi' the commission. I'm not taking the fricking suspicious-ass job, understand?"

Patrick and Suze were looking slightly startled because I didn't usually lose my cool. And I had definitely lost my cool. But it was turning into a stressful day and I could really do without the endless phone calls when Jorja could be trying to contact me.

"*Ide?*" I paused before I could continue my rant because only people I knew called me Ide; the dodgy modeling jobs called me Mr. Bjornson. And more than that, I realized I recognized the way that suspiciously irritating southern posh-boy voice said my name.

"What the hell! Trys, is that ye?"

"*Yeah it's me, what the fuck was that about?*"

I opened my mouth to explain and apologize, but then I remembered who I was talking to.

"No. What the hell, Trystan? Why the hell are ye even calling me?"

This was worse than talking to a modeling agency, and I didn't want Jorja to get an engaged tone. And then I realized... that my sister had probably been calling me for Trystan Jackson. Which pissed me off all the more.

I hung up.

We'd come to a stop and I realized Patrick and Suze were staring at me with slightly shocked looks on their faces.

"You okay, Ide?" Patrick asked softly.

I realized that I was furious. Actually genuinely wanting to hit someone furious. I took a deep breath and dropped my face into my hands, obscuring the seething anger that must have leaked into my eyes.

"Shit, sorry, guys, I'm fine. It's been a long day."

"What's going on? Who was on the phone?" Suze asked gently as she linked her arm through mine and leaned against me in a reassuring way.

What was going on, indeed? My sister who I'd been desperately trying to make up with over some unspecified transgression had finally called me. But the suspicion that she had called me for Trystan would not go away, and I hated that man so much right then that with Suze's half hug pressed against me I genuinely thought I might break down in tears on the street.

In my hand my phone started to vibrate once again. And it was with grim acceptance of the truth that I saw Jorja's name flash up on the screen. This time I hung up on her. The gesture wasn't unnoticed by Suze.

"I thought you wanted to talk to her?"

"Yeah, I changed my mind." My voice was gruff and hollow and I palmed through my call history to pull up the last unknown number. "Guys, I need to make this call. It's probably going to be messy, so ye should go ahead."

Both of them fixed me with concerned looks. Suze reached up onto her tiptoes and pressed a kiss against my cheek.

"You're a lovely man, Idrys, and when you decide to settle you'll make someone very happy. Don't forget that. Or let anyone tell you different, okay?"

I took a deep breath and swallowed down the lump that balled in my throat. Suze was too nice to be a friend of mine. I managed to smile down at her, even though I didn't believe a word of what she'd said.

"Thanks, love," I said and gave her a brief squeeze in return before she detached herself and went to Patrick's side to hurry along down the pavement.

I hit the Send Call button before I lost my nerve and raised the phone to my ear. It was answered on the second ring.

"*You spoke to your sister?*" the voice on the other end of the line said, a voice I had hoped to go at least a year, preferably two, before hearing again—Trystan.

"No, if I speak to her now I'll lose my cool. What d'ye want, Trystan?"

"*You in a prissy mood again, Ide?*"

"A—" I cut myself off before I could explode at that. I was almost home, and I didn't know whether that was a good thing or a bad one; in public I had a reason not to start shouting.

"Trystan, thanks to that whatever it was in Scotland, my sister isn't speaking to me." I was a little more calm this time. "When she finally decides to call me it's because of ye... so yes I'm in a 'prissy mood,' ye fricking arrogant bastard. Now tell me why yer calling before I head into town to change my number."

"So you do act like a fag sometimes; you go in a mood like a girl."

By my side I balled my hand into a fist and fought the urge to punch the nearest wall as a replacement for the face of the man on the other end of the phone.

"Last chance, Trystan," I said instead and remembered the fat paycheck I'd get if I turned up unscathed on Saturday.

"I need a favor."

"Hoh? Well, newsflash, Trystan: if ye wanted me to do something for ye, ye should have fucking been nice to me, ye—argh!" I cut myself off again because the people walking down the street were giving me funny looks. I tried to calm my breathing.

"Look, you think I like *calling you? You think I* enjoy *having to call up and beg after you made a fucking fool of me?"*

"Oh my *fricking* God, Trys! It was a *game*. And it was *ye* who fricking started it, so don't give me that shit. Now what do ye want?"

The other end of the line went quiet for a moment, and I lifted my phone from my ear to see if he'd hung up. He hadn't and eventually I was greeted with a sigh.

"Fucking hell, you really are shallow, aren't you? Jorja said as much but—"

"Oh, I'm so *sorry*, Trystan Jackson, that my personality offends ye. I'll be sure to make sure I'm more normal next time I see ye. Shall I be all virginal and pretend to quake when ye press yer morning wood into me?" Sarcasm was laid thick on my words but my voice had lost its venom because this time it wasn't just Vince he'd been talking to about me, but my sister too.

I was home and I wanted to go inside so I could cry or scream in private. But I'd have to walk past James's room, and if he was in, I wasn't sure I could cope with him and Trystan at the same time. But I could hardly hover outside my own house. I stared up at the building in indecision.

The choice was made for me as a hand slid around my neck and grasped my jaw.

"Looking for me, *faggot*?" James's words slid into the ear that didn't have my phone pressed against it. I snatched my face from his grip and hissed at him as I spun to face him. I wondered how long he'd been following me.

"I've warned ye once already, James, if ye touch me again I swear I'll slice yer dick off while yer sleeping," I snapped back, but I know there was an edge of fear in my voice because the look in James's eyes was actually beginning to concern me. My phone was completely forgotten as James backed me into the door.

"Ha, empty threats," grunted James.

"Stay away from me, James!" I hissed.

"Ide? Idrys? You still there? What's going on?"

I actually wanted to laugh, because the one person who might be able to help me I disliked almost as much as James right now.

He pulled something out of his pocket. It flashed in the sun, and for a moment I thought it was a knife.

He laughed at me as he saw the ashen horror wash through my face and body as I slumped back against the door.

He continued his dark snigger as he wove his keys through his fingers before he pressed them into our front door. I stumbled backward through the doorway as he opened it. In a flash I was rushing up the stairs, straight to the top of the house. I locked my door and slid down the wall with my thighs pulled tightly to my chest and my head dropped against my knees.

It had been a long time since someone had scared me like that.

"Ide…? Ide…?"

"I'm here," I whispered, because that was all I could get my voice to do, and although I really didn't want to talk, Trystan actually sounded kind of worried.

"What the hell was that?" he asked.

"New housemate—he makes ye and Vince look like fricking gay rights activists."

"You live with him? Is that really safe? What does Jorja think?"

"Jorja doesn't know, because she's not talking to me, because of ye, so… tell me what it is ye want and go t' hell, Trystan. I don't need yer pity."

"*It's not pity. Fucking hell, Ide. My placement in Oxford fell through at the last minute. I got a new one in York, and I need somewhere to stay while I find a house.*"

I laughed, and it was slightly hysterical. "Ye know? Right now I'd actually rather deal wi' ye than that guy; at least I know what shittiness to expect from ye."

"*I'm not asking for you to kick anyone out. I'll just sleep on a couch until I get a place sorted; it shouldn't take more than a couple of weeks.*"

"Ye for real?"

"*Unfortunately, yes.*"

I really hoped that sometime soon his answer to that question would be no.

"When d'ye start yer placement?" I asked, because it seemed like the sensible thing to say.

"*Monday*" was his blunt response.

I sighed. "When d'ye need to come up?"

"*Friday.*"

"Friday? As in tomorrow?"

There was a pause. "*Yeah.*"

"Yer kidding?"

"*Nope.*"

The emotional rollercoaster ride that had been the last forty minutes of my life was beginning to take its toll, and I felt myself shiver slightly as adrenaline started to mess with my regular body function.

"Trys?"

"*Yeah?*"

"If ye try any o' that shit ye pulled in the tent, I'll kick yer ass out on the street."

"*That's fine.*"

"I'll be sleeping around, a lot."

"*That's your choice.*"

"I know. I'm not asking yer permission. I'm preparing ye so ye don't have a hissy fit again when ye see me kissing some other guy."

"*I didn't—*"

I cut him off before he could say anything. "I don't want to talk about it. I just wanted to make sure ye knew."

I heard him sigh. "*When is a good time to arrive?*"

"I have lectures eleven 'til three, so before or after," I answered automatically.

"*I'll be there at ten. Text me your address.*"

I hung up because I couldn't think of anything else to say and I didn't want to say good-bye like this was some normal phone call. I stared at the hand wrapped around my phone—it shook lightly. All of me was shaking. I laid my head back against the wall and stayed where I was until the shaking stopped and my breathing returned to normal.

I had three missed calls from Jorja. I ignored them all.

7—BUTTERFLY

UNSURPRISINGLY, I slept badly. By the time I was sitting in the kitchen watching the minutes to ten tick down, I'd already been to the gym, showered, and spent a couple of hours on the essay I had due in next week. I sighed as the knock on the front door thudded through the house.

Trystan looked the same as the last time I'd seen him except his outdoor gear was replaced by jeans and a T-shirt, his walking boots by trainers—much the same as me.

"Trystan," I said by way of greeting as I held the door open for him and stepped to one side.

"Ide," he replied just as wearily as he clocked my hostile look and less than welcoming tone. He had a holdall slung over his shoulder. "Do I need a parking permit?" I pressed a booklet into his hands and returned to the kitchen.

I sat back down at the table, flicking a piece of junk mail absently through my fingers while I waited for him to deal with his car. I heard the front door click shut and someone pause in the doorway to the kitchen. I was being a dick, but I honestly couldn't bring myself to be civil. Simply agreeing to this ridiculous situation was almost more than I could cope with. My chair screeched against the floor as I pushed it back.

"I'll show ye upstairs," I muttered as I passed him without meeting his eye. With my foot on the first step I groaned as the door to the front bedroom opened. "Fricking great."

"Got a fag friend come to stay, Idrys?" James slurred. I didn't look round at him. I didn't have to look to know that there would be a sneer on his fat lips.

"James, Trystan. Trystan, James." I waved a hand over my shoulder without looking round. "I'm sure ye two'll get on like a house on fire: Trystan hates *fags* too. He's staying with me because he has no choice," I continued in a monotone as I made my way up the first flight of stairs. "Trystan's favorite pastime is also making my life hell—yer like a match made in heaven."

James actually laughed, but I was on the first landing by then and I continued round to the next floor without reacting. Trystan remained silent, and heavy footsteps followed me up and into my attic bedroom. Floorspace-wise it was big, but the walls sloped down near the edges and the parts I couldn't stand in were used as storage space for a range of outdoor equipment: camping, hiking, climbing, and biking. There was a large double bed pushed against one wall. One wall was mostly covered by a collage of OS maps, pieced together to give a detailed map of the area between York and Derby, one other was decorated by four blue chunks where my other poster had fallen down.

"I'll put a roll mat out and ye can sleep on the floor. Unless ye think ye can keep yer hands and legs to yerself, then ye can sleep on the bed."

"I'll take the floor."

"Sensible choice." I glanced at my watch. "I'm going to have to go in ten minutes." I fished a set of keys out of my pocket and finally forced myself to face him again. Have I mentioned how irritatingly attractive he was? I think I have. Well he was scowling, and he still managed to look good. I had a sudden urge to drag him downstairs and kick him out on the street. Instead I held the keys out.

"My room, the front door," I explained and pointed to the respective keys. "Make sure ye lock this room when yer not in it." God knew what James would do if he got in here, and I did not want to find out. "I wrote an *I* on my milk, so if ye want tea use that one. I'm sure ye can find what ye need. If it's been chucked out again, just steal someone else's. The bathroom is downstairs. Ye can use my laptop." I waved in the general direction of my desk. "The Wi-Fi password is on the back of the box that is next to the fridge. I'll be back at about four." He continued to stare at me like he was expecting something else. "Have I missed anything?"

"Your room is more normal than I expected."

"I took the gay porno down." I grimaced as his eyes drifted to the suspiciously empty square between the four lumps of Blu Tack. I rolled my eyes, scrambled over my bed, and dug the poster out from where it had slid awkwardly down the side. I flattened it pointlessly and stuck it back to the half-dried Blu Tack. It was an autumn landscape, the only green was the muted tent in the foreground against a backdrop of sunshine ochre. "Happy?"

He ran a hand through his dark hair, and I noticed that he looked pretty tired. "Not really, Ide. Look, I get that you're pissed with me, and although I'm not sure why you agreed, I'm very grateful for you helping me out. But I'm kind of annoyed about what you said to that guy downstairs."

"Yeah, well, yer'll get over it." I started to collect the stuff I'd need for uni. "What're ye doing today?"

"I'll keep looking for places to stay," he said with a small shake of his head as he dropped his holdall in the middle of the room. "So this is it? You're just going to ignore me?"

"I'm not ignoring ye, Trystan. I'm letting ye stay in my room and drink my milk; that's as far from ignoring ye as it gets."

"So that's why you're calling me Trystan again?"

"It's yer name. Not my fault if ye don't like it."

"Fucking hell, Ide. You're like a petulant child."

"Yeah well, yer the one that decided to stop talking to me over a fricking kiss, and yer the reason that my sister hasn't spoken t' me in two months, and yer the one that called me up and asked for this. So if ye can't deal, then go book yerself into a b-n-b." I stuffed notebooks and pens into a bag.

"Ide."

I flinched as he grabbed my shoulder. I'm not sure why, maybe because I'd gotten so used to being on the defensive with James around, but I felt a jolt of fear stir itself in my gut and I slapped his hand away. I stood and twisted round to face him and something must have shown because the irritation that had been narrowing Trystan's dark eyes changed to concern. "Shit, Ide. I'm not going to hurt you, for fuck's sake. Are you all right?"

"I'm fricking hunky-dory," I replied as I sucked down a deep breath through my nose. I was far from fine; I was wound up like a child's toy and ready to go spinning in any direction if I let myself go.

"Has that douchebag downstairs done something to you?"

"*Trystan.*" I fought to keep my voice calm. "I fail to see how ye think he is *any* different to ye? I've dealt with ye all my life; one more asshole is no big deal."

"I'm not—"

"Yes, ye were. *Are.* Ye can spout some nonsense like ye did in Scotland, but yer still the same at the end o' the day. How's Josh? He seeing guys yet?"

"How's that important...?" He scowled as I raised an arched brow up my forehead. "He decided it was a phase," he said reluctantly.

"Well he's lying to ye. That boy is gay, and he won't tell ye because he's scared, and he has good reason to be." I glanced down at my watch. "I'm going to be late. I've got to go."

And with that I stepped around Trystan and left him standing in the middle of my room.

"YOU'RE JOKING?" Patrick said as we made our way between our first and second lectures. On his other side, Suze was looking wide-eyed as I finally got a chance to explain what yesterday's phone calls had been about.

"Yeah, I really wish it was a joke." I balled my fists into my eyes against the rare autumn sunshine.

"So he's in your house right now?" Suze asked.

"Yep," I said and pulled my phone out of my pocket in case he'd texted me about something. Thankfully only the unopened messages from Jorja flashed up and I shoved it back in my pocket—I didn't need my sister if this was how she was going to treat me.

"Why didn't you just say no?" Patrick asked.

I shrugged. To be fair to him, it was a good question. The answer was that I wasn't usually very good at saying no to people—the modeling gigs were an exception. Which was kind of what had got me into this situation in the first place, wasn't it? The other reason was that although I was ignoring my sister, I wanted to use taking in Trystan to prove something. As for what, I wasn't quite sure.

"Isn't it a bit dangerous? Having two people who don't like gays in your house. What if they gang up on you?" Suze asked, looking genuinely concerned.

"Ha, I don't think Trystan would *physically* hurt me." I was mostly sure of that. "And if he wanted to, he certainly wouldn't need James's help." I might have been taller than Trystan, but that was more or less my only advantage and wasn't much of one given there was only about a centimeter in it.

"Oh, Ide, I'm worried. Do you want to come and stay at my house until he's gone?" Suze said.

I shook my head slowly. "Nah, I think that would probably be worse. But thanks, love." I gave her a brief one-armed hug as we arrived at our next lecture. The next few hours were a welcome respite from having to think about anything nonacademic, but that seemed to be over in a flash and suddenly it was time to head back to my home.

Once again I paused outside my front door and had to psych myself up before I put the key in the lock. The kitchen was blissfully empty, and I made myself a drink before heading wearily up to the top floor.

"Ide?" Penny's door was open and her voice called from inside when I reached the first floor.

"Hey, Penny, good day?" I asked as I stuck my head round the door. Penny shrugged and I nodded to Matt, who was sitting on her bed with his laptop on his knee. "Ye guys met Trystan yet? He's going to be crashing in ma room for a couple of days."

"Oh yeah. I didn't realize he would be staying." She gave me a funny look. "Don't you think it's a bit silly, with how James is?"

I ground my teeth. "Well, ye may remember I was here first. But Trystan isn't gay, he's just a fr—guy who's friends with my family. So James shouldn't have a problem, or does he get to say whether I'm allowed guests now?"

Penny pouted. "Ide, you know that wasn't what I meant. I'm just worried."

"Yeah, well, maybe instead of being worried we should kick that jerk out" was my unkind response.

"You know we can't afford to do that," Matt piped up. He was being reasonable, but it didn't make dealing with James any easier.

"Yeah." I heaved a sigh.

"Horseshoe as usual later? You coming for a couple before you go out?" Matt asked as he dropped his laptop to one side of his knees. He was referring to the pub round the corner to our house.

I pressed my eyes shut for a moment, because back before my life had been picked up and dropped on its head with an addition of Trystan Jackson I'd organized to spend my evening with Dan. Which usually meant a few drinks, possibly a dance, and then hopefully back to his house for some *exercise*. I usually went out with my housemates for a pint or two beforehand because he worked in a bar and wasn't usually free until ten or eleven.

"Meh, yeah, I'll come. Mind if I bring Trystan? Ye guys can talk to him for me; damned if I have anything t' say to the guy," I replied.

"Not a problem, eight-ish as usual?" Matt said with a chuckle, and I nodded and left with a faint wave as I headed up to the attic.

Trystan was sitting at my desk; he'd pushed my laptop to one side and was on his own, flicking through housing websites with one foot up on the edge of the chair. He swiveled around as he heard me. He had an unamused look on his face. I imagined it mirrored mine.

"Ye coming out for drinks wi' me and my housemates? Eight-ish?" I asked as I dropped my bag and myself onto the end of my bed.

He looked marginally surprised at my question and I rolled my eyes. "If I introduce ye to more people, I don't have to deal with ye and ye don't have to deal wi' me: solves both our problems."

"That dickhead from the ground floor going to be there?" Trystan's tone was curt and a flash of irritable anger darkened his eyes.

"James? Not usually, he's got his own friends," I answered honestly and wondered briefly what James had done to piss Trystan off.

"Then yeah," Trystan said.

I actually chuckled and the sound surprised me, but Trystan didn't look amused at my reaction. "I'm kind of offended you'd even think I'd get on with him. Then again, I guess you have a pretty low opinion of me."

"Something like that. Any luck with houses?"

"I managed to book a couple of viewings for next week," Trystan replied, looking thoroughly unamused by my dismissal.

"Good" was all I could think to say.

He gave a weary shake of his head. "Look, Ide, we were getting on pretty well to begin with in Scotland. We're going to be stuck together for a few days at least; can't we try and sort this shit out? I know your sister is worried about you as well. She wants you to call her back."

"First off, what's going on between me and Jorja is none o' yer business. Secondly, what is there to sort out? As far as I'm concerned, ye used me for a good time, then had the nerve to get jealous over a fricking kiss—like a teenage girl—when two days earlier ye'd been practically begging me to take the boy's virginity. I have no problem wi' what we did, Trys; it was fun watching ye squirm and battle wi' yerself over whether it was worth it. What I have a problem with is yer fricking jealous, holier-than-thou attitude that ruined the end of the holiday, which my family assumed was my fault and now aren't talking to me."

"Why *wouldn't* I be bothered? I think it's weirder that you think it's fine. Yeah, I said that stuff about Josh, but that was *before* I'd kissed you and offered to fuck you; then you start hitting on my brother—in front of me. I'm sorry if I have some pride."

"And this is why straight guys are a pain in the ass," I said through clenched teeth. "Ye think it's different because I'm gay and yer not? Because ye *forced* yerself to kiss me by thinking I was a girl and because ye *deigned* to consider fucking me? Was I supposed to feel super honored and fall at yer feet, Trys?"

"I didn't—" He dropped his head back so he was staring up at the ceiling. He took a deep breath and turned those dark brown eyes back on me. "You have some messed-up relationship habits. If I'd done what I did with you with a girl—even if it was just for a bit of fun—I still wouldn't kiss someone else in front of her the next day."

"Said the guy that asked me to fuck his brother after I sucked him off? I honestly didn't think ye were bothered. Seriously, ye just wearing good drag and yer actually a girl?"

"I don't think it's me that has the attitude problem here," Trystan muttered.

"Ye didn't think my attitude was a problem when ye asked me to blow ye. Twice."

Trystan's frown was reluctant and slightly insular, but really, there wasn't much he could say about that.

"So you're saying it was all my fault?" he began again eventually, his tone arched.

"No. I should've said no—to ye *and* Josh. Yer a pair o' teases and I should've known better than t' mess with a straight guy or to get involved in the hassle of a guy who isn't out o' the closet."

Silence settled over the room. Trystan considered me and I glared right back. Eventually his shoulders deflated. "Shit, you really think Josh is actually gay?"

"Would ye like me to explain how I know?" I asked archly. Trystan grimaced and looked away.

"So you did do stuff in the end?" he asked, and a frown lowered my forehead because Trystan had dropped his gaze away from mine.

"No." My tone was weary. "Just the kiss. Know many straight guys who get hard from kissing a dude? Well, apart from ye."

He flicked me the finger. "I didn't get hard from kissing you, fag; I got hard 'cause of a dream and I stayed hard 'cause of your mouth. The second time I was drunk."

"Whatever, Trys." I rolled my eyes at him and was surprised by the smile that quirked the edge of his lips.

"So I'm Trys again now?" I returned the finger and he chuckled, then sighed. "Poor Josh; he's been dating girls these past two months and everything."

"Yeah, well, I can't imagine it'd be easy to admit yer gay wi' ye and Vince as brothers and Jerry as a dad."

Trystan's weary resignation was replaced by a flash of irritation. "Honestly, Ide, I don't know how many times I have to explain to you that I have no problem with gay guys. It's really starting to piss me off. I was a teenager, I did some shitty stuff, and I'm sorry, but I don't have a problem with it anymore. I would have thought that was pretty obvious by now."

"Ye say that, but yer attitude still sucks. Ye still call me a fag—just like that dick downstairs does—which is pretty insulting, by the way. And yeah, maybe it's in jest, but does Josh know that?"

"I just—"

"Say it 'cause that's what yer've always said, 'cause that's what yer dad said," I finished for him. "But yer dad's a homophobe, and ye know it."

He let out a slow, deep breath and ran a hand through his hair.

"Fuck." He glanced round at the time. "Shit, is it too early for a beer?"

I laughed because it was only about five, and I'd already experienced that Trystan was a bit of a lightweight. But given the circumstances I decided we both deserved a beer.

Several beers later I was in the pub round the corner from my house with my housemates and Trystan Jackson. I leaned against one of the partitions that split the bar and stared at the table of chatting people. Honestly, if someone had asked me when I had woken up yesterday morning what I'd be doing this evening, it would not have been drinking in a pub with Trystan. Hell, if someone had asked me this afternoon, I still would have said anything but this.

I watched from my removed position as Trystan demonstrated one of the many talents I resented him for and was chatting with my housemates as if he had known them for three years, not three hours. He had integrated himself with smooth comments, witty banter, and a dark look from beneath those thick eyelashes. I rolled my eyes as I sat back at the table.

"Trys?"

"Hmm?" He looked round at me from Matt and took a swig of his beer as he did.

"I'm meeting someone. Ye want me to leave ye here or d'ye want to go home?" I asked as I glanced down at the time; I'd already cut it pretty fine. I glanced back up and caught the end of him rolling his eyes. "What? I made plans days ago, and I told ye."

"Yeah, yeah," he cut me off. "Do what you want, Ide, I can find my way back or go with these guys. You don't mind if I stay, do you?" He turned to Matt, who shrugged.

"Sure, no problems here," Matt said to Trystan and then he turned to me with a wry look, but his words were for Trystan. "Idrys is always like this. You'll get used to him eventually."

I shot him the finger and downed the rest of my pint. "Whatever, see ye tomorrow. Ye"—I turned to Trystan—"remember, if ye come on the bed, keep yer fricking hands to yerself."

A ripple of interested chuckles and arched brows swept around the table, and I left Trystan to explain his curious sleeping habits.

THE BAR where Dan worked was still busy, which was lucky for me because it meant he wouldn't notice I was late. I wove through the crush of people clamoring for cocktails with the practiced ease of someone who grew up short. I leaned against the bar and found Dan among the servers; he was six foot with charcoal hair that he kept shaved and dark Mediterranean skin stretched over his swimmer's body. He and the other waiters and waitresses practically danced around each other as they collected elaborate bottles and made a show of creating the beautiful drinks. Dan hadn't seen me and I watched him with a smile as he performed for a pair of midtwenties women who were watching him with unabashed appreciation—if only they knew.

"Can I get you a drink?" an unfamiliar voice asked from next to me. I kept my body leaned on my arms against the bar and just turned my head, fixing the guy who'd spoken to me in the depths of my pale eyes. He smiled a little nervously.

"Ye realize I'm a guy, right?" I asked. If my height didn't make it obvious enough, my jeans and shirt should have made it clear. But the lighting was low and it wasn't like it was the first time I'd been mistaken for a girl.

"Ah, yeah, sorry I thought…."

I could see he wanted to go, but also didn't want to break eye contact.

"Oh, yer gay." I was faintly surprised because even looking how I looked it was unusual to be hit on in a regular bar—York was a city, but it wasn't exactly a metropolis. Maybe I should clarify: I was dressed in a simple gray shirt and jeans, I talked like any other guy, and I didn't wiggle my arse or wear some kind of rainbow bracelet or some shit like that, but with my neutral features no one is ever particularly surprised to find out I'm gay. Plus my odd blond hair is still shoulder length—thanks, Meredith—and though I don't do much more with it than tie it back when I get out of the shower, leaving it to dry in a bit of a mess, it does unfortunately look like I dye it. I turned my ice blue eyes on him and let my gaze skim up and down over his body. He wasn't bad-looking, a bit tall for my usual tastes, but some other evening I probably would have taken him up on his offer.

The whole thing took less than twenty seconds, but the guy's cheeks were blooming red and the color was spreading quickly down his neck— kind of amusing given that he came on to me. I tried to soften my face into a smile because there was an edge of worry mixed in with his embarrassment. "Sorry; ye made the right call, but I'm waiting for someone. Some other time?"

He let out a long breath. "Shit, you had me scared for a moment there." He relaxed his smile and dropped his shoulders.

"Can I get you a drink, Ide?" Dan's voice came from the other side of the bar. I turned to say yes, but then he tangled his hand through my collar and pulled me over toward the beer taps, and then Dan's lips were pressed over mine. He kissed me aggressively, all teeth and demanding tongue, but I didn't mind.

I laughed lightly as Dan let me go. He was glaring at the guy who'd offered to buy me a drink. And I wasn't surprised when my would-be suitor mumbled a good-bye and disappeared into the packed bar.

"I'd already said no." I let my mirth show and Dan pouted slightly. I couldn't really blame him; it wouldn't exactly have been the first time I'd dragged someone else into our evening, but we always agreed on it first, and really it was Ashlie who liked that shit.

Behind him, his colleagues were rolling their eyes. It wasn't like Dan was camp, but neither was it the first time they'd seen us together— although usually he waited until we were somewhere a little less public before he pounced on me.

"They've asked me to stay for an extra half hour, until the rush dies, that okay?" Dan added after a moment, and suddenly he looked a bit nervous about his outburst.

"It's fine, chill, Dan; finish yer shift. I'll have a Grolsch, or do ye only offer drinks when yer jealous?" He clicked his tongue and poured me a drink. I drank it and watched him flirt with men and women alike as he made a startling array of cocktails in a short space of time.

"Come on, then," he murmured against my ear when his shift was finally done. He wrapped a hand through mine and pulled me out the staff entrance. His mouth covered my lips as soon as the door clicked shut behind us, and he pressed me up against the wall of the back alley. His body meshed up against mine, and he rolled his hips in suggestion of what was to come.

"Ashlie text me." We were both breathless as he broke the kiss but left me pinned between his body and the wall with his hands shoved up my shirt. "He's got some friends over."

"Yeah, I saw him yesterday. I'm not really in the mood," I said between nips of his bottom lip.

Dan grinned at me and ran his tongue over his teeth as he let his hand slip down my spine and toward the waistband of my jeans.

"Echo'll be there…," he whispered.

"Yeah, but if I wanted both of ye, I'd just have my own threesome, wouldn't I? I don't want to have t' share ye with those greedy little boys."

Dan sniggered and his grin widened at the image my words had put in his head. But I knew he didn't really want to join Ashlie's party, he just wanted to make sure I knew he wasn't trying to keep me for himself.

"Want to go somewhere for a drink?" he asked. I could see him trying to pull himself together.

I chuckled as I let my hands dust down his back and nuzzled my face into his neck, and then I was sucking, dragging his flesh into my mouth as my fingers pressed into his ass, holding him tightly against me.

"Come on," I whispered against his ear after I'd pressed a soft kiss against the mark I'd left against his collarbone. "Take me home and fuck me, Dan." He groaned and pressed me back against the wall, getting thoroughly distracted and definitely not getting me any closer to the bed. I pushed him off and dragged him toward the main road and the prospect of a taxi. After my last two days, I really needed the stress relief.

We stumbled through the door to his flat, stripping as we went and leaving a trail of clothes behind us. I dropped to my knees and took his penis in my hand, and the flesh hardened fully as I stared up at him through pale eyelashes. Then I parted my lips and let my tongue slip out to taste his cock. He grunted something unintelligible and pressed himself into me, his eyes closed in bliss as I brought him right to the very edge.

"Fucking hell, Ide." He tugged me to my feet and pressed me back onto the bed. He grabbed a bottle of lube and he was grimacing as his body bucked—trying to find something to rub against and take him the rest of the way over the edge of his orgasm. But he held himself away from me, moaning as he worked his lips down my chest. "You're the worst fucking bottom—how the hell am I supposed to concentrate now?"

I gave a throaty laugh as his teeth closed around my nipple. I was the worst bottom because I wasn't a bottom; I generally liked to fuck rather than be fucked. And even if I loved being topped by this guy, it was hard to sit back and do nothing. A trail of marks unfurled like bright pink wings down my chest as Dan took out his frustration with his lips and teeth. And then he was repaying the favor, closing his mouth around my flesh as he slid two slick fingers inside of me.

"Ah," I panted and my body bucked against him as he went straight for the spot he knew better than anyone. He was massaging and stretching as he toyed with my dick with his tongue, and soon I was on the edge and he was pulling away and sliding a condom over himself. Then I was being filled again, the slight edge of pain washed away almost instantly as his cock took over where his fingers left off. I moaned and thrust up into him as he wrapped his hand around my dick to palm me off, doubling the sensation. My spine arched in bliss and my eyes slipped closed.

"Oh God…," I cursed as a slither of pure pleasure spiraled out of my spine, because behind my eyelids my brain had decided to gift me with an image of Trystan, and he was in Dan's place. Pressing into me, filling me, as he stared down at me through smug eyes and drove me over the edge. I forced my eyes open and fixed Dan in my sights, but it was too late. My cock pulsed and juddered in Dan's grip, and he milked me as he thrust inside my arse and was drawn over the edge by my sudden orgasm.

"Shit," I groaned as Dan dropped his weight on top of me. Luckily he mistook my genuine annoyance for surprise at my sudden finish— usually we lasted longer than that.

"You were really stressed, eh?" He chuckled and brushed a strand of wayward hair out of my eyes. He kissed me lightly, then sat up to pull out and dispose of the condom.

"Want a beer?" he asked as he went through to the kitchen of his apartment.

I felt like I needed one after that—whatever the fuck that was. I pulled my boxers back on and followed him.

"So what's up?" he asked as he handed me an open bottle.

"Remember my holiday from hell?" I asked as I helped myself to the contents of Dan's cupboards, specifically the kitchen roll he stashed under the sink, and started to clean myself up.

"Oh yeah." He laughed lightly and a warm grin spread across his face, because whether he remembered me telling him about the holiday or not, I knew he would remember the sex we'd had when I got back—let's just say I'd been insatiable and leave it at that.

"Well the guy from said holiday is going to be staying wi' me for a few days." I toed the bin and leaned back against one of the sides—clean enough for now.

"The homophobe you shared a tent with?"

"Meh, I don't even know if Trys *is* a homophobe or just messed up."

Dan eyed me curiously and crossed the room to wrap an arm around my waist. He pulled me against him and pressed a kiss against my lips.

"Well, you know you can stay here if shit gets bad."

I smiled at him but I couldn't keep the small sigh from my lips. I'd been sleeping with Dan for two years. The story of how he got me to bottom for him is one for another day, but suffice to say he put a lot of effort into getting me into bed, a hell of a lot. And once he'd shown me that I didn't hate bottoming as much as I thought, we came to a kind of agreement—because liking to be fucked and trusting any old idiot to do it were completely different things. That had led to him introducing me to Echo, and then I'd met Ashlie, and we'd kind of fallen into the odd open and group type relationship we now had. But from the start we had made it very clear that whatever was between us was just for sex.

I did stay over at his place sometimes, after a particularly epic session or if I was too wasted to get myself into a cab, and I was probably almost as comfortable in his house as I was my own. I still didn't think staying with him for a few days was a great idea, because it had the potential to shift the dynamic of our relationship, and at the moment I liked it just the way it was.

"I'll let ye know if I need ye," I said as I kissed him lightly and glanced at my watch. "I should probably get going after this. I have work tomorrow."

He chuckled and let me go. "Send me some pics, eh?" Dan asked as he dug through our abandoned clothes to find something to wear while we finished our beers.

"IDE?" TRYSTAN was still half-asleep as I opened the door to my bedroom later that evening.

"Yeah, only me, sorry," I whispered. I was faintly surprised that he'd woken up, because from sharing a tent with him in Scotland I'd got the impression he was a heavy sleeper. But it wasn't that late, so he could have only just got in. I used the light on my phone to make sure I didn't stand on him. I swore as I tripped over a spare sleeping bag that had tumbled from its pile. And then someone flicked on my bedside light.

Not someone: Trystan.

He flopped back down and then rolled over to watch me through eyes that I wasn't sure were narrowed with sleep or in annoyance. I stared, because I'd briefly forgotten how gorgeous he looked sleep-tousled, and my flash of memory while I was under Dan had really not done him justice.

I realized he was staring back at me.

"You smell of sex," he announced after a moment.

"No shit? I wonder why that would be?" Irritation flared in my chest because I'd said no to Dan's offer to use his shower, but right now I was wishing I hadn't and it annoyed me that I cared.

I tugged my shirt off over my head, then frowned because Trystan sniggered and I suddenly remembered the marks Dan had left. They'd be gone in the morning, but right now the pale pink trail of butterfly kisses were still clear against my ivory skin, even in the low light.

"Did tonight's underage boy get a bit carried away?" he jeered as he continued to watch me strip to my boxers and pull a pair of pajama bottoms on over my lower half.

I let a languid smile curl the edge of my lips as I stood at the bottom of his roll mat. He was propped on his elbows, staring up at me with that holier-than-thou smirk of his, and I really wanted to wipe it off his face like I'd done when I'd called his bluff and blown him and like I'd done when he'd let me stick my finger in his ass. He seemed perfectly happy to forget all of that—well if he thought I was just going to take his shit, he had the wrong idea about me. We weren't in Scotland surrounded by our families now; he was in my house.

"If I had sex with underage kids, then I would have fucked yer brother in Scotland." I kept my voice level as I dropped over him. I enjoyed the fact that in his sleeping bag he couldn't struggle away as I fell on my knees straddling his hips and I dropped my hands on either side of his shoulders. He collapsed his elbows, lying down to open up a bit of space between us, but I followed with a smirk, driven on by the beer sloshing round my system.

"I would've taken him somewhere private." I kept my voice a low hiss. "And I would've sucked his little cock and stuck my finger in his arse, just like I did to ye." I watched his reaction with smug satisfaction as those lovely chocolate-brown eyes of his darkened. "And he would've begged me for more...." I dropped my head down and he flinched as I skimmed past his lips and left my mouth against his ear. "Just... like... ye... did," I whispered very deliberately against his ear and enjoyed the ripple of irritation I could feel underneath me.

"You're such a fucking whore, Ide."

I laughed brightly and pushed myself up so I was kneeling.

"Hey, it's not my fault everyone finds me irresistible." I trailed a hand along his sleeping bag where I knew his chest was; then with a last smirk, I got to my feet and clambered into my bed.

"Sweet dreams, Trys." I kept my voice low and suggestive, holding his gaze with mine until I flicked the lights off. I turned over and was glad the dark would hide my own irritation as I was left to stew in sexual frustration of my own making.

I could only hope he found somewhere else to live quickly.

8—FLY

THERE WAS something to be said about the fact that it was the middle of the afternoon when Theo rang me next. It was Friday, I was done with uni for the week, and I was on my way home from the gym, so I relaxed my stride into an easy stroll as I answered the call.

"Ye moved to a new time zone and not told me?" I answered cheerily, even though I knew that there was only going to be one thing this was about.

"What the hell are ye doing, Idrys?"

I rolled my eyes at him for good measure and feigned ignorance. "Nice to hear from ye too, Theo. I'm currently on my way back from the gym, why what're ye up t'?"

"Not funny." He was right, but I chuckled anyway. *"Why the hell is that dickhead in yer house, and why is Jorja ringing me, asking me t' get ye t' answer her calls when just last week we had a conversation exactly the other way around."*

I shrugged even though he wouldn't see and sighed even though he *would* hear.

"Trystan's staying wi' me while he finds somewhere t' stay."

"Aye, I know why. I want t' know why the hell ye said yes."

Wasn't that just the million dollar question? Trystan Jackson had been living in my house—more specifically my room, for a week now. After an awkward Saturday and Sunday I'd hardly seen him. He left at six every morning and he didn't get back before seven every evening, and after stuffing his face with food he'd crash on the roll mat to search for houses. I'd been out the door at nine most evenings and he'd been asleep by the time I got in, but the little conversation I'd had with him I'd found out he'd seen a couple of places in his lunch hour and that none had been any good.

But I let out another sigh, because right then it wasn't even Trystan that I was pissed off with.

"Ye know she tried t' call me last week, the day I talked wi' ye." It was Theo's turn to sigh, which told me that if Jorja hadn't told him straight up, then he'd worked it out himself. I carried on regardless. "After two fricking months o' ignoring me because o' that self-centered asshole, she wants t' get in touch t' ask me t' do him a *favor*. She can go t' hell, fer all I care." I'd trailed off to a hissed whisper because thinking about it was making me lose my temper all over again.

"Then why not just say no. He's a bullying asshole an' I think it's a bloody ridiculous idea having him around. Especially with that douchebag James still on the scene."

Theo's anger stilled some of my own, leaving me feeling a strange mixture of agreement and a need to defend my guest. All week Trystan had been more than fine. I mean, sure, I hardly saw the guy for more than two hours a day, and he was still kind of acerbic, but he hadn't called me a fag, he hadn't belittled my sexuality, or my late nights. If I was honest it was kind of disconcerting.

I found myself entertaining the notion that he might have actually listened to what I'd said last week. As I walked I stared at the gray-coated sky and wondered when I was going to see my first flying pig.

"The guy just needs somewhere t' stay. I know the only reason Jorja called was 'cause she thought I'd leave him hanging wi'out her t' talk me int' giving him a hand. Well ye can tell her that I'm not a complete twat."

"Yeah? Well I think yer an idiot."

"I've known the guy fer most o' my life, he needs a favor, it's not like I can't cope wi' him fer a week. An' if he pulls anything, I'll kick his ass on the street. I'm a big guy, Theo. I can look after myself."

"We all know how well that turns out."

"That was uncalled for," I deadpanned back and Theo sighed a quick apology.

"Sorry, sorry. I've had yer sister on the phone t' me for like an hour already, an' the hunt have been on my ass because the grouse are apparently—" He stopped with a weary chuckle. *"Which ye really dun need t' know about right now."* He was quiet for a moment and I listened to the sound of Theo clicking his tongue and the silence of him sorting out his head. The guy really needed to spend less time worrying about me, but it was nice to have someone to talk to who wasn't instantly enamored by Trystan and his infuriating charm. *"What ye up t' this evening?"*

"I'm going out wi' Ashlie." I couldn't keep the smile from returning to my face, especially when Theo responded with predictable distaste. His reluctant truce with Dan did not extend to the other members of my bizarre relationship.

"*Urgh, I should know better than t' ask. I dun know what that boy must do in bed, I wouldn't put up wi' Scarlett Johansson if she was as irritating as he is.*"

"I'll tell ye next time we have a chance for a few beers, eh?"

Theo did a very unattractive snort down the phone and barked something at Tess in the background. "*I think it'll need t' be more than drunk. I take it this shit wi' Jorja means ye still have no plan t' come back?*"

"Ask me again in a couple o' days."

"*I feel like an abandoned wife,*" he mocked in a disturbingly accurate gay lisp.

"I'll bring ye flowers t' cheer ye up?"

He laughed and switched back to his regular gruff tones. "*Beer works better, dickhead. Look after yerself, and try not t' do anything more stupid than usual, eh?*"

"Love ye too, Theo."

"*G'bye Idrys....*" Theo hung up and I was chuckling to myself for most of the way home.

AT ONE in the morning I paused in the doorway to my bedroom and gave a weary shake of my head. Since the first night Trystan hadn't woken up when I'd come in late, not for Dan again last Sunday or Echo last Wednesday or that random whose name I'd already forgotten. Tonight was no different, and I surveyed him for a moment with reluctant appreciation as he lay there, irritatingly good-looking and oblivious, with one leg cocked out of the duvet and his neck arched like it was inviting a kiss. No different from every other night this week, except for the duvet.

My duvet.

I pressed the door shut behind me as I weighed up my options. I'd spent the evening with Ashlie and all I really wanted to do was get into bed and go to sleep, but I stood in the middle of my bedroom for a moment and studied the dark-haired sleeping form. He hadn't been a pain, and he hadn't made any comments—snide or otherwise—about my frequent late nights. In fact all week, he'd been unnervingly *nice*, and now he lay there dead to the world. In my bed. Looking exasperatingly molestable.

But I kind of wanted to laugh, because, in what I could only assume was some kind of attempt to keep himself from straying, he was lying like a bloody sarcophagus along one side of the bed.

I couldn't really blame the guy for getting up there. I mean, it was fine sleeping on a floor when there was no other option, and probably when the bed was full, but I know I would have been tempted by a bed I knew was going to be empty for most of the night. Still, it was funny that after everything, he was trying so hard to obey my rules and stop himself from straying.

I was torn, because I was tired and I just wanted to get into my bed. I glanced at the roll mat and seriously considered sleeping on the floor. But it was my damn bed, and I'd just had quite the workout with Ashlie, and my hips really didn't like the idea of sleeping on the floor. I couldn't quite believe what I was doing as I pulled my shirt and jeans off and tugged on a pair of pajama bottoms.

He'd gone next to the wall, so at least I didn't have to climb over him. I lay there next to him in a similar pencil-like position and couldn't help but think about the last time we'd slept next to each other. The last night in Scotland the rain had beat down on the tent, but it had still been so hot and muggy. I'd slept badly for four nights, jerking awake at every small movement because the one time Trystan had woken up near me, he'd punched me and it had hurt.

I sighed because Ashlie had asked me to stay at his, and right now I was kind of wishing that I had.

"Urgh, sorry, Ide, my back," Trystan's voice was muffled as he shuffled a little closer to the wall. At least his arms and legs were pointed away from me.

"Whatever," I muttered and flicked onto my front. Thankfully it didn't take long for me to slip into oblivion.

I woke up feeling odd, and I wasn't sure why. It took me a moment to realize it was because I'd fully expected to wake up with a six foot two guy pawing at me in his sleep. I flicked my head to where Trystan was obediently curled up on one side of the bed. Well, that made life just a little simpler at least. I rolled out of bed to head down for a shower. I had a job to get to.

"Mmm, morning, Ide," Trystan greeted me as I got back from the shower. He was perched on the edge of the bed looking sleep-tousled and gorgeous with his pleasant six-pack sticking out of the top of his pajama bottoms—I'll admit there are worse things to come back to.

"Yeah, morning," I replied as I kept my back to him and tugged boxers and jeans on under my towel and a shirt on over my chest.

"Look, about the bed, I'm sorry, but my back was killing me and I knew you'd be late, so I figured you'd just kick me out when you got in."

"It's fine, Trys. I told ye: ye can sleep on the bed as long as ye don't touch me, which ye didn't, so?"

"Oh, I guess you did. Hmm, good night?"

"Yeah, ye after details? First of all we—"

"No," he cut in, and I sniggered because I'd had no intention of actually telling him what I'd done to Ashlie. Mmm, that boy was delicious; his slightly irritating personality was more than made up for by his sweet, sweet ass.

"So, what ye up to today? I've got to work," I asked quickly to distract myself from memories I did not need to be recalling right now.

"You still modeling? I wondered why you'd kept your hair long." I nodded as I tied it back off my face. Other than washing there was no point in me doing anything to myself as I'd be polished, primped, and generally made up once I got to work.

"Yeah, well, the money is good and the work is easy: go to the gym, then stand and have my photo taken."

"Fair enough; I've got a couple of house viewings this afternoon, what time do you finish? Fancy coming with?"

"Oh," I bumbled because I hadn't expected the question. "Sure, I should be done by three; that work?" Trystan nodded absently, he was palming his phone.

"Yeah, first one is at half past."

"Okay, well, I've got to dash, but I'll text ye the address, come meet me. Ye know where everything is; help yerself." I grabbed my bag and headed out. There was a taxi waiting for me at the front of the house, and I slipped into the backseat and got the address from the driver so I could text it to Trystan. I couldn't help but feel slightly like I was organizing a date or something.

The job was a pain in the arse. There were supposed to be three models, but one of them turned up late and the other one was a no-show. Then halfway through the shoot, Meredith decided that if there were only two of us, our outfits and makeup weren't quite right so we had to go and change completely.

"Guys, I need a break," I announced as the latest *discussion* between the photographer and designer dissolved into yet another bickering session. I didn't wait for an answer. The clock on the far wall said it was five to three, and with a rumble of annoyance I went through to the reception. Trystan was sitting on the far side; one of his ankles was slung over his knee, there was a portfolio on his lap, and the receptionist was sitting next to him fawning and batting her eyelashes. I rolled my eyes.

"Trys," I grumbled because I was in a bad mood anyway and I was going to be in a worse one now because I was dressed in a fucking ridiculous suit and I had more makeup on than my sister wore on a night out. But at least I looked like a guy this week.

He looked up and laughed. "Ide?"

"Who the hell d'ye think it is?"

"Well, I don't know." He stood and looked me up and down and his eyes were filled with mirth. "You look like one of those puffy magazine boys."

"Yeah, and I'm getting paid three-fifty a day. How much do ye get paid, Trys?"

"You got a pay rise?"

I shrugged. "Yeah, I threatened to cut my hair. They almost started crying."

"You coming to look at houses dressed like that?" His eyes drifted down to my chest that was bare beneath the satin suit jacket I was wearing.

"Yeah, 'bout that. We're running late, so I'll have t' stand ye up. Sorry."

"Eeee-drys," the whiney voice of the design artist came through from the studio, and I ground my teeth as the small woman came into reception.

"Have ye finished arguing yet?"

"I pay you to look pretty, not give me lip, now…." Meredith trailed off as she saw Trystan and I literally saw her eyes light up. "You called someone else from your agency?"

"No, Trystan is a friend." I could almost see exactly what was coming and it pissed me off. She came over and Trystan watched wide-eyed as she pulled his T-shirt up and revealed the pleasantly tanned and toned muscle of his chest and abs.

"So when I asked if anyone knew a nice torso model this morning and you stayed quiet, you were just lying?" she asked me.

"Trys isn't a model, Meredith."

"Would you like to be?" She ignored me.

"He has somewhere to be," I answered for him.

"Will you pay me as much as him?" Trystan nodded in my direction.

"No, you're just a pretty body—your face is too Abercrombie for Idrys's paycheck." Right then I actually could have kissed that irritating woman. "You can have half; that's still almost two hundred quid for an hour's work…." And then I was right back to hating her.

"Trystan," I growled. "Yer've not been a pain yet. But I want ye out o' my house."

"Well, the flats I was going to look at were above my budget anyway."

I cursed and marched back through to the studio. Behind me Meredith was pulling Trystan through to the makeup rooms.

"Do ye have any idea how irritating ye are, Trystan Jackson?" I muttered as he came into the studio wearing satin suit trousers and nothing else. They only wanted his chest, so his face looked like normal, but his torso gleamed like someone had already been to work on it in Photoshop.

"Hey, you really thought I was going to turn down two hundred quid?" he asked as he obediently let himself be positioned.

"Ooh, *Idrys*?" the other model uttered as he blatantly eyed Trystan up. "Where have you been hiding this guy?"

"Kieran, this is Trys, family friend. He's staying with me for a bit. He's also not gay so don't get too excited."

"Oh, well if you can't be tempted by our gorgeous Ide, I suppose you must be as straight as they come." Kieran grinned like a Lewis Carroll creation as he was directed into the shot.

Trystan quirked an eyebrow as he lay out across the studio, lounging back against his hand as Meredith directed.

"Idrys, like this morning with Kieran," Meredith called. I rolled my eyes because this was fine when it was just a room full of arty types, but it was bloody embarrassing with Trystan around. I dropped my head into Kieran's lap and stared up at him as the shot was taken. "Great, that is so much better with the body in the background. Lean against Trystan please, Idrys."

Luckily the shoot only required Trystan to be in the background, so apart from resting an arm against him, I was still mostly just interacting with Kieran. I managed to slip back into the detached mindset I used for work. We had a couple of outfit changes, but the rest of the shoot proceeded without a problem and we were finished up by four thirty.

"You two coming out?" Kieran asked as I finished having my makeup removed and returned to my usual jeans-and-T-shirt-wearing self. Kieran was a little more flagrant about his sexual preferences, and I caught Trystan's eye and rolled mine as the other model pulled on a hideous pink top.

"Did ye miss all yer viewings?" I asked Trystan, and he gave a guilty shrug. "Then sure, we'll come; they pay," I added for Trystan's benefit and then the three of us were ready.

We went across town to a nice little bistro restaurant, and as a group we were probably a sight to behold as we piled in. Usually it was only me looking out of place with eight or nine arty types, so it was actually kind of a nice change to have Trystan there, looking as relatively normal as Trystan Jackson ever can. Although I guess I'm not one to talk.

"So, is Trystan your boyfriend, Idrys?" one of the makeup artists asked. I spluttered and beside me Trystan just laughed.

"Sorry, Jules, it's just I don't really do boyfriends, and Trys is straight," I explained when she looked puzzled at our reaction.

"Huh?" A smile lit up her face and I actually sniggered as she turned to Trystan in one of the most blatant changes of attitude I have ever seen. I cocked an eyebrow at Trystan, but he actually looked kind of weary. I guess with a face and body like that it was probably a relief when girls assumed he was gay—yeah, right.

"So, you two are just friends? How do you know each other?" Jules asked.

"Our parents are holiday friends is the easiest way to explain it, I guess," Trystan said.

"Yeah, Trys has ruined a lifetime of summer holidays," I added and Trystan rolled his eyes. "He's just staying with me while he finds a place to live."

I realized the design artist was staring at Trystan with a look on her face that I knew I didn't like.

"What is it, Meredith?" I asked.

"I'm thinking about next week's shoot. I've got the guy who stood us up booked in, but you two looked good together—your colorings are such a great contrast. Would you be willing to stand in again, Trystan?"

Trystan was staring at me, and with a start I realized he was actually waiting to see whether I was bothered. "It's up to ye, Trys. Ye should check the designs, though; make sure yer comfortable with whatever Meredith is going to want ye to do."

"It'll just be you, right?" he asked me and I looked round at Meredith, who had pulled out her diary and was flicking through it.

"Yeah, I've just got Idrys and the no-show booked in next weekend."

"Then sure. I could do with the extra cash."

Well, I was beginning to simply resign myself and go with the flow of crazy that seemed to be my life at the moment.

MY BODY was hot, but instead of flinching from the heat that was wrapping around me, I moaned pleasantly and pressed myself closer into it. It felt nice; fingers were dancing down my chest, skipping across my skin but leaving behind pulses of pleasant warmth behind. And then lips were being pressed against my neck and a hungry mouth was making short work of my pale skin and turning the pleasant warmth into a growing throb of arousal. My moan as I was rolled firmly onto my back was deeper and throatier than the first. Those lips were working along my collarbone; then they were devouring my flesh desperately as they worked down my torso, hands and mouth keeping pace as they drove me to a state of distraction.

There was something wrong with this situation. Somewhere in the back of my head I knew that, but the bittersweet pressure pulsing in my hips was drowning out that small concern. And then there was no more room for thoughts as lips quested over the head of my cock. They sucked lightly at first, drawing that pressure in and releasing it in pulses that drove me quickly to heady heights that had my body quivering. When I was balanced beautifully on the knife edge of steadily building pleasure and the cavernous fall of bliss on the other side, the mouth deepened its draws and I groaned and thrust up as the head of my cock was cushioned against a warm throat.

The eyes that held mine were the color of the shaded depths that lurked in the empty spaces between the trunks of a forest, bright and crisp and deep, smug and dark with lust.

I pushed my hand through tousled dark hair, and my body shook as it tried to bask in the pleasure and drive me quickly into my release at the same time. I whimpered, a low noise in the back of my throat that did nothing to help the inevitable ecstasy as I was suddenly plunging down into my orgasm.

"Shit." I jolted awake as my body thrummed with the crest of my pleasure. I bucked against nothing, and I fought to hold myself still as I pumped my load, not into a warm and receptive mouth, but into my boxers—like a fricking teenager.

I stared at the ceiling, breathing heavily and massively conscious of the mess in my pants and the arm thrown possessively across my chest.

"Ide? You okay?" Trystan's voice was groggy, thankfully he was too close to sleep to have noticed more than my odd thrashing.

"Fuck," I swore under my breath, rolled out from beneath the pressure of the arm, and sat on the edge of my bed with my head in my hands.

A week. He'd managed a whole fucking week of staying on his side of the bed. I'd spent a week waking up with an odd sense of ridiculous misplaced loneliness and relief that he'd kept his promise. And the one time he messed up I had a fricking wet dream? I hadn't come in my sleep since I was sixteen, for God's sake.

"Oh shit." I pressed my face into my hands as the memory of that dream caused my cock to stir. I'd come, but hardly enough, and in my dream Trystan's mouth had been amazing. I quickly reminded myself that it was just a dream and focused on the uncomfortable dampness in my crotch instead.

"Oh bloody hell. Sorry." Behind me Trystan was beginning to wake up properly and had clearly realized he wasn't where he was supposed to be. "Ah crap, Ide. I didn't do it on purpose."

"*Notaproblem*," I garbled. "I'm going to get a shower." I stood up and tried to keep my back to him as I grabbed my towel. But Trystan was jumping from the bed with far too much energy for so early on a Saturday morning. He snagged my upper arm and he spun me around.

"No, seriously, Ide. I'm not trying to mess shit up again." He sounded serious and concerned as he tried to catch my gaze with his. "And the flat I saw yesterday wa...." He sniffed once, then looked down, and his eyes darkened as he finally realized what had happened.

"Oh fuck, sorry." His voice was gruff as he stepped away from me.

I laughed—because my life was laughable at the moment and this situation seemed to sum it up perfectly. Plus, laughing helped to distract me from the memory of the sultry look the dream version of Trystan had given me as he'd dropped his mouth over me.

"I'm going t' shower," I repeated as I pressed a hand against Trystan's chest to shift him out of the way and headed down to the bathroom. It didn't help that I'd somehow ended up kind of busy and hadn't slept with anyone since Ashlie a week ago.

I came back to my bedroom via the kitchen. It was Saturday and still early so I could walk around in a towel and not worry about bumping into James. I dropped two mugs of tea onto my desk and leaned against it.

"Ye need t' shower; the taxi will be here in half an hour."

Trystan was still sitting on the edge of the bed with a funny look on his face.

"Hmm?" he asked absently, and I rolled my eyes.

"Ye told Meredith ye would work this week. If yer've changed yer mind, it's a bit late, and ye'll be screwing me out o' my wages too."

"Shit. I haven't changed my mind, just forgot." He shot me a last funny look before he got up to get ready.

Half an hour later we sat in the taxi in silence.

"Look, Trys," I said eventually, because he still had an odd look on his face. The fact he wasn't ribbing me about this was actually kind of concerning, and it was going to be a pain if this caused shit between us again, because his house searching was going surprisingly slowly. "I'm sorry about this morning, not much I could do about it. So just forget it, 'kay?"

"No, I...." He grimaced, gave a shake of his head, and then fixed me with his more usual smug grin. "Can't control yourself around me when you haven't seen any of your fuck buddies?" he asked archly.

Unfortunately I couldn't deny anything, because sharing a room with him meant he knew I hadn't been out for a week.

"Been keeping tabs on me again, Trys? Dun go getting yer hopes up, straight guy," I cut back as I flicked him the finger. Still, I much preferred dealing with arrogant Trystan, and I settled into the seat of the cab feeling a little relieved.

They got Trystan ready first because his outfit, makeup, and hair were all much simpler than mine. I didn't mind waiting, because it was faintly amusing to watch him huff and complain about all the work the makeup artists and costume designers had to do to him. I wondered what he'd think if he had to put up with what they did to me. Although I think the fact that he was actually straight made the crew worse than usual. He went through to do lighting checks and a couple of test shots while I finished up so he didn't see me until I was completely done up. His face when I came into the studio was a picture, and I kind of wish I'd gotten someone to capture it so I could laugh again later.

"Stop laughing, Idrys, you'll ruin your makeup," Meredith snapped as I tried to catch my breath. The hair girl grumbled something, too, and came to tuck something back in place. Trystan was standing in the middle of the studio, and he looked great even though he was only wearing stonewashed jeans. They hung well off his tidy hips, and that subtle six-pack of his was practically begging to be tenderly caressed as it gleamed in the lighting. By contrast I was in suit trousers and a fitted white dress shirt, but I knew that my face didn't match. The confusion was why Meredith paid so much for me. They'd primped and primed my hair until the strawberry tone gleamed out against the platinum, and then they'd tousled it around my face, which was basically done like a girl's.

I stopped in front of him. My gaze locked on his in faint amusement and a touch of curiosity. His dark brown ones were creased in puzzlement as he got over his surprise. He dropped his head to one side, looked down at my body, then up at my face until finally down again. "You *actually* look like a girl. A girl with no boobs, in men's clothes. It's weird as fuck."

I heard the shutter start to go off. I didn't know if they were doing test shots or just liked the natural scene, but I'd been doing this long enough that I knew to just ignore them.

"Trystan, onto the step, please," Meredith directed, and Trystan stepped back and suddenly I was forced to look up at him again, which I kind of didn't like.

"Ooh nice, Idrys, just stand there and look at Trystan like that; it's great," I heard Meredith mutter in the background. Which was fine with me, because looking at Trystan like he drove me crazy was pretty easy. "Like I said, Trystan."

He bent his head to stare down at me and there was a really irritating smirk on his face. And part of me was certain it was because he was thinking about when I'd been shorter than him. He tucked his hand under my chin, tipped my face up, and lifted slightly so I had to strain up toward him. In the background Meredith was practically exploding with joy.

I barely registered it because I was so fricking turned on by that smirk in his eyes—so similar to the one in my dream—and the way he was forcing my body to balance so I could keep staring up at him. I could feel all my senses humming to life as lust slipped round my body in response to him. All of which was wholly unprofessional, massively inappropriate, and so *unbelievably* irritating.

Somewhere behind me Meredith was about to have a heart attack. She was muttering something about coloring and chemistry and the photographer was scurrying around like a bloody fly clattering against a window as she tried to be everywhere at once. I barely noticed because all my senses were only tuned in to the man that had me balanced against his hand, forcing me to reach up toward him. A man that was staring down at me with a smirk, because he thought I looked like a girl.

"My wet dream was about ye," I whispered, trying not to move too much. "I dreamed ye were sucking ma cock; shitting hell, ye were good at it…." I parted my lips slightly so he could just see my tongue darting in the darkness of my mouth. "So if yer having trouble remembering I'm not a girl; ye just imagine me coming in yer mouth."

I let a smile touch the corner of my lips as I stared up at him and I watched Trystan's eyebrows rise up his forehead as he processed what I was saying while still trying hard not to shift positions too much. I was impressed at that. Then he smirked again, raised my chin higher, and dropped his head so his mouth was next to my ear. I was practically balancing on just my toes, and as he disappeared from view, I felt my body leaning into him and the single point of contact against my chin.

"It's okay, Ide," he whispered against my ear. "You don't have to worry; I think you're more attractive when you're a guy anyway."

And at that I almost fell over.

I was expecting Meredith to shout at me as I lost my balance, but the odd woman actually giggled in glee as I stumbled over and Trystan reached out to steady me.

"Oh my God, Trystan; can you come every week? I've never seen Idrys look so sultry."

What? I wasn't looking sultry, I was looking pissed off!

"Bloody hell, Meredith; can ye not inflate his ego any more than it already is?" I glared up at Trystan, who was grinning back.

Meredith and the photographer both laughed. "I think you're doing a fine job of that by yourself, Idrys," Meredith said, her tone slightly mocking; she was enjoying this far too much.

"It's okay," Trystan crooned as he dropped his head to one side with a wry grin curling one side of his lips. "It's only a game, eh, Ide?"

I sighed because I had the distinct impression that I had just lost that round.

9—Snake

We went out for the free food and beer after the shoot. I honestly don't think I have ever seen Meredith in such a good mood and I'd been working with her for six months by this point. She actually sat at the dining table cackling with glee as she went through the photos. She showed me one, and I actually groaned; it was so fricking embarrassing. You couldn't really see Trystan's face; he was bent over me, looking all rugged cowboy type with his broad shoulders, gorgeous tan, and unruly hair. I, by contrast, looked delicate and ghost-like in my formal wear as he held my chin so that I could stare longingly—yes, fricking longingly—up into his face.

"That's my angry face," I said as I handed her camera back and helped myself to more of my beer.

"Hah. Then I pity the boys you try and look sexy for; they must just fall at your feet," Jules giggled. I rolled my eyes.

"Something like that." I have never been so glad for the arrival of food.

After we'd finished there I arranged to meet up with my housemates in town. Trystan and I ended up arriving early and we found a table and got drinks to wait. Trystan didn't seem all that bothered by the day so far. He didn't even bring up what I'd said in the shoot and was his usual smug self as we chatted about areas to live. Apparently he'd booked in to see a house on Monday that was immediately available and looked perfect on paper, so hopefully he would be out of my hair by the end of next week.

"Ide?" My name was a question but it was followed instantly by a hand sliding onto my waist and a kiss pressed against my neck. "You ignoring me, dickhead?" Dan mocked in a poor imitation of a gay lisp. He laughed and pulled my face around to press a chaste kiss to my lips. "Or have you just got yourself a *boyfriend?*" His tone turned back to his usual low drawl and he shot a grin in Trystan's direction, assessing his reaction, no doubt.

"Fricking hilarious, Dan," I said with a roll of my eyes, because of all my friends, gay or straight, Dan knew best that I did not do boyfriends.

"So, a new recruit?" he said with a mocking lick of his lips as his gaze drifted blatantly down Trystan's body. "Please tell me you found a new catcher, mmm-mmm."

"Dan, this is Trystan; Trys, Dan." I waved my hands between them as I did the introductions.

The sardonic smile on Dan's face dropped into a look of astonishment. "Trystan? As in?"

"I only know one Trystan," I said by way of explanation. Dan's head whipped back round to the dark-haired guy next to me, who was watching with a look of wry amusement. He gave Dan a wave as he took a swig of his beer.

"You didn't tell me he was hot," Dan whispered against my ear, watching Trystan with an outraged smile. "Why exactly were you bothered about sharing a tent with him? I feel that you have done a disservice to homosexuals the world over by not using that infamous charm of yours to convert him."

I pressed Dan out of my personal space, met his amused smile, and gave him a weary shake of my head—he wouldn't be so amused if he knew what had happened.

"So you're one of the guys Ide keeps abandoning me for?" Trystan asked with his trademark smirk.

"Yeah, not recently, though," Dan said and shot me a slightly peeved look. "You over your bottoming phase, then? I'm sad, but you know I don't mind switching. Surely I'm better than Ashlie's loose ass?"

I chuckled. Ashlie was a little promiscuous even by my standards, but sometimes it was nice not to have to worry.

"Nah, not over it, just been busy," I answered—mostly honestly. I hadn't been any busier than usual, but with Trystan around in the evenings, I'd just never got round to organizing anything.

"Ooh, then are you busy later? I've got work in half an hour, but I'll be off at eleven."

"I'm shattered, actually. Tomorrow?"

I watched him think about it; then he nodded and pressed a kiss against the side of my lips. Happy, he turned his attention back to Trystan, who had watched our exchange with something bordering on amazement.

"Did you guys just discuss who else you were sleeping with, then organize a sex date?" Trystan asked.

"Sure, why?" Dan responded with a grin. Trystan was staring at him, not frowning exactly, but not smiling either. Dan chuckled. "You shouldn't get the wrong idea; it's not always that easy. Me and Ide just have an understanding, and I've learnt from other's mistakes that if you're possessive of Ide, he'll leave you high and dry, so"—Dan turned back to me and shot me a slightly sad grin—"better to share than have none of him."

"Don't make it sound like ye save yerself just for me, ye fricking hypocrite," I cut back with a roll of my eyes, and Dan's usual grin returned.

"So, Trys?" said Dan, and I groaned silently at the mischievous look on his face. "Have you enjoyed a taste of our lovely Idrys?"

"Dan," I warned. "Trys is straight."

Dan hooked his hand around my waist and pulled me affectionately against his side. "Yeah? But we all know that every man has a little bit of gay inside of him reserved just for you, Ide."

Trystan sniggered and seemed as unbothered as ever. "Well, he gives good head, I'll give him that."

I thought Dan was going to choke on his beer. When he finally stopped coughing, I wasn't sure who he looked more annoyed with: me or Trystan. He settled for Trystan.

"You! First off, how *dare* you claim to be straight and get a blow job from Ide? Secondly, how dare you call it merely *good*? I'm offended for him."

Trystan just shrugged and drank down some more of his beer.

Then Dan turned to me, and his irritation was a little more serious. "And *you*; you wonder why you get into trouble when you go around blowing straight guys?"

"It was complicated," I muttered, thinking of the weird events that had led to me sucking Trystan off, and the negative consequences.

Still looking peeved, Dan glanced at his watch.

"I need to go," he said reluctantly. He leaned forward and scooped a hand behind my head, pressing his lips to mine. I felt the gentle pressure of his tongue and let him have his way because he was pissed off, even though it had been he who brought up the conversation. "Text me about tomorrow," he said as he broke away. Then he downed the last centimeter of his beer and left with a chaste kiss for me and a wave for Trystan.

"Do you have that effect on all men, then?" Trystan's tone was wry as I looked back round.

"Dan was just in a funny mood," I said, which was true. Trystan considered me.

"Do you really have no idea? He was jealous; he clearly has a thing for you."

I rolled my eyes because Trystan didn't know anything.

"Dan doesn't get jealous; that's what I like about *him*." I left a little emphasis on the last word on purpose, and the slight ripple of tension across Trystan's forehead told me he hadn't missed my point. Yet he continued anyway.

"He was clearly—"

I cut Trystan off with an angry scowl.

"Ye know what the difference between ye and Dan is, Trystan?" I kept my voice furiously low as I leaned across the table toward him, capturing his gaze with mine. "Dan understands our situation. And yeah, maybe he's annoyed that I did something stupid—because that's what messing around with you was: *stupid*."

Dan had been right about that, and I wondered when I would learn my lesson.

"But ye know what the difference between his feelings and yers are? Dan's feelings aren't *completely fricking arrogant*." I quirked a pale eyebrow; I was being cruel and mocking, but he was still staring at me with that holier-than-thou smirk of his. Like he thought he knew, like he had any idea about me and about my relationship with Dan. Like it had been perfectly within his right to get so bloody annoyed about me kissing his brother. And it was fricking infuriating.

But not nearly as exasperating as the fact that the same arrogant smirk had turned me on so much in my dream this morning.

"Dan didn't waltz into my life, my bed, and then *presume* I belonged to him; he did me the courtesy of asking what I wanted before assuming anything. And ye know what?" I reached forward and caught Trystan's jaw in my hands. I felt the rasp of his evening stubble against my fingers as I tugged so he was leaning toward me across the table. I dropped my face down to the crook of his neck, taking an exaggerated breath as I ran my lips millimeters from his skin and settled with my mouth next to his ear.

"I could take ye home right now and fuck ye, and turn up at Dan's tomorrow and *he wouldn't care*," I whispered against his ear, letting my tongue dart out to run against the curled ridge of flesh. "We'd laugh together about how sweet yer virgin ass was and about how clingy straight guys are. I could kiss ten Joshes in front of him, blow ye right there in the same room. And it'd be like it always is between us: I'll fuck him or he'll fuck me and we'il both love it."

I released my hold on him and pushed him back across the table. I met his gaze, he stared straight back, and his brown eyes were unflinching and indifferent.

And then he laughed. Big peals of laughter that shook his shoulders, and he caught his breath enough to knock back the last of his beer.

His dark chuckle trailed off, but the smirk remained with one eyebrow cocked. "So he doesn't care who you fuck? I guess if he hangs out with a whore, that should be obvious. But do you think he'd get jealous if he knew the reason you've not been calling him is so you can share a bed with me?"

"What the hell? That's not—" I growled, but the rest of my argument was cut off by Penny wrapping her arms around my shoulders and squeaking excitedly in my ear.

"Eeeeedrys," she squealed and tried to squeeze the breath from my lungs.

Matt and Jason were behind her. Jason was carrying a tray of drinks, which by the look of it included fresh beers for me and Trystan, and a round of what I suspected was tequila.

"Trystan," Matt laughed as they all sat down at our table. "We've come to save you from Ide's excessive campness."

A pint, a shot, a wedge of lime, and a small packet of salt were dropped in front of me. I eyed the slammers with reluctance. Although frankly, their appearance was a welcome distraction from a conversation that had been teetering precariously close to ending in me and Trystan not speaking again. I looked up from the shots; Trystan wasn't looking at me anymore, but the edges of his conceit remained in the creases at the corners of his eyes.

He was seriously deluded if he thought I'd not been sleeping around because of him.

"You guys coming out with us later?" Jason said. "We just saw Dan so I know you're not busy, Ide."

"Yeah," Penny cooed as she grabbed my arm in mock begging. "It's been ages since you came out with us, and I miss having someone to dance with."

"And besides." Matt grinned. "Surely we have to get Trystan laid before he starts getting confused."

"Well there's no worry of that happening," Trystan laughed.

"Bit late," I mumbled so only Trystan would hear. He just laughed again.

"Seriously, though, how?" Trystan said with a chuckle. "Unless northern girls are so different that they take you to *their* place? I think I'm already stepping on Ide's toes enough."

Which was a fricking understatement and a half.

"Ha-ha, threesome." Matt grinned and my housemates burst out into fits of drunken laughter—probably at the thought of me with a girl; even I sniggered at the thought.

"Don't boobs just get in the way? And how d'ye choose which hole t' use?" I tried to sound serious, but the others were drunk enough that I didn't need to try too hard.

"Oh God, Ide, there is no way a random girl would let you do her ass," Jason mocked.

"Why? I'm good at it, and that way I wouldn't have t' look at her weird flobby chest."

Penny cuffed me and clasped her breast in mock indignation.

"Right, shots!" Matt announced.

I groaned. The three of them had clearly been drinking before they met us, but if I was staying out I was going to need Red Bull, not tequila. I humored them anyway and grimaced as I knocked the shot back and squeezed the lime wedge between my teeth to get rid of the sharp tang of cheap Mexican liquor.

"Right, now you basically *have* to come out," Penny chimed.

"Fine, fine, I'll come out." I gave in—after all, it'd been a quiet week, and I was suddenly feeling like getting laid.

"Trys? It's not a school night...?" Jason asked as he tried to sound more sober than he was.

I quirked an eyebrow at Trystan across the table. I was still pissed off, but I'd find some other way to get payback.

"Come on, man, we'll definitely sort you something." Matt egged him on.

"What do you take me for? Course I'm going to come. You think I'm going to sit at home by myself, or worse, with James?"

I chuckled. Despite my insistence that Trystan was straight, James had still been a twat to him just for being associated with me.

"And if ye need a lay so bad, ye can just have the bed," I added for good measure. "I'll sort myself out."

Trystan shot me a funny look. But that didn't stop him from taking me up on the offer.

BY THE time I'd got around to remembering to text someone about a bed—and associated activities—I'd had far too much tequila to really think it was a great idea. I'd sent Trystan off with instructions on where my condoms—and lube if he wanted—were stashed and for him to leave my sleeping bag outside the door.

"Dun missss me too much," Trystan had managed to only slur slightly as he'd stumbled out of the club with a rather sexy brunette tucked under his arm. My assessment of him being a lightweight had been confirmed—to be honest, I was impressed he was still standing. I gave the brunette a cheery wave as they left.

When I finally arrived home with Penny and Jason—Matt had left early as well—I was equally impressed that Trystan had actually remembered to chuck my sleeping bag out onto the landing. My amusement was dampened slightly by the fact that the couch in the kitchen was pretty uncomfortable, and too short. But I'd drunk enough that I only had about thirty seconds to think about that before I was unconscious.

I was woken up by a hand sliding up my side.

"*Ferfucksake*, Trys," I grumbled as I tried to push the hand away. "I'm sleeping." A cold hand snared the wrist that I'd been using to free myself, and suddenly I remembered where I was and that Trystan was upstairs with a girl, and therefore very unlikely to be pawing at me.

My eyes snapped open. Suddenly the hands on me felt disgusting; in the dark I saw James leering down at me.

"I knew you two fags were fucking."

"Shit, James," I tried to keep the drunken edge of fear from my voice and struggled to sit up. But then there was another hand on my shoulder, pressing me down. My shout of protest was muffled by a mouth pressed hard against mine. He bit my lip and I tasted the tang of my own blood as I shrieked and he pressed his tongue into my mouth.

I managed to get my other hand out of the sleeping bag, but he had all his weight on top of me and I couldn't get enough leverage. He grabbed my other wrist and tugged them both up over my head. His free hand ran down my torso. It was cold and clammy, and I shrank away from it as it slithered over my skin. I thrashed desperately as I tried to get free of my sleeping bag.

"James, what're ye trying t' do, ye fucker," I shouted as I bit down on the tongue that had forced its way inside my mouth. He shouted out as he flinched away from my face.

"Shut up, whore. This is what you like, right, faggot?"

He punched me in the face and I saw stars. The dregs of the alcohol in my system and the pain in my face was blinding. I was being rolled over. Hands pressed into my shoulder, and I could feel the skin breaking. I shouted out and he hit me again. Clammy fingers tugged at my boxers. I kicked out and finally I felt something connect. The weight left me and I scrambled off the sofa, stumbling to the floor. But he was already on his feet and I was still struggling to mine as my head continued to spin. A garbled shout scorched my throat as a foot connected with my stomach and I collapsed back onto the cheap lino flooring.

"Stay down, you fucking tease, we both know you were waiting for me…."

Ohgod.

Ohgod.

I could hardly breathe. I thrashed and nothing happened. The hand was still tugging down my boxers, and all I could think about was the last time I'd been like this… ohgod. When I was fifteen. It had been the first time I'd had sex with a guy: a man had gotten me drunk and taken me into the toilets of a seedy club, and he'd fucked me with no prep and… ohgod. Someone had found me when the bar closed. I hadn't bottomed for four years, not until Dan.

And now cold hard fingers were stripping me and my face was being pressed into the dirty lino and I was going to be raped in my own kitchen.

I was shouting something. I was fucking shouting as loud as my lungs would let me. There was a houseful of people. Probably unconsciously drunk people, but I kept shouting.

Then suddenly there was a break in the weight above me and I kicked out. I twisted round and managed to land a hand in James's face. I scrabbled backward as he reeled back from me.

Only it wasn't James; it was a slightly pissed-off looking Trystan.

He was breathing heavily with anger and concern shimmering in those brown eyes of his. His lip was split. His knuckles were bruised.

I stared as I tried to work out what was happening.

It had definitely been James a moment ago.

He grunted and rubbed the side of his face as he dropped down in front of me. He seemed faintly surprised by the blood, but not bothered.

He turned those brown eyes back to me and the anger was almost completely gone now. "You okay?"

I was not okay, I was about as far away from okay as I could get. He edged toward me and I scrambled back, tugging the sleeping bag over me as I went. Trystan sighed and stayed where he was.

"I've locked James in the downstairs bathroom. The police are on their way," he explained in a slow, quiet voice.

I nodded blankly, unsure whether I was glad I wasn't going crazy or.... Suddenly everything swept back in and hit me. I rolled over as stomach acid, beer, Red Bull, and tequila forced their way up through my throat, and I threw up all over the kitchen floor.

An hour later I was on the sofa with my legs tucked up against my chest and my sleeping bag wrapped around me. I was staring at a policewoman who was trying to ask me what had happened, and I was trying to explain but my body had other ideas. Despite having already evacuated everything from itself over an hour ago, my stomach was still insisting that it wanted to be sick, and I had to keep stopping to dry retch. I wanted to tell her what had happened because all I wanted was to go to bed and be alone. I had been seen to by a couple of paramedics, and James had been taken away. The girl Trystan had been with had been sent home in a taxi and all that was between me and bed was the woman in front of me.

I must have finally managed to say whatever it was she wanted to hear, because she gave me a last pitiful smile and told me she would contact me tomorrow and then she was leaving with the other police officers and I was finally alone. Except I wasn't, because Trystan was still here.

He'd spent the last hour sat at the kitchen table. My other housemates had gone back to bed. I stared at him across the room.

He sighed.

"You're actually a magnet for trouble, aren't you?" He spoke gently, and although his words weren't harsh and I knew he didn't mean them unkindly, it was exactly how I felt right now.

I let my head loll against the back of the couch. I heard shifting and then felt someone sit at the other end of the sofa.

"Sorry, Ide," he said with a sigh. "I knew what he was like and—"

"It's fine." It wasn't fine. "I knew too. Nobody could've known he'd go that far." I whispered because that was all my throat could cope with.

"What's wrong with me? What do I have to do to get people to just leave me alone?" I felt completely sober but the dregs of the alcohol in my system were still loosening my tongue. A faint wave of anger hit through the wallowing self-pity that clung to me. "I make sure I talk like a straight guy, I wear the same clothes, do the same stuff. So why? Why can't people just leave me alone?"

Trystan wrapped an arm around my shoulder and I let him tug me against his side. "Sorry, Ide. I'm as bad as the rest of them, aren't I?"

I didn't know what to say because he was, yet he wasn't.

"I want to go to bed," I said instead.

"Want me to sleep down here?" he asked.

I shook my head; I'm not sure why. I wanted to be alone, but the thought terrified me.

"Come on, then." He slid himself out from underneath me. He didn't carry me; he just walked next to me as I made my slow way up to the top of the stairs.

In my room I stared at my bed and my face crumpled. The bed was a mess. I could smell the brunette's perfume.

"Oh, fuck my life," I snapped, because all I wanted was to sleep in my bed, but I didn't want to get anywhere near it when it smelled of some random girl. I crossed my room and riffled through the piles of camping equipment, pulling out the roll mat I had lent to Trystan.

"I'm going to sleep on the floor. Have the bed if ye like."

Trystan heaved a weary sigh and held his hand out for another roll mat. I pulled a face but didn't say anything as he laid them both out on the floor. I found two summer sleeping bags I'd got for a festival. The cheap nylon felt horrible against my skin as I slid into one and lay down. Trystan lay down next to me. I didn't complain as he tucked me under his arm. I don't think either of us slept for a long time. But neither did we speak.

10—Cat

TRYSTAN MOVED into James's room. Did you see that one coming? Maybe you did, but I didn't. I would have said no, I still wanted to, but we needed someone to pay the rent.

I can't explain to you what happened over the next two weeks. It passed in a blur. James got charged, but only for assault because Trystan had managed to stop him before anything actually happened. I was still shaken. I still hated sleeping and being touched. After that night in sleeping bags with Trystan, I couldn't stand it. I hadn't seen Dan or Ashlie or Echo or any of the other guys I sometimes called. I'd gone to lectures. I'd handed in my essays. I'd cancelled on Meredith. I think her reaction was one of the worst. Because she didn't shriek and complain, she just told me it was fine, and from her more than anyone, that meant I wasn't.

"Ide? You coming out for a drink?" Penny asked from the door. They asked me every time, even though I always said no and had no intention of saying yes anytime soon. She knew, and she asked anyway. But she'd slept through my screaming, just like Matt and Jason. They'd ignored James, ignored me when I said we should get the girl. And I could hardly look at them.

"Not tonight, thanks, Penny," I said without looking round from my desk. I wondered how long I'd been writing the same paragraph.

"Ide?"

I sighed. "I'm not coming out."

Behind me I heard the sound of someone sitting on my bed. "I'm not asking you to come out, Ide," Trystan said in his soft southern accent. Or maybe he'd picked up a touch of a northern twang on some of his vowels already.

I twisted around to face him. He was the same as always.

"Then what's up, Trys?" I asked, trying to make my face look neutral.

"I'm going home for the weekend, to see my family and pick up the rest of my stuff." I waited blankly for him to get to the point.

"And?" I pressed when he didn't continue.

"You going to be okay?"

This seemed like an odd question as I hardly saw Trystan anyway. He worked pretty long hours in the week, and at the weekend I'd been spending a lot of time walking or biking with Patrick and some of the other guys from my course.

"Maybe you should call Jorja; it'd be nice to see her," he continued with the same look on his face.

I considered him across the room. "I'm not a kid, Trystan." There was a flash of something in his eyes, and I was sure he noticed my use of his full name.

"I'm not suggesting you are."

"Then go home and stop worrying about someone who isn't yer problem. Yer not my boyfriend; hell, yer not even my friend out o' choice. So leave me alone."

He considered me in silence for a moment. A sad smile pulled at his lips, then he exhaled, stood up, and left me alone. I stared at the door after he'd gone. A breath escaped from me. I spun my office chair back around, grabbed my car keys from my desk, and headed downstairs.

It took almost two hours to get home, and it was dark when I arrived, the kind of dark that sets your nerves on fire and lets the sky shimmer with stars. I sat in my car for a few moments as I pulled to a stop in the farmyard. The back door opened and my mum stood framed in the golden glow that spilled out of the kitchen. Her suspicion turned into a look of concern as she recognized the car.

"Idrys?" she called in confusion. She was crossing the yard, there was bread dough all over her hands, and her hair was a crazy red halo around her head. Her feet were in those ridiculous yellow Crocs she loved, and the cats danced around her ankles, almost tripping her. I wasn't crying when she pulled the car door open. I simply had my head dropped against the steering wheel. A rush of air that smelled like home washed over me, cold and damp and safe.

"Sorry for just turning up, Mam." I forced the words out of a chest that felt too tight and turned my face slightly so I could see her.

She looked like I'd just broken her heart as she wrapped her arms around my shoulders.

"Oh, Idrys, love; what's wrong?"

She bundled me out of the car—a feat because she was only five four—and then I was being sat at the kitchen table. The kitchen smelt of yeast and cats and wellington boots. Mum had washed her hands and made tea and she silently pressed a cup into my hands and went back to her bread. She let me sit in silence while she finished, simply glancing over at me with a soft smile every now and again. When she had slid the raw dough into the Aga, she pulled out a chair to sit next to me, and then she waited patiently while the smell of fresh bread overpowered everything else.

"Is Jorja home this weekend?" I asked when I was sure my voice wouldn't break.

"No, love; want me to call her?"

I shook my head, because I needed to sort out whatever had happened between me and my sister. But I didn't want to see her quite yet. "I'll call her in the morning."

"Good; she's missed ye."

"I'm sorry, Mam—" My voice cracked as I dropped my head, and I fought to hold back the wash of pressure that was mounting an assault upon my face, threatening to overwhelm two weeks of keeping myself together and send all my control spilling down my cheeks.

"Shit, I fricking mess up everything." I dropped my mug clumsily onto the table to hide my face in my hands, as demons I thought I had laid to rest surged up through my chest. "I'm really sorry. Why couldn't I just be normal and make everyone's life easier?"

"Oh, Idrys, what's happened?" She shuffled forward and pulled me into an awkward hug. "Yer dad and I dun want ye to be normal; have we ever said we dun love ye just the way ye are?"

"But—" I tried to speak but she wouldn't let me.

"No! No buts! Ye are jus' fine, and if something's gone on, then it's nae yer fault, so dun yer go blaming yerself. People're idiots, jealous idiots, 'cause ye have what they think they want, and they think it's easy. Well ye jus' ignore them, dun ye dare let them get ye down. Okay?"

I took a slow breath as I pressed my forehead against my mum's shoulder. The air that filled my lungs smelled of her, and the feelings she embraced me with were warm and unconditional. She ran a hand through my hair, soothing me as she hummed something soft and tuneless. There were so few people in my life who wanted nothing from me, who could live beside me and remain unfazed by jealousy or untwisted by coveting me. It was a sad state of affairs, and maybe it sounds conceited, but honestly, I wish it was just in my head. I was used to dealing with it, I had dealt with it all my life, but right then I hated it again. I hated the way I looked and the way people looked at me.

But my mum's arms around my shoulders, her hands gently rubbing my head, her humming filling my ears and the cats dancing for attention around our ankles, all of it allowed me to slip away from the self-hatred.

"So it would be someone else's fault if I'd robbed a store?" I managed to laugh through the pressure in my chest.

"Why ye...," she growled affectionately, then pushed me to arm's length as a loving smile curled her weathered but beautiful face. A timer went and she tittered. "I swear yer homin' device only activates when I've been baking," she said as she got up to pull a tray of perfect bread rolls out of the Aga. She gave one an experimental tap, and satisfied with the sound it returned, she tipped them gently onto a wire cooling tray. She squeaked as she picked one up, tossing it between her hands before she dropped it onto the table next to me, then proceeded to fish out butter and find a knife from the drying rack.

"Just dun tell yer dad," she said with a grin as she broke apart the still burning hot bread roll and proceeded to butter half before offering it to me.

"Thanks, Mam." The bread was almost hot enough to scald my lips, but it was the nicest thing I'd tasted in months. For the first time in two weeks, I felt a genuine smile slip over my face.

THE NEXT morning I woke up to help my dad with the chores. He didn't ask me why I was home because he was a "you'll feel better after a hard day's work" kind of guy rather than a "talk it out" kind. Which was fine with me. Because my dad was fine with me being gay, but I wasn't sure I was fine with him knowing I'd been almost raped. I wasn't fine with anyone knowing, so when we were done with the early morning stuff and it was a reasonable time to call my sister, I sat in the kitchen and stared at my phone with a growing sense of dread.

I knew she'd been talking to Trystan; he'd said as much last night. I wondered how much he'd told her.

"Idrys?" she answered breathlessly before the first ring had even finished. So Mum must have told her I was home and was planning to call.

"Hey, Jorja," I said just because I couldn't think of anything else. It had been almost four months since I'd spoken to her. We'd never gone that long before. Our arguments generally lasted a couple of weeks at most, but usually no more than a couple of hours.

"Oh my God, Ide, I'm so sorry about being a bitch over the whole Scotland thing. I know what yer like, but sometimes yer just so stupid that ye come across as arrogant, and I'm sorry for suggesting Trystan call ye even though I know ye hate him because ye hate straight guys crushing on ye, but he's…."

"Jorja, shush; I don't hate Trystan."

"Ye don't?"

I sighed because I didn't know what I thought about Trystan anymore.

He'd saved me.

He'd looked after me.

Since that night he had been careful not to touch me, and his brown eyes had held nothing but concern.

I didn't want to think about Trystan.

"I'm still not sure I'm his biggest fan. But I don't hate him." My voice was embarrassingly hesitant but that was the best I could manage at the moment.

"What happened, Ide?" she whispered. "Trys wouldn't tell me, but I know there were police involved."

"It doesn't matter, Jorja."

"It does to me."

I stared out of the window at what should have been a drab autumn day, but it was made beautiful by the rainbow of reds and oranges and browns. One of the cats came into the kitchen. It gave a cursory mew and jumped onto my lap, giving me little choice in the matter as it curled up and pushed its head under my hand.

"Just another straight-guy incident," I said as I concentrated on the cat instead of the memory. And the distorted gasp at the back of Jorja's throat let me know that she knew exactly what I meant. I heard a muted sob rattle down the line.

"Oh my God, Ide, fucking hell, I'm so sorry I wasn't there for ye."

"It's fine, nothing happened, Trys stopped him, so…." I sighed as I realized what a truly ungrateful prick I had been last night. "Please don't tell Mum and Dad. The first time was hard enough on them."

I could tell she didn't want to, but she agreed eventually.

"How did he get into yer room?" she asked quietly when she had collected herself together.

"I was sleeping on the couch. I'd lent the room to Trys because he'd picked up a girl," I explained slowly. Talking about it wasn't as bad as I had expected; the explanation just slipped out like I was talking about any old thing. I let my fingers caress the cat on my knee, and it purred gently in my lap. I realized both me and my sister had been silent for a while. "Jorja?"

"Sorry, I'm here; that surprised me, were all. I thought Trys was still…."

"Well, I don't think he would have unless I'd offered, but I did, so… anyway, it was fine." I tried to lighten my tone. "He got his lay and to be a white-fricking-knight, and I'm just a bit shaken." Which was an understatement and little unfair on Trystan, but Jorja managed a soft chuckle down the line.

But I *was* messed up. I felt better right now surrounded by the familiarity of home, but just like the time in the bar toilet, the experience had changed me. Last time it had put me on the path to the strange group relationship I was now part of with Dan and Ashlie and Echo and all the others that drifted in and out of our core group. And this time I wasn't sure what would happen, but I was certain I wouldn't be able to go back to how I'd been.

"So Trys is living wi' ye now?" she asked eventually, and I muttered confirmation down the phone. "And ye guys are okay?"

"Kind of. We were up until the shit with James… but I've been a bit of a tosser lately."

Jorja chuckled, although I could still hear the edge of sadness in her voice. "Well, yer usually a dickhead, and that doesn't seem to have made much o' a difference so far…." She hesitated as if she wanted to say more; then with a sigh she changed topics. "I'm coming home in a fortnight, ye going to be there?"

"Yeah, I'll come." In the yard I heard the distinctive sound of a battered old Jeep, and a smile touched my lips. "Theo's here, so I'm going to go. Love ye, Jorja, and I'm sorry too: for being an idiot and a dick and everything else."

She giggled. "Love ye too, see ye soon."

I hung up as Theo called an absent, "Knock, knock…?" through the open kitchen door as he paused to take his wellies off. I don't know why he bothered because his dog rushed straight in with her paws covered in the same mud and jumped on my chest. The cat on my lap gave Tess a haughty look as I pushed the dog back to the floor.

"Heya, Tess." I ruffled the collie's head affectionately.

"Decided t' finally grace us wi' yer presence then, did ye, city boy? And ta very much for letting me know ye were back," Theo grumbled as he ignored the cat and tugged me to my feet and into a one-armed hug.

"Sorry, Theo, it was kinda unplanned," I answered honestly as my oldest friend pulled away, rolled his eyes, and set about making himself a brew.

"I thought it must be as Jorja ain't here." There was a note of weariness to his tone, and I felt a pang of resentment for my sister that she was still stringing the poor guy along. Maybe I didn't have the best attitude toward relationships, but at least I always made my intentions clear so nobody got hurt.

I'd had a crush on Theo when I was younger. The kind of crush you have when you're so young that you don't really understand what husband and wife—or husband and husband in my case—really meant. Back when "gay" was an insult you used because you didn't quite dare to say "shit" for fear of your parents hearing. But nothing had ever come of it; I'd got over it by the time I realized I was gay, and I could honestly say that Theo was one of the only straight guys who I have never caught looking at me with curiosity.

"Ye two kissed and made up yet?" he asked as he dropped a mug of tea on the table next to me and took a seat.

"I just got off the phone to her; so, hopefully."

"Good, she sulks when ye two aren't speaking; and it's been bloody ages," Theo said with a wry chuckle. "So what's been up? Yer dad showed me some modeling photos tha' I wish I could erase from ma memory."

I groaned. "That man needs his head checking, seriously. But I haven't been up to much, to be honest."

"Tha' southern dick found himself a new place yet? I still can't believe he had the cheek t' ask ye in the first place."

I gave a weary chuckle. "Funny story: he's living in my house share these days."

"Yer shitting me?"

"Nope, someone had to move out, we couldn't afford to be fussy, and I was outvoted." Which was mostly the truth. It had been Matt who suggested Trystan take the room, and although Trystan had been reluctant because I was so against it, he still said yes. But at least I had my bed to myself again.

Which was definitely a good thing. Because I definitely didn't miss having anyone in my bed. Definitely.

"Ye had any more trouble?"

"Honestly, Trys is a pain, but he's better than the last guy, so...." I gave a small shrug. Thinking about James still caused a ripple of tension across my chest, but it wasn't so bad that I thought I couldn't breathe anymore, and I'd got over worse in the past.

"Oh dun ye listen to Idrys, Theo; Trystan's a lovely boy," my mum chimed as she came through the kitchen door with a basket of eggs under one arm.

I caught Theo's eye and rolled mine, letting him know what I thought about that without having to actually contradict my mum.

"I'm just about t' make a bit o' lunch, love; ye staying?" my mum asked Theo as she bustled around the kitchen.

"Aye, if ye dun mind, that would be lovely, ta," Theo said bashfully, and I grinned because suddenly it was just like we were twelve again and we'd been discovered scaring the chickens.

When we'd eaten I went back with Theo to his farm and helped him with his evening duties—well, I did most of everything to prove I still could and Theo mocked me. Then we drove to the local pub in Theo's Jeep and sat in the corner with Tess at our feet as a stream of locals came over to say "Hi" to Theo while they gazed curiously at me as if I were an exotic animal. It was just like old times, except with pints instead of juice and a Jeep instead of bikes.

The next day I ate my body weight in roast dinner—by the time I got in the car to drive home I was really wishing I hadn't had a second helping of blackberry and apple pie. Mum gave me a hug; my dad muttered something I couldn't quite hear and patted me on the back—the closest to a hug he could manage. And then I pulled out of the drive and even though it was almost two hours back to York, I was feeling really okay for the first time in a while.

It was eight o'clock by the time I got up to my room on Sunday evening. It was just how I'd left it. The notes for the essay I'd been struggling with were still next to my laptop that had managed to shut itself down at least. The essay was due in on Tuesday, and thanks to me having done nothing on it over the weekend I was probably going to have to sort it out tonight. I found I didn't really mind. I went downstairs to make myself something to drink and was glad that everyone's doors were closed. I felt like I could face them again now, but I didn't particularly want to.

There was a knock at my door around nine. And I looked round absently for a moment. Penny, Matt, and Jason rarely came up to my room, and even after everything that had happened Trystan tended to forget that this wasn't his room anymore and usually walked straight in. I heard feet shuffling away on the other side.

"Sorry, come in; it's open," I called, still curious.

"Oh, hey, Ide." My curiosity turned to surprise as Josh Jackson stuck his head around the edge of the door. "I wasn't sure if you were back yet."

"Huh, Josh?" Of all the people I'd expected to see, I could honestly say that Josh was the last person.

He being here made absolutely no sense. Because the only way he could get here would be via his brother—who *had* gone home this weekend. But it still made no sense, because hadn't Trystan blown a fuse when I'd kissed the boy in Scotland? And now he was bringing Josh to my house and letting him come up here by himself?

I realized I was staring, and while I'd been silently trying to work out what was going on, Josh had crossed the room and stood opposite me. His knees were just apart from mine.

"How come yer in York? Trys know yer here?" I asked stupidly—it wasn't like the guy could have hidden in his brother's boot for the four-hour car ride.

Josh nodded, his brown eyes still fixed on mine. He looked nervous, terrified even, but there was a note of determination there too.

"He said I could come," Josh said as he licked his lips, and his eyes flicked down to mine as his knee brushed against me. "I'm sixteen now," he added quietly, and everything else that was different from the last time we'd seen each other was also written across his face.

"Josh, I don't think—"

"You promised." He leaned over me, and without giving me much more choice in the matter, he pressed his lips against mine.

The last person to kiss me had been James. And since then just the thought of kissing someone had been enough to make bile rise up my throat and sour my thoughts. But Josh's kiss was okay. Maybe because he looked so scared. Maybe because as he leaned over me he kept his hands clasped to his side—like some kind of old-school toy soldier—or maybe it was because it was so sweet and tender.

His lips were ever so soft against mine. He mewed quietly in the back of his throat, and it was as if reality had twisted and it was me that was the unsure-of-himself kid and Josh was desperately trying not to scare me away. Maybe life *had* switched. I returned his kiss softly, parting my lips so he could let his curious tongue taste my mouth. I pushed one of my hands through his hair, rubbing my fingers softly against his scalp, as I let the other drift up to rest against his hip. I could feel him struggling to keep control of himself; it was in every hitch of his breath and almost nip of his teeth and increasingly eager questing of his tongue.

I let my hands leave gentle pressure where they rested against him, and I guided him forward so he wasn't at such an awkward angle. He didn't break the kiss as he straddled me. His hands sprang suddenly into action but I wasn't worried. His touch was featherlight at first as he quested over my shoulders; when I didn't flinch away he let them slide down my spine around my back, and when I continued to let him kiss me, he slipped those hands under the hem of my T-shirt and I felt his fingers clutch at my flesh. He moaned in the back of his throat as he straddled my lap and ground his hips forward into mine in time with his kisses.

And it was okay because I wasn't feeling sick, and he was sixteen now. So it was fine.

But I felt nothing.

Not nothing exactly. I felt tenderness and affection as I held one hand against his hip and used my other to gently caress the back of his head. Josh's lips against mine were soft and demanding and full of lust. But as I kissed him back, not a jot of desire stirred inside of me.

I heard the door handle twisting. I broke the kiss. Josh gave an impatient mew as he tried to find my lips again with his that were already flushed and damp. Mine must have looked the same as I ignored Josh and stared blankly over the boy's shoulder.

Trystan was framed in the doorway to my room. His face was like thunder.

I stared into furious chocolate-colored eyes, and I realized the reason I felt nothing for Josh. It was the same reason I hadn't called Dan or Echo or Ashlie, even before the incident with James. It was the same reason my gut was twisted right then, and the same reason that I had to stop myself from chucking Josh from my knee.

I laughed. Because my life was laughable.

I didn't hate Trystan.

I was falling for him.

I wanted him to lock me in those brown eyes of his, teasing, joking, laughing, I didn't care. I wanted to curl up next to him on a sofa. I wanted to kiss his lips and have him devour my body, and I wanted to sleep beside him and wake up with him snuggled next to me.

If the fury on his face was anything to go by, the feeling wasn't mutual.

How the hell had I let this happen?

How had I let myself get attached to a straight guy?

And why, of all the men in the world, did it have to be Trystan?

"Josh." Trystan was beyond furious, his voice so cold it should have been terrifying. "Get off him right this second."

"No," Josh said, his voice firm and slightly petulant.

Trystan stalked over and I thought for a second that he was going to haul his brother from my lap. Instead he bent down so that his face was right up in Josh's. I retreated into the back of my chair, oddly terrified of having him so near.

"Ignoring the fact that this guy is a serious whore"—Trystan's voice was deadly low as he glared at his brother—"he's a fucking mess. Now get off him."

"He was fine; he kissed me back," Josh grumbled. He still had his hands up my T-shirt and my calm of a moment ago was beginning to wear off under the dark gaze of Trystan.

I reached round to extract Josh from my shirt.

"Actually, Josh, yer brother is right; ye need to let me go." I clamped my hands on either side of his arms and gently forced him back away from me. I met the hurt in his eyes and guilt joined the churning disgust and apprehension in my stomach.

"Go downstairs," Trystan snarled.

"Trys—" Josh tried, but his brother cut him off.

"No! You promised me. You *fucking* promised that you wouldn't bother him, and he's back for what? An hour? I'm putting you on a train home first thing in the morning, and don't look at me like that, Josh; I *wanted* to help and you couldn't fucking keep it in your pants, could you?"

Josh bristled. He shot me a last hopeful glance that crumpled into desolation as I just stared back. And then he stormed from my room. The sound of his feet clattering down the stairs filled the silence.

"Trys," I exhaled, and wondered what the hell was wrong with me. "I'm sorry, I just...." I dropped my head into my hands. He'd backed away, but I couldn't look at him anymore.

What kind of masochistic idiot was I?

"I wasn't going to do anything, but he kissed me and...."

"Just shut up, Ide. You're such a fucking whore; I thought you'd be bothered by what James did, but I guess that's probably just a bit of fun for you, eh?"

I hissed a breath between my lips.

"Ah...." The chuckle that rattled my chest hurt. "Yeah, I guess so."

I lifted my head and stared beyond Trystan, to the door Josh had left through. I took a deep breath and tried to remember how I'd been feeling when I got back from home. A small slither of calm returned and I forced my voice not to crack. "Ye brought him here 'cause of the gay thing, right? So don't send him home, I'll take him out, find a nice guy for him and...."

"Oh my fucking God, Ide!" Trystan exclaimed. He looked angry and exasperated as he stood in the middle of my room. "He doesn't want a *nice guy*. Nobody does: everyone fucking wants *you*! How're you the only one who doesn't see that?"

I dropped my head to one side, still staring slightly beyond Trystan. A bitter smile quirked the edge of my lips.

"Ye think I don't know? Ye think I *like* it? Ye think that shit wi' James was the first time something like that has happened?" I spoke softly and I discovered that the slither of calm I'd found allowed me to meet Trystan's gaze with my own. He flinched slightly. "Well, it wasn't. And the first time there was no one to stop him. So shut the fuck up, Trystan."

"Oh shit, Ide." He stepped toward me and I snatched myself away.

"No! I don't want yer pity; yer as bad as all of them."

I dropped my head back into my hands because the problem was that Trystan wasn't like them. I wanted him to want me, and he didn't. He hugged me in his sleep because that's what he did, and he had looked after me with that shit with James because he was a nice guy, and he flirted with me because it was a game, and my head had converted that into something it would never be.

11—FOX

"IDE, THIS is stupid," whined Josh against my neck. I nuzzled him playfully as he sat between my legs.

"No, it's not. Tell me who takes yer fancy, I'll tell ye if it's a good idea."

"Meh, Ide, I want *you*."

"Well, ye can't have me; so pick someone," I replied, not unkindly. Because when I'd convinced his elder brother to let him stay, I'd also explained to Josh that under no circumstances was I going to sleep with him.

"No one's going to think I'm free if I'm on your knee anyway," Josh moaned, but he didn't seem particularly inclined to leave my lap.

By my side Dan chuckled. "Don't worry about that; being with Ide probably makes you more desirable."

"See," I chided. "Now sit still and point."

"Him," Josh pouted.

I rolled my eyes as I saw the thirty-year-old businessman that Josh had pointed out.

"The idea is t' find someone closer to yer own age, idiot."

"You're close enough." Josh sulked.

"Ye want me to take ye back to Trys?" I whispered in Josh's ear and the boy shuddered, which could have been in a good way in response to my hushed words in his ear or in a bad way at the thought of his brother.

Trystan had reluctantly agreed to let Josh stay. He had even more reluctantly agreed to let him come out with me this evening. But he had been in a filthy mood since he'd found Josh in my room on Sunday—it was now Friday. I didn't particularly care. I just needed to get over this stupid infatuation, and I needed to do it as fast as possible. Trystan walking around with a face like thunder was as good a reason as any to ignore him when we crossed paths in the kitchen, and in the five days since I'd convinced him to let Josh stay, I hadn't said more than a handful of words to the guy.

I already felt like I was making progress.

"Fine," Josh huffed, and for the first time he actually took a serious look around the bar that was quiet so early on a Friday evening. I watched as a blush rose up over his cheeks and he dropped his head, hiding his face in his hands. "Oh my God, this is so embarrassing: everyone is staring."

"They're staring 'cause they think we're cute," I said softly into his ear. "Because they see ma face and assume I'm a catcher, and it turns them on imagining us together—like straight guys thinking about lesbians. They're staring at Dan and wishing they were him, so they could do ye."

"You're *not* helping, Idrys," Josh grumbled. His face was so red it was beginning to spread down his neck.

Dan chuckled and caught my eye when I went to take some more of my beer.

"Speaking of which, when *can* I do you again?" Dan reached to press a kiss against my lips. I think the whisper of lust that went round the bar was a physical thing as everyone's heads went into overdrive—and I knew Dan had done it on purpose.

"I told ye; I'm not in the mood at the moment," I replied as I broke away. Once such a display would have had me riddled with excitement and desire. Now I just smiled warmly and pressed a chaste kiss on his lips. I found I could cope with Dan's kisses, but just like Josh's, I found that they did very little for me.

"You know I don't mind switching." He smiled back and I rolled my eyes and looked pointedly at the guy in my lap.

"If I was in the mood for *that* we wouldn't be sitting here, would we?"

Dan gave a weary sigh and a shrug. "Guess so." His eyes narrowed and I knew he was going to try and ask me what had happened, but I didn't want to talk about it—even with Dan. I pressed my lips back over his.

"Leave it, Dan." I turned back to Josh. "So?"

"Thanks to that display you two just put on, I think *actually* everyone is now staring."

"Meh, narrow-minded, the lot of them. Hmm." My attention was caught by a guy at the other end of the bar who wasn't watching. He seemed cute and tallish, although it was hard to tell exactly because he was sitting down. There was a drink in front of him, but it looked like juice. I checked out his face; he was young—about nineteen if I had to guess—and his mousy blond hair fell over his face as he messed around on his phone.

"What about him?" I whispered to Josh.

"Oh…." Josh clammed up, but he didn't dismiss the guy completely. I pressed a kiss against his cheek and stood up from behind him.

"Cool, I'll go vet." I crossed the bar before Josh could say anything to stop me.

I tried to pull my most charming—and least attractive—smile onto my face as I pulled up a stool next to him. It took him a few seconds to look up from his phone, in which time I had noticed that his drink was indeed juice and didn't look like it was diluted with anything alcoholic. As he finally looked up and saw me next to him, his eyes widened in genuine shock then slight panic as they darted over my shoulder to the corner where I'd been sitting. I followed his gaze in time to see Dan give him a friendly wave. Josh had twisted around so his back was to us and had his forehead pressed against the table.

"Ah…," the guy garbled as he looked back at me. It was a fair enough reaction; Dan was a big guy and my height more than made up for my lack of breadth. Plus, it wasn't like I never came here, and although I'd never noticed this guy before, I knew that me and the group I usually hung out with weren't exactly easy to forget—Ashlie: tiny, gorgeous, and exceptionally camp; Echo: the seemingly emotionless giant, his voice as low and loud as thunder and with skin as close to obsidian as mine was to white; Dan: boisterous and beautiful and prone to getting into fights over me. So unless he'd never been here before—unlikely given how comfortable he'd been sitting at the bar—he probably had some idea of what I was like. Which was a fact I often used to my advantage, but this time was probably working against me.

"Relax, I'm not trying to pick ye up; I have a favor to ask ye. And it's not a gang bang, so don't look so scared."

"Oh."

"No need t' sound so disappointed either." I chuckled and the guy blushed. "Anyway, first off, it's not for me. Yer not my type. See the guy over there? The one that was on ma knee?" I added because we now couldn't see Josh's face, but given the guy's reaction to me, he must have noticed us.

"Yeah, I saw him before. Your boyfriend is cute—but did you check his ID?" I laughed because the guy had gotten over his shock and he had a sparkle in his eyes as he finally put his phone down.

"Yes, but he's not my boyfriend. Which is the point. He's just recently come out, and he begged to come here wi' me." The guy's eyebrows flicked up his forehead in mirth. "Yeah, I know; poor guy doesn't have a clue. I promised his brother I would look after him, and well, I dun really need to try, do I?"

"No, no one in their right mind would approach you guys."

I smiled because I knew it was the truth. "Well, just so ye know, we're not that bad, or at least, not always." I gave an absent wave to cut off whatever he was about to say. "The point is, I can't—won't—let him come on his own, but I'm not about to sit here and let him think he's not gorgeous. Which he is, by the way."

"So you're pulling guys for him?" He looked slightly aghast and kind of impressed at the same time. "If he's so gorgeous, why not just bring him into your group?"

So he definitely knew who I was and what I was like, and he was still playing hard to get. That meant he probably wasn't going to come over just to get in with me and Dan, which meant he might be a nice guy.

God knows I'd been tempted by Josh once. And if I wasn't off sex, the chances were I would have damned myself further to hell and taken the boy to bed. But I *was* off sex because of the James thing—because it was definitely the James thing; there was no way I was hung up on a dick like Trystan. Even Dan had offered before he'd even met Josh—and slightly more enthusiastically when he finally met the gorgeous youngest Jackson. And although I knew that Dan would have made it great for Josh—I knew firsthand after all—and despite the fact that I was happy with my sex life—or had been before I'd seemingly lost my ability to feel lust—it wasn't like I didn't realize it wasn't particularly normal.

"Pah, not a chance in hell; ye think that's healthy?"

He frowned at me; he clearly hadn't expected me to belittle my own habits, and I gave him a small shrug in return.

"So, are ye meeting someone or would ye like to come and chat to an awkward and embarrassed friend o' mine? He's a nice guy, gorgeous eyes, likes camping and Xbox," I added with a grin.

The guy chuckled, and he glanced over my shoulder once more. He was seriously thinking about it, which in my books was probably a good thing. "Why the hell not? I'm Chris."

"Nice t' meet ye, Chris," I said and shook his hand as he got to his feet. "I get the impression ye know already, but I'm Idrys, and the handsome man at the back is Dan. Yer cute blushing date is Josh." I let my smile slip slightly and stared down at him from my full height. "And if yer screw over my friend, yer'll be dealing with me, Dan, Echo, *and* his brother. His brother's scary as hell. Understand?"

Chris met my gaze and shrugged. "Sounds fair."

I mediated some brief and amusingly awkward introductions, and then I deposited Chris and Josh on a table in watching distance and made sure the barman knew not to serve Josh anything alcoholic. Then I went back to Dan. There were plenty of curious looks as I leaned against Dan with a small sigh and returned to my beer.

"Even for us, this is weird," Dan said softly as we kept a surreptitious eye on the pair.

"I guess so, but I feel sorry for the kid. Ye would too if ye knew his family."

"So this has nothing to do with him having a massive crush on you?"

"Well, it would make my life easier if he could get over that, yeah."

Dan said nothing for a moment, but I could feel him building himself up.

"What's going on, Ide? I spoke to Ashlie and Echo and a couple of the others, and from what I'm hearing, you haven't been with anyone for, like, a month? I mean, there's nothing wrong with that, but why now? You got a guy you like?"

"It's complicated," I said softly.

"You know all of us would do anything for you, right?"

"Mmm, I know, Dan, and I'm sorry…." I looked round at him, and he held my eyes in his as he pressed a kiss down over my lips. It was soft and tender and full of love; but I knew already. I didn't need him to tell me; I knew that he would go exclusive for me. I knew that what had once been nothing more than a mutually beneficial agreement had turned into something more on his side. And I hated that after everything he had done for me, all I was able to do was hurt him.

"Wow, I kind of want to meet the guy that's finally tied you down." Dan gave me a sad smile as he broke the kiss.

"It's not like that, Dan."

"So this has nothing to do with Trystan?"

I shrugged, because it had everything to do with Trystan and nothing at the same time.

"I just don't feel anything, Dan. It's worse than when ye first met me; then at least I felt *something*, even if it was only lust. But last Sunday, the cute little piece of ass I've just sat at the table over there with another man practically threw himself at me. Josh was practically begging me to take him, and I felt nothing."

Dan pressed a kiss against the side of my head as we watched Josh across the bar.

"It happened again, didn't it? You should've just told me, Ide. I guess I can't help you this time?" He spoke gently, and although his words were a question, I knew I didn't need to answer.

I'd gone a bit mental after the disaster that was my first time. My ass had healed, and after a bit longer so had my head—to a degree. I'd sworn never to bottom again and proceeded to fuck as many guys as possible. Which had been fine when I lived in the middle of nowhere, but when I moved to York, I'd had a practically inexhaustible supply of willing partners. I'm not suggesting that the me right now is some chaste little angel, but I'm practically a saint these days compared to how I was before Dan sorted me out.

Dan had never hidden the fact that he'd done the whole thing just so he could fuck me and that he knew I was scared behind my callous attitude. I'd fucked him once, in a toilet I think, and then he'd basically stalked me, cock blocking me over and over, giving me little choice but to sleep with him again or go without. I think at one point I'd fucked him about five times in a single evening in an attempt to get him to back off. He hadn't, and then one day I'd woken up in his bed with his finger up my ass. He was real clever about the whole thing. He'd started with just the one finger. He'd not pushed for anything more, just fingered my prostate when he sucked me off. Then after a week or so he moved up to two fingers. When I'd got used to that, he'd stopped doing it altogether. He'd simply waited for me to ask for him to start again. And when I did he'd fucked my brains out.

Dan had made it clear from the start that he didn't want to date; he just wanted to fuck me. And once I'd discovered that I quite like being topped every now and again, it worked quite well for both of us. Dan introduced me to Echo via a threesome, and I introduced him to Ashlie. And others have come and gone on the edges of our messed-up sex lives, but the four of us have more or less remained the same for two years.

Except that now Dan was in love with me.

"Looks like the date is going well?" Dan said softly. I followed his gaze to where Josh and Chris were laughing together, and the doe-eyed look I'd only ever seen Josh use on me was now in full force on the poor unsuspecting Chris.

"Those bloody Jackson eyes; honestly, they should be illegal," I said gently, and at my back Dan heaved a sigh.

DESPITE DOING nothing much more than sit, drink beer, and watch other people flirt, I was surprisingly exhausted when I finally got back home. I'd had maybe four pints, and despite what had gone unsaid between Dan and me, I had ended the night with a nice warm glow from a job well done. It wasn't late but I was ready for my bed.

So I was kind of irritated by the angry big brother waiting for me on the other side of the door.

"Where the hell is Josh? You fucker." He didn't grab me and slam me up against the wall. I could tell that he wanted to, but instead he glowered at me and backed me into the wall just by stepping into my personal space. It had much the same effect. And although I knew he was resisting the urge to manhandle me because of all the shit with James, it amused me that he thought this was any better. It didn't matter anyway; I wasn't scared of Trystan. I knew he could hurt me if he wanted to, but that was just one of the many things I knew he didn't want to do to me.

I leaned back against the wall and stared into those gorgeous brown eyes. Even narrowed in anger they should still have been illegal.

The beer I'd drunk was merrily making its way through my veins. He was so close I could smell him and just about feel the heat of his body as he stood over me. I stared into angry brown eyes and felt about ninety percent of the progress I had made by ignoring him this week dissolve into a soft wash of warmth. So I let a languid smirk spread my lips and tucked my hand around his waist. I ignored the flash of irritation on his face as I pulled him slightly closer to me.

"Well, I found a suitably old, debauched, and decrepit pervert and left them to it," I whispered with a smile. "Would ye like me to show ye what they were up to when I left?" I ran my tongue over my bottom lip and reached forward slightly, so that my lips almost touched his. "Unfortunately for the pervert, yer mam rang, so Josh is on the phone to her outside," I finished in a more normal voice.

I laughed lightly, only the problem was that Trystan's look of irritation hadn't wavered and he hadn't moved his face away from mine. And as I stared at him, it was becoming harder and harder to convince myself to lean back against the wall and open up some space between us.

"It went something like this."

I touched my lips against Trystan's. It was the softest almost-caress I could steel myself against, and I could have cried at the fire that my body finally decided to release.

Why? Why not the lovely Dan who would have done anything for me? Why not even Josh who would have at least been fresh and willing? Why this immobile man who stared down at me with hard eyes? My head didn't know, but my blood sure as hell didn't care about that, and it flooded my body with delicious bliss. And it demanded more. And I was going to give it more.

"Right, so *you're* allowed to pester Ide but I'm not?" Josh complained as he appeared in the doorway. "How exactly is that fair?"

Trystan jerked back from me and I was left reeling. Josh had his arms crossed over his chest and he was kind of joking, but I could see an edge of irritation in his eyes that his good night wasn't quite able to soften. With a smile dusting my face, I gently raised my hands to Trystan's chest and pressed him the rest of the way out of my personal space.

"Don't worry, Josh, yer brother likes playing gay chicken," I said with a smile that I didn't really feel but was helped along by the beer in my system. "He doesn't quite get that I'm gay and am therefore always going to win," I finished with a wink.

Josh looked at me and then turned his puzzled frown on his brother.

"Was Mum okay?" Trystan asked. He had backed away from me, and despite the considerable evidence that I had looked after his brother, he was still scowling.

Josh nodded absently, and he was frowning too; what was it with these two? "Yeah, she just wanted to know I was home. Text her and let her know I'm with you, please."

I wanted to go to bed, and yet I knew that the echoes of lust that I felt were going to keep me up.

I tried to work it out; it really had been four weeks since I'd been with anyone, and the only action I'd had was that wet dream. Sheesh—no wonder I felt so on edge. Yet I couldn't deny that last weekend I'd kissed Josh and felt nothing while I'd hardly touched my lips to Trystan and had rarely felt so high on sexual energy. It was obscene—and annoying.

"Come on, Josh." I held my hand out to him with a smile. Half because I knew it would piss off Trystan and half because I had a feeling Josh was not the kind of guy to go slowly and getting advice in quickly was going to be a necessity.

"Where're you going?" Trystan snapped irritably as Josh took my hand and a smile returned to the younger brother's lips. I paused at the bottom of the stairs and shot Trystan a wicked grin over my shoulder.

"Isn't it obvious? After spending the evening introducing Josh to other guys, I'm taking him t' my room to ravish him." I rolled my eyes and let my sarcasm slide away. "I'm going to talk to him about gay sex. Come if ye want."

"Please don't," Josh muttered. His brother ignored him and followed us upstairs.

At my room Trystan paused in the doorway and looked suddenly awkward. I cocked my head to one side and shot him a questioning smile. He met it with a scowl and so I waved him over to the bed. He sat on it, shuffling back so he could lean against the wall and his legs were spread out across the length of it. I found I had mixed feelings about the whole thing as I sat in my office chair and called Josh over to sit between my knees. On one hand this was almost certainly going to be awkward for Trystan— which I liked—but unfortunately having him here would also be a pain for Josh. Having him on my bed also meant there was a chance his scent would remain, and that could be a good or bad thing, depending on my mindset.

I decided to just stop worrying about it. Trystan wasn't about to leave, and Josh needed to know what he was getting himself into.

"Right, what was that website called?" I mused as I fired my laptop up and pulled up a web browser. I had to go to an e-mail Jorja had sent me in the end, and eventually I found what I was looking for—mangafox.

"What the hell is that?" I could practically hear Trystan's raised eyebrows.

"This is yaoi. It's mostly completely unrealistic, but it's less offensive than porn," I explained as I reached around Josh to find a suitable case study.

"What the hell? That *is* porn!" Trystan exclaimed from behind me as I flicked past a particularly graphic—and unrealistic—sex scene.

"It's *cartoon* porn, or would ye rather me pull up some actual porn, eh, Trys?" I arched round to meet his gaze. He was scowling at me still, but he'd shuffled to the edge of the bed so he could get a better look.

He grumbled something that I took to be a no. So I turned back to the computer to locate what I was after.

"Right, this will do. Fortunately for us they make it super easy: the one that looks like an underage kid is the one going t' be the bottom—probably ye—and the one that looks like an actual guy will be the top," I said to Josh. "This part's exactly the same as when ye were with a girl: kissing and petting. Guys are generally a little more enthusiastic." I was kind of enjoying myself, and Josh was leaning forward, staring at the pictures.

"What *is* this stuff?" Josh asked.

"Dunno, Jorja reads it. Apparently girls like reading about gay guys—go figure. But it seemed useful for what I needed." I flicked to the next page. "This is where it gets a little different. So." I paused because Trystan had dropped into a squat next to the office chair. I looked down at him and he gave me a brief glance from under his eyebrows.

"*What*? I'm just curious," he muttered. I shrugged and turned back to the laptop.

"So when ye were with a girl, ye had to get her ready, right?" I framed it as a question because I had a vague idea, but I'd kissed a girl once, and that was as far as my experience with women went. Although I did know a little more than I'd actually experienced thanks to when I'd researched to help Jorja plan her first time—if hell ever froze over and I had a change of heart about the whole boobs thing I'd be sorted. I mean, it's so bloody straightforward compared to anal; hetero guys have no idea how easy they have it.

"Erm, yeah," Josh stuttered slightly. By my side Trystan sniggered, and I reached round and cuffed the back of his head.

"Ye, be quiet or I'll kick ye out," I grumbled. Trystan gave a perturbed scowl but nodded as he directed his attention back to the computer.

"So it'll be the other way around this time, *and* if he *doesn't* try, ye get out o' there as quick as ye can, understand?"

Josh was oblivious as he cocked his head to get a better look at the screen. "Sure."

From the corner of my eye I noticed Trystan glance up at me, but this time I didn't look back.

"So, ye'll kiss and cuddle and touch each other. I don't think I have to explain that part, right? His bits will be the same as yers, and I guess ye know how they work."

Josh said something irritable and wordless under his breath.

"I feel obliged to recommend that ye don't go any further for the first couple o' dates. I also recognize that's pretty hypocritical."

Trystan snorted. "Way up there."

"What did I say about being quiet, eh?" Trystan rolled his eyes. "And I said no to *ye*, didn't I?" I added archly as I looked down on him. The paling of his cheeks as he looked up at me was fairly pleasing.

"Hah, *yes*! Fuck you, Trystan," Josh chortled on my knee. He twisted round so his face was in his brother's, and he was grinning so wide I thought his cheeks must hurt. Trystan's expression creased into a look of irritation, and he put a palm over Josh's face and pushed him away. But Josh was still laughing with glee behind Trystan's hand. I watched with a faint look of amusement.

"Anyway, I'm not sure why me turning down yer brother is quite so hilarious. I'm not *that* bad, at least not with straight guys," I said with a smile. That set Josh chuckling again. "So, back t' the lesson: at some point he's going t' have to stick his fingers in yer ass."

Josh's laughter finally petered out, and he gave an awkward little shuffle against my chest. I rested my chin on his shoulder. "Well, it doesn't sound great, but it's fine. Right, Trys?"

"What the fuck, Idrys!" Trystan rumbled and I looked back down at him with a smirk. Josh's nervousness had once again evaporated, but he wasn't laughing this time, he was looking down at his brother with a faint look of outrage on his face.

"Why would you even…," Trystan grumbled, but he was looking at his brother and I swear there was a smirk trying to curl the edge of his lips through his irritation.

"Well, yer here; might as well make yer little bro' feel better, eh?" I decided I was just seeing things, and I reached down to ruffle a hand through his hair. That was a mistake.

He turned those dark eyes on me. Looking down at him with my hand tangled through his hair while he stared up at me with a look that was definitely a mixture of irritation and arrogance, I had a sudden flashback to my dream. I tugged my hand away, because the look he was giving me was causing a coil of pressure to unfurl deep in my hips, sliding like silk through my senses, reminding me what I'd been missing for the best part of a month.

"What the hell?" Josh asked, glancing between us with a look of horrified fascination.

I dragged my eyes away from Trystan, and I took a deep breath. I was annoyed that it sounded more like a hiss than I had wanted it to, but I tried to smile nonchalantly at Josh.

"Just a joke, don't worry about it." I wondered how I'd ended up more bothered about what I'd said when it had been Trystan I'd been trying to make uncomfortable. I placed my hands on either side of Josh's cheeks and turned his attention back to the manga.

"Ye just need to know that one finger doesn't—shouldn't—hurt. It may be a little odd, two might sting a little, same wi' three. But the more time ye take over it, the easier it will be. Easier said than done because if he's any good, ye probably won't want to go slow. Although I imagine if it's Chris he will know to take it slow. For yer first time ye should definitely make sure he uses lube. Some people don't bother once they're used to it, but personally I always use it." I took a slow breath and let Josh digest what I'd just said. "I'm not going to lie, Josh: for yer first time it will probably hurt, no matter how good he is or how slow he goes. But… it's hard to explain, but wi' a good partner it's kind o' easy not t' think about the discomfort."

"Nnn. Ide, why can't you just do it? Then I wouldn't have to worry," Josh said in a small voice.

I let the side of my head press against Josh's. "Ye heard what Dan said, right? I'm not doing much of anyone or anything at the mo; so don't take it personally, eh?"

Josh grumbled, still unsatisfied, and I pressed a chaste kiss against his cheek. "Don't worry, it'll be great, more than great. Being bottom is awesome, honestly."

"You say that, but don't you usually top?" Josh grumbled.

I chuckled. "I go through phases. At the moment I'm a *uke* through and through, mmm." I laughed and pressed my face into Josh's neck. By my side Trystan made a disapproving grumble, but he didn't actually say anything so I ignored him.

"What's a uke?" Josh asked, sounding puzzled.

"Japanese term for the guy that receives." I waved at the screen vaguely. Josh turned back to the pictures and he flicked backward and forward through them a few times.

"What was your first time like, Ide?" Josh asked quietly.

"Ah… well." I let out a long breath. "My first time isn't a very good example; it was stupid and ah… rushed. Neither of us knew what we were doing." Which was the truth, but not the whole truth. "I like to think of my actual first time as wi' Dan, and that was pretty epic, so…."

"Dan?" Trystan piped up, and I turned to look down at him. "As in the guy I met at the bar that time?"

"Yeah, why?"

Trystan held my gaze and he was scowling at me, but it seemed more questioning and irritated rather than angry. "How many guys have you slept with?"

"I dunno, I lost count," I let a wry grin spread my lips, because it was the truth: I'd lost count of how many guys I'd fucked way back in my first year of uni. But I knew that wasn't what Trystan had meant.

His face twisted in frustration.

"But if ye mean how many guys have I been fucked by? Then three: Dan, Echo, and I never caught the first guy's name."

Trystan stared up at me with a frown on his face.

"Not a very good whore, eh? My ass is probably almost as tight as Josh's here." My laugh that time was for myself—because even with four weeks off, that most definitely wasn't true. "Speaking o' which: ye make sure ye use a condom."

"What? But we're guys?" Josh moaned.

"Yeah, and guys *can't* get pregnant but they *can* get STIs, plus condoms generally have extra lube, so…." I chuckled again. "Honestly, this is kind o' fun."

"I think you're the only one having fun here, Ide," Josh grumbled.

"Oh, I dunno; yer brother looks surprisingly interested," I stage-whispered into Josh's ear, and we both turned to stare down at a suddenly backing away Trystan.

His defense was cut short by Josh's ring tone.

I watched as a faint look of nervous excitement washed over Josh's face.

"It's Chris," he breathed.

"Well, before ye answer, best ask big brother here if yer allowed out on a date, eh?" I raised an eyebrow at Trystan, daring him to say no.

"Do what you want," Trystan sighed. Josh squeaked with glee and then he was jumping up from my knee, pressing the phone to his ear as he ran out of the room.

I turned back from the door to find Trystan staring at me. "Did he seem all right?"

"You mean Chris?"

He nodded.

I'd got the feeling that Chris had said yes to humor me, and that he'd intended to say hi to Josh, chat to him for a bit, then go back to the bar. Unfortunately for Chris, I hadn't really been lying when I said Josh was gorgeous, and once the youngest Jackson had gotten over his embarrassment and turned on those puppy-dog eyes, Chris's nonchalant attitude had done a bit of a one-eighty. When a new guy had spotted the couple, he'd approached with a smile for Chris, but had quickly left to sit at the bar by himself, looking kind of peeved.

Both Chris and Josh had looked slightly irritable when I had approached their table to point out that it was getting a bit late and X-rated for Josh to be hanging around. I'd felt a lot like a brothel Madam as Chris had quickly exchanged numbers with the boy and then rewarded the doe-eyed Josh with a kiss that I imagined was not nearly as much as either of them wanted. But he'd not complained, and now he'd called, so all in all I'd decided he was a decent guy.

"Yeah, he's nice, seems smitten. Then again, it's not hard when the subject is Josh."

"He's my brother, you know."

I let a long breath slip out from between my lips, and I busied myself at my laptop for a moment before turning back to Trystan. He was sitting on the floor leaning back against the side of my bed. He stiffened as I got up and I chuckled at him as I went past him to lie across my bed.

"Stay up here wi' me," I mumbled as I lay back and tucked my hands behind my head.

"Well I'm not going to go downstairs and listen to my brother flirting on the phone, am I?" I could almost hear the roll of his eyes as he spoke. That wasn't what I had meant, but the misinterpretation was probably a good thing.

"Shove over." I jumped half out of my skin as hands pressed into my side and pushed me farther across the bed. I turned my head to see Trystan sitting back against the headboard in the space he'd made for himself. My body thrummed where his hands had been.

I couldn't think of anything to say. I stared up at him as he looked out across my room, and all I could think about was the mounting excitement in my chest and the way my blood felt slightly electric, so that suddenly I was hyperaware of every part of me. Maybe it was just pent-up lust, maybe if I just got it out of my system it would go away and I would return to normal. I licked my lips and suddenly only the top half of my lungs were working as Trystan turned his gaze down onto me.

I shouldn't want him.

There were so many reasons that I shouldn't be feeling what I felt right then. But I suddenly realized I didn't care. My one major defense, the last stand of my head, the thought that would always still wayward notions of receiving for someone other than Dan or Echo, was stilled completely by those dark eyes fixed on mine. Eyes that I had spent most of my life hating and fearing, I realized that I now trusted.

I didn't want to think about that.

So I concentrated on the swirling desire that warmed my body and pulled a smile onto my lips.

He said something, but I wasn't listening. I was sitting up, twisting around, dropping one of my legs to the far side of Trystan's hips. I could hear my ragged breathing and I tried to calm it as I straddled Trystan's lap and slid my hands up his chest to rest against his shoulders.

"What're you doing, Ide?"

My face was so close to his and his voice was low and breathy. I wanted to kiss him, I wanted to devour his lips, to taste every inch of him, and then have him press himself against me, into me. But I knew that wasn't how this worked; I'd have to bait him a little.

"Ye were curious, right? Of the manga? Want me to show ye?" I leaned forward to whisper against his ear and let my hands exert gentle pressure against his shoulders. Everywhere our bodies touched, mine pulsed with pleasure.

I yelped as a hand wrapped through my hair, and reluctant acceptance washed through me as I was tugged from Trystan's lap. I was tossed back on the bed, the mattress bowed slightly under the force of it. But my brain must have been running on slow motion because the hand was still wrapped through my hair and Trystan hadn't stormed off. He was hovering over me, and his face was creased in an irritable scowl as he glared down at me.

"You're a fucking whore; you think I'd want you after you just spent the night with some other guy?"

"Didn't ye hear what I said to Josh? I'm not sleeping with anyone, haven't for four weeks. So if that was *really* all ye were bothered about?" I shrugged and strained up, ignoring the faint pressure at the back of my skull from the hand there. I pressed my lips against Trystan's: they were wooden and unmoving. But I was still smiling lightly as I dropped my head into the pressure of his hand.

"I saw that Dan guy come and pick you up," Trystan cut back.

I shrugged my shoulders against the mattress. "*And?* We sat and watched Josh all night. He was just there to keep me company."

My body was still on fire at having Trystan pressed down over me, but I felt kind of weary now.

"Come on. I'm horny after all that cartoon porn," I lied with a lazy grin. "It'll be just like the blow job: I'll do all the work, it'll be easy, yer'll get off, I'll get laid. Job done."

Trystan stared down at me. He had me pinned with his hand through my hair and his body half covering mine, and he looked angry and exasperated. I was an idiot because I loved the feeling of having him over me. I also knew that if anyone else held me like this I would be terrified— even if it had been Dan or Echo, which was ridiculous because they had never hurt me, and unlike Trystan, they knew exactly what they were doing. But I didn't want them. I wanted the man who was staring down at me through narrowed, suspicious eyes.

I resisted the temptation to press up into the body covering mine. But there was an odd look blossoming across his face that had me worried.

"I thought you said my 'anal-virgin ass' couldn't get you off?" he asked archly, and I remembered what I had said in the tent when I had turned his offer to fuck me down so flatly. I kind of wished I'd chosen my words more carefully, but at the time I really hadn't expected to want exactly that so damn badly.

"So," he continued in a whisper, "now I'm wondering why you didn't ask Dan when you were out?"

"He was busy," I lied. "And now he's not here, but ye are, so ye'll do."

He was scowling down at me, and his hand was still in my hair, but it seemed looser now.

"I'll do?" He stiffened and I was certain he was going to lift off me and leave me cold and horny. Instead, he shifted and slipped one of his legs between mine. I stifled a groan as his thigh slid up against my groin, pressing into me through the material of my jeans. I thought I was going to stop breathing as he lowered his head and I felt the unmistakable brush of lips against mine. I tried not to reach too desperately and I tried not to strain too hard against the hand in my hair and the weight against my hips, and I really hoped that I wouldn't get hard just from a kiss.

It was a close call.

12—LION

THE THINGS Trystan's kiss did to my body were as far away from nothing as it was possible to get. My body was incandescent with lust: it flickered down every nerve and pulsed through every muscle, all in time with the insistent caresses of his lips and the curling pressure of his tongue as he sought entrance into my mouth.

As he pulled away, my body was strumming, and I couldn't help but pant lightly with the effort of keeping myself in check. I fought down the mew of annoyance that tried to force its way from my throat. I willed my body not to buck up into him, and I refused to let my lips strain to follow his.

"So you just decided you want a fuck?" he asked softly with lips that were still flushed from our kiss. "After four weeks cold turkey?" With each word his tone was getting firmer, turning slowly to mocking skepticism as he stared down at me. "And it just *happens* to be only me that's around?"

I wanted to groan because the angry look had gone from his eyes. Now the chocolate-brown that stared down at me was pure arrogance. An idle smirk curled the corners of his lips, and it caused a delicious lick of desire to churn against my hips—fuck my life—he was so fricking gorgeous. I hated him for it, for being handsome as sin *and* nice to me and making me feel all this stupid shit that I should feel for anyone but him.

"Piss off, Trystan. I just want sex."

His grin didn't waver as his fingers loosened slightly to tease my scalp. Oh God, how I wanted to push my head up into that hand and my lips up against his and have his pressure and heat never leave my body.

"Then I shouldn't feel at all smug that I'm the only one you want to have sex with?"

"I didn't say that." My tone was clipped and, I hoped, not too desperate because that was exactly the case, but how the hell could he know that?

He sniggered lightly, fixing me in cool chocolate eyes.

"I've met Dan, Idrys." He leaned down to whisper against my ear. "There is no way in hell he would *ever* be too busy to help you out. You stopped sleeping with him weeks ago, as soon as I started sleeping in your bed…." My eyes widened as I realized what he was saying.

"Did you think I didn't notice? I can tell you; it took a lot of effort not to touch you once I realized what you were doing. When you managed a whole week, I thought I'd relax a bit… and then you had that wet dream, straight off, after only a little hug." He hummed lightly in my ear. "You even admitted it was me who had you so riled up." He chuckled again, but then his tone turned a little heavier and the gentle rolling he had been keeping up against my hips stilled. "I don't mind admitting that I really regret taking that girl home. But she was pushy and it was nice to have someone honest for a change. So there I was, waiting patiently for you to feel better about that whole fucked-up evening, and then I find you happily making out with my fucking brother—*again*."

He covered my lips with his once again and my retort was sealed away as he pried my mouth open and slipped his tongue inside. Oh God, his lips were silk and the faint pressure of his stubble was such a contrast and I wanted to wrap my hands around his head and never let him lift off. But my hands were pinned next to me as his tongue dominated my mouth, pressing into it, tasting every corner, and meeting mine, and all I could do was think of that tongue doing the same thing to my dick.

Somewhere, my head was trying to tell me I needed to start damage control, but that thought was being completely drowned out by every other sensation in my body. That electrified feeling was returning. It was leaving me light-headed as he darted his tongue against mine—practically fucking my mouth. He slid his hand down my neck and shifted his thigh against my groin, just enough to drive me to the edge of my inexorably fracturing sanity.

He lifted away. And that time I definitely leaned up to follow him with my lips, and God help me if the sound that left me wasn't a little gasp of longing as he lifted out of my reach.

"So here's the deal, Idrys." His voice was husky. "If you want me to fuck you, that's fine." He pressed his face into my neck, nuzzling and licking and nipping between his words. "You just admit that you want *me*. Admit that it's not Dan—or any of those other sluts—you want to fuck you, but me, and I'll see if I can't help you out." He lowered his head slightly and ran a tongue across his bottom lip as he watched me strain up to meet him. His eyes seemed to turn entirely black as he paused just out of my reach.

My brain had been short-circuited and was being used purely to tell me exactly how fricking turned on I was right now. And somewhere deep inside me, I was still trying to control the throbbing reaction my groin was having to a few fricking kisses.

"Oh God...." I think I said that out loud as he pressed his hands down over my chest and abs and rested them against my hips.

"And just in case you think you're not getting value for money; I'll let you know that you're most definitely *not* going to do everything. I really like that desperate look on your face right now, and you have no idea how much I'm going to enjoy teasing you." He slid his tongue down my neck, and his hands just missed my cock.

I groaned—at myself and in pleasure—as I thrust up into him. It was too much: my head gave up, my body gave up. I didn't care if he knew how much I wanted him, I didn't care if I was getting turned on from a kiss and a couple of hands through some clothes. I was on fire and my dick finally hardened between us.

"That's better," he whispered as he pressed himself down onto my erection and pulled a mouthful of the flesh at my neck between his lips. He sucked and nibbled and caressed with his tongue as his thigh ground against my dick. "Now, are you going to tell me you want me, or do you want me to leave?"

I tried to suppress the strained groan of desperation that was working its way up my throat as he worked on the buttons of my shirt. He spread the sides of my top open as he left my neck and made his way down to the dark circle of my nipple with his mouth.

"Fricking hell." I arched up toward him as he pulled away from me, leaving me cold and gasping. He was really going to leave. The stubborn look in his eyes was daring me to test him.

"Fuck it." I wrapped a hand around the back of his head, rising up off the bed to reach his mouth as I dragged him back down over me. I kissed him: I didn't hold back. It was desperate and I ground our lips together, our teeth clashed and I sucked down on his tongue. I used my other hand to force his hips back against mine, rolling myself up into him as my groan of pleasure and surrender rumbled through the kiss.

"Fuck me." I wrapped my hand through his hair and tugged his mouth from mine. "I want ye t' fuck me." I reached up to nip at his lips. "And if ye chicken out after making me say that, I'm going to flip ye over and fuck that virgin ass of yers and show ye what ye need t' do, understand?"

The arrogant bastard actually laughed.

Then his lips and hands were back against my skin and they were running down over my chest and abs leaving behind a trail of bright red marks against my pale skin. And everywhere his lips touched was the start of a string of lust that connected to my cock and made it throb in the confines of my jeans.

"And just so you know, I'm not pretending you're a girl; I'm going to touch your dick and stick my fingers in your ass and I'm going to fuck you *because* you're a guy."

I felt his dark smile against my skin. His lips were past my belly button now. I knew that something he'd just said was probably a big deal, but I really didn't want to think about anything but the sensations accosting my skin. I was panting pathetically and completely lost in my own body. Fingers were working the buttons of my fly, and Trystan undid my jeans and pulled them off with my boxers. I was naked, Trystan was still fully clothed, and he was kneeling between my legs with a feral grin on his face as he released my straining erection.

"Oh fuck." I balled my hands into fists against the sudden onslaught of Trystan's mouth around my cock. It wasn't like he knew what he was doing, but my God, I almost came just from the idea of what was going on. I stared down, burning that memory into my mind because I so wanted to remember how his face looked parted around my cock and the glint that remained in his eye as he caught me looking. I dropped my head back and tried not to thrust up into his mouth as he worked me, suckling and stroking and teasing with his tongue and lips. And *shitting hell* you wouldn't know that he had never sucked cock before. I was panting and grasping blindly at my bed as I tried to keep myself in some semblance of control.

The pressure around my erection relented briefly and I gasped and tried to catch my breath; I was almost glad for the respite because I was so close to the edge already that it was almost painful holding back. No matter how fucked up this situation was, coming in Trystan's mouth was a no-go for two reasons: because even brain dead with lust as I was, I wasn't far enough gone to think coming in a straight—bi maybe?—guy's mouth was a good idea, and there was no way I was giving him the satisfaction of me coming so soon.

I groaned and dropped my head back as his hand replaced his mouth, sliding over the saliva he'd left behind.

"You said I needed lube; you have some, right?"

"Nnnn," I garbled something incomprehensible. Trystan chuckled and seemed to get distracted from his original quest as he dropped back over my erection. He kept his hand fisted around the shaft as he took just the head into his mouth and let his tongue explore my cock like it had explored my mouth earlier.

I really needed to string a sentence together.

"Shit, stop, Trys," I gasped as his tongue slipped into the small cleft at the tip. "Or ye want t' taste another guy's cum?"

"Hmm, well, I wouldn't mind." He lifted slightly, then licked across the head of my dick. He sat up and ran his tongue over his lips, as if taste-testing me. "But seeing you squirm is kind of fun; where's the lube?"

"Where do ye think it is, idiot." I waved toward my bedside table— where he knew I kept my condoms because he'd used one on that fricking brunette—as I fought to get my breath back and my body under some semblance of control.

He grinned at me as he unfolded himself from the bed. He caught my gaze in his and held it with a languid smirk on his face. I went to sit up as he tugged his shirt over his head.

His lips snagged mine, and he forced me back against the bed.

"Stay… put… and watch," he whispered between kisses down my neck and my hips bucked slightly at his words as a groan left me.

And I did as I was told. I never did as I was told. But I lay there and his eyes on me were almost as much of a turn-on as his hands as he went to work on the buttons of his jeans. My breath stilled in my throat as I took in his toned-to-perfection torso that I really wanted to decorate with a set of marks to match the ones he had left against my skin. Shit, he was hot. But that wasn't why I felt a shiver of divine tension run through me and felt my face darken suddenly with lust. Trystan dropped his boxers to the floor with his jeans—and he was hard. One side of his lips curled up as he saw my reaction and then he was riffling through my draws. His dick stood proudly away from his body, and I couldn't keep my eyes from it as he came out with a bottle of lube and a condom.

Trystan had gotten hard for me, from kissing me... from sucking my dick.

I wasn't sure how the world had got so fucked up. Right now I didn't care.

"Stay p...." His words trailed off as I twisted up off the bed and wrapped my mouth around his cock. He grunted wordlessly and dropped his hand to thread through my hair as he thrust between my lips and deep into my throat. I glanced up; he was staring down at me, and he looked pissed off and in ecstasy as I moved up and down his shaft. I gave hungry pulls at his flesh, devouring his cock and the delicious mote of bitter chocolate precum that I had caused. And my dick ached between my legs, and my ass really wanted some attention, but I loved the feeling of his flesh between my lips, and I would have sucked him until he pumped his cum right into the back of my throat. But he tugged my head away and pressed me back onto the bed, his smile dark and dangerous as he slid between my legs.

"Stay put," he managed to finish this time.

He didn't hesitate, didn't ask what to do; he just poured a load of lube onto his hands, wrapped one around my cock and slid the other back between my ass cheeks.

"Mmmpht" was the distorted noise that came from between my lips as Trystan's finger slid inside me. It was cold because of the lube, and it was such a contrast to the heat that filled me, and it was absolutely the fricking best thing I had ever felt, and he hadn't even hit my prostate.

"So there's some kind of button in here, right?" His tone was mocking but I could hear the slight strain to it as he fought to keep himself in control.

And right then it honestly didn't actually matter to me whether he found my prostate or not. I was so fricking turned on from the blow job and the hand on my dick. Never mind just the mere idea of what Trystan was doing to me was enough to make my cock twitch if I thought about it too much.

"Two fingers, I'm not a virgin, so—" I was cut off by a snigger and a wave of pressure as a second finger joined the first. It gave him a better angle and allowed him to go deeper, and he took full advantage of that; he started to move his fingers inside of me, stretching and questing in time with firm strokes of my dick. I wasn't sure how much of this I was going to be able to take.

There was a knock at the door.

There was only one person it was going to be.

"Sorry, Josh, I'm kind of—" I chucked a hand over my mouth to silence the strangled groan that interrupted my words. "Shit, Trys, there," I whispered, gasping as my hips jacked up to force his finger back against the point that had just sent my nervous system into overload. And as I moaned and bucked uncontrollably against his hand, Trystan stared down at me through hooded eyes, watching me with his lips parted in a self-satisfied smirk.

"Guess I'm not doing too badly, then?" he hissed at me quietly. I couldn't answer because if I took a breath to speak right then, I was going to come.

"Ide? You okay?" Josh called through the door, and he sounded concerned. "Is Trys...?"

"I think he's in the bathroom," I cut him off and my voice came out as a shout as I fought not to sound like I was on the brink of coming—it was taking all that was left of my tattered self-control to hold myself together.

"No I'm not; I'm here," Trystan said, pitched perfectly to be heard through the door. I could feel him inside of me as he tried to find the exact point once again with his head cocked to one side as if his brother wasn't standing on the other side of an unlocked door and his only concern in the world was proving me wrong.

"Oh fuck...." I tried not to shout as I jacked up again when he once again found what he was looking for. My cock was weeping in his hand, and his grin was smug and possessive as I groaned and was unable to stop myself from thrusting against his fingers.

"Now piss off, Josh, Ide is mine."

"What? No, I'm coming i—"

"Fuck, no, Josh! Don't come in," I shouted again as I tried to catch my breath and glare at Trystan. "Stop a second." I tried to sound firm, even though stopping was definitely the last thing I wanted to do, a fact that was made more obvious by the way I was still grinding my hips against his hand.

But what had Trystan just said?

He laughed at me as he pressed his fingers back against the spot that caused me to see nothing but white and feel as if my blood had been replaced with pure pleasure.

And holy crap, I so desperately wanted to come, but I never wanted this feeling to end. I grasped empty-handed at the duvet as I held myself back.

"Go away, Josh," Trystan said. "Go think about your new boyfriend while I look after Ide. He tastes great, by the way."

I wanted to be angry at Trystan as I heard footsteps hurrying away from my door. But it was difficult when he had my body balanced on a tightrope.

"So? Three fingers?" he asked with a lazy smile that was contradicted by the flush on his cheeks and the erect flesh at his hips.

"Ah." I arched up into his hand yet again.

One look at his face told me he really was thoroughly enjoying doing this to me, not just fingering me, but watching me try and hold back in this agonizing verge-of-coming state. But he was still hard, and his breathing was slightly hitched; he was holding himself back too.

I took slow breaths through my nose and shot him a smile. "Two's fine. Ye can fuck me now."

Darkness passed over his face and for a moment a twisting uncertainty radiated out from my stomach. It washed away all the bliss and tension and replaced it with a cold fear that he had suddenly realized what he was doing and was going to stop, or worse, that this was just a joke.

Then suddenly I was on my stomach. Fingers were pressed firmly into my hips, tugging them up. One hand was sliding down my spine, and against my ass pressed the firm and unmistakable pressure of Trystan's erection.

The fear retracted, and I was left reeling in the wake of the rush of lust that made my arms and legs tingle and my cock throb. I pressed my hips backward.

"Urgh, how slow do I need to go?" he muttered as he finished putting on a condom. I arched my head over my shoulder to see the tension on his face as he breathed heavily through parted lips.

I pushed myself up off my hands so I was kneeling in front of him and I let my spine slip back against his chest as I reached around to pull his lips against mine. I kissed him slowly at first, encouraging him until his tongue slid in against mine. I pressed my hips back into his cock, rolling them slightly. When I broke away, we were both panting.

"Don't worry, just don't rush; ye won't hurt me."

I don't know why I believed that. I definitely shouldn't have done, but I dropped back onto all fours and pressed my hips back toward his. His hands came up to part my cheeks, and the tip of his cock pressed against me. I dropped my head down between my arms, panting heavily as his cock split me and I had to resist the urge to drive myself back because he was going so fricking slow and I really wanted him buried inside me.

"Urgh." I muted a moan, because apparently four weeks was long enough to make a difference and it was so fricking tight. Pain like fine needles scurried across my hips and up my spine. It clashed against the pleasure, sending my head into overload, and I was arching my spine as Trystan's fingers dug into the flesh at my hips. I pressed backward and our low gasps merged together as his cock finally slid against my prostate. I could feel myself shivering around him, and he pressed his fingers tighter as he held himself still.

I risked a glance over my shoulder, and the sight of him buried inside of me with a look of blissful agony on his face sent yet another delicious wash of pleasure through me. The faint whispers of discomfort were suddenly nothing.

"Holy crap, Ide," he hissed when he'd finally caught his breath.

I dropped onto my elbows as little jolts of electricity fired up from that contact, and then I couldn't think, because he was drawing out and I arched my hips so he'd reach the spot I needed. And then my body wasn't a body anymore, it was just a mass of tension and a continuous wave of pleasure that I wanted to never stop and yet wanted to end quickly.

"*Ohmygod*." I dropped my head completely onto the duvet as he continued to drive into me harder and harder, just how I wanted. My world splintered, and I could hardly breathe as I fought to keep myself in one piece. "Yes, Trys, fucking hell, yes...."

My orgasm crested, and it turned each of Trystan's thrusts into a supernova of sensation—I couldn't pull away, but each agonizing thrust was killing me in the best possible way. I groaned and bucked and still Trystan was pressing into me.

His hands were holding me up now and I panted pathetically as I was drawn back into the depths of my pleasure over and over. I was completely lost in the bliss as he continued to fuck me, his groaning and panting and unintelligible curses mixing with mine as he drove into my ass again and again. I drowned in wave after wave of something so fine my brain couldn't even label it and had stopped trying and was just basking in it. Hoping it would never end. And shitting hell, I could feel the agonizing rise of pressure that meant I was going to come again, because Trystan was finally swelling inside of me, and I could feel his orgasm building as he tugged me almost painfully back onto him. I shouted out in divine protest and abandon as my second wave hit.

I groaned as he shuddered to a stop inside of me. My body trembled as sparks of ecstasy flickered like motes of water dropped onto a flame, dancing along the desecrated fibers of my nerves. He was holding me up, and I whimpered in delight and regret as he pulled us both over to one side so we were lying spooned together.

"Did you just come twice?" he whispered against my ear.

Fuck my life, I really had.

"That was definitely yer imagination," I replied, but I was too languid in the throes of my orgasm to really care too much about sounding convincing.

"Hmm, I must have a very good imagination."

"Do ye always talk this much after sex?" Then I sighed because I was a mess and my duvet was a mess, which was a stupid rookie mistake to make.

I edged my way off him, reaching round with weak limbs to hold the condom in place. He got up to dispose of it, and I stared at the mess I had made of my duvet and myself. Seriously—twice? Too late to worry about that now. I sat on the bed and stared at Trystan's back as he tied off the condom and chucked it in the trash.

"So I take it my ass is safe?" He shot me a smug smirk, but I took a small amount of solace in the fact he sounded a little breathless.

"For now," I chuckled, then soured slightly as I glanced toward the unlocked door. "But what was that shit with Josh? Don't ye think that was a bit much?"

Trystan growled at me. He stood there in the middle of my room, still naked and half-hard and he actually pulled his lips back, bared his teeth, and snarled at me as if we were animals and I'd just tried to take something he thought was his.

Well that wasn't quite the reaction I had expected but I pressed on. "And what was that shit about me being yers? Hmm, straight guy?"

"You are a. *Fucking*. Pain. In. The. Ass." He carefully enunciated each word as he stalked up to me and pressed me back on the bed. He climbed over me so his knees were on either side of my hips. And then he bent down and started pressing kisses onto my cheek and giggling like a girl, nuzzling my neck and pawing at my chest—no, seriously!

"*This*! This is what I've had to put up from you two for a whole *fucking* week," he seethed between mock giggles and chaste kisses. "Josh rubbing my bloody nose in it while you two 'gay guys' paw at each other like it's perfectly fine. Josh mocking me every evening while he tells me how many times you've kissed his cheek and how you brushed past him while he was making tea, watching him smirk at me while he sits on your fucking knee. So don't give me that shit. Josh got what he deserved: you chose me."

"Huh? Wait." I pressed him away from my neck because it was kind of distracting and there was some messed-up shit being said. "Ye brought him here as some kind of fricking competition?"

Trystan shook his head, still looking a little peeved, but he had stopped the ridiculous kissing at least. "I brought him here because it was half term and when I went home I have never seen anyone so down and out. I told him you were off-limits because of the James thing." He rolled off me and lay out on his side with his head propped on his hand. "But he didn't bloody listen, did he? He just marched up here and threw himself at you, and you were fine with it."

"I wasn't *fine*," I said as I got myself back together. "I really wouldn't have done anything other than that kiss."

Wait, why was I defending myself to him?

"Yeah, well, that was enough, and then Josh worked out that I liked you and has spent as much time as possible rubbing my face in the affection you've piled on him. Why are you only like that with gay guys?"

I laughed a little at that, and it was like floodgates opening up and suddenly I couldn't stop.

"Seriously?" I spluttered and tried to catch my breath. "Because most straight guys I know don't like to be kissed by other guys in public," I explained when he still looked like he wanted an answer.

"No. Wait... ye *like me*?" I couldn't help the skepticism in my voice. "What the hell, Trys? Ye've been living wi' me for a month and done nothing and now ye expect me t' believe ye suddenly *like me*? After one fuck? I mean, I know my ass is great and all. But seriously?"

He stared at me, and I got the impression he was really hoping that I was joking. "You're such a head case, Ide. I liked you in Scotland. Do you really think a straight guy would kiss another guy just for a blow job?"

"Ye wouldn't be the first straight guy to get confused by me, Trys," I answered honestly, my voice droll.

"Yeah, well, I wasn't confused. I'm still not; I know you're a guy, it doesn't bother me. I find it kind of hot, actually." His voice was a low growl. He let his eyes skim down over my body, and there was nothing but feral appreciation for what he saw. When his gaze arrived back at my face, he noted my still skeptical look with a slight hitch of his shoulders.

"Okay, I realize this might seem weird for you, but ignoring the fact that you think I'm straight: why *wouldn't* I like you? You're hot as sin. We enjoy the same shit. When we're not arguing—usually about your fucked-up lifestyle—we get on well. As for why I've not tried anything, I would've thought that was fairly self-explanatory: having some other guy's leftovers doesn't appeal to me. Jorja let me know what you were like after that shit in Scotland, so despite the sudden realization that I was probably bi, I decided to just steer clear of you."

"So yer suddenly bisexual now?"

He rolled his eyes. "Hardly suddenly."

"Fine, but if ye were so adamant about staying away from me, why the hell did ye come and stay in my house?"

"I really did need somewhere to stay," he said with a shrug. "If I hadn't been so fucking desperate I would've left that first night when you came in reeking of some other guy. In fact, that whole first week was really fucking irritating."

"I warned—" He didn't let me finish.

"But then I got in your bed one night, and just like that you stopped. And if I thought ignoring you was hard when you were whoring around, it was damn near impossible when you weren't."

"That had nothing t' do wi' ye."

"Whatever, Ide."

I ground my teeth together. "So if ye *liked* me so fricking much, why did ye take that girl home?"

"Because you'd spent that whole bloody day taunting me with stories of me blowing you in your dreams and staring at me like you wanted me to fuck you right there in the studio, and then you went and made out with that Dan guy—*in front* of me. I was as pissed off with myself for thinking you'd changed as with you."

"Yer such an arrogant bas…." I trailed off because suddenly something that had been lurking in the back of my head when he mentioned my sister had finally slipped into place. "Jorja knew!" I didn't ask because I didn't need to. Everything she'd said on the phone last weekend: the half-finished sentences and the confusion when I'd told her Trystan had been with a girl. It all pointed to one thing: that she had known Trystan "liked me"—whatever the hell that meant when it was said with such a condescending smirk.

Trystan was staring at me with a look on his face that let me know he thought I was a bit simple.

"Ide, *everyone* but you knows. Your sister worked it out in Scotland, because she's not a messed-in-the-head idiot who would assume a guy would start fooling around with another guy on a whim."

I opened my mouth to argue, but he reached forward and pressed his lips over mine.

"Chill, I understand. If nothing else living with you has certainly made you make sense. But yeah, Meredith guessed straight off: she made some fairly blatant comments—mind you, you were there for a few of them." He laughed lightly. "Josh knows, of course. Penny, Matt, and Jason know I'm bi, and I'm pretty sure they know I like you. Oh and I'm fairly certain Dan guessed, if the evil looks he was shooting me were anything to go by."

I stared at him and he stared right back. The smug amusement in his chocolate-brown eyes was exaggerated by one arched eyebrow.

"So," I spoke slowly, because it was a lot to get my head around. I lifted myself up so that I was on my side, mirroring Trystan's pose. "Yer *bi*… and despite just calling me a 'messed in the head idiot', ye *like* me?"

"Isn't that what I just said?"

I considered him. The words that had come out of his mouth had been a lot more complicated than any confession that I had ever received, not least because it was the first one in a long time that I was actually kind of interested in.

I stared at the man stretched out on the bed next to me. He was still butt-ass naked and yet seemed perfectly fine with it. He was staring at me with that same twinkle of arrogant amusement in his dark eyes. But it was softer than usual, toned down by what I could only assume was the result of this "like" he apparently had for me. Either way, he was seemingly happy with himself and what he was feeling and was comfortable with what we'd just done. Which had been pretty epic. And which I kind of wanted the chance to happen again. But he'd been pretty specific in explaining he didn't like that I slept around.

Despite my own feelings for Trystan, there were a million reasons that having a jealous guy attach himself to me was a bad idea.

Yet I already knew I wasn't really interested in other guys at the moment.

And hadn't he been coping for the last month?

So maybe, just for now....

"So 'like me' as in ye don't want me to sleep with other people?" I said after a long moment of comfortable silence had passed between us.

Trystan cocked his head to one side and a small frown passed over his face.

"Is this going to have anything to do with what Dan said at the bar that time? About you having a problem with people getting possessive of you?" He let out a slow breath and his smile was definitely slipping away. "Honestly, I get it: you're like a magnet and honey and light all mixed together and you turn everyone around you into obsessive iron-wasp-moths."

"What?" I asked, wondering how my simple question had turned into this—probably quite accurate—assessment of the chaos that seemed to follow me around.

"People are *drawn* to you. And I know at the end of the day that I'm as bad as everyone else. But...." He flopped back onto the bed and a weary, out of character sigh slid between his lips as he stared up at the ceiling. The lost look of resignation on his face wasn't right on him at all.

"Bollocks. What the fuck did I think was going to happen?" he muttered mostly to himself. "I can't ask you to stop being what you are; I know that. But fucking hell, Ide, I don't think I can cope with...." He made an irritated sound at the back of his throat. "Ah *fuck*. Maybe we should just forget this or something."

"Just answer the fricking question, Trys." I snapped a little and rolled my eyes before calming my voice so my question was clear and precise. "Do ye or do ye not want me to stop sleeping wi' other guys and only sleep wi' ye? Which just so ye know, even in my limited experience, sounds an awful lot like dating."

Trystan grumbled and sat up. "We already live together and go out together and now we've slept together. I just want you to not sleep with any fucker that asks you."

"So that's a yes; ye only want me to sleep wi' ye?" I pressed as he stared down at me.

His face contorted, reluctance ingrained in every muscle, but he nodded.

"Okay," I said.

He stared down at me, and I stared right back. He opened his mouth to say something. Then he shut it again, and I felt a smile creep over my lips, because his astonishment was hilarious and I had finally left him speechless. I sat up and arched an eyebrow.

"Ye can kiss me now if ye like, straight guy," I suggested gently. "Or do I need to change yer name to bi guy...? Hmm, doesn't have quite the same ring to it. And if ye think that ye can go off and shag girls whenever ye like just 'cause ye give yerself an indecisive label, then ye are—" I was cut off by lips sealing over mine. And I wasn't too bothered.

He pressed me back onto the bed, covering my body with his.

"Did you draw that out on purpose, you pain in the ass?" he muttered as he broke the kiss and stared down at me. He was brushing his hand gently through my hair, and I found I quite liked the possessive connotations of it.

"It's not ma fault ye started going on about iron wasps and refused to answer ma perfectly clear question."

"Why you little...." He kissed me again and I grinned into it. My body felt amazing: exhausted and content and warm and protected as he lay over me.

"But ye should know—" I broke the kiss and grinned up at him. I ran one hand through his dark hair, and the other I let drift down his back and rest against his ass. I took a handful of that solid muscle between my fingers and squeezed. "—if yer going to keep me t' yerself, I'm not going to let ye get away wi' not switching."

"Oh fuck." His eyes darkened. His tongue came out to dart over his teeth, and I watched his cheeks blush and his pupils dilate.

"Pardon?" I asked archly, because he'd mumbled something so quietly that I hadn't been able to hear it. Although if the flush on his face was anything to go by, I could hazard a guess at what he'd said.

"That's fine."

"Only fine? Ye seemed kind o' into it when I tried it out before."

"Fucking hell, Ide. You can do me if that's what it takes." He struggled to get the words out and I laughed gently at him.

"Don't look so scared. Believe me, when ye tried to recruit me to deflower yer brother, ye picked an expert, eh?" He scowled a little at the mention of his brother, and I reached up so I could whisper in his ear. "If ye thought a finger was nice, yer've no fricking idea...." I pressed a kiss against the side of his face. "But not tonight. I'll surprise ye with it one day, eh?"

"Fucking hell, I think I'd rather get it over and done with."

This time my laugh was edged with a smirk to give Trystan a run for his money. "Now where's the fun in that?"

13—MOUSE

I WOKE up with a smile on my face. And I may have been an idiot for it, but I ignored the voice at the back of my head and snuggled into the body pressed against the side of me. I had missed it, and I knew that was almost as ridiculous as the warm contentment inside of me because it had been months since Scotland and he'd only broken his promise not to touch me once when he'd been living in my room. So how my body had decided in five or six mornings that this was what it wanted, I do not know. But I inhaled and filled my lungs with the scent of Trystan.

I unwrapped myself with a last look at Trystan's sleeping face. I would have loved to stay right there and wake him up slowly—maybe tease him a little about bottoming—but I had an essay to write, a duvet cover to wash, and I'd agreed to meet Patrick at the climbing wall at midday. I made sure the sleeping bag was draped back over him as I went to shower and turn the washing machine on.

"So."

I winced as Josh's single syllable wove through the kitchen and stabbed me straight through the back of my neck. I eyed my cup of tea and wished the kettle had boiled faster so I could have avoided this. But I also suspected that Josh had probably been waiting for me.

Josh wasn't an idiot, but it didn't take a genius to work out what had happened: Trystan hadn't gone back to his room last night, my sheets were in the washing machine, and I'd just got out of the shower even though I'd had one last night before I'd taken Josh to the bar. And that wasn't even including Trystan's words through the door or my rather breathy reply.

I turned with a sigh and fixed my gaze on the sixteen-year-old that had—through no fault of his own—caused me quite a lot of trouble. Well maybe he had some fault, as he definitely hadn't had to throw himself at me all those times. But I was fine with admitting that it had mostly been my less than standard attitude toward sex and relationships that had caused the vast majority of the problems I'd found myself with. I knew I wasn't generally that nice a person. The problem was that the way Josh was looking at me—had always looked at me—made me think he didn't realize that.

"So…. I get to hear what you sound like during sex, with my *brother*?"

I gave an imperceptible shake of my head at the timing and because Josh looked angry but also like he was about to cry. I wanted to hug him, but I wasn't sure if that would make it better or worse.

"So you really were just not interested in me? It wasn't because you were getting over James." He stalked over to stand in front of me and glare up into my face. His eyes were ringed with deep gray circles, and I wondered how much he'd slept last night. "Was it just a game to you this whole time, like Trys said? You're just a fucking whore?"

"Meh." I cuffed him lightly round the head then bent down and pressed a kiss to his forehead. "One, ye came on to me, remember? Two, don't try and badmouth yer brother to get to me again—he called me worse to my face last night." I was kind of irritated but I kept my voice neutral as I stared down at him. "And three, yes I am a whore, but I wasn't messing; I would have fucked ye—happily. Do ye feel better now ye know that? I would've fucked ye, and ye would've liked it, and ye would've wanted more, and I wouldn't have been able to give it to ye. And we'd still be here having exactly the same conversation. And the only way ye'd get t' be wi' me is joining the group with Dan and the others? Ye think ye'd be okay wi' that?"

He stared at me in silence and I could see my words trying to get through to him, but he was still pissed off.

"I wouldn't mind…."

"The hell ye would. Ye think how me and Dan were last night was embarrassing? That was toned down, like to nothing, and ye were still squirming. Ye'd never cope wi' Dan on normal mode, never mind Ashlie and Echo, for God's sake." I leaned down into his face because he looked like he was going to argue. "Ye want to know how many times I've been fucked by Dan in the toilets of that bar?" I whispered. "Ye want to know how many times I've sucked Echo off while doing it or watched Ashlie do the same while I fuck some random…? I can't tell ye 'cause I've fricking lost count."

To be fair to him, Josh only flinched a little.

"You're telling me Trystan is fine with that?" he cut back archly as I straightened.

"Trys didn't ask me to stop," I answered simply. "I offered."

"What about Dan? He likes you, and he's never tried to change you. I could understand Dan, but Trys isn't even gay!"

I really just wanted to drink my tea and go back to my room and possibly spend an hour in bed with Trystan before I had to get on with everything else. But Josh still looked upset and angry, and while part of me wanted to leave him to stew, there was a part of me that felt responsible for him now.

"Look, Josh, I get it, ye'd probably never met anyone like me before, right? Gay and out and not bothered? And ye threw yerself at me because ye wanted to try, and that is fine. But think about it for a second, what kind o' guy does that make me that would accept that? That would make out wi' a kid and think about doing stuff to them. Even if I resisted, I still thought about it."

"But I...."

"Yeah, I know; ye would've been fine with it. Ye've made that clear enough. But ye were—still are, really—a kid. And it's like yer brother said—I should o' known better. But that's the kind o' guy I am. And that's the kind o' guy ye want to sleep with, right? The one that would think it's okay t' sleep wi' ye, the whore who would sleep wi' anyone? 'Cause that is who ye'd get. Not the Ide that sits ye on his knee and looks after ye and talks ye through what yer first time would be like. The other me wouldn't have done that for ye; I would've taken ye to bed and just done what I wanted, and ye would o' liked it, but ye probably would've been scared."

"You're just saying all this to put me off."

"No, I'm not."

"Why else would you make yourself sound so horrible?"

"Because I know what I'm like. I know I'm messed up; I just didn't mind being that way. But...."

But what? But I was going to change? Because Trystan had asked me to. Was that what I was going to say? I ran an absent hand through my hair.

"Look, Josh, it's not like I don't know yer brother isn't gay, he said as much to me. But I'm not sitting here imagining he's going to want me for the rest o' his life or some shit like that. He'll get bored and he'll go back to girls, or maybe he'll find himself another guy, one who's less hassle, maybe. I'm not an idiot."

"I'd never get bored with you! And what about Dan? You guys have been together in that stupid fucking relationship for over two years, and is he bored?"

I sighed. "Josh, yer young, of course ye think ye'll feel this way about me forever, but last night I watched ye look at another guy in exactly the same way ye look at me; I watched ye grinning like an idiot when he called ye. Ye only like me because I was the first gay guy ye ever met, the first guy ye could be open about yer feelings with."

"No, I—"

"And as for Dan," I interrupted. "Ye have no idea, so don't even try and talk to me about D—" My words were drowned out as a mouth was pressed over mine.

He squeaked as I forcefully removed him from my face by tugging a handful of his hair and thudding my hand into his shoulder. I scowled and dropped his hair to scrub the back of my hand across my lips as I glared at him.

"What the fuck, Josh?" I kept my voice furiously low. And he just stared up at me with his eyes narrowed in defiance.

"What the hell, Ide…?" I looked up and Trystan was standing in the doorway to the kitchen wearing just his sweatpants, with his perfectly toned abs and arms and, well, everything. His eyes were still creased half with sleep, and a couple of days of stubble dusted his chin. He looked totally gorgeous and thoroughly pissed off as he took in the scene of Josh standing up against me with my hands pressed against his shoulders.

"Oh for fuck's sake." I was done being nice.

I shoved Josh out of the way, sending him stumbling to one side as I stalked across the kitchen and kissed Trystan. I pressed my lips against his, and I wrapped my arms around him, pulling him against me, backing us against a wall. He got the idea, and I moaned as he parted my lips and drove his tongue into my mouth. I ground my hips against him as I let my hands tug at his arse.

"Ye think ye can give me what I want, Josh?" I deadpanned over Trystan's shoulder when he let me up for air. "Ye think ye can fuck me like yer brother fucked me last night? Well ye can't: yer too fricking young and yer too fricking small, understand?"

Josh was alone in the middle of the kitchen. He held my gaze for a moment and then dropped his eyes to stare at the floor.

"Not that I don't enjoy being kissed like that, and not that I don't enjoy rubbing Josh's nose in it, but do you fancy explaining to me what is going on?" Trystan asked against my ear. There was a faint note of amusement in his tone and beneath it a husky undertone of desire that was only enhanced by the ever-so-subtle roll of his hips against mine as he kept me pinned against the wall.

"Later, Trys," I said as I reluctantly peeled myself from underneath him. I crossed back over to Josh, and he flinched slightly as I dropped a hand on his shoulder.

"Piss off."

"Look, Josh, I'm sorry it had to come to this."

"I can't believe you made me listen to you having sex with my brother, then made out with him in front of me. I think I'm scarred for life." Josh's voice was just loud enough to make out. I could hear him trying to keep his tone light, and then he turned his back to me and busied himself riffling through cupboards.

"Yeah, well payback's a bitch, isn't it?" Trystan said, his voice cheery as he appeared next to me and pulled me against his side. He caught my jaw and pulled my face around to take my lips with his. "You left me hanging this morning. You owe me a morning fuck," he added under his breath.

And holy crap, his words slid straight down my spine and into my groin. And his smirk as my face slackened and I pushed myself into him wasn't nearly enough to counteract the lust I felt right then.

"Well this is a new level of messed up, even for you, Ide." A half-asleep Jason was standing in the doorway to the kitchen. He rubbed absently at his bleary eyes as he looked pointedly between the brother I was kissing and the brother who had just hastily turned away to pretend he wasn't watching. Then with a flick of his eyebrows for me, he waltzed into the kitchen and helped himself to some breakfast.

With his cereal bowl in hand, Jason dropped himself on the couch and cocked his head to one side. "Sorry, please continue, I thought this was a public incest show?"

I flicked him the finger and detached myself from Trystan's side.

"So you two finally fucked? Or have you been fucking this whole time and you've only just been caught?"

I went back to my tea. Unsurprisingly, it was cold, so I set about making more.

"None of yer business, Jason," I said cheerily as I waited for the kettle to boil. Josh had made himself some toast, and he sat himself at the dining table with his feet tucked up on the chair and stared at his knees as he ate.

"Well, it will be my business if you two have some bitch fight and hate each other and I have to live with you."

"Well, look at it this way," I began pleasantly enough, but I let my voice drop as I caught Jason's eyes in mine. "Nothing could be more fucked up than the housemate ye guys chose, so…."

Jason had the good grace to look a little sheepish. So I let him be and set to making two teas for me and Jason and two coffees for the Jackson brothers. Then I sat opposite Josh. Trystan sat down too, looking thoroughly unimpressed that I was not heading upstairs to bed—which quite honestly I would have loved to do. Instead, I turned to Josh.

"So, what did Chris say?" I asked as I stole a bite from one of his bits of toast. After three months of getting my food frozen or thrown out, I'd gotten into a habit of not having much in that I hadn't shaken yet.

"Doesn't matter."

"Does sulking like a bitch usually solve yer problems, Josh?" I asked archly as I returned his toast.

"You're such a bastard, Ide," Josh grumbled back, but I watched as he straightened his shoulders a little. "He offered to take me out on Monday." He turned big brown eyes on his brother. I wasn't sure what was going on, but then I realized Trystan had said Josh was here for half term. Which meant he probably had to go back home tomorrow.

"Can we run interference?" I asked Trystan, who glanced up at me with a disapproving frown creasing his forehead.

"Josh needs to go to school."

I laughed lightly. "I'm not suggesting he drop out or something, just that maybe he could get a bit sick for a couple of days and head back later in the week?"

"I can't believe anyone would trust you to be a responsible guardian," Jason added from the couch.

"Hey, I took him out and brought him back in the same state o' deflowerment; what more do I need to do to prove myself?"

"The fact that you think that's an achievement kinda proves my point," Jason said.

"Well then ye don't know our little Josh very well, do ye?" I mocked lightly. Josh winced a little but looked like he was trying not to smile at my comment. I turned my eyes on Trystan. "Come on, Trys, think of it as making up for scarring yer poor little brother."

"Fine, you can stay. I'll call Mum and tell her you're sick."

For the first time all morning, Josh managed to look a little happy.

"Right, I need to get some work done before I meet Patrick," I said, getting up. I shot Trystan a grin.

"I left my phone in your room," Trystan said as he got up to follow me.

"Course you did." Jason looked as thoroughly unconvinced as he sounded. "Can you guys try and at least not make out in the communal spaces?" he shouted up after us when we were halfway up the second flight of stairs.

Having Trystan following me made me oddly self-conscious. I could feel his eyes on my spine and arse, and the expectation that he might reach out and touch me was killing me. Well not killing me exactly, in fact it could probably be described as the exact opposite. I could feel every inch of skin on my back; every nerve waited impatiently for the contact.

I pushed the door to my room open and the sight of my bed brought back a tumult of memories of last night. They had a dream-like quality to them already. I had a moment to wonder how long this twitchy breathless feeling and the self-consciousness was going to last. Then Trystan's breath was against my ear and I was melting from the inside out, the core of me filled with something like the color of his eyes.

"I'll leave you to work, shall I?" His words stroked my ear, but the touch I'd longed for was still absent as he drew away and sidestepped around me to pluck his phone from where it lay on my bed.

I laughed and came up behind him, wrapping my hands around his waist, pulling his spine back against my chest, and taking my time to whisper into his ear.

"Ye should be careful playing games wi' me, Trys; if I ye don't keep me *entertained* I might just pounce on ye...." I let my hand slide down his side and slip between us. Over his sweatpants I pressed my fingers into the firm muscle of his ass and traced the crevice of his backside as I hummed into his ear.

He twisted round in my grip and my lips were suddenly under his. He kissed me aggressively, all teeth and plunging tongue, and I kissed him right back. I could feel myself already melting inside as his tongue ravaged my mouth and sent me spiraling down somewhere dark and delicious. I already loved this, I loved the games, the desperation, and the things he did to my head and body. I was definitely going to fuck that sweet virgin ass of his at some point, but right now I was in ecstasy as he dominated me.

"Suck me off," he ordered and he brought his hand to my head, pushing me down onto my knees.

I didn't hesitate, just dragged his sweatpants down as I went. I wrapped one hand around the already half-hard flesh of his cock and grinned as it came fully erect in my grip. I did that to him; the knowledge made my own cock throb in response.

I started slow, tasting and licking his head, enjoying the impatient moans and little halfhearted jerks of his hips as he tried to get more. I held myself back and my hand still as I worked just his tip. And then his grip was tightening in my hair, and he was cursing under his breath as he forced my head down over him and I didn't mind that either. My own body bucked as it craved him doing that to a very different part of me. I dropped my hand so it was just circling his base and sucked and suckled and pressed my tongue against him as he drove himself into my throat. He pulled me back with a handful of my hair, and I was groaning with him, dropping my free hand down to my hips and taking my own straining cock in my grip. I worked myself as Trystan pumped my mouth against his cock, and I was in bliss. I glanced up and grinned at him round his erection as I struggled to suck in air and never let off the pressure around him.

When he started to strain, I felt myself uncurling in response; I felt my cock shudder at the memory of how he'd felt coming inside of me, and then I was spraying my load into my pants as Trystan rammed my head onto him and juddered to a stop. I stroked myself a little more gently as I continued to suck on his now overly sensitive flesh, drawing out groans that bordered on agonized as his hand tightened in my hair. He didn't stop me or pull me off; he just twisted in tormented pleasure and gave a reluctant sigh when I eventually drew off with a last gentle lick that sent a visible shudder through him.

"Ye want to come to the climbing wall wi' me and Patrick?" I asked as I stood up and kicked my trousers off into the washing pile. I chuckled as he pulled me half-naked against him and pressed kisses into my neck.

"Shitting hell, you're so fucking amazing at that."

"Yeah, I know." I reached for his lips, and he surprised me by deepening the kiss, taking the taste of himself with a chuckle as he brought his hand up to hold my head against his.

"Yer really taking this gay/bi thing pretty easily." I was a little breathless as he let me go, and despite my recent release that was definitely the stirrings of desire churning in my hips again. Perhaps Trystan coming to the climbing wall wasn't such a good idea. I had a sudden image of staring up at his back, the muscles twisting and bunching under his flesh as he made his way up, and that was enough to convince me that it was probably best if we didn't do any public physical activities together until I'd gotten myself back under control. I didn't tend to hide what I was or what I liked, but I wasn't about to start rubbing people's faces in it in places where I genuinely liked to go just to relax and have fun.

"It's not like I just decided I liked guys yesterday, you know," Trystan said with a chuckle as he pressed a last chaste kiss against my lips and stepped away from me to pull his sweatpants back up from around his ankles.

"So yer've really been crushing on me since Scotland?" I asked as I dug out some clean underwear and trousers. "I'm not trying to be cocky or anything, but—"

"You're going to anyway?" Trystan cut in.

"Well yeah, but seriously, I'm not used t' guys not just throwing themselves at me. It's probably because I'm a bit, ah, *promiscuous*, so people just figure they'll play along."

"*Promiscuous?*" Trystan laughed. "You're completely lacking in morals and pretty much a dirty little man-slut…." He squared himself in front of me, and he met my arched look with a smirk. It wasn't like I could—or would—get offended by what he said; it was true and had never really bothered me.

"Yeah, *and*? I know what I am. I like sex and guys take advantage of that and just throw themselves at me."

Trystan gave a small sigh as the playful sparkle to his eyes turned serious. "Yeah. Look, Ide, I'm not an idiot; I know people don't just change because some guy starts sleeping in their bed. It's not like I don't realize that some of why you haven't been sleeping around is down to that shit with James. But… I guess what I'm trying to say is: when you get your head sorted, can you just warn me or give me a chance before you just start throwing yourself at other guys again?"

Shit. Less than twelve hours, that was all he'd managed before my past had snuck into the conversation.

"Look, Trys." He looked surprisingly despondent, which was odd on him. But I was struggling to find the right words to say what I wanted. I wasn't used to this. I slept with people and then I left them and slept with someone else. I didn't make promises to be exclusive, and I didn't care when people got upset with what I did. Or at least I hadn't.

"I get what yer saying, but—" I tried to start again, but yet again Trystan cut me off.

"I know, shit, sorry, it's fine. Don't worry about it." He turned away from me to finally scoop his phone up off the bed.

"Ye going to emote like a girl or listen to what I'm going t' say?" I asked archly.

That pulled a look of irritation onto his face that was much more like the Trystan I was used to dealing with. He turned back to me and crossed his arms, looking peeved but still concerned.

"Look, ye said ye like me, right? Is it just that ye like how I look? Because if it is, I really think ye should try experimenting wi' some other tall blond," I said as I backed away to lean against the edge of my desk.

"It's not like I haven't considered that," Trystan grumbled, looking and sounding annoyed. "After Scotland, I messed around with a couple of guys, and it was okay, but nothing special. I find guys attractive, but I haven't put up with this past month of shit because of how you look, Ide. Like I said last night: I'm probably an idiot for it, but I like you. Being with you is fun, the craziness and the teasing—and the sex was fucking incredible. But I'm a possessive guy and I just... Ah shit." He drifted his gaze up to linger on the damp-marbled ceiling as his explanation faded to a muttered curse.

Well I definitely couldn't deny the sex part. As for the rest of it.... I considered him as he stood cross-armed and defensive in the middle of my room. I let my gaze slip down the sculpted lines of his torso, and just watching him made my blood simmer. The sight of him always had, from when we'd been kids and he'd been a bastard, to now when he was standing there asking me for something he didn't really believe I could do.

He didn't even know the half of it.

Still leaning back against my desk, I pressed my palm against my forehead. This was ridiculous. Even if I changed, everyone around me would still be the same. This thing with Trystan was going to end exactly how every other relationship I'd been in had ended—the whole two of them.

I cracked an eye open; Trystan was watching me, a mixture of resignation and annoyance contorting his features.

"I'll go." He reached for the T-shirt he had discarded last night, a long breath escaping through his nose as he snagged it from the floor.

I knew exactly what I should do. I should tell him he was right and let him go, and then I should go to the bar and fuck this stupid fixation out of me with someone whose name I didn't know.

But I didn't want some random with no name, and I didn't want Trystan to go find some other tall blond to experiment on.

With a click of my tongue I reached out and snatched his top from his hand.

"I didn't say that shit last night just so I could blow ye again." I gave him a pointed look and irritation joined the other emotions playing across his features.

My laugh was slightly bitter and I tried to get control of the frustration that was making it hard not to scowl at him. I sucked in a deep breath through my nose and leveled my gaze on him.

"Look, Trys, I didn't say I'll go exclusive t' soothe yer fricking pride, and I didn't let ye fuck me on some kind of whim." I held his gaze, making sure he believed what I was saying because there was no way I wanted to do this twice. "Ye were right, if I wanted Dan I could've had Dan or Echo or yer brother or anyone I fricking wanted. Anyone who wasn't some irritatingly possessive, bi-curious straight guy who's bullied me for half o' ma life."

I cocked an eyebrow as I watched him bite back some comment. But he kept his thoughts to himself and his arms crossed against his chest as he waited for me to continue. I shifted slightly against the desk, feeling the familiar warmth in my hips and lower back that came after good sex, slightly more of a sting this morning because it had been such a bloody long time since I'd last been with someone and Trystan had really gone to town.

He took the number of guys I'd been topped by to four, and that was a number that I really didn't want to think about.

"I like sex—love it in fact—but I don't *do* being fucked, Trys. I don't know what Jorja has told ye and what ye've worked out for yerself, but I wasn't being stubborn in Scotland: I just don't bottom. Yer the third person I've let anywhere near my ass, and frankly, the idea that I let someone fuck me who has never given or received anal before is fricking laughable."

Trystan had dropped his arms from across his chest and was looking at me with his head cocked to one side. A range of emotions played across his face that I would rather not decipher, but I kept going because I needed to get this over and done with.

"So I'm not likely t' go out and pull some random to fuck me anytime soon. Plus, I think we've already established that if I was in the mood for fucking around yer brother's chastity might be another degree less intact."

He scowled at me in silence. I gave a hitch of my shoulders and carried on even though I really needed to shut the hell up.

"Whatever, Trys. At the end o' the day, it's yer fricking choice whether ye trust me or not, just like it was last night when ye decided t' fuck me even though ye knew what I was like. I'm not saying it's going t' be easy; in fact yer probably going t' hate it and dump my ass like every fucker else. Just don't dance around it like a twat. I let ye top me because I'm a fricking idiot, it's like ye said: yer fun to be around, I enjoy messing wi' ye and waking up with yer ugly mug pressed into my neck and yer fat sweaty legs tangled in mine. And possibly just a little bit because ye have a fucking great body."

I finished with an exaggerated leer as I realized I had said far more than I had intended to. But I must have said something right, because despite everything I could see him trying not to grin. He took a half step forward and fixed me in those satin eyes of his; there was a mixture of smirk and curiosity in them that was hot and kind of disturbing.

"What?" I snapped to stop myself from spouting more nonsense.

"I'm just trying to work out if you just said you liked me."

"Pfft," I squawked as I pushed myself forward off the desk so that I was square in front of him, meeting him eye to eye as I pressed my tongue against my teeth and his shirt against his chest. Then I leaned forward and ghosted a kiss against the corner of his lips, feeling soft mouth and the faint rasp of his stubble before I lifted off and met his smirk with my own. "Don't get carried away. I don't 'like ye;' yer a convenience."

Trystan wrapped his hand round the back of my head, tugging my lips down on top of his. He started it rough, bruising his lips against mine, forcing his tongue straight into the cavern of my mouth. I melted against him, humming slightly against the pleasant wash of warmth inside of me. Then he got softer and softer, his tongue gently pressing against mine, his lips teasing and caressing and his other hand slipped around my waist, pulling me gently and possessively against him. I followed his kiss as he broke it off, and I realized I was staring up at him with rather too much affection mixed in with my annoyance.

"Well I'll just have to try harder, then, won't I?" he said with a soft smile.

14—Leopard

WELL, GETTING some work done before I met Patrick had gone down the drain. Quite literally, because I'd ended up having to take yet *another* shower. That made three in a single twelve-hour period. Even by the standards of my worst pre-Dan days that was impressive. So I'd been rushing and Trystan had taken me up on the offer to come climbing that I'd given before I'd really thought about it. Which is how I found myself staring up at exactly what I hadn't wanted to: Trystan's Greek-god-back stretching and contorting as he made his way up one of the more challenging courses at the local climbing center.

I grimaced and turned away just as Patrick finished and dropped down from his run. Because there were three of us, we were using the automated belay equipment, and it was probably a good thing as my concentration was all over the place.

"You want to come out for some bluffs this weekend?" Patrick asked, talking to me and watching Trystan. "The weather is supposed to be pretty nice."

"Sorry, Patrick, I told my sister I'd go home for a visit. I've not seen her in a few months, so I can't really cancel."

"Fair enough. So—?" Patrick glanced round at me with a curious look on his face. "He's pretty good?" he pressed when I didn't volunteer anything further.

"Yeah," I added rather unhelpfully and resisted the temptation to turn back and stare at Trystan as he made the course he was on look completely effortless. We hadn't climbed this summer because the end of the holiday had been too wet, but I'd climbed with him back in the day, and I knew he still did it because he'd mentioned it a couple of times. I just hadn't gotten round to inviting him out because either one or both of us had been busy or we'd not been talking to each other.

Patrick got to the point. "Any reason this is the first time you've brought him out? You could've invited him the other weekend."

"We weren't really getting on then," I answered honestly.

"Why does that not surprise me?" said Patrick with a roll of his eyes. His gaze drifted over my shoulder and looked appreciative. I kind of wanted to see what Trystan was doing that was good enough to impress Patrick. But I kept my gaze fixed on the guy on the floor.

"What *is* going on, Ide?" Patrick asked as he finally looked back down at me. "You turn up with him like you're best buddies, when the last time you mentioned him you were bad-mouthing him. Of course the time before that you seemed to be getting on okay, and then there's your reaction on the phone when he called you that time."

Well hell, didn't that just sum up mine and Trystan's relationship?

"Poor Ide is just emotionally retarded, can't accept that he finds me irresistible, eh, Ide?" Trystan's amused tone sounded behind me.

I twisted to find he'd already managed to finish one of the hardest courses in the complex. Which was fine, but it was only his third run of the day, he'd never done this particular ascent before, and it wasn't like anyone had been pointing him. I glanced at the course behind him and sighed; what had I really expected? Of course Trystan wasn't going to be merely good.

"Oh, I'm sorry, Trys." My voice was dripping with sarcasm. "Were we not paying ye enough attention? Do it again and we'll clap this time, promise."

Patrick just sniggered.

"What?"

That only made Patrick laugh some more. "I get it now."

"Get what?" I replied, probably not just a little bitter.

"The love-hate thing," Patrick elaborated, and I raised a single eyebrow at that. He glanced at Trystan and shot him a proper grin for the first time since I'd introduced them. "Because apart from Dan, he's the only guy I've met who's into you and doesn't just roll over and fawn at your feet."

I blanched a little at that. "Trys isn't—"

But I was interrupted by a hand landing on my head, scratching gently at my crown, and pulling wayward strands of my hair loose to fall over my eyes. Trystan twisted me round by the top of my head and he fixed me with a mocking grin.

"Told you. It's only you that's oblivious to the feelings of everyone around you. Your friend here worked it out in forty minutes, and we haven't even been speaking." He turned that mocking smile on Patrick. "And if that doesn't prove my point that he is emotionally retarded, I don't know what will."

"Never said otherwise." Patrick didn't lose his smile, but concern tugged at his temples. "Good luck with him, mate."

"Don't worry, I've got him covered; he'll be a model member of society in a matter of weeks."

"Pfft." I wasn't alone in my dismissive laugh, and I tugged Trystan's hand from my head so I could retie my hair. "If I don't get bored o' ye in a couple of weeks," I said archly. "Ye'll need to learn some new tricks if ye expect t' keep me entertained for more than a couple o' days."

"Challenge accepted. Care to take a bet? Or do you only bet when there are Yorkshire puddings involved?"

Bloody Jorja.

"I'll take that bet," Patrick chortled. "Twenty quid says you don't last past next Wednesday. And that's *only* because Ide is going home at the weekend so he can't go out."

"Yer supposed t' be my friend," I muttered. Although, I imagine there weren't many of my friends who wouldn't take that bet.

"Aye, which means I know what you're like." Patrick was still looking thoroughly amused.

"So, twelve days is what I have to beat?" Trystan's smug smile was not wavering.

"I'll ask around, see if we can't get a sweepstakes going, closest wins or something," Patrick said as he pulled out his phone to text everyone else.

I gave Trystan the benefit of a condescending smile as I passed him to take my turn on the wall. Patrick was busy sending out texts. The distraction was a welcome one as I concentrated on getting my body to the top of the room. I enjoyed the strain on my muscles, the all-consuming concentration, and the flash of triumph as I reached my goal. The flicker of adrenaline in response to the split second of free fall before the auto belay engaged was familiar, and I kicked off back down to ground level.

"Nice work," Trystan said as I got back to their side.

"Not as fast as ye," I said as I glanced at the time with a weary shake of my head.

"I'm twice as strong as you, easily," he said with a shrug, and though he was smiling, he didn't look like he was rubbing it in.

"And I've done that run so many more times than ye," I replied.

"Well, you had nice form on it, looked really tidy and in control."

"Huh? Oh thanks, I guess." I chuckled as I realized he'd actually just complimented me. "Ye weren't too shabby yerself."

"Oi, *lover-boyz*, Suze says she's feeling generous and is giving you two months," Patrick said as he glanced up from his phone and saw what probably looked a lot like me and Trystan grinning inanely at each other. "I think she's just playing the odds and figures no one else will risk going that long."

Trystan laughed at that, and I pulled my far too cheesy grin into a weary look as I shook my head at him.

"Ye realize they're betting on me leaving ye or cheating on ye, right? Why do ye look so pleased wi' yerself?"

He just continued to smile with his lips split wide, his tongue darting over the clean white flash of his teeth as he met my gaze. He was completely unfazed.

"You were the one who told me to trust you, right?"

I blanched as I remembered our conversation this morning. Why the hell had I said that shit? More importantly, had he really believed me, just like that?

"So they can bet to their hearts' content; I'm still going to win," Trystan continued, his voice still low and perfectly confident.

"Jason's going for fifteen days, reckons you'll fail next weekend," Patrick reported from his phone.

I collected my surprise that Trystan seemed to have taken my words to heart and let one of my eyebrows arch up my forehead. "Yer going to win against *two months*?" I didn't bother to hide my skepticism.

"Ide, you're such a head case," he said at a normal volume and then leaned forward to whisper against my ear. "I just waited four months for you... you think I'm going to let you escape in anything less than that?"

I pressed my hand against his chest, easing him away from me, and my smirk was almost as dark as his.

"Well, I'm glad t' see yer so confident. But if ye think I'm going four months without switching...." I let my voice trail off suggestively.

Trystan just gave a little chuckle as we readied ourselves for the next ascent.

"I'm still going to win," he said softly.

"JOSH GET off all right?" Trystan asked on Wednesday evening as he marched into my room like he still lived there and dropped himself onto my bed.

"I really thought ye might have learnt yer lesson about knocking by now?" I replied as I spun round in my desk chair to face him.

"Well, it's not like you'd be up to anything I wouldn't enjoy seeing." His voice was suggestively low, and it rumbled straight through me and settled in my—frankly aching—hips.

"Not now we've finally got rid of Josh at least," he finished in a more normal tone as he sat back up and undid the first few buttons of the shirt he'd worn to work.

"Something you like?" he asked.

I realized I'd been staring, watching his fingers work the buttons and the slow revealing of his flesh underneath.

Shitting hell, why did he have to be so fricking gorgeous?

"Perhaps." I let my tongue slide out between my teeth as I pushed myself out of my chair and stalked across the room. I clambered onto the bed and mounted my knees on either side of him, holding his eyes in mine as I nudged his hands away so that I could release the next button myself. I drifted my fingers across the flesh I exposed, before I slipped my hand inside his shirt with a slow smile.

"Hmm." He reached around, pressing his fingers into the muscle of my ass and tugging me firmly against him as he let his lips dust across my neck. "So I guess I beat the couple of days challenge?" He blew the words against my neck.

"Well, ye stepped up t' the table; who knew ye were such a fast learner, eh?" I hummed as I let my hands slip down his spine and the memories of last night's antics brought another wash of warmth rushing down my spine. I could feel my body reacting. My ass kind of ached because even before my break I wasn't used to being fucked five nights in a row, and right then I really wished Trystan had been a bit less defensive about the whole switching thing. But he'd certainly been very imaginative in his willingness to keep me entertained, and it wasn't like I couldn't cope with a slither of pain here and there. I didn't need to push it yet.

"Such a talented tongue," I whispered as I pressed my mouth against his and let my own tongue plunge between his lips.

Trystan's hands were underneath my shirt and we were both breathing heavily into the kiss when my phone buzzed on my bedside table.

I glanced over to see if it was ignorable, then stepped off Trystan with a faint sigh when I saw the caller ID.

I gave a little cough to clear my throat and straightened my sweatpants as I answered the call and settled on the bed next to Trystan.

"Hey, Mam." I put a little emphasis on the last word as I batted Trystan's hand away from my groin.

"Idrys, love, how are ye?"

"Good, thanks, just been trying to get an essay finished." Beside me Trystan gave a faint chortle that I hoped didn't carry.

"Oh good. Did Josh get home safely? I can't believe ye let him catch a stomach bug."

"He's fine, Mam, and it wasn't like I infected him on purpose or something." Another chuckle from Trystan at that.

Of course Josh hadn't been ill, although he'd been grumpy enough to seem ill when I took him to the train station this afternoon. Chris had taken him out on Monday; I think they'd gone for Nandos and to see a film. In my limited experience, it seemed like a good first date; however, Josh had come back looking thoroughly irritated. It didn't take long for Trystan and me to work out why: Chris had refused to do more than kiss the boy. I had almost felt sorry for him, but my apparently blossoming responsible side admitted it was probably a good thing. Josh hadn't tended to agree and had spent the last two days sulking.

"And how's Trystan? Are ye two fighting or friends at the moment?"

"Trys is fine, Mam, he's just got in from work and we're getting on. But I'm coming home on Friday and I can tell ye all about the son ye wish ye'd had then."

"Oh well, that was why I were ringing really, Ide love. I was talking t' Samantha this morning and we were saying how hard it is for her havin' Trystan so far away so she can't feed him up, and I suddenly realized it's so silly for him not to come too. It'd be lovely t' see him and yer sister gets

on with him anyway and...." She was still wittering reasons why Trystan coming back with me at the weekend was such a fabulous idea. I'd zoned out and I twisted round to fix my wide-eyed gaze on Trystan. He was smirking, as if he'd planned it, and I honestly wouldn't have put it past him right then.

"I think he's got plans actually, Mam."

"Oh, no, nothing that can't be changed," Trystan said loud enough for his voice to carry.

"Oh Idrys, yer such a one." Her tone was amused, and then she raised her voice so she was shouting down the phone, even though Trystan had clearly heard her perfectly well when she spoke at a regular volume.

"Hello, Trystan love, we'd love to have ye come visit. Ye don't let my rude, dastardly son keep ye away, ye hear? I promised yer mam I'd feed ye up."

I slapped my free hand over his mouth as he went to speak, and he grinned at me from the other side of my palm. Then he slid his tongue out, running circles against my flesh as he reached forward, taking advantage of my busy hands to slide his fingers into the waistband of my sweatpants. I glared at him in silence, and though I couldn't see his mouth, I could see the smug smirk in his eyes as he slid his fingers against the flesh between my legs.

With a grimace I dropped my hand from his lips and tugged his hand out of my trousers.

"Thanks, Mrs. Bjornson, I'd love to come," Trystan said as soon as his lips were free. The whole thing had taken less than five seconds and my mum hadn't noticed a thing.

"Oh, wonderful. Do ye have any food preferences?"

I gave a weary sigh as I held the phone toward Trystan so he could speak to her. While they compromised on lasagna for Saturday evening, I lay back on my bed. When he was done he held the phone out to me. I took it, and I must have said something sensible and then good-bye to my mum, because she hung up with a brief "love you" and I was left staring at a grinning Trystan.

"Come on, Ide?" he whispered as he crawled over the bed, dropping a knee on each side of my hips and his hands on either side of my shoulders. I stared up into his smug, amused face that got closer and closer as he dropped his lips to rest against my neck. He sucked my flesh into his mouth, letting his teeth grate against me gently.

"What could you possibly have to worry about?" He pressed the words against my neck. "It can't be not being able to keep your hands off me, because you're going to be bored of me by then, remember?"

He ran his tongue up my neck and dropped his hips against mine, rolling lightly.

"Yer such a fricking pain in the ass, Trys."

"Mmm, indeed, and I'm the only pain in yer ass at the moment, right?"

"Seriously?" I couldn't help the faint chuckle at his words, but then his hands were drifting down my torso, sliding back to my waistband. His lips returned to my neck briefly before he dropped his mouth down to take my nipple in between his teeth through the cotton of my T-shirt.

"So?"

"Hmm?" I asked absently as I arched into the double assault on my senses.

"I can practically see how bored you are already." His voice was low as he relented in his attack on my nipple and raised his head back above mine.

"Has anyone ever told ye, ye talk too damn much, Trystan Jackson?" I growled as I pulled his lips down over mine.

"Only you; most girls love my sweet talking."

"Ye still not got in yer head that I'm not a damn girl." I wrapped my hand around his neck as I grasped his upper arm and rolled us both so that I was over him.

His tongue darted out between his teeth, but his smug smile remained.

"You just confuse me, see…." He pressed the gentle swelling of his groin up against mine as he drifted his hands over the slight curve of my hips and then up my body. "Gentle curves here, narrow waist here, sensitive nipples." He grated his nails against the slight damp patch he had left against my T-shirt. "Sexy hole, perfect for my dick right here…." He continued to explore my edges, he left a faint trail of warmth as his touch skipped around my back and over my ass. "Just a shame about that stubble of yours, and your face of course, nothing sexy there. Not hot at all." He ran the fingers of his other hand through my hair and urged my lips against his.

He rocked his hips against mine, slipping his hands between us and catching the waistband of my sweatpants. His kiss deepened as he reached past the globes of my ass, his fingers digging into my flesh as he bit and nibbled at my lips and drove his tongue into my mouth.

Then suddenly he wasn't underneath me anymore. My chest was pressed against the duvet, my ass hanging over the edge of the bed, and Trystan was over my back, rolling his still clothed hips against my suddenly bare ass as his hands came around to palm my dick. His teeth were against my neck, sending shivers down my spine as he knelt down behind me, and then those teeth were against my backside.

"Ow, fucking hell, Trys." I bucked against him as he used his free hand to hold me still as he bit down on my ass. He chuckled darkly as he ran his lips and tongue against the mark he'd no doubt left, and the juxtaposition was odd and soothing. His hand was still against my dick, and soon I forgot about the pain. Until he did it again.

This time I just moaned as the ache washed out through the muscle, the tension clashing against the pleasure of his hand against my dick.

"Such a flawless ass shouldn't exist; it's too fucking gorgeous." His words whispered against a third mark, adding a shiver of cold to my rapidly heating ass.

"Nnn." I garbled something incomprehensible as he bit down again, and as my hips bucked against the sting of his teeth, I wasn't sure whether I wanted to press up into him or away from him. "Trys…." I was fully aware that my voice sounded pathetically pleading as he bit down yet again.

"What, Ide? Something I can do for you?" he whispered again as his hand continued on my cock and his teeth set my ass cheeks on fire.

"Ah, yer such a twat…." My senses were completely overwhelmed, and this time I definitely arched my hips into his teeth. "Just fuck me already," I gasped as he went back over one of the marks he'd left and I felt the sting of pain all the way down through the soles of my feet.

He laughed darkly as he half lifted off me just enough to find lube and a condom, and then he was back. He kept up his intermittent assault with his teeth and tongue on my cheeks as he slid his fingers inside me just enough to lube me up, and then his heat was over my back. My ass was hot and stinging as his weight pressed down through it. My trousers were still only just pulled down past my cheeks, so were his by the feel of things, but I couldn't twist round to see as I was pinned completely. He ran his lips up my neck, biting and sucking again, only slightly more carefully than he had against my backside. And his cock was nudging against my entrance that ached for him, but I couldn't reach for him, I could only lie there trapped beneath him as he urged his way inside me.

He slid his hands round to the front of my hips, taking my cock between his palms as he rocked against me. He was breathing heavily against my ear, his weight pressed me down into the mattress, and his arms pinned me against his hips, leaving me feeling completely trapped by him. And my ass burned inside and out as he pumped into me.

"Oh God, Trys...." I felt the slow, incessant building of pressure in my balls. I wanted to push back against him, but I couldn't move, and it was driving me even wilder as he took his sweet time fucking me right to the edge of sanity.

"Shit, Ide, you're so—*fucking*—good," he groaned and dug his teeth into my shoulder as his languid pace finally picked up a little.

Pleading slid out of my mouth as my body desperately tried to buck up to meet him. His hands sped up on my cock, giving a little twist each time he got to the head. I shouted something incoherent as my body seized up and my pleasure erupted in thick cords. While behind and on top and inside of me, Trystan shuddered to a groaning halt as he joined me.

He rolled away, and I lay where I was for a moment to catch my breath and readjust to the lack of weight on top of me.

"Ye really need to remember to use the fricking towel or buy me a second duvet cover," I complained, but my harsh words were betrayed by the faint smile on my lips and the breathless tone to my voice. I flopped backward from the bed and then cursed and rolled over as my ass cheeks hit the coarse carpet.

"Trystan, ye fucker, what've ye done to my ass?" I arched over my shoulder and was hardly surprised to see my usually pale skin was looking remarkably similar to a red version of one of those Dulux paint shade palettes: each dark red teeth-shaped circle faded out to paler shades of pink until it hit the next mark.

I glowered at him as I placed my palm over one of the marks and it glowed hot beneath my hand.

"Well, you said I was a pain in the ass.... I thought I'd make it literal." He was still laughing as he chucked me a towel to clean up with.

"Ye...." I couldn't even find words to insult him with so I concentrated on cleaning myself up. I winced as I pulled my sweatpants back over my ass and decided to lie on my front when I got back to the bed. "Don't ye fricking dare." I grabbed his hand where it had just been reaching toward my backside.

He grinned, looking the picture of sarcastic innocence.

"I was just going to rub it better."

"Yeah, course ye were." I pulled his hand away from me. "Seriously with the duvet, though, Trys; I can't be bothered to wash it every fricking day because ye get carried away."

"I didn't hear you complaining about getting carried away a few minutes ago."

"Yeah, well, when I'm top I'll be in charge; ye want t' play the man, ye get to do all the fun shit that comes wi' it."

He chuckled and leaned over me to press a coy kiss to my cheek.

"You can come and sleep downstairs in my bed to make up for it if you like."

I pressed my eyes shut at the faint leap in my heart rate that thought caused. We'd had sex plenty since last Friday, but we hadn't shared a bed again, and I begrudged the excitement in my chest that having an excuse to sleep next to him caused.

"Great, so I get t' wake up at six when ye go to work. I'm a lucky guy, eh?" I grumbled, but Trystan just laughed lightly and shifted his lips against mine.

"You're such a head case, Ide; you already told me you like sleeping with me."

"That was last weekend. I'm way over that."

"Oh, since when?"

"Since ye molested me while I was on the phone to my mam, and made it so I can't sit down."

Trystan's eyes glistened with mirth as he lay out next to me with his head propped on his hands, and he looked deliciously disheveled in the now rather crumpled outfit he had worn to work.

"Why were you even freaking out about me going home with you? It's not like I've never met your parents before."

"What if they find out, Trys?" I said in all seriousness.

He shrugged. "What difference does it make? Aren't your parents really cool about that kind of thing?"

"Yeah, too cool." My voice was a little droll. I honestly couldn't ask for a more supportive family, but that was the point, *my* family wasn't the issue here. "But what if they say something to yours?"

"Oh." Trystan cocked his head to one side, but instead of looking worried, he just smiled softly. "Aw, were you worried about me? You're so cute, Idrys."

I yelped as he dropped his hand onto my ass.

"I am going to kill ye, ye fricking irritating man."

He just laughed and gave my ass a gentle squeeze that sent a wash of warmth and a sting of pain through me.

"Isn't that what you like about me?"

"I don't fricking like ye."

"Course not, my mistake." He grinned at me and leaned forward to catch my cheek in his hand and urge my lips against his for a brief kiss. He hummed contentedly as he pulled away. "Anyway, don't worry about Jerry. I'm not going to tell him yet, but if he finds out, I'll just deal."

His phone buzzed in his back pocket and he tugged it out. I considered him as he flicked through the text that had come through. "Oh yeah, I'm supposed to be going out with some of the guys from work tomorrow for a few drinks; want to come?"

I checked over his face, my own satisfied smile once again slipping into a look of concern. "Won't that be weird?"

"Nah, they're bringing other halves. They asked specifically for you, to be honest. I think they're curious."

I let the silence hang, and I rolled onto my side to match Trystan's pose and meet his gaze with mine. "Are ye being *serious*? Ye haven't actually told the people at yer work placement that yer dating a guy?"

"Sure I have, why wouldn't I?"

I stared at him, searching his face for any clue that this was one of his jokes.

"Because we've been *dating* for less than a week, and my friends are having bets on how quickly I'll cheat on ye." I kept my voice slow, but I couldn't help the mote of exasperation that clung to my words. "Do ye have no sense of self-preservation?"

"Should I be worried?"

I opened my mouth to say yes and then pressed it closed again. Because I couldn't lie. And more importantly; I didn't want to.

He watched the whole thing, and a languid smile slipped across his lips. He shuffled closer, slipping his hand into the small of my back as he held our bodies gently together and took my lips in his. His tongue quested over mine and caressed my lips, and he dropped his hand to run gentle soothing circles over the burn of my ass cheeks.

I realized the faint humming was coming from me this time as he pulled away.

"So do you want to come?" he asked, his lips flushed and damp and his eyes half-closed in satisfaction.

This man was clearly crazy. I wondered how I hadn't noticed.

"THIS IS a monumentally bad idea," I muttered as the boot of my car thudded shut. I let my head loll back against the driver's seat headrest and started the ignition. The passenger door opened and Trystan hopped into the seat next to me and buckled up.

I had now been *dating* Trystan for a week. And after a whole seven days, the guy still turned my insides into liquid gold. I honestly could not get enough of him, to the point where even *I* thought it was obscene—and I feel you know enough about me by now to realize that is pretty impressive.

"Don't be daft, what could possibly go wrong?" mocked Trystan, and I shook my head, jammed the car into reverse, and headed in the direction of the A1(M)—and home.

The fact that Trystan thought it was funny proved to me how much of a lack of understanding he had of this situation. When my mum had called on Wednesday, I'd just decided to let it go for the time being. I'd figured I'd come up with an excuse to leave Trystan behind and it'd all be fine. Clearly, that hadn't quite gone to plan.

We'd gone out with his friends from work last night and it had been fun. It's not like I walk around expecting everyone to be homophobic, but let's face it, I might not dress or act the part, but no one is particularly surprised to find out I'm gay, whereas Trystan really doesn't look like he bats for the other team. Plus, we're not exactly a normal-looking couple—given that we're both over six foot two—and we're not going to be winning any awards for being affectionate to each other. So I had expected a bit of weirdness from his colleagues, or at least that they might take a while to get used to it. They hadn't batted an eyelid.

After quickly establishing that, despite occasionally being a model, I wasn't into shoes or clothes any more than the average straight guy, conversation had turned rapidly toward sports and beer and Trystan's shockingly low alcohol tolerance. And as such the evening had been whiled away and when we'd gotten home we'd fallen into bed—both of us in Trystan's—and I'd completely forgotten that I was supposed to be thinking up reasons for him not to come home with me the next day.

I tried to concentrate on the road rather than the pleasant wash of warmth that was brought on by the thought of how I'd woken up this morning: far too hot yet perfectly content, with Trystan's body curled up around my back.

Right now I didn't feel content at all. I felt anxious and stressed. I really did not want my parents to know about me and Trystan.

Not because they'd be bothered, on the contrary, I was perfectly certain that they would be ecstatic I had a boyfriend for the first time since I was fifteen. And they loved Trystan. I'd only been slightly sarcastic when I'd made that comment about the son they wished they'd had when I'd been on the phone to my mum. As if being bullied by him for two weeks a year for most of my life wasn't bad enough, I also had to put up with frequent reports on how wonderful he was from Mum when she had her weekly phone calls with Samantha.

My parents finding out we were together wasn't the problem. It was how they'd react when it ended. I didn't think I could cope with the disappointment they'd look at me with when I inevitably messed up.

Then there was Jorja.

And the fact that keeping my hands off him for a whole weekend so they didn't find out was going to actually kill me.

"You heard from Josh today?" I asked because I needed to distract myself from the shit in my head.

"Yeah, he's doing fine—fully recovered from his stomach bug," Trystan said with a knowing smile. "He text me today to ask if he could come and stay again next weekend."

"Oh did he now? I wonder why, hmm?"

Trystan laughed darkly. "Indeed."

"Can't he find some cute guys back in Kent? A weekend to ourselves sounds quite nice at some point."

"Huh? Planning on sticking around for that long, are we?"

I gave a small roll of my eyes and flicked the radio on to fill my thoughts as we cruised southward.

My anxiety didn't lessen, and I gave an unenthusiastic sigh as an hour later we pulled off the M1 just north of Sheffield and switched to the narrow winding lanes that would lead us into the depths of the Peak District. Outside it was raining, and the windscreen wipers were a squeaky drum beat in the background.

"You're actually really worried about this, aren't you?" I glanced briefly across at Trystan. He was staring at me with an unusual amount of concern. "But why? Your parents know you're gay. Aren't they cool with it?"

My face crumpled.

"Yeah, they know I'm gay, and they also worship the ground ye walk on."

He grinned. "So what's the problem?"

"The problem isn't this weekend, or maybe it will be with Jorja… urgh. The problem will be when I mess this shit up and they hate me for leaving ye/cheating on ye/whatever."

"Hmm, so if your parents find out, then you won't be able to leave me; is that what you're saying?"

"Don't sound like that's a good thing. Ye've only had t' deal wi' me for a week."

Trystan just laughed, and then he reached over and gave my thigh a quick squeeze.

"You shouldn't worry so much. But sure, if you don't want them to know, we'll just keep it quiet. Easy."

"Except it's not, because my sister has no brain-to-mouth filter sometimes, and if she notices something, she's bound to just blurt it out in front of them."

"Well Jorja already knows I like you, so she's not likely to say anything about it in front of anyone." He gave a nonchalant shrug, and then his tone turned sly. "And of course, you don't really like me, so why would she notice anything on your part?"

"Yer such a pain in the ass, Trys."

"Hmm, what was that? You want me to bite your ass again?"

"Fricking hell." The thought of Wednesday evening sent a wash of heat down my spine, and I shifted against the still not completely healed marks on my backside.

From the corner of my eye, I saw Trystan's smug smile slip into a sigh. "If you're really so worried, I'll just call your sister. If we tell her, she'll know to keep it a secret."

I made a strangled noise in the back of my throat. She was never, *ever* going to let me live this down.

"Fine; call her. Just brace yerself for squealing," I relented, because one of them knowing was better than all three.

I tried to concentrate on the road and breathing to the bottom of my lungs as Trystan pulled his phone out and hit call. He switched it straight to speaker, which I wasn't sure was a good thing or not.

"*Hey, Trys, ye guys stuck in traffic or some'at? Dinner is stew so it can wait.*" My sister's voice came down the line, and I kept quiet and my eyes on the road.

"It's been pretty clear so far. You by yourself? I need to ask you about something."

"*Nope, but give me a sec... right, all alone, what's up?*"

"Hmm." I saw Trystan glance in my direction. "Well yer brother is freaking out about me coming home with him."

"*Ye guys still not sorted yer shit out? This is getting stupid. Why don't ye just tell him ye like him already?*"

Trystan laughed. "You're on loudspeaker, Jorja."

"*...oh, crap! Shitting hell, I'm sorry, Trys, I didn't.... I mean I kept my mouth shut and... bloody hell.*"

"That's pretty mean, even for ye, Trys," I added when Trystan left her panicking.

"*No, Ide, I didn't mean.... Wait, why aren't ye freaking out?*"

"I already know," I said at a normal volume, then waved for Trystan to continue because we were getting to a rare bit of dual carriageway and I wanted to overtake the retired tourists who were crawling round every corner at fifteen miles an hour.

"Look, Jorja, we'll tell you about how and why later, but Ide was worried you'd work it out and say something in front of your mum and dad, and he doesn't want them to know."

"*Hold on; how and why what? How and why Ide knows ye like him and is okay with it? Or... wait.... I'd work it out? Work out wha... holy crap are you two... dating? No, no....*"

I could practically see her shaking her head as her forehead creased in confusion and she frantically pushed her fringe out of her eyes. Trystan was holding the phone out with a faintly amused look creasing his eyes as he let her witter on.

"*No, that's impossible because Ide doesn't date. So wait, are ye just putting up wi' his whoring? Or... no ye wouldn't. Would ye? No... no* fricking *way? Yer actually dating, aren't ye? Yer Ide's* fricking *boyfriend...?*" The predicted screeching occurred and the phone's speaker could barely cope.

"*When the hell did this happen, Idrys! If ye dare tell me that it was longer than thirty seconds ago I swear I will tell Mum it was ye who replaced her scones wi' shop-bought ones that time and make sure ye get no Yorkshires from now 'til Christmas.*"

Trystan was laughing and trying to stifle it as he watched me heave a weary sigh. "Ide is driving at the moment, Jorja, so he can't defend himself. But it happened last weekend, and well, I'm sure if you think about it you can probably guess why neither of us would tell you straight off. So if you could find it in your heart to not mention anything in front of your parents, that would be great."

"*Fricking hell, Trys, ye sure ye know what yer letting yerself in for?*"

"Still here, Jorja," I piped up in the background. "And yer supposed to be on my side, not his."

Jorja spluttered something under her breath that didn't make it down the phone. "*Fine, I'll keep schtum, but if ye two think yer getting out o' explaining this shit t' me, then ye have another thing coming. I need to go, drive safe.*"

"See you in forty minutes," Trystan replied and hung up. Then he looked back round at me. "She's an odd one, your sister."

We pulled into the drive of my parents' place fifty minutes later after getting stuck behind an out-of-season caravan for the final ten miles. I stopped the car halfway down the drive and turned to Trystan with a questioning look.

"So, this is it. If ye want to pull out, I'd probably say something now, because once we stop in that yard, yer—" I was cut off by a pair of lips pressing over mine, suckling at them, then prying them open so a tongue could force its way inside. I groaned and struggled against my seat belt as I tried to claw him closer. Then he was pulling away, leaving me slightly breathless and with a sudden perfect awareness of my blood and the heat it was pooling in my groin.

"This is going to be a long weekend," Trystan said with a small sigh and just a touch of a smirk as he sat back in his chair.

I stared down at myself and wondered—not for the first time that week—when my body had been switched with a younger version of itself, the one that had got hard from a kiss.

"Can ye at least try and look less attractive or something for a couple o' days, I dunno, don't take a shower or wear some clown clothes?" I asked as I fired up the car and drove the last two hundred meters to my parents' back door.

"Hmm, you saying you like the way I look?"

"Shut up, Trystan," I muttered as I pulled the handbrake on, flicked off the ignition, and steeled myself for the upcoming mayhem.

"I don't know why, but this really isn't where I imagined you growing up," Trystan said as I fished our bags out of the boot and tossed him his.

"What did ye imagine?" I asked as I watched him twisting round to examine the endless expanse of pitch-black nothingness that stretched out beyond the illuminated farmyard. There wasn't a single other light visible in any direction; there wasn't much of anything visible in any direction. Even when it was daytime, it was just rolling hills.

"More towny. You were so small and I know you were hard as nails, but I don't know.... I just thought it might be a village at least."

"I had t' be hard as nails 'cause someone kept beating me up," I replied and gave Trystan a level look over my shoulder. Trystan shot me a wolfish grin.

"Maybe it was like that stuff you hear about where you beat up the person you like."

"No, Trys, ye were just a bully." I let a smile quirk the corner of my lips as I pushed the back door open.

"I'm back," I called as we came straight into the kitchen. I came to an awkward stop in the doorway and forced Trystan to step around me so he could get a look at the farm kitchen that currently smelled of the most amazing things.

My mum and dad greeted me, and I accepted and returned a hug and a gruff man-pat from each of them respectively, but I wasn't concentrating. I was staring at Theo, who was sitting on the other side of the kitchen table with Tess at his feet. He had a glass of ale in one hand and one ankle slung over his other knee, and he was staring at me with a pissed-off look that was matched by the girl behind him. Clearly my sister had kept her promise not to tell our mum and dad, but I hadn't been quite specific enough in my request.

"Oh, Trystan, I'm so glad ye could come. Idrys's student house is so awful, and I know he doesn't eat properly. How could he when he's so skinny? I swear I've spent my life tryin' t' fatten the boy up. And I promised Samantha I would feed ye properly before I sent ye back." My mum was wittering as she managed to give the impression that she was wrapping the man considerably larger than her in her arms. Then Trystan was treated to the same greeting as me from my dad, and I was left with having to introduce him to Theo.

"Hey, Theo," I tried to pull a grin onto my face because I knew the gormless look I was currently sporting was going to lead to questions.

"Ide" was Theo's monosyllabic response. And right then I honestly felt like having my parents know and Theo not would have been a better situation.

15—Ostrich

I STOOD just inside my parents' quaint farmhouse kitchen with the cats dancing curiously around my ankles. Mum was still wittering things at me and Trystan that I didn't, couldn't, really pay much attention to. Jorja was glaring at me—that wasn't much of a surprise. But honestly I wasn't prepared for Theo. I'd been so focused on my parents not finding out that I had hardly given my best friend a second thought. Now that I finally did, I realized the mistake I'd made.

When had I ever thought that my best friend was going to take it well that I was dating a guy who'd bullied me for a large portion of my life?

"Ah, Theo, this is Trys." I seriously wanted the ground to open up beneath me right then. "Trys, this is Theo." I hoped I didn't sound quite as shell-shocked as I felt as Theo stood and came round the table to shake Trystan's hand. "He lives on the next farm over, we've been friends since—"

Trystan was shooting me a confused look, clearly wondering what the hell was going on because Theo practically stalked round the table and the look on his face was pure fury as I watched their hands clasp together.

"…since we were four. *Nice* t' finally meet ye, Trys; I've heard a *lot* about ye."

I saw the sudden flash of understanding in Trystan's dark eyes, and his confusion switched to amusement—which did not help.

"Yer dad and I already ate, sorry, Ide love." My mum seemed completely oblivious to the tension between Trystan and my best friend. "There's a quiz on in the pub, yer welcome t' come down when yer done, but we're going t' shoot off." My mum smiled up at me and pressed a warm kiss against my cheek. "We'll catch up properly tomorrow. The stew is in the warming oven wi' some jackets. There's plenty for ye as well, Theo, so feel free t' stay."

"I could do with a hand in the morning, if you don't mind, Idrys," my dad asked as he shrugged his jacket on.

"Sure, Dad, no problem." I jumbled my words as I tried desperately to think of a way to get them to stay. They left anyway with an absent wave, and silence settled over the little kitchen while we waited for the sound of my parents' 4x4 humming to life.

"Right." I broke the silence—because it was ridiculous—and went round to the Aga to fish out the food—because I was hungry. "Trys, the fridge is on yer right. If I were ye I'd get some beers because we're about t' get an earful from this pair."

I dropped a couple of spoonfuls of beef stew on top of a perfectly bronzed potato and slid it onto the table behind me. "I take it yer staying, Theo?" I added as I proceeded to set out three more.

"So." I sat down and waved to a chair for Trystan to take a seat, and I looked pointedly between the two spare bowls of food. "Ye two going to preach on an empty stomach?" They sat down.

"Ye want me t' tell ye what yer both going t' say?" I asked as I finished my first mouthful. "Jorja, yer going t' tell Trystan he shouldn't trust me, and yer probably right. And, Theo, yer going t' tell me I'm an idiot for seeing someone who ruined a large part o' my childhood, and yer probably right."

"Aren't you just jealous?" Trystan smirked at Theo, and Theo bristled. I rolled my eyes because the idiot was not helping.

"I'm not gay. And if I was, ye think Ide would choose ye over me, dickhead?"

I couldn't help but snigger at that because Trystan's face had dropped and Theo was probably right: I didn't fancy him and he didn't fancy me, but if my best friend were gay, I'm almost certain we would have ended up together.

"Sorry, sorry," I hurried because all three of them had glared at me when I laughed. "Theo is a bit right, though, sorry, Trys."

If Trystan thought he could get a rise out of Theo by teasing him about his sexuality, he was sorely mistaken. Me and Theo have had many a conversation about the nature of each of our states of being—hetero versus homosexual—the first of which was probably when we were about eight and had no idea of the significance of what we were talking about.

"So what's the problem?" Trystan said with a slightly toned-down version of his usual smirk. "You don't fancy Ide, I do."

"Ma problem ain't whether ye fancy each other or not; it's the fact yer a prick," Theo growled. "And if I didn't think so before, I'm certain now."

Trystan laughed a little at that and turned to Jorja. "I'm not that bad, am I?"

Jorja gave an awkward little grimace, and I could see her warring with herself. "Well no, Trys, yer fine now, but ye *were* a bit of a twat t' Ide when we were younger, and Theo is Ide's best friend, so he knows all the shitty stuff Ide told him when we got back from our holidays."

"So you're judging me based on some stories from five years ago when we were all still kids?"

"Look," I cut in before Theo could respond because Trystan was still not helping—I was just guessing but I imagined that Theo did not find Trystan's smirk sexy enough to distract him from the smug tone beneath his words. "Trys is a bit of a dick, I'm not denying that, but seriously, Theo, I'm not exactly going t' be winning any awards anytime soon, so… can't ye just be happy that ye won't have t' tell me off for sleeping around?"

"Well that's ma point exactly," Jorja piped up and I rolled my eyes; this was like some twisted version of tag-team wrestling. "Are ye telling me that yer've gone from sleeping with like ten people a week straight to dating?"

I tutted. "Jorja, I haven't been that bad for *years*. It's only been three or four recently." I stuck my tongue out at her bristling rage, but she'd turned her eyes to Trystan. She was looking at him with a mixture of pity and disbelief.

"I know people think my brother is hot, everyone does, for frick's sake, but come on? I'm sorry, Ide"—she flashed a look in my direction—"but ye don't need t' put up wi' that shit, Trys."

I laughed at her softly, and my dismissal of what she'd said pulled a look of annoyance and guilt onto her face.

"Honestly, Jorja, I get what yer saying," I said softly with my head cocked to one side. "But as ye seem so desperate for details: I haven't slept wi' anyone other than Trys here for over a month…."

That definitely shut her up.

"A month?" she clarified after quite a long time of staring at me like I was a stranger.

"Five weeks," Trystan added—trust him to count.

"How d'ye know?" my sister asked, her doubt still evident.

"Because I shared a bed with him for the first week of it, and now I live next to the front door…."

Jorja looked between us, then leaned across the table, staring at me. Her head was cocked to one side, and she was inspecting me like I was a particularly curious and exotic animal.

"Yer not actually shitting wi' me, are ye?" I shook my head. "This t' do wi' what that piece o' shit housemate did t' ye?"

"He stopped before that," Trystan cut in before I could say anything. My sister slumped back in her seat, her face going slack as she turned her astonishment onto Trystan.

"Yer a fricking miracle worker, shitting hell, Trys." Jorja shrugged and sat forward to start on her food. "Fine then, ye have my approval. Just dun come running t' me when he goes back t' how he was."

"Jorja," Theo admonished as he turned to my sister with a look that said he definitely did not agree with her sudden approval.

"What, Theo? Ide is right: Trys is no more of a prick than my damn brother. So if Ide's not sleeping around, then I've got no problems."

Theo sighed and looked back at Trystan. "I just dun understand how ye even had the nerve t' try anything in the first place after the shit ye pulled as a kid."

"Yeah, well, people change." Trystan gave a small shrug.

"It's fine, Theo, I'm a big guy now, I can look after myself," I added with a tight smile for my best friend. He grumbled something and finally started on his food.

We ate in silence for a bit, and then I picked some random conversation just to break the silence. I wasn't even sure what it was. Then dinner was being cleared up and we went through to the living room. Jorja put something on the TV, again I have no idea what it was. At some point I went through to get some fresh beers, and as I came out of the fridge Theo was waiting for me, leaning against the front of the Aga and scratching Tess's head with a frown on his face.

"Ye still annoyed?" I asked as I handed him a full bottle and leaned against the fridge.

"Yeah, I'm still annoyed, mostly that I had t' find out from yer sister. This is a pretty big deal, Ide. Ye haven't dated anyone since that Phil guy back in year eleven."

"Yeah, I know."

Trust Theo to even remember the guy's name. Then again, it was Phil breaking up with me that had put me on a train to Manchester and in the path of the guy that'd stolen my virginity, and Theo had played a big enough part in picking up the pieces of me after that whole debacle.

"I'm sorry I didn't tell ye. But honestly, right now I'm still getting my head around the whole thing; I just didn't want t' make a big deal out o' something that might be going nowhere."

"I get that." Theo ran a hand through his dirty blond hair and turned his eyes up to the ceiling. "What happened, though? It's not like I'm not relieved that yer not going t' be risking yer life and health by sleeping around anymore. But last time ye were home, ye weren't exactly singing the guy's praises, and now ye've apparently decided t' change yer lifestyle completely to date him?" He hesitated as he looked at me. "What Jorja said, about yer housemate...."

I let out a long breath and saw off some of my fresh beer.

"Just some unwanted attention; not like it's anything new."

"As bad as last time?"

"Trys stopped him."

"So ye've got a hero complex?" Theo's resignation was kind of frustrating, but I could hardly blame him.

I gave a little shrug. "I dunno, I'd...." I clicked my tongue against the roof of my mouth; if I couldn't tell Theo, who could I tell? "Ye know I always had a crush on him, even when he was being a tosser t' me." It wasn't a question but Theo nodded anyway. "Well in Scotland he kinda started coming on to me, so I just went along wi' it."

"Ye kept that one quiet."

"Yeah, 'cause I knew ye'd disapprove. Anyway, he does this weird thing when he's sleeping."

"Remember: I don't like details, Ide," Theo said with a grimace.

I laughed and ran a hand over my face. "Ha, if only it was something like that, it'd be less embarrassing. He kind of snuggles, and I guess I got used to it. When he first moved in with me, he was on the floor, but he just moved up to the bed one night, and it wasn't like I thought about what I was doing, or that he'd said anything to me...."

"Ye just stopped fucking around?"

I nodded, and for the first time Theo's face lost some of the background irritation. "Anyway, then that shit happened with James and I was even less up for fucking around, except for with Trys. I mean, I know it's a bit messed up, and hell, he's only bi, so it's not like I really expect much to come of it in the long run, but I don't really feel like sleeping around, whereas I do like sleeping with Trys, so I figured I'd just go with the flow for a bit."

"Hmm," Theo said, and he was considering me with a weird look on his face.

"What ye doing about Dan and the others?" he asked eventually.

That was a good question.

It wasn't like it was the first time "you're jealous because Ide likes me, not you" had been sent in Theo's direction. Theo had been to stay with me a few times at uni, and Dan and Ashlie had made comments along the same lines on separate occasions. Each time Theo's response had been more or less the same: "If I were gay, are ye *really* dense enough t' think Ide would choose ye over me?" I found it oddly comforting to know that he was fine enough with me to feel happy saying such a thing. But still, what I'm getting at is that Theo knew about Dan and Ashlie and Echo. And while his approval of that situation was about as significant as his approval of what was going on between me and Trystan, he had at least acknowledged that Dan had made a marginal improvement in my mental state. Dan had other significant advantages over Trystan, too, in that Dan had never hurt me, and I hadn't spent most of my life badmouthing him to Theo.

"So far I've been avoiding them," I answered honestly.

"Course ye have." Theo sighed. "Look, Ide, ignoring the fact that I disapprove o' yer choice o' guy t' do it wi', I'm glad yer not fucking around. And it's not like I really think what ye had going wi' Dan was a picnic o' health, but ye can't just *ignore* him. Maybe ye never sat down and said 'Hey, we're going out,' but ye had a relationship, and ye need t' end it properly, not just leave him hanging."

"Shit, yeah, I know, but I'm kind o'…." I took a deep breath. "Shit, Theo, I'm pretty sure Dan's in love wi' me. Two fricking years he managed, and he decides t' fall for me now? It was hard enough facing him when I wasn't with Trys."

Theo stared at me across the room. And I wondered if I'd said something wrong.

"Honestly, Ide, of all the things ye've said this evening, the fact that ye suddenly care so much about the feelings o' someone that isn't ye, yer family, or, at a stretch, me, is the most convincing argument yet that yer've been replaced with an alien version of yerself."

"Yer such a tosser."

"Maybe, but since when do ye care about letting down the dickheads that fall for ye? Now suddenly yer dating one o' them and worried about hurting another? So what's different, Ide?"

It was a good question. What *was* different? Was I going to delude myself into thinking that I could get attacked again and suddenly the world would treat me differently? I shook my head slowly and took another drink of beer. I was surprised to see I'd somehow finished most of it already.

Theo shook his head and glanced over his shoulder toward the living room where Trystan and Jorja were watching some awful Friday night TV.

Was anything really different?

No, I knew what was going to happen. What was different was that I didn't want it to.

I pressed my eyes shut and that thought from my head as I hastily downed the last of my beer.

Theo turned back to me and his serious look melted away as he quirked an eyebrow. A mocking smile played against his lips as he dropped his head to one side.

"So yer telling me that ye being with him has nothing t' do wi' the fact that he looks like one o' those Italian statues?"

I let a smile slip onto my face and pressed down the oppressive thoughts that weighed on my chest.

"I've absolutely *no* idea what ye could possibly be talking about." I grinned, flashing all my teeth, as I twisted round to fish out a fresh beer.

I kept my face schooled in a faint smile as we went back through to the living room and dropped onto one of the sofas. Jorja shuffled in next to me, and Trystan caught my eye, a small questioning look behind his grin as he sat on the floor in front of my chosen spot. I shifted so my hand could rest on his shoulder, enjoying the small contact while I could. Conversation turned to bikes and front shock absorbers, while faint whispers of warmth spread up through my fingers as I considered the back of his head and the tanned lines of his neck.

Theo settled on the two-seater couch and Tess jumped up instantly to settle beneath his knees while the cats divided themselves between his lap and Jorja's. I was suddenly struck with how surreal the whole situation was: Trystan was in my parents' house, chatting with my best friend. And he was going to spend the night in my bed....

I jerked upright. With all my worrying about my parents finding out about me and Trystan, I had completely neglected to think about bedroom situations.

"Do ye know what Mam had planned with sleeping arrangements?" I leaned down to whisper in my sister's ear, and she craned over her shoulder to look at me, a grin thinning her lips.

"I think she's put a mattress in yer room."

"Is the spare room...?"

"Full of furniture again."

"Oh crap." I leaned back and realized Trystan was peering up at me, a puzzled look on his face. I dropped a hand over my face and wondered how I was going to resist him when he was staying in my room.

"You need to go take down the gay porno?" asked Trystan, and Jorja and Theo sniggered.

I was busy considering whether it was possible to die from lust in two days.

Theo left at about eleven with a wave and a promise to see us tomorrow. Jorja pottered off to her room in the attic, and I led Trystan through the house to the room at the back that was tucked into the hill my parents' house was built against. One of the walls was still raw, rough grit stone, the others were clean and white, and the roof sloped slowly into the stone wall at the back. It was plain and unadorned except for a couple of family pictures and a diagram of different climbing knots.

My dad had brought the mattress from the bed in the spare room—that was currently full of antique furniture my mum had bought from random house sales to clean up and sell off—and it was on the floor made up with a duvet decorated with pale pink roses. My bed was a regular double: it seemed excessively large compared to the single mattress and yet impressively small if I considered having to share it with another full-grown guy—who I really needed not to touch.

"No need to look so scared," Trystan whispered into my ear and skimmed his hand over the small of my back.

I pressed the door shut behind us, and the click was surprisingly loud in the silence of the countryside. Outside the sound of an owl screeching pierced the thick stone walls of my room. I turned to Trystan and grinned at him as I reached for his lips with mine. I let my hands slide down his spine, my fingers slipping and sliding over the ridges of his back and then diving beneath the waistband of his trousers. I let my hand slide deeper and squeeze beneath the elastic of his boxers to clutch at the flesh of his ass, and I tugged him against me as I grinned into his lips.

"If ye try anything, Trys, I swear I'll take yer virgin ass right here. So please, try something, because I'm starting t' fancy fucking someone...." I pressed another kiss against his lips, pulled away, and got ready for bed.

Saturday morning was one of those mornings where I woke up with perfect clarity. I knew I was in my tiny but comfortable double bed at my parents' house, and I knew that despite sending Trystan to sleep on the mattress, he was currently spooned around my back. I wanted to be angry with him, but I knew the mattress from the spare bed was lumpy and too short for someone Trystan's size. Just like I also knew that the size or uncomfortableness of the mattress had nothing to do with why Trystan had got into my bed. So I wanted to be annoyed, but instead the sensation of him pressed up against my spine and his hands wrapped possessively around my chest filled me with a strange sensation that made it really difficult to be angry, which in turn made it really difficult not to get turned on.

I tried to shuffle away, but my attempt was met with a tightening of the arms around my chest, a sleepy chuckle in my ear, and Trystan's hips pressed more tightly against my arse. I tried not to moan.

"Not funny, Trys," I muttered as I tried once again to pull away.

"Who said I was trying to be funny?"

One of Trystan's hands slid down my chest, nudged its way under the waistband of my pajama bottoms, and wrapped itself around my rapidly hardening cock.

"Ye are *so* dead," I cursed as I tried to gulp down the groan of lust that was attempting to escape from my lips. My complaint wasn't particularly convincing because my hips had taken on a mind of their own and were rolling back into Trystan's groin in time with his thrusts. And right then I suddenly didn't give a damn where we were, as long as the feelings curling inside of me didn't go away. I was beyond caring as I ground back into him and arched up into his hand, gasping and swallowing down thick gulps of air so that I didn't shout out as I was drawn down through layer after layer of pleasure. Trystan was hard at my back, and he was tugging down the thin cotton covering my ass, and my God I was going to let him fuck me in my parents' house with no lube and no condom, and I honestly didn't give a shit.

This man at my back made me crazy, and I didn't care.

"Ide, you want a brew?" I froze as my dad's words wove through from the other side of my bedroom door, slicing through my lust with the perfection that only being caught by your parents really can.

"Oh, ye are *so* fricking *dead* when we get home, Trystan," I whispered as I sucked down air into the bottom of my lungs.

"Yeah, thanks, Dad, I'll be out in a minute," I said at a more normal volume and could only hope the slightly gravelly tone to my voice would be interpreted as me having just woken up rather than anything else.

I wrapped my hand around Trystan's wrist and pulled it away from my groin, and then I rolled over and wrapped the fingers of my other hand around the firm lines of his jaw as I stared into his face. I was slightly glad to see that he looked just a little bit pissed off at the interruption.

"I can only assume," I said slowly as I leaned in and skimmed a ghost of a kiss over the fine stubble on his chin and the flushed skin of his lips, "that this means ye *want* me t' fuck ye." I ran my tongue over my lips as the idea sufficed to make my cock throb yet again. "Well dun worry, Trys; I'll see t' yer sweet virgin ass as soon as we're home." I brought my lips to a stop against his ear. "Ye might want t' book Monday off work."

And with that I chucked a leg over him and pressed a chaste kiss against his stubbled cheek as I rolled my weight onto my other leg and ended up standing at the edge of the bed. I glanced down at my hips, where my cock was still impatiently demanding that we carry on with what Trystan had initiated. Unfortunately, if I didn't turn up in the kitchen soon, my dad was going to bring the tea to me, and I really did *not* want him to walk in to see Trystan in my bed.

I chucked on one of the old T-shirts I kept at home and a pair of jeans. Trystan was lying on his back watching me through hooded eyes, and he looked sexy and frustrated.

"Serves ye fricking right," I grumbled, blew him a mocking kiss, and went through to the kitchen.

"I was just about to bring it to you," my dad said as he nodded toward the steaming mug of tea on the side without looking up from his newspaper.

"Ta, Dad," I said as I scooped up the tea and sipped at it as I riffled through the kitchen. I found a loaf of my mum's homemade bread and cut myself a chunk before sitting at the table to load it up with butter and jam. "How was the quiz?"

"Same as usual; we always do awfully but your mum likes to go, so...." Thanks to the barest edges of a Swedish accent, my dad's voice is strangely emotionless and yet oddly melodic. He shrugged as he folded his newspaper. I glanced up and realized that the pale blue eyes I had inherited from him were considering me, unblinking, across the kitchen table.

"I'm glad to see that you and Trystan are getting along again."

I tried not to look too surprised.

"Well it was too much hassle not getting along when we've ended up living together," I replied slowly. I was wondering how he had worked out we were getting along when he'd only seen us together for all of five minutes when we got in last night.

My dad continued to stare, his face unchanging.

"Your boss sent me some of the pictures from that shoot you did together."

What? Oh my God, I was going to kill Meredith. I was honestly going to refuse her money and her tears and her begging.

"That's just work, Dad," I said carefully and looked at my tea.

"Well, that's fine, and if it wasn't, that's fine too. Trystan is a nice boy."

And if you're thinking that this response is a bit tame considering the big deal I had been making about it—that was very, *very* extreme for my dad.

I could only pray that he hadn't said anything to my mum.

"Dad," I began slowly, "Trys and me are just living together."

"That's fine, Idrys, everything's fine as long as you're happy." I risked a glance up at my dad and resisted the temptation to groan, because he was actually smiling. My dad never smiled.

He proceeded to smile faintly the whole time we went about the morning chores. And wasn't that just fricking wonderful.

When I got back into the kitchen a few hours later, Trystan was sitting at the table with my sister drinking coffee and tucking into a bacon sandwich that was filling the small room with its gorgeous salty tang. I grinned as a plate containing a similar sandwich was handed to me by my mum, and I sat down to devour it.

"I didn't realize you were getting up to work. You could have told me. I would've helped," Trystan grumbled. He looked a little irked, and I wasn't sure whether it was from me leaving him to sleep or leaving him to stew. Well the latter served him right, so I just smiled and shrugged.

"Would've taken longer t' explain what needed t' be done," I said between mouthfuls of bacon and soft fluffy bread.

Trystan still looked slightly peeved, and I chuckled at him.

"If yer so desperate t' help, ye can give us a hand this evening. But it's really not that exciting, Trys," I said and then I realized that my mum and sister were staring at me with odd looks on their faces. I scowled at my sister, and she flicked her eyebrows up her forehead in a look of mock innocence before turning back to her food to try and hide her amusement.

"What?" I hissed at her across the table when our mum and dad finally left the kitchen.

She sat back and crossed her arms across her chest, and her nonchalant façade cracked a little when she let her eyes drift over to Trystan.

"Nothing," she replied in a way that left me in no doubt that it was anything *but* nothing.

"No, it wasn't nothing. What were ye going t' say?"

Jorja rolled her eyes and shot another brief, and amused, look in Trystan's direction. "Mam and Dad aren't idiots, Ide. If ye want t' keep it a secret, ye should be more careful."

I thought about my dad's words to me this morning and his completely out-of-character smile, and grimaced.

"Careful about what?" I asked anyway.

My sister stared at me, and I could see her trying really hard not to burst into fits of laughter as once again her eyes flicked over to Trystan.

I looked at him too, but he was just sitting pretending to pay attention to the newspaper while he finished his coffee.

"About looking at Trys like yer fricking besotted wi' the guy," my sister said softly as she turned back to me with a dark gleam in her pale eyes.

I sat back in my chair and held my sister's gaze. "Whatever, Jorja."

Like Trystan winding me up about that wasn't bad enough, now I was going to get it from my sister too?

"The only reason I don't want Mum and Dad to know is so they don't get pissed with me when I dump the guy's ass, so don't give me that shit."

Jorja's face dropped a little and she turned a concerned look to Trystan, who gave a wry little chuckle that turned Jorja's worry to confusion.

"Wow, yer actually as mental as Ide, aren't ye?" she said to Trystan with a shake of her head. Then she sent a final dark look in my direction. "Ye two going t' be together long enough t' come for a bike ride this afternoon?"

"Sure, sounds like fun," I agreed. Trystan nodded, and conversation turned to which of the many spare bikes would be most suitable for Trystan.

I joined in, but my head wasn't completely in it.

Besotted? *Seriously*? I mean I'd already admitted that I kind of liked Trystan, and not just the sex—which got no complaints, regardless. But *besotted*? I considered Trystan as we chatted about bikes and which of our favorite routes would still be rideable at this time of year. He caught me staring, and a little smirk curled on the edge of his lips.

Liking the guy was one thing, but *besotted…* wasn't that just another word for love?

There was no fricking way I was in love with the arrogant bastard. No fricking way.

I LEANED against the door to my damp-stained attic room and stared at the ceiling. The rest of the weekend at my parents hadn't gone badly, exactly. It had contained all the things I generally enjoyed about going home: eating too much food, helping about the farm, getting out on the bikes with Theo, and having a—long overdue—catch up with my sister.

Yet her words on Saturday morning had lurked at the back of my mind the whole time, making me consider every look or comment I sent in Trystan's direction.

Because I did not want to be in love, or even falling in love. And I definitely did not want to be doing it with a guy who was still insisting he was bisexual and was likely to decide to switch back to women as soon as he won a bet and got bored with my ass.

My phone rang in my back pocket and I tugged it out, glad for the distraction from my thoughts. However the caller ID made me sigh lightly.

"Hey, Dan." I pulled my hair back off my face, dumped my holdall, and sat on the edge of my bed.

"*Ide, how you doing? I was starting to wonder if you were ignoring me,*" he chatted lightly, and there was no double meaning behind the words because why would Dan ever have reason to think I was ignoring him? Other people had come and gone, but in more than two years, we had always ended up back with each other. I had a sudden flash of realization as I imagined what it must be like for Dan these days, watching me sleep with other guys when he was in love with me and now not even able to see me.

"I've been at my parents' this weekend."

"*Nice time? You make up with your sister?*" I murmured an affirmative. "*What you up to tonight? Fancy coming out for a quick drink?*"

I glanced at the time. It was almost eight and it was a Sunday night, so wherever Dan fancied going was probably going to be quiet. I wondered if Trystan would be annoyed, then got irritated with myself for thinking about it. And then I was thinking about what Theo had said.

"Yeah sure, where d'ye fancy?"

"*The pub round the corner from mine, half an hour?*"

"Sure, see ye in a bit." I hung up and really disliked the odd fluttering sensation in my stomach.

"Trys?" I stuck my head around his bedroom door, and he glanced up, looking apprehensive, which was odd for him. "I'm going out for an hour."

His odd look didn't go away, and he held my eyes for a moment.

"It's just Dan…." The words slipped out of my mouth before I could stop them. I watched his hand tighten around the handle of the bag he had been unpacking.

A surge of irritation washed through me. And it was as much for my reaction as it was for his.

"Why do I even fricking bother?" I slammed Trystan's door shut between us before he could respond.

Outside I drove my hands into my pockets and tried to calm the angry beating of my heart as I walked beneath the orange glow of streetlights.

"Hey, stranger." Dan wrapped an arm around my shoulders and pressed a neutral kiss against my cheek. I'd walked here on autopilot. When I'd answered the phone to him half an hour ago, I'd fully intended to take this opportunity to tell him about me and Trystan. I was going to tell him and break the heart of the guy who, other than Theo, was my closest friend.

For Trystan?

For a guy who no matter his pretty words and smug smirk couldn't even trust me to go out for an hour. He hadn't said anything—he didn't need to. I had seen that look enough times to recognize it: the flicker of doubt of me and those around me.

Dan let me go with a chuckle, and I sat down in front of a pint he'd already got me. And right then I wanted this. I had enough awkwardness and confusion at home with Trystan. I wanted this selfless, easy friendship. I didn't want to stare into Dan's eyes and see pain or resignation or weariness. I wanted the look that he had always given me, easygoing acceptance of exactly who I was.

He pulled me against him, and despite the fact that I was taller than him, he tucked me under his arm, forcing me to half lounge down the bench we were on. We'd been here a few times and the management had no problem with us, but a few of the customers shot us a mixture of curious and disapproving looks.

"You seem stressed. I thought you said you sorted out the shit with your sister?"

"Oh… yeah we did, but…."

"This got anything to do with that new housemate of yours? Trystan? He looked like trouble."

I couldn't help but chuckle at that, and I tilted my head up to meet Dan's mocking disapproval.

"When will you ever learn, eh?" He leaned down and pressed a kiss against my lips. It was just a gentle caress of his lips against mine.

I jerked up and away from him, ignoring Dan's startled look as I scowled at nothing and took a long gulp of my beer.

Because I hadn't felt "nothing."

But what I had felt *hadn't* been desire. Or lust. Or even the faint affection I'd recently felt when Dan kissed me.

Instead my stomach had churned and my breath had frozen in my lungs, sending a pulse of simmering discomfort through my limbs.

I swallowed down the awkward wave of nausea that was closing my throat off and drank some more beer. I dropped my head into my hands and my elbows on my knees.

Next to me Dan shifted to rest his palm in the small of my back.

"Sorry, Ide. I didn't mean to push you or anything, I...." He took a deep breath and I heard it slip out between his lips as a soft sigh.

Guilt churned through my stomach: guilt that I was letting Dan think I was still getting over an attack I hadn't even told him fully about, guilt that I had betrayed Trystan's trust. And disgust at myself wove it all together.

"Shit, sorry, Dan, it's not—"

"Don't worry about it," Dan cut me off with a faint smile and a gentle hint of pressure in the small of my back. "Come on, tell me about your weekend."

I knew I should tell him.

I knew this was the perfect time.

But the words never left my lips. Instead we spent the hour chatting about the weekend I'd just spent with my family. And about the ridiculous new cocktail that Dan had to learn to make because it was a new fad. And about what stupid things Ashlie had said when Dan had been out with him last weekend.

And then it was late and Dan was saying he had to head off because he had an early shift tomorrow and he pressed a chaste kiss against my cheek and a brief hug around my shoulders and he was waving good-bye.

It was about half ten when I walked home with my hands thrust in my pockets. But for the return journey, instead of anger, the sluggish motes of guilt returned to curl their way up through my lungs.

The light was still on in Trystan's room when I got back. I pressed the front door closed behind me and then a hand was wrapping around my wrist. I stumbled briefly but I was caught and bundled into the front bedroom. Hands were running down my back, trying to remove all space between mine and Trystan's bodies as I fought to suck air into my lungs because his mouth was covering mine. I was forced up against a wall, my body sandwiched between it and Trystan as he jammed his leg between mine and his teeth worried my lips as his tongue drove into my mouth, claiming it as his.

And it felt so fricking good.

I mumbled something wordless into the kiss as my hands came up to pull Trystan closer still, as I let my body melt in against him.

I was addicted to him and to the feelings he stirred in me.

With a grimace I pushed him off me and tried not to frown as I caught my breath.

This was stupid. I was exaggerating. Whatever this was between us was just regular lust.

And when he left me I'd be fine.

Trystan didn't frown exactly as he leaned forward to press a quick chaste kiss against my lips. Even that sent little messenger bundles of sensation down through my body.

"Ah, I have a nine o'clock," I muttered as I tried not to scowl at the worn carpet.

Several emotions flashed in quick succession across Trystan's dark eyes, and it finished with annoyance.

"For fuck's sake, Ide, did you fuck him? You said you would let me know, at least give me a fucking chance."

He didn't shout; in fact, he sounded more resigned than furious, but I felt irritation bristle inside me anyway.

I stared at him through hard, pale eyes.

The contorted tension Dan's kiss had caused inside of me returned as I raised my hands to Trystan's shoulders and firmly pressed him away from me. He stumbled a bit, but didn't resist.

"Go to hell, Trystan," I whispered and I sidestepped out of his embrace as he stared at me. Then with a last withering look, I turned and left his room.

It really fucking hurt to breathe. I could feel anger burning up inside of me as I took the stairs on autopilot.

What the hell had I expected to happen? Had I really been so fricking stupid as to think I could tell him a couple of stories and he would suddenly trust me? I was the idiot here for giving any weight to the shit that the guy had spouted these past few days. Given what he knew about me, trusting me would make him a moron.

And hadn't letting myself be kissed by Dan just proved him right?

"Fuck...." I slid down the wall inside my bedroom door as it clicked shut behind me and dropped my forehead to rest against my knees.

Kissing Dan had felt bloody awful.

Trystan's lips against mine had caused an explosion of relief and desire and something hot and frighteningly tender.

I pressed my fingertips to my head as I groaned. How the hell had I been so stupid? I knew better than this. This is what I knew was going to happen. This was what always happened.

So why did it hurt so fricking much?

I wondered absently who had won the sweepstakes.

And what my dad's face would look like when he realized I'd messed up again.

And in the end, didn't it just serve me right?

My phone buzzed and absently I pulled it out of my pocket. A dark and weary chuckle wove its way out of my chest as I answered the call.

"Jorja."

"What're ye laughing for ye fricking idiot? I cannot believe ye dared to spout me all that shit on Friday and then went straight home and screwed it all up. Yer such a twat, Idrys."

"Nice to know I've got someone on my side."

"Fuck off, Ide. I am on yer side; the only fricking reason Trystan talks to me about ye is because all of his friends quite rightly think yer a complete fricking wanker and that he should steer well clear of ye. Unfortunately I'm related to ye, so I feel obliged not to be instantly dismissive."

My sister paused, clearly waiting for me to defend myself.

"Come on, Ide, give me a fucking crumb, something t' work wi'."

"I don't need my fricking prude of a sister as a relationship coach."

"*Oh... ye absolute arsehole. And yer such a contradictory twat, would ye prefer me to be like ye? But no, ye want me to be wi' Theo, so ye think he'd like it if I spent my years at uni sleeping round do ye?*"

"Don't pretend like yer saving yerself for him. Ye don't even like him."

"*Don't ye fucking try and tell me what I'm doing, Idrys, or who I like.*"

"Well right back at ye, Jorja! I didn't fricking sleep with Dan. Did either of ye feel like clarifying that before ye started judging me? No, ye both just asked the question and assumed the fricking answer, so fuck ye both."

"*Oh—my—fucking—God! Why the hell did ye not just* tell *him that, ye complete and utter moron!*" My sister was shouting at me down the phone, and she sounded completely exasperated.

"What's the point, Jorja?" My tone was dismissive, and it was taking all my self-control not to just hang up on her. "Because eventually it probably will be true, and because of that he's never going to trust me, and I just can't be arsed."

"*Ide, ye—*"

"No, Jorja," I interrupted softly. "Just leave it, all right? I'm sorry for calling ye a prude, but seriously, I don't want or *need* yer help. This thing between me and Trys was going one way only, we both knew it; it's just gone that way faster than we expected, is all. So just... I'm not going to tell ye not to talk to him. But stay out of this, understand?"

"*Yer such a fucking head case, Idrys.*" But her words were followed by a resigned sigh. "*Just don't leave it four months again, eh?*"

"Sure thing."

"*Love ye, Ide.*"

"And ye." I hung up. I dropped my head back down over my knees and breathed slowly.

Now everything could go back to normal.

16—SQUIRREL

NORMAL WAS kind of boring. It entailed me waking up in my own bed on Monday morning. I stared at the ceiling while I floated in that innocent moment between waking and sleeping where certain facts elude you, and thought that it was kind of cold.

Then I remembered that I wouldn't be sharing my bed with possessive southern men anymore.

And life ticked on by as usual.

It really wasn't an exciting day. I walked past Trystan's locked door to go to the kitchen to get my breakfast, and I walked right by it to go upstairs again. I passed it on my way out of the house to lectures, and I walked straight by it when I got in again that afternoon. He was at work anyway, so I had no reason to be bothered by a rectangle of wood.

I had an essay to write for next week that I should've probably got on with, but instead I lay on my bed and stared at an episode of *Top Gear* on iPlayer.

My phone went and I gave a weary shake of my head when I saw the unknown number.

"Hello?" I answered simply, because even though it was almost certainly a modeling job I didn't want, I had learned my lesson about answering with a rant.

"*Idrys? It's Meredith.*"

Well that was a surprise, although I wasn't sure whether it was a good one or not. It was, after all, still a modeling job. After James I had told my agency I didn't want anything at the moment, even Meredith's well-paying shoots, and despite feeling better, I'd not got around to telling them that I was happy to take work again. I hit pause on my laptop and dropped to sit on the floor propped up on the side of my bed.

"Hi, Meredith, how'd ye get my number?"

"*Ah, well, I asked your dad for it.*"

I gave a roll of my eyes. "Of course ye did. Speaking of which, I cannot believe ye sent him pictures of me and Trystan. I've told ye to check wi' me before ye send him anything."

"I know, but you were out of contact and the agency wouldn't give me an e-mail or number or anything so I just went with it. They were cute."

"Yeah, well." I kept my tone droll and tried not to think too hard about the subject of our conversation or the anxious pain thinking about him caused in my chest. "Trystan is the not-out-of-the-closet son of one of my dad's oldest friends...."

"Ooh, okay. Crap." She had the decency to sound sincere at least. *"Sorry about that."*

"Hmm, it's done now, just check next time, yeah?"

"Yes, sorry again, Idrys. Next time, you say? Does this mean you're going to start working again? I'm sorry to be pushy, but I have this job coming up that I just know you would be perfect for, and I don't want to book anyone else before making certain that you cannot be persuaded to do it."

I laughed lightly down the phone that this was Meredith's idea of trying not to be pushy.

"I can offer you a little more money?"

"No, Meredith, it's fine, I don't need any more money. I didn't stop because of that."

"Well, yes, you sounded... never mind, I'm glad you're well again now. When are you free?"

"All my weekends are okay up 'til Christmas."

"Fabulous, I'll call your agency and organize it through them anyway." She gave a relieved sigh down the phone, and I wondered, not for the first time, why she put up with me. *"And shall you be bringing along the lovely Trystan? He did make your eyes sparkle something wonderful."* She sounded happy and mischievous, and I remembered Trystan saying she had worked out that he liked me. Then again, I also remembered him saying he would trust me.

I forced my chest to expand and pull the stifling air into the bottom of my lungs.

"No sparkling there anymore, sorry, Meredith."

"Oh, what a shame." She did sound genuinely surprised and just a little sad, and I wondered why when she had met Trystan all of twice. *"You were lovely together."*

"I'm sure ye can find someone else with his coloring."

"Of course. Well, I'll be off. See you soon, Idrys."

I smiled absently at the phone in my hand, lost in my thoughts and the churning of my stomach. I should get up and start *Top Gear* again or begin work on that essay. Instead, I sat on the floor and stared at the blank screen of my phone.

My head twisted round of its own accord as the handle to my room went.

I don't really know who I expected, because there was only one person who wouldn't knock. Still, I stared at him blankly as Trystan appeared in the doorway.

Why couldn't I remember to just lock the damn thing?

I let my head loll back onto the bed and stared up at the ceiling as my mind was flooded with a thousand thoughts that it couldn't sort through because my heart rate felt like it had just plunged and skyrocketed at the same time, and the whole thing left me feeling suddenly exhausted.

"What d'ye want, Trys? Have ye come for all the juicy details, like the old days?" I kept my voice low and my eyes fixed on his, and I was well aware that what I was saying made it sound like something had actually happened. I twisted my head so I could fix him with a mocking smile, but he just continued to stare down at me.

"We went to a bar." Nonchalance was surprisingly easy to feign. I held him in my gaze, and an elaborate lie danced on the end of my tongue. I would tell him that we had a drink, that I had gone back to Dan's, that I had fucked him in the doorway to his house. The lie would be easy, because it wasn't like I didn't have memories of doing exactly that to work from.

But I stared at him. And the lie wouldn't come out.

"Yer such a tosser," I said instead, and my tone was harsh but weary. "I went there to tell him about us, ye know. But I *didn't* because I was pissed at ye for *doubting* me, and because Dan is my friend and I didn't want t' hurt him. And he kissed me. I didn't let him, but I didn't stop him either, and I hated it." I was angry at him for doubting me and with myself for even letting myself get to the point where I cared.

"That enough for ye? Or would ye like a blow by blow of our conversation too? Or maybe ye would only be happy if ye could check my ass…. But of course it's a bit late and there's no way to tell if *I've* fucked *him*, so I guess yer screwed."

Trystan was scowling at me, his frown getting deeper with every word that came from my lips.

With a final grimace, he stepped through into the room and pressed the door closed behind him. I watched him as he came round the edge of the bed and dropped into a squat in front of me.

"I'm sorry," he said simply as he held my gaze in his.

I just stared back at him, and he gave a weary sigh and ran a hand back through his dark hair.

"Fuck, Ide, I'm sorry, but…. I mean there's no excuse. I really am trying to trust you…. I *do* trust you." His gaze flicked back to mine, and then he dropped his forehead to rest against my bent knees.

"If you tell me you haven't done anything, then I believe you," he muttered quietly. "I don't want to just give you some lame excuses, but I'm a possessive guy, Ide.

"When you told me you were going to see him, it wasn't that I didn't trust you, but rather I was *jealous* that he'd get to spend time with you when we'd had so little over the weekend. And it annoyed me that I seem to want you more than you want me: you hardly bat an eyelid this weekend at your parents, while I could hardly stop myself from pushing you down and fucking you against every wall we saw regardless of who was there." He gave a wry little chuckle that held no amusement. "Plus I was—*am*—seriously freaking out about bottoming for you. And when you shut me down… *fuck*, you've never shut me down, Ide, not here, not for no reason. I just… my head short-circuited and my mouth opened and that shit came out."

I stared at the top of Trystan's head where its faint pressure rested against my knee.

He lifted his face, finally meeting my gaze with his. He held it for a moment and gave a small sigh when his search found nothing but me staring blankly back. He shifted away from me. And he was getting back to his feet before I'd had a chance to pull the frown from my face or get the words out that I needed to say. And he was walking toward the door, his shoulders slightly bowed.

The defeated look didn't suit him at all.

Shit…. I had said I would fuck Trystan because of that little stunt he pulled on Saturday morning. I'd completely forgotten about it, and he'd been stressing.

What the hell was wrong with my chest?

It wasn't like I'd never fucked a virgin before; I'd just never had to care about anything other than the physical shit, never mind the mental prep that must come with suddenly switching teams.

I stared at his back and there was that weird tension feeling again. It felt a bit like lust, but it was higher up on my spine, just between the points of my shoulder blades. It had that same tingling slightly electric feeling, just softer and somehow more intense.

I was on my feet, rounding the end of the bed in two quick steps. I hooked a hand around his waist, twisting him round to face me just as he was about to reach for the door handle.

I didn't even have time to feel embarrassed about the words that were about to come out of my mouth.

"Can ye trust me when I say it's only ye that I want t' sleep wi'? I still feel nothing for anyone else."

It was my turn to stare down the blank look, but I gave him time and the resignation in his eyes softened just a little. I felt the tension beneath my hand relax slightly as he gave the smallest inclination of his head. I stepped a little closer to him, holding his gaze and giving him a soft smile.

"I'm sorry, too, for flipping out and not explaining. It's just... fricking hell—" I sealed my lips over his. Kissing him was easier than trying to explain that it was easier to assume Trystan was just the same as everyone else. Because thinking that he wasn't was terrifying.

"Just so ye know." I drew away just enough to murmur breathless words against his lips. "Keeping my hands off ye at the weekend was killing me." I wasn't quite ready to explain that my sister's words had also had a part to play in my odd mood that weekend, but Trystan's air of dejectedness was retreating. With my hands resting against the firm muscles of his waist, I could see the dark smirk returning to his lips as he stared at me.

I needed to say this quickly, because I didn't think I could say it to smug Trystan.

"As for the sex thing...." I swallowed and forced myself to meet his eyes, and then I kissed him again, softer and swifter this time. "I know what I said, but I don't want ye t' stress about it. It's supposed to be fun; yer supposed t' want it. So if yer really that bothered, I'll leave it be for now."

I had never, *ever* said that to anyone. If I wanted a fuck, I'd fuck, and even if they weren't that into bottoming, I'd railroad them into it. I was good at topping, I always made sure my partners got off, but that was because watching someone squirm in pain doesn't do anything for me, not because I really cared.

But I wanted Trystan to want me; I craved that look of glazed lust I had seen on his face so many times when he took me. I wanted it to be on his face while I fingered him and spread him and pressed into him. And I wanted that look because I knew it would only be mine. I could horde it away, and no one else would ever be able to have it.

Wait, *what*? When had I started thinking like that?

My confused thought was sidetracked as the idea of him begging for my cock sent little fireworks of excitement and lust dancing through my stomach, a feeling that was completely inappropriate given that we were just making up, and he'd just told me he was worried about exactly that.

But I stared into those satin brown eyes of his and he looked... what? Kind of disappointed?

A slow smile spread itself over my lips. I couldn't believe what I was thinking about. Because the idea I'd just had definitely wasn't going to help me to get over the borderline too-intense feelings I was having.

No, the thought made that odd feeling in my chest pulse and sent a little prickly shimmer out along my limbs. But I didn't care right then, because the idea of getting Trystan to beg for me was enough to drown out the little warning voice at the back of my head.

I leaned in to scoop my hand around the back of Trystan's neck, I pulled his reluctant form closer to me, and I kissed him gently. I think he was a little startled, because the only gentle kiss we had exchanged had been the one initiated by him last weekend.

"Guess I need t' trust ye too," I whispered against his lips as I broke the kiss but left our lips touching slightly so my sight was full of his eyes and the warmth that filled them.

"You're such a pain in the ass." He pulled my lips back against his.

I urged him back against the door, letting my hand slip down his neck and the other rest against his hip as I kissed him as softly as I could manage. I could feel his lingering nervousness between our lips. It was heady, and I hadn't really anticipated how hard it would be not to grind down into him and mash my body against his and paw at every piece of flesh I could find.

I pulled away with a deep shuddering breath and stared at an equally breathless Trystan. A faint ember of irritation rekindled in his eyes as he stared at me.

"You think you can just kiss me and expect me to forget you shot me down?"

"Who said I was just going t' kiss ye?" I grinned and pressed another kiss against his flushed lips.

I'd enjoyed the last week of being completely dominated by this guy. But staring at him as I pulled away again—with his cheeks flushed as he leaned back against the wall, under me—definitely reawakened the part of me that up until this point had been happy to sit back and bask in the pretty impressive orgasms. But it was out now. I stared at Trystan and straightened to use my extra centimeter of height to my full advantage so I could reach down to kiss him.

He wanted to be fucked: that flicker of disappointment had definitely told me that. He just needed to admit it to himself first. And it was probably going to kill me, but I was going to help him realize it.

I kissed him with my body held over him, and I didn't let him take charge. I grabbed his hands as he brought them up to touch me and pinned them against the wall as I drove my tongue into his mouth, tasting him. I hummed lightly at the back of my throat as he struggled slightly, then gave up trying to free his arms and just pressed his body up into me instead.

God that was hot. How had I thought it was normal to live without that?

I groaned as he arched his back to roll his hips against mine. This man was definitely going to kill me.

"Come here." I tugged him away from the door as I broke the kiss, backing us across the room and toward my bed. I twisted slightly and threw him down across the duvet with a smile tugging at my lips for the mixture of apprehension and lust that dusted his face. I only wanted one of those emotions.

"Relax, Trys." I crawled over him, pinning him underneath me as I brought my mouth up to his neck. I made short work of his shirt and moved swiftly onto his jeans as I kissed him deeply. I had to stop undressing him a few times to press his hands away from my own clothes. And finally I knew why Dan got so annoyed with me when I didn't just lie there and behave like a good passive catcher.

"What're you doing, Ide?" His voice was low and slightly breathy as I pushed his hands away yet again and finally stripped him of his last item of clothing, leaving him naked and gorgeous and me fully clothed. I sat back on my ankles and took a moment to appreciate the gift I had unwrapped.

"Just looking," I replied with an honest grin.

Hell, he was actually divine; just looking at him like that made my blood hum slightly. His neck and shoulders and chest had a pleasant hint of a tan, the muscles that shifted beneath were nicely defined, and all of it was dusted with a faint red blush where I'd worked his skin with my lips and teeth. His stomach—that perfect balance of just enough muscle to give definition but nothing too over the top—led down to tidy hips where his dick waited for my touch, half-hard from my kisses. I bit my lip and made a small rumble of appreciation as I dropped back down over him. I went straight for his cock and made him jerk slightly in surprise. I palmed him slowly while I pressed kisses down the ridge of hair that ran from his belly button to his cock, then down his thighs.

My own cock was responding, pressing uncomfortably against my jeans, begging for something to relieve the pressure that had been building since the start of the weekend. But I was going to have to wait, because even if I undressed just to get myself off, I wasn't sure I would be able to resist the gorgeous body that was now writhing under my hands and begging for me to wrap my mouth around him.

"Fucking hell, Ide." Trystan's confused curse was music to my ears as I finally pressed my lips around his cock and worked him at a leisurely pace that would build him up but wouldn't get him off. His hand went for my head, pressing down, urging me on like he usually did. And God, part of me wanted to just let him take control. Instead I brought my hand up, wrapped it around his wrist, and tugged his fingers from me. Driving that hand into the duvet, I held it there. I glanced up and met his eyes. I could see him working out what was going on, and that flash of apprehension returned. I smiled at him around his cock and deliberately held his gaze as I used my free hand to push his knees up and then reach between his ass cheeks.

"Calm down, Trys. I've been here before, remember?" I whispered as I released his erection from between my lips. Catching a bit of the leftover moisture, I pressed my finger lightly against the ribbed hole that was hidden between the firm globes of his ass. He'd stopped trying to get his hand free and had gone a little slack, his face screwed up in a mixture of leftover lust and what was definitely something verging on fear. He'd been a little drunk last time, and I hadn't been able to see his face, but I really hoped that he hadn't been this scared.

"I'm not going to fuck ye, Trys," I whispered lightly as I ran my tongue up the underside of his still bobbing cock, while my finger kept up gentle but firm pressure around the ridged hole.

His groan did not help the throbbing pressure in my hips.

I wasn't going to fuck him, but fricking hell I really wanted to. I wanted to press my fingers inside of him, stretch him slowly, bring him right to the edge over and over while I took my sweet time with him. And then I wanted to bury my cock inside his ass that I knew would be almost too tight and absolutely divine, and I wanted to drive him back to the edge and show him exactly how amazing it was to be gay.

But I wasn't going to. I massaged his ass while I toyed with his cock, and I waited for that lingering tension to unwind. Then I made sure my finger was coated in as much saliva as it would hold and pressed a little more firmly. I felt his muscles flicker and release and then my finger was inside of him. I held it still and increased my work on his cock while he got used to it.

"See, no different than last time," I whispered as I lifted off his cock again to check his response. I kind of wish I hadn't, because Trystan's face was screwed up, and as I looked down on him I could see the trembling tension in his spine. And it wasn't in a bad way.

"Nnnn, much better… than… last time." He shuddered between his words, and I could see the little jerking movements in his hips that were him trying to hold himself still.

I sucked in a very deep breath and folded over on myself so I couldn't look at him anymore, because my cock had just made a very loud complaint about its current constricted position while my head had gently suggested a much better constricted position it would rather take up. I dropped my mouth back over Trystan's erection, and his strangled gasp didn't help, nor did the uncontrolled jerk of his hips right to the back of my throat, or the ripple of pressure around my finger. But concentrating *did* help and I ravaged his cock with my mouth as my finger curled and I started gentle movements that would loosen… only I couldn't think about that, so I just concentrated on finding his prostate.

That didn't help much either, because the noises he made were rumbling straight through my cock. I was honestly wondering if I was turned on enough to climax without any stimulation at all as Trystan begged me to let him come.

The begging was divine; his voice was low and desperate and broken by moans, and God how I wanted him to beg for my cock inside of him. My hips were arching and grinding against nothing, pressing my erection into my own jeans, and I was so turned on that it was almost enough to get me off.

"Oh... fucking hell.... Ide, make it... just let... fuck." Trystan's voice was pained and gorgeous. I felt his ass ripple around my finger, and he was pressing down into my hand almost as much as he was arching up into my mouth, and with a last thought for my sanity, I picked up my pace just enough to finally drive him the rest of the way into his orgasm.

He shouted something incomprehensible as his cock shuddered in my mouth. And Holy Mother of God, his ass was so hot and so fricking tight around my finger as I swallowed down the hot rich cords of his pleasure.

I stayed where I was for a few minutes after I had finally licked him clean. I had to, because I was still dancing along the edge of my self-control, especially with the way his ass continued to spasm around the digit still pressed inside of him.

"Ide?" Trystan's voice was hoarse and questioning as he lifted his head to look down at me.

"Nnnn" was all I was able to mutter back. I took a deep breath. Fricking hell, his muted gasp as I finally withdrew my finger *did not help*. I pressed my eyes shut as I sat back on my heels and then I heard him sitting up and.... Fuck. He was climbing on top of me, his bare ass spreading over my lap as his hands came round my back and his mouth found mine.

I pushed him hastily away, and as I opened my eyes, I was met with confusion.

"Sorry, Trys, I'm just a bit... on edge."

His confused frown morphed into a grin, and he crawled back over to me.

"Think you can control yourself while I help you out?" He was hurrying at my jeans and I groaned unintelligibly as he freed me and wrapped his mouth instantly around the seeping, sopping head of my dick. And I had the most amazing view of his ass as he bobbed down over me. I didn't last more than a minute until I was jacking up into his throat and whimpering at the beautiful unfurling of pressure.

OH—MY—*fricking*—God. I had no idea how I had resisted Trystan for so long before. I had no idea how I had gone four whole weeks without a fuck. And I had absolutely no idea if I was going to be able to survive another five minutes, never mind however bloody long it was going to take Trystan to give in. The last time we'd had sex had been the Thursday before we went to my parents... oh God, I was so bloody ridiculous. Just thinking about it was actually making my blood thicken, a situation that was not at all helped by the fact that currently my lips were carefully, gently—and bloody infuriatingly—caressing the lips of the object of my desire as I struggled to hold his hands away from my body. I had to keep pushing Trystan's hands off me and ignoring his increasingly aggravated commands when all I really wanted to do was comply.

It was now Friday and given the options of pushing him down and devouring him, or being pushed down so he could do whatever the hell he goddamn wanted with me, I honestly didn't care. My body was literally singing. Every ounce of willpower I had was being taken up with not pushing him down and not letting my body react.

It wasn't like we'd done nothing all week. There had been a lot of petting and groping and humping and blow jobs and palming and everything except dicks being pushed into asses. I'd moved up to two fingers on Wednesday and that had taken Trystan a bit longer to get used to, but he'd still got off, and on Thursday—last night—he had actually moaned in pleasure as I pressed that second finger into him, and I had almost cracked and carried on. But drawing on reserves of self-control that I had never known I had, I had resisted and the man moaning against me was still a virgin—at least where his ass was concerned.

I was a bit slow, and one of his hands skimmed my spine and I melted into the touch just a little before I managed to grab his hand and bring it back round to my front.

"What the fuck, Ide...," Trystan tried to deepen the kiss and ravage my mouth with his. For just a moment I gave in to the sensation that turned increasingly frantic at an alarming rate. Trystan picked up on that chink in my armor; his hand snaked out of my grip to snarl through my hair and press my face into his. I managed to pull away—but shitting hell I was not built for self-control—to drop kisses along his jaw and use my suddenly free hand to skim over his torso and down over his jean-covered ass. I was rewarded by a reluctant groan—but it was a groan nonetheless—and he pressed himself into my hand. Such a simple thing, such a small movement, and just like that I was on the verge of pressing him down and fucking him right then and there. Instead I squeezed his arse and let my lips leave a trail of pale pink marks like jewels down the line of his neck and into the collar of his shirt.

The problem was that being submissive did not come naturally to Trystan. Not at all. And being patient did not come naturally to me. So all in all this was a bloody stupid plan, but in a weird twisted kind of way, I was enjoying it. The heady perpetual state of arousal was kind of addictive, and it was like all the colors had been turned up so the smallest things had my blood churning. I'd always been into sex, but this was a whole new level, and while I'm not saying I wanted it to go on forever, I was almost enjoying the torture.

Almost.

Trystan abandoned my hair and skimmed his hand down my neck, round over my collarbone, and dropped over my nipple. I gasped at the jolt of energy his touch caused even through the cotton of my T-shirt. I bit down lightly on the flesh I had against my lips, drawing it into my mouth, sucking and biting and caressing the blossoming red mark that was developing against his collarbone. His fingers pressed into my flesh, grasping through my clothes and rubbing against the taut bud of my nipple, and in response I shifted my lips and started again on another mark. And this was quickly getting out of control. My tenuous hold on my own arousal slipped and my cock throbbed, aching for anything.

With my hand still pressed into Trystan's ass, I pulled him against me. I growled lightly against his flesh as I shifted my hand so I could dig my fingers down the waistband of his jeans. The bare skin of his ass was hot against my palm. There wasn't much room for movement, but I slipped my hand down there anyway, moving my lips back up his neck and finding his lips, finally kissing him how I wanted to kiss him. It was desperate and messy and I could feel little bursts of tension and release through his kisses and his body. I pressed my hand between his cheeks and was rewarded with a small growl of satisfaction as my finger pressed up against the firm hole I had grown very familiar with over the last week.

He didn't shift away, didn't tense up; he just carried on kissing me and pressed his hips into mine. I gave one last roll of my hips against the bulge that was his erection. And then I stepped away from him.

He reeled slightly. I didn't begrudge him it; I would have, too, if I hadn't been psyching myself up for it for the whole thing. As it was, I was still breathing heavily as I grinned at him and removed my hand from his boxers.

"What the fuck, Ide?" He glared at me, and tried to step closer to me again. I took another step back, distracting myself from my own frustration by taking a small mote of amusement from his pissed-off look.

"Don't ye have t' go pick yer brother up from the train station?"

He glanced at his watch. "Not for another—shit, yes I do." He jumped away from me and grabbed his car keys from where he'd discarded them when he'd got in from work. He shot me an evil look over his shoulder as he unhooked his jacket from the back of the door. "Are you trying to prove some kind of point, Ide? Or just to drive me crazy?"

I grinned.

"Right, so both, then?" He adjusted his jeans with a sour look as he crossed back to me to scoop his hand behind my head and pull me into a brief kiss. "I'll take solace in the fact you're probably hurting more than me." He smiled against my lips and met my self-pitying grimace with a wry one of his own as he left to go pick up Josh from the train station.

I pulled a deep breath into the bottom of my lungs and headed up to the top of the house and my own room. I busied myself checking e-mails and grabbed a shower to cool my head, and the sound of the front door and Josh's excitable voice wound up through the house as I went back upstairs to change. With a last question for my sanity, I pulled on a pair of jeans and dark blue fitted shirt as I headed back down to Trystan's room.

I was greeted by a pair of arms wrapping around my shoulders. Josh kept the hug brief, which I was thankful for because I really wasn't in the right mindset to deal with Josh in a clingy mood.

"Hey, Josh, how's things?"

"Chris wants me to go meet him at that bar you took me to. Will you take me?"

"Ah, sure?" I phrased it as a question as I glanced up at Trystan because it was kind of late, but he just shrugged. "Ye eaten? Or is he taking ye out for something?" I asked as I tried to gauge how much of my evening was going to be taken up babysitting. I hadn't been to the local gay bar since the time I'd first introduced Chris and Josh, and the thought of spending my evening there left me feeling kind of weary.

"Nah, just meeting up, but I ate before I left home. Mum sent me up with some cakes. Make sure Trystan doesn't hog them all."

I glanced up and Trystan was watching me with a mixture of annoyance and amusement.

"I can be bribed to share," Trystan offered with a quirk of his eyebrow.

I grinned back at him; at least I could look forward to coming home. "I'll claim mine when we get back, then. We won't be late. Ye ready to go, Josh?"

Josh nodded and headed toward the door.

I paused with my hand hovering at Josh's shoulder. Trystan was pulling off the shirt he'd been wearing for work, only it wasn't the view that brought me to a standstill.

"Give me two seconds, I'll come with you," Trystan said with his back to me as he riffled through his cupboards.

"Ah... erm, I'm not sure that's such a great idea." I stumbled over my words.

"It'll be fine, I promise not to be an overbearing big brother. Besides, I need a drink." He turned back, pulling a fitted stone-gray tee over his head, and shot me a droll grin as he swapped work shoes for something more casual. He looked good, but then Trystan looked good in pretty much everything he wore. The top set off the nice tone in his arms and did nothing to hide the definition of his abs. If I saw a guy come into the bar wearing that, I would have looked twice, and that wasn't even thinking about his face.

But I'd kept Trystan away from gay clubs for a reason, and it wasn't because of the attention *he* would get.

I glanced down at Josh. He met my gaze and gave a little shrug. It wasn't nonchalance that was framed in the eyes he shared with Trystan, there was pity and just a touch of disdain. It wasn't really hard to guess why. I wondered what Chris had told Josh when he had asked about me, half of the truth? Some of the truth? It was enough of the truth that Josh looked at me differently now.

Trystan said he knew what I was like. But how did he know? From seeing me with Dan just once, from watching me come home smelling of sex for just a week. From Jorja, from my housemates; people who didn't know the half of it.

I could change all I wanted to. Just like I could dress a certain way, talk a certain way. And whatever I did, however long I left it, everyone else around me would still be the same. Would still treat me exactly the same.

Only this time Trystan would see. The guy who had admitted he was possessive, just the same as he'd said he understood and would trust me anyway, when really he didn't understand anything at all.

I really didn't want Trystan to come.

But what could I say?

17—Magpie

I WATCHED Trystan change and then the three of us walked into town, chatting about what Josh was up to at school and where our parents were planning on going on next summer's camping trip. I joined in, but I was slightly distracted. Suddenly my sexed-up body didn't seem like such a great thing. I wondered what the chances were of it being quiet on a Friday night at this time.

The chances were slim to none; it was heaving. The bouncer gave Josh an odd look as we got to the front of the small queue, but waved us all through without bothering to check IDs when he saw me behind him. The three of us walked into the press of people and music and I felt as if the air was being drawn from my lungs. I paused just behind Trystan, hovering in the shadow of his heat, and for the first time ever, I felt oddly self-conscious.

Josh spotted Chris and we were instantly abandoned as he wove through the men and women that filled the bar. He slowed at the last moment and tried to pull his face into a more relaxed grin as Chris leaned down to greet him with a short, sweet kiss. I lingered to watch a moment, to notice how no one paid them any mind at all, and I realized that the tension across my shoulders was jealousy.

"Let's get a drink and find somewhere out o' the way," I said to Trystan and stepped ahead of him to lead the way through the crush of people. One by one I felt curious glances turning my way, their thoughts were like physical things sweeping over my skin as they considered this new person who walked by my side like they belonged there.

It was inevitable. It was the same as always. And for the first time in a long while, I truly hated it.

"You seem a little on edge, Ide?"

"Yeah, well." I waved the barman over and ordered up two pints and two chasers. Trystan raised a wry eyebrow as I handed him the shot. "Yer not going t' like this." I spoke under my breath, but I knew Trystan had heard me because his curious grin soured slightly.

I watched Chris and Josh at the other end of the bar. Chris caught my eye and even he gave a curious glance at Trystan.

Then all hell broke loose in the form of Ashlie and Echo.

"Idrys! Oh my g-*oh*-d.... Idrys, what are you *doing* here?" Ashlie's touch dusted my cheek, exerting just enough pressure to urge me down so that he could reach my lips; he kissed me playfully, his tongue flicking against my lips as he pulled away. "So you're out and it's Friday; does this mean you're back on form? Oh I've *missed* you, Idrys; it's just not the same without you." He slipped his hand down my neck and over the small of my back as he leaned his upper body away from mine. He was touching me like he always had done, his fingers dancing and mischievous as he teased my skin. Then his eyes flicked over my shoulder and settled on Trystan. Ashlie's eyes lit up and he pursed his lips in appreciation.

"Oh, *Ide*! You really do find the best guys," he added in a hissed whisper that I imagine Trystan heard perfectly well.

I did not want to turn around and face Trystan right then. I reached back and unpeeled Ashlie's hands from my spine. Behind him Echo was standing with a barely there smile just touching the edges of his lips. He gave me nothing more than a tiny inflection of his head as I caught his obsidian eyes in mine.

"Sorry, guys, I'm not out t' play tonight," I said as I brought Ashlie's hands round and raised them up to my lips for a brief kiss before letting them go.

"Oh? But Dan's working, isn't he?" Ashlie sounded puzzled, and he didn't look any less confused as he eyed Trystan up again.

I wondered what his face looked like. But I didn't want to turn and see.

"Dan has taken your absence badly, Ide. You should talk to him." Echo's voice rumbled through the background chatter, and he was clearly talking to me, but he was watching Trystan. "Has this guy gotten a bit attached, my friend?" he added after a moment, still talking to me and still considering Trystan. "You shouldn't get the wrong idea, Mr. Tall-Dark-and-Handsome. Idrys only belongs to you for the night; he'll always be ours in the end."

I sighed. "Look, guys, I'm here to keep an eye on this guy's baby brother. I'm not in the mood for playing, and I probably won't be for a while."

Echo gave a faint hum of curiosity but didn't press for details. Ashlie cocked his head to one side. And his bright smile dropped slightly as he considered me.

"You okay, Ide?" he asked, sounding a little more serious than usual. I appreciated his concern, because it wasn't like it would have been the first time I'd got mixed up in something dodgy.

"Yeah, I'm fine, honestly."

"You seem different?"

I bent down, pressed a kiss to Ashlie's cheek, and then reached to whisper against his ear. "Go have fun, Ashlie; think o' me when ye get fucked by some hotties, okay? I'll call ye next week and we can chat, but I need t' speak t' Dan first."

"That sounds pretty serious, Ide," Ashlie said, a slight crease forming between his eyes as his gaze darted over my shoulder once again. Then he stepped away, his smile flicking back into place as he backed against Echo, pulling the guy's hand over his shoulder. "Guess it's just us again, Echo. You best find me someone hot t' suck off while you fuck me." He shot a wicked grin over my shoulder and then they slid off into the crowd.

I watched their backs, and then I turned to watch Chris and Josh, who were laughing together, their bodies tucked in close to each other like normal lovers on a date. I turned to face Trystan. He met my gaze, and it was hard to read his face.

"I told ye, ye wouldn't like it," I said with a barely restrained sigh.

"Who were they? And why are so many people staring at you, us? Why do they look so interested? Or is this just what happens in a gay bar up north?" Trystan's words came out in short bursts. I stared at him, waiting for him to add something about the kiss Ashlie had pressed on me. But Trystan just held my gaze in his and waited patiently for my answer.

"That was Ashlie and Echo," I said softly.

"That was Echo?" Trystan's gaze darted over my shoulder to settle briefly on the huge black guy. "He's fucking huge."

I couldn't help but snigger a little at that.

"That still doesn't explain why so many people are staring," he pressed softly when he finally turned back to me.

"Maybe it's just 'cause yer hot?" I grinned at him, although I'm not sure my whole face was in it.

"Well of course," he said with a mocking smirk, but it slipped a bit as he turned to look over the room again. "Everyone looks... curious. Even the guy with Josh."

"Do ye really want me t' explain?" My voice was quieter than I had meant it to be, but at least the words hadn't caught in my throat. Those brown eyes locked on mine, and I knew the answer.

I let out a long, slow breath. "Look, I know ye thought I just fucked around, and I did. But those two, plus me and Dan, we were.... I guess the simplest way t' explain it is we were a kind of open, interchangeable relationship." I pressed my jaw together, because Trystan knowing about Dan didn't bother me half as much as him knowing about the rest of this shit. His brown eyes remained the same as I explained, and all he gave me was a small incline of his head, as if it didn't bother him. Which was great, but that wasn't really the bad part.

"And you haven't told them you're seeing me now either?" he asked.

I shook my head and swallowed. "I like Ashlie and Echo, but Dan is... he needs to know first."

Trystan nodded slowly. "That still doesn't explain why half of the bar is staring at you. I mean, people always stare at you, but this is—" He glanced around briefly and a faint crease appeared between his eyebrows. "—*extreme*, even for you."

"The reason people are staring at us is 'cause yer not part o' the group, yet yer with me. So they're wondering." I waited for Trystan's eyes to drift back to mine. "They're trying t' work out if there's someone new in the group... or if I'm collecting people."

"Collecting people?"

I nodded slowly. "For group sex."

"Oh." Trystan raised his beer to his lips and managed to see off about half of his pint.

"I told ye, ye wouldn't like it."

"I know, but I asked. Thanks for being honest." He glanced over his shoulder back at his brother and Chris, and I could see what he was thinking.

"Chris knew. I think he's told Josh, but if he was after an in, he's never spoken to me about it, so I don't think he's interested."

"I see, ah… could you get me another beer?" He surprised me by leaning over and pressing a kiss to my cheek, and then he was weaving through the groups of people heading to the toilets at the back of the bar.

I watched him go with a puzzled frown: for him and for the wash of warmth his kiss had caused. Apart from that first morning in the kitchen, the only time Trystan had kissed me was when we were alone. But it wasn't so much that as much as the fact that the brief, affectionate kiss had meant more to me than if he had tried to kiss me properly. It was as if he had understood that here some overt display of lust would have meant nothing.

For the first time since we arrived, a smile tugged at the corner of my lips, and I leaned back over the bar to order some more drinks.

I sipped my new beer and watched Josh and Chris with one eye while I let my gaze flit over the rest of the bar. There were plenty of curious glances still being sent my way. I was careful not to make eye contact with anyone more than necessary, even though the chances of someone approaching me were pretty slim. My attention caught on Echo and Ashlie, who had settled themselves at a table. Ashlie was chatting animatedly to a guy I recognized but didn't know by name. Echo was staring toward the back of the bar, and then his gaze flicked to me, and there was a slight frown marring the edge of his eyes. He held my gaze in his, and suddenly I realized that Trystan had been gone for far too long.

"Oh fuck."

I abandoned the pints on the bar, not caring that they would be undrinkable after leaving them unattended. I danced through the groups of people, shoving them out of my way.

How could I have been so fricking stupid?

The feeling in the pit of my stomach was nauseous and hollow at the same time, burning even as dread froze my thoughts. It was all of those things at once as I tried not to punch a guy who accidentally went the same way as me when I tried to get by. He spilled half of his drink as I shoved by him with a grimace, and his shouted curse followed me as I finally got to the back of the bar.

The door to the men's toilets clattered against the wall. The line of cubicles along one side of the white and fluorescent purple room were short, so you could see over the top, and they didn't have locks. But I didn't need to check them because Trystan was there, in the middle of the room. He looked pissed off but in one piece despite the two guys facing him.

"What the fuck are ye two playing at?" I snarled, and Trystan actually looked a little startled, though whether it was to see me or by the low threatening tone to my voice I didn't know. The two guys twisted round, more people I recognized but didn't know by name. I realized that I had fucked one of them, and he shot me a disgusting smile as he saw recognition flare through my eyes.

"I said… what the fuck are ye two playing at?" I repeated when I got no answer.

"Just putting this guy in his place," the first guy said.

"We want to play," the second one added, and he stepped a little closer. "Come on, Idrys, we just want in."

I snarled because he knew my name. And because they had clearly been threatening Trystan. I stalked toward the second one and he was smiling until my hand wrapped round his throat.

"If ye guys so much as look at him askance, I'll make it so ye never fuck another guy again, understand?" I finished as I left just a little too much pressure on the guy's neck.

"What the fuck! You think you're so high and fucking mighty! Well your pimps aren't here this time." The first guy cursed as he started toward me. He looked slightly surprised to see Trystan's hand wrapping around his arm.

"I guess you're talking about Dan and that big guy they call Echo? But if you think I'll let you lay a hand on Ide, you've got another thing fucking coming—"

"No wonder my ears were burning." The low rumble of Echo's voice filled the toilets.

I glanced over my shoulder, and obsidian eyes briefly held mine before they drifted past me to settle on the other two guys.

"I think you gentlemen shouldn't get confused." His words were slow and precise, and a slight accent lingered in his tone, sharpening just the very last second of each word, making them slam through the air despite the fact that he hadn't raised his voice. "Just because Idrys is not with me this evening does not mean that I will fail to protect him from fawning little pricks like you. Now you will both leave. Or would you like to stay and see what I do to people who threaten my friends? I can assure you I am much more imaginative than the lovely Idrys." His voice trailed down to a whisper that was barely audible over the thick rumbling bass that came through from the bar.

The would-be attackers detached themselves from mine and Trystan's grasps, and much to Trystan's surprise, they scarpered. I wasn't concentrating on Trystan right now, though, I was staring at Echo.

"Thanks, Echo." I sighed.

He nodded and his eyes drifted to where Trystan had just come to stand next to me, his shoulder almost-but-not-quite touching mine.

"May I assume this is Trystan?" Echo asked in his slow, deep voice. His face didn't change when I nodded. "Dan mentioned him. May I assume you are quite fond of him, Idrys?" I nodded again. "I see. I won't tell Ashlie yet, but please, you should speak to Dan, explain to him properly. I'm afraid he has broken the rules."

I didn't need Echo to explain what he meant. There was only one official rule: always use a condom, but that wasn't what he meant. He had meant the unspoken rule: don't get too attached.

"I'll call him tomorrow."

Echo nodded and he turned his gaze back on Trystan. "Maybe I have broken the rules as well. So listen, Mr. Tall-Dark-and-Handsome, the same goes for you as for those two idiots who just ran scared: if you hurt my friend, I will hurt you. Very simple."

He flicked his eyes to me, a rare smile dusted his lips, and then he was gone. As always he moved surprisingly quickly and lightly for such a big guy.

"He is fucking terrifying," Trystan muttered.

"Ye don't need to worry about him, he won't hurt ye. Well as long as ye…. I guess ye got the idea."

"Yeah, I got the idea." He turned to me and let a long breath slip from between his lips. "But, Ide, what the hell was that about? Those guys…."

I scowled and took a short pacing step toward the door. "We should go and check on Josh." A glance over my shoulder said Trystan wasn't going anywhere.

I pressed my eyes shut for a moment, trying to sort out my head and calm the odd feeling in my chest.

"Fuck, Trys. *This* is why I didn't want ye t' come." I waved a hand in a vague circle that encompassed the whole bar, the people, the memories, everything—although quite frankly just this room had far too many memories in it for me to be comfortable standing there with Trystan. I wanted to escape, but Trystan still wasn't happy with my answer.

"This place is all the stuff ye don't like about me. And when I come here, people will treat me like the person ye don't like; they'll treat me like the slut that collects guys for a gang bang or fucks his friends in the toilets or whatever the fuck else ye can think of and dislike. And I can brush it off; I have been for the past month. But it's not just me. By coming here ye get tarred with the same brush, and that's what just happened: they thought ye were like me."

And that really bothered me.

Trystan was scowling and I could see his face turning slowly to eye up the insubstantial toilet cubicles. I winced, grinding my teeth together as I turned to leave the room. Washing through me was that same feeling of awkwardness that I'd experienced when I first arrived with Trystan.

I pushed open the door and breathed deeply, but even out here the air was just as heavy, just with beer and cloying aftershave, and eyes still watched me curiously. I sought out Josh, and I panicked for a moment when I couldn't find them, but they had got a table and were making out, slow and sensual, and nobody paid them any mind at all.

I wanted to leave. And I realized with a strangling feeling that if I went over and told Josh, he too would be contaminated by associating with me—if he wasn't already. I ran a hand through my hair and stalked through the bar, my eyes fixed on the ground as I pulled out my phone to text Josh instead.

Outside, the early November air was crisp with cold that turned my breath into white puffs, but even that wasn't enough to clear the thick heaviness that seemed to have settled in the bottom of my lungs. Out here I was just another gay guy leaving the club early, but people were still eying me with curiosity as I began to pace. Not because they knew me and what I was like, but because everyone always watched me. Whether I cut my hair or hid my eyes, whether I wore tracksuits or outdoor gear or the simple high-street jeans and shirt I was in now, people always stared, their eyes buzzing over my skin incessantly. Whether I was pacing anxiously outside a regular bar or a gay club, night or day, rain or sunshine, people watched me, and they always had.

Had I really forgotten what it was like? Had I really believed this was going to work?

Even before my head had been so messed up by what that guy had done to me in Manchester, the only two relationships of my life had fallen apart. Both for the same reason: neither of them could cope with the way people stared at me, with the relentless and unending attention that always drifted my way.

What was it Trystan had said? I was magnetic-honey-light, and the rest of the world were the iron-wasp-moths: forever drawn to me.

For twelve months after I was raped I had been with no one. While I had locked myself away from the world and men, I had grown over a foot. And if anything it had gotten worse.

I remember the moment I became who I am now with perfectly clarity. It was Jorja's fourteenth birthday, and we'd gone to the fair in the local town. It had been a baking hot first of June, almost two months before my seventeenth birthday and just over a year since I'd lost my virginity. I hadn't been with anyone in that time, but I could feel myself starting to wake up from the lustless slumber the experience had put my body into.

The field full of dated disco music had smelled of rotting garbage beneath the scent of chip fat and sweat and popcorn. Theo had had to stay home to help out his dad on the farm, and I had been left with the elder brother of one of Jorja's friends to look after a group of about ten girls. I wasn't scared of people, but I resented being left with the stranger and had hardly said five words to him all afternoon. I had spent most of the day watching the people around me. For the first time in my life, I was enjoying the hot weather because it meant a significant number of guys had gone topless, and I drank it in, getting reacquainted with the thick stirrings of lust my body produced, so much darker and stronger than anything I'd had before the incident, when I had basically still been a child.

"D'ye want some beer?" the guy had offered as we'd waited for the girls to finish on some ride or another. I was leaning forward on a fence, not bothering to hide the fact I was watching the half-naked ride attendant with rapt fascination. I'd twisted my head to look over my shoulder and caught his eyes flicking up quickly from my ass.

There was a brief flash of panic inside of me, but it faded quickly as I straightened up, stretching to my full height as I looked at him properly for the first time all afternoon. I realized that even though he was a couple of years older than me, I was the taller of us; he wasn't short, probably just under six foot, but nevertheless I was already able to look down on him.

His skin was golden bronze and dusted with freckles from working outside and stretched over lean muscle from the same work that kept him outdoors. He'd kept his shirt on despite the heat. I could smell his sweat, and the scent was familiar after being with him all day.

"No thanks," I muttered as I pressed my hands into the small of my back, arching up onto my toes to straighten the kinks from leaning on the railing. To my surprise, his eyes darkened.

"You're such a fucking attention whore." His breath was a hiss, and he flicked his gaze away from me, but I watched a faint flush rise up on his cheeks beneath pale brown eyes that were half-hidden by a flop of blond hair that looked like dirty straw compared to mine. He downed another mouthful of his beer. "Like sex walking around on two legs."

I'd looked beyond him, and it was the first time I realized that more or less everyone was a bit shorter than me. And as I let my eyes skim the crowd, I had noted gaze after gaze for just a second. Most hastily turned away when they caught me looking, a few returning dark glances.

I turned my eyes back to my companion, and I considered him as he stared determinedly toward the ride our sisters were on.

This guy didn't know me, he'd never met me before, and even he resented the attention I got.

"Ye want me t' fuck ye?" I asked with a laugh as I turned back to lean against the railings as if my comment had been no more significant than when he had offered me the beer.

"I'm not gay."

"S'fine; ye think I look like a girl, right?"

"Why would I want t' be fucked by a guy who looks like a girl?"

"Don't ask me. It's ye that wants it." I glanced over my shoulder and caught him staring again. I let my face relax into a nonchalant smile as he glanced hurriedly up.

"I don't—" I'd cut him off by pressing my lips down over his. He'd tasted of cheap lager and candy floss. Our teeth had clashed and he'd shoved me off him *almost* instantly, but not before he'd let my lips linger for just a moment against his. I'd not fucked him that day; it had taken me maybe a month.

I'd realized that if even a stranger could get jealous of the attention on me, then I had no chance at an actual relationship. I couldn't change the way I looked: I had already tried dressing, acting, and behaving differently back when I'd been dating. That day at the fair I decided to just embrace it. I couldn't change myself, and I couldn't change others, so why bother worrying about it, why not just welcome it? And I had, completely: I had accepted every flirt and come-on and discarded them once I was done, before I could be discarded. And that had been what I had been doing when I met Dan: fucking every guy that looked my way.

I dropped my head into my hands as it suddenly hit me what a fuckup my life was and how much I was screwing Dan over just a little more thoroughly with every day that passed and I didn't tell him about Trystan. Theo was right, maybe we'd never sat down and said we were going out, but Dan had given me what no one else had ever given me. He had never once made issue of the way people were around me, the way people watched me, lusted after me—coveted me. He had embraced it, enjoyed it, *used* it with me for games and conquests. And for the past two years, because of Dan, I had let myself forget.

I had ignored the unspoken rule that had governed my life since that day in the fair when the grass had been burned and golden and the air had been full of dust and pollen and the buzzing of wasps. *Don't get too attached.* A rule that had never been meant for application on those around me, because that's just what people did, they got attached to me. That rule wasn't for them. It was for me.

Because no matter what I felt or how hard I tried, the jealousy and doubt would eventually drive everyone away.

I wasn't even fooling myself anymore when I pretended I didn't understand the odd shimmering feeling that buzzed through my nerves when Trystan was around. Or that I didn't know the reason why I was suddenly willing to spend a week, a month, however long it took, building up to having sex with him. Or why I suddenly felt this churning nauseous feeling of emptiness when I thought about the look that had passed over Trystan's face when he had eyed up the toilet cubicles.

I hated that place right then.

It was everything I was, everything I had embraced about myself as protection. And I suddenly hated it all. Because in the end, I could say that I was different, but to the rest of the world I would always be the same.

I didn't want Trystan to leave.

I didn't want him to see this and realize what a mistake he was making.

But I had nothing to offer him to stay.

I twisted round to continue my pacing and realized Trystan was standing next to the door, leaning back against the wall with his arms crossed against his chest and a frown darkening his eyes.

18—HUMMINGBIRD

"IDE?" TRYSTAN said when he saw me notice him. He gave an irritable huff when I turned on my heels and paced away from him again.

Seeing him scowling at me did not help. All it did was reinforce the awful gnawing sensation in my chest. I felt a hand wrap around my upper arm, forcing me back around and giving me no choice but to meet Trystan's eye.

"Ide? What the hell is wrong with you?"

I glared at the ground and pushed his hand from my arm. I didn't bother trying to turn away; I just opened up half a step between us and glanced in the direction of the bar as I waved a hand toward it. "I told ye, ye wouldn't like it."

I ground my jaw together. "But it won't change, Trys. It's always going t' be the same, whether it's here where people know me or in some place I've never been before. It never stops, the looks and the come-ons, men and women, yer brother, ma friends, strangers… it'll just keep happening. There's nothing I can fricking do about it, so ye should just quit while yer ahead."

He stared at me, his head cocked to one side, and his irritation turned to a genuine look of puzzlement.

"Seriously?" A quick series of emotions flashed across his face as he stared at me, and then with a sigh he reached forward and hooked a hand behind my neck, not pulling or demanding, just a gentle pressure against my skin, almost like he was reassuring me that he wasn't going anywhere.

"Why are you being like this all of a sudden, Ide? You've never been bothered before. Hell, you paraded it in front of me the first week I was here." An odd, tight smile thinned his lips, but there was still a frown tensing his forehead. "You know I'm not exactly some chaste little virgin, right? I've slept around plenty, and it's not exactly like I care what people think of me." He gave an irritated huff and clicked his tongue. "Hell, if fucking in a public place does it for you, then you just have to get me drunk and I'd probably be on board."

"Huh?"

"Ide." Trystan stepped toward me, holding me in place with the hand that remained against my neck as he let our bodies slide together. "You told me to trust you, right? So I'm trusting you. And I told you to give me a chance to be what you want, so don't just make decisions by yourself. Give me a chance."

"Nnn." I groaned something low and incomprehensible even to me. "But this—"

"You think I didn't know what you were like?" he interrupted with a weary shake of his head. "You think your sister and your housemates didn't tell me all of this shit to try and convince me what a bad idea dating you was? *I know*, Ide, and yeah it's not ideal, and yeah I'm kind of possessive usually, so it's not been easy to turn down the urge to punch every guy that looks at you or kisses you." A wry smile flickered across his face, and he gave a soft chuckle. "But I don't care what you did, or who you did it with, or how many people you did it with. I just want the stuff you do now to be with me."

Trystan was staring at me with such a look of determined frustration, his eyes gleamed in the yellow lamplight as he held me against him on the edge of the road. People just walked around us. A few catcalls and insults came our way, but we were mostly ignored. His body was pressed up against mine, feeling as divine as ever. And finally I admitted to myself that the reason it felt so good wasn't because of his muscle or bone structure—I'm sure it helped—but because it was Trystan, and because my messed-up head had decided to fall in love with him.

Which was *such* a bad idea.

Because he was going to leave me. He'd get jealous and leave.

But he was staring at me with his hand cupped gently behind my head. Staring at me with conviction and just a little bit of hope and a lot of regret, and he didn't look jealous, just worried.

"Oh fuck it." I slid my hand round his back and up his spine, enjoying the faint sparks of pleasure my body created from that simple touch as I wove my fingers up through the hair at the back of his head and pulled his lips against mine.

I'd never kissed someone like that.

Or maybe I had. Maybe I'd been kissing Trystan like that this whole time and I hadn't wanted to admit it to myself.

He looked slightly dazed as I broke away. I imagine I looked much the same.

"I don't want t' fuck ye in the toilets of some shitty bar, and I don't want ye t' fuck me there either." My voice was low and breathy as I spoke. "I want ye all t' myself, I want t' be the only one allowed t' look at ye and touch ye, understand?"

He understood. I could see the inexorable realization blossoming in his eyes, spreading through his face and curling up the edges of his lips in a self-satisfied smirk. He pressed his lips against mine, kissing me just how I'd kissed him, and I was in ecstasy.

"Just tell me, Idrys. Come on, I told you right from the start, so tell me... tell me this isn't just a fuck, tell me the reason why you suddenly care so much," he whispered against my ear as he broke off the kiss. He pressed his lips against my tragus, dragging his teeth slightly against the flesh. "Tell me, and you can take me home right now and fuck me."

I hissed a breath between my teeth as his words slid straight down my spine and into my groin.

"I know it's been killing you." His voice rumbled straight into my ear. "I know blow jobs aren't enough for you, and you've been holding back for me; it's so fucking cute...." He grasped my free hand and guided it to his back before sliding it down over his ass and pressing it against the firm muscles there. My fingers gripped his flesh through his jeans, pulling us closer together so I could feel the faint stirrings of his erection twitching against mine.

Was I really going to say it?

"I like ye...." I held my lips against his, speaking the words straight into his mouth.

He chuckled and pulled me closer.

"You're such a head case."

Then he was pulling me down the side street the bar was on and toward the main road where we'd be able to get a taxi. His face was split in the biggest, darkest, and sexiest grin I had ever seen. It left me speechless and horny as hell, and it couldn't have just been me, because other people were staring at him too. People paused, their eyes widened, their breath hitched as they watched the gorgeous guy dragging me by my wrist. I could have been imagining it, my head was so messed up the whole thing could have been some kind of twisted dream. Or maybe my drink had been spiked.

"Shit." I stumbled to a halt, forcing Trystan to a stop. He stuck his hand out to flag down a taxi. "Josh," I said, and the boy's name brought me out of the lust-filled haze I had been inhabiting.

A taxi pulled up to the curb and Trystan gave our address and tugged me toward the door. I tried to hold him back, and he shot me a dark look before using his extra muscles to drag me inside.

"I asked that Echo dude to keep an eye on him, but my brother can do what he wants. If he wants to fuck that guy, then that's up to him. Hell, I'd be a bit of a hypocrite if I tried to stop him." He jerked the door shut behind me and the taxi pulled off.

"But I thought…."

"I don't care who my brother fucks, as long as it's not you." He gave a small shrug. "Besides, that Chris guy seemed sound enough."

"How could ye possibly tell that from across the bar when he had his tongue down yer brother's throat?"

Trystan grinned. "I went over and said hi before I came out to find you emo-ing your pretty little brains out."

"I was not—" I was cut off by a mouth pressed over mine. I had a moment to hope that the taxi driver was open-minded before my blatant lie along with all other thoughts were drowned out by Trystan's tongue working my lips open and pressing against mine, drawing it inside his lips so he could suck down gently on it. I groaned and pulled him against me.

Suddenly we were home. Breathlessly I pressed twenty quid into the front of the cab, letting him keep the excessive amount of change to say sorry, and then we were stumbling through the front door.

"Come on, your room, so no one can hear me scream," Trystan growled against my lips as he tugged us toward the stairs.

I laughed against his lips. "The only screaming yer going to do is when ye beg me for more."

We detached to make our way up the stairs. The house was empty anyway.

We made it through the door to my bedroom before I attached myself to his lips, hitting the latch across just in case. I devoured him as I undressed him against the wall: with hands and tongue and teeth I touched and caressed every inch of him as I stripped him down. I kept my own clothes where they were, because I was already strung out, and my cock was already aching beneath my jeans. I pressed myself up against him, grinding against his nakedness, and he moaned into my lips, grinding right back as I pulled us both from against the wall and backed us the rest of the way onto the bed.

"Ye remember how this works, right?" My voice was hoarse as I whispered the words against his neck. I alternated between sucking and lightly biting the sensitive flesh as beneath me Trystan ground his hips against my clothed form.

"Slow; three fingers; gonna hurt," he breathed between moans, summing up the bare bones of what I had said to Josh what felt like a lifetime ago but was only three weeks.

"Going t'hurt gooood," I breathed and dropped down his body, skimming lightly down his chest and abs and setting a delightful shudder down his spine as I wrapped hands and lips around his seeping flesh. And holy fricking mother of all that is good, the sounds he made: low growling mews and a hiss of anticipation as I lowered my hand to his ass, teasing lightly at the flesh. And he was lifting his hips for me, I could feel him relaxing and pushing back against the gentle pressure and holy fuck that was the sexiest thing I have ever seen or felt or been part of.

"Mmmm." He hummed as my finger penetrated him, grinding down against my hand as I alternated between working his prostate and stretching him for the second finger that drew a muted groan from his chest.

By the time he was ready for a third finger, he was as strung out as me.

I pressed it against the thick ring of muscle, and he groaned, urging himself up into me, lusting after more and more sensation. He hissed a little as I pressed it inside him, but not nearly so much as when I'd moved up to two fingers on Wednesday. A ripple of tension washed through him, and he froze for a few moments as my digits finished their journey. I held still too, lessening the draws on his cock, humming lightly against his flesh, and using my free hand to soothe him.

"Ye okay, Trys?" I whispered. "I know what ye said, but we can stop if ye want." I pressed kisses against the faint ridges of his hipbones. My own groin ached with need.

He sucked a deep breath down into his lungs and then lifted his hips, pressing himself against my hand and causing my fingers to shift slightly inside of him.

"S'fine, *morethanfine.*" His words strung together as I moved my fingers once again. "Holy fuck, Ide," he groaned as I spread him, but he didn't stop thrusting against me.

I was dissolving into a mass of strung out nerves, and I was still fully clothed. I just tried to concentrate on my hands and mouth. I glanced up occasionally to check Trystan's face, swallowing down a wash of desire each time I did. At some point I stopped, at some point I stripped, and usually I took that time to calm myself the fuck back down. But it didn't help, because Trystan arched up off the bed as I pulled out of him, and then he lay sprawled and panting across my bed, holding my eyes in his as I stripped.

"*Hurrythefuckup,*" he breathed as he lay there, hands clenched, body coated in sweat, breaths tugging through parted lips, eyes half-closed with lust. His cock was coated in my saliva and dripped with that delicious bitter chocolate-flavored precum of his.

I sucked down a mouthful of air as I got back between his legs; rolling the condom on had been a nightmare. I pulled him down toward me, hitching his legs up on either side of my chest. I used more lube, enjoying the way he shuddered as I slipped my fingers just inside of him. It was like dying from something beautiful. I was so far gone the pleasure had blurred into something hot and tense, and as I finally slipped the tip of my cock between his ass cheeks, it was me who was grimacing at the little shocks of pleasure that were so intense they overloaded my nerves, shifting it through to pain.

"Ide... oh fuck... please, Ide, I need to come...."

The sound that tore from my throat was a confused mess of noises as my head and body warred about what they wanted.

Begging... holy fuck that was what I'd wanted and that was what I got, and sweet, blissful, boiling hell, it was so fricking hard to go slow as he moaned and pleaded with me.

I groaned and leaned forward, mashing my hand over his lips.

"Please stop," I whispered, my voice hoarse with need as my cock head rested against his ass and I fought the incessant jerking of my hips as my body sought its release.

"Shitting hell." I mangled something that didn't make any sense as he lengthened his spine, pressing his ass down, and the hot warmth of him spread over me. At the same time he rolled his head, his lips catching on the edge of my fingers to draw them inside his mouth. He sucked on my fingers, and I simply obeyed, pressing my hips forward, urging my cock into his ass as he drew my fingers between his lips. His teeth bared around my digits, worrying my skin, he hissed in a breath as his muscles clenched around my cock, dragging me in deeper.

"Shh, relax." My voice was strained, and I was unsure whether I was telling myself or Trystan. I pressed my finger against his tongue, massaging it gently, as with my other hand I stroked his hips and thighs and down to soothe the thick ring of muscle that was currently the only thing between me and coming right then, before I was even halfway in.

"Nnn." He panted around my fingers, his teeth pressed firmly against my flesh and his body a twitching mass of tension as I finally filled him.

"Ye okay?" I was as breathless as he was. "I'm going t' wait, so get yer, fuck...."

My fingers curled against his mouth, pressing into his teeth as my other hand dug deeply into his hip.

And around my fingers and between his breathless sucks of air, Trystan was fucking smirking at me, because he'd just clenched his ass around my cock, and the sudden sensation had nearly driven me over the edge.

"Shut the fuck up and move," Trystan growled, and the fucker did it again.

"Oh, ye are so fricking dead," I sneered as I drew most of the way out and slid back in in two smooth, firm strokes.

Holy mother of fricking everything, he was divine.

He shouted something incomprehensible as his back arched up off the bed. I grinned and tugged him roughly forward so his hips were propped up against my thighs, and then I bent over, plucked my fingers from his mouth, wrapped my arm behind his head, and pulled his lips up to mine.

"Relax and breathe slow," I whispered mockingly as I dropped him back against the bed, pulled out, and drove into him again.

Two utterly impossible instructions.

He groaned and shouted and ground back against me as I pushed into him again and again, a little harder each time. His hands were straining forward to clutch at my knees—the only part of me he could reach.

He was so fricking tight and so fricking hot as he writhed underneath me, split around my cock. I could feel every judder of pleasure as I angled myself to assault his prostate with each thrust, over and over. I could hardly breathe for the tension in my body.

"Nnn, Ide, so… fucking… close." His voice was a mess as he switched between shouting and whispering as I continued my unrelenting assault on his body.

"Oh crap." That was my limit; the tattered shreds of my self-control disintegrated completely. I wrapped my hand around Trystan's seeping erection, jerking him off in time with my thrusts. I felt him shudder around me and his cock twitch in my grasp.

"Oh my… *fuuuck.*" The words tore from my throat, almost a scream, as my body dissolved and exploded. And I was lost in one of the best orgasms of my life as Trystan jerked in my hand and spasmed around me as I milked thick hot streams of cum across his chest.

I don't know how long we stayed like that, as we both twitched and shuddered our way down from whatever plane we had driven each other to. I reached down and pressed a kiss against his knee where it was still propped against my chest. And then reluctantly I eased out, leaving Trystan sprawled on the bed while I went to dispose of the condom and get something to clean him up with. He was still lain out with his eyes pressed shut when I got back to the bed, and with a soft smile I cleaned him up. When he was passable, I climbed up next to him and tucked my body in next to his.

"Ye okay?"

"Mmm, that was… intense." He lifted one eyelid and glowered at me. "Can we not draw it out so much next time? A week is a little excessive, hmm?"

I chortled at him, leaning down to press a kiss against his lips. "Talking about next time already?" I pulled gently at his lips, still smiling as I leaned away and propped myself up on one elbow.

"Urgh, how did you do this every day?" He winced as he tried to sit up, and I laughed at him a little.

"Seriously? Because I've been having sex for years; ye get used to it, idiot. Well, actually every day for a week was... sore, but what can I say: ye just make me a little crazy."

"I make you crazy? I just let a guy stick his dick up my ass, *that's* crazy."

"'A guy'? Why, Trys, ye could break a boy's heart with that cold attitude."

"I'll break more than your heart," he growled, and I ended up laughing at him again as he tried to reach for me and ended up just wincing and lying back down.

I took pity on him and wrapped my hands around his shoulders, rolling him over so he was lying on top of me. I liked the way our bodies fit, hip to hip, chest to chest, lips to lips.

I just liked Trystan, more than liked him.

"Hey, Trys?" I whispered as he stared down at me, his brown eyes like satin in the low light and his hand curled around my head. "Don't leave me, okay? Yer've fucked me over completely with yer smirks and yer too-cool-for-school understanding of all the shit in my life. Ye need t' take responsibility for yer actions."

I swallowed slowly and reached up to kiss him again, slower this time, letting my hand drift up to feel the tousled strands of his hair, down his neck and back, still flushed and slightly damp from our sex, then down to dance ever so lightly over the no-doubt sore globes of his ass.

He chuckled at me as I broke the kiss.

"You think I'd let any old hot as hell, gorgeous, sexy guy who likes all the same shit as me fuck me in the ass?"

"Well from experience, ye do tend t' just throw yerself at them," I replied, trying not to smirk quite as much as Trystan was.

His smile fell away just a little. "Promise me: promise me you'll tell Dan, promise you'll call him tomorrow and explain to him that you're with me now, that you're serious about me, and you're not going to be able to play those games with him. I don't mind you staying friends with him, with anyone, I'll trust you. Just promise me you'll do it... and I'll tell you."

I stared up at him, and that wash of tension flooded through me, drowning my nerves with tingling light like the static of a summer evening, charged and ready for the storm of all storms to hit.

"I'll call him. Pass me my phone. I'll do it right now."

He shook his head gently and pressed his lips briefly against mine. "No, you should go and talk to him face to face. Just promise you'll do it tomorrow."

"I promise."

He grinned at me. "Then here you go." He leaned down and pressed a long, slow kiss to my lips, stretching it out to dust kisses across my jaw and down my neck and up to my ear. Then he tucked his head in next to mine, relaxing over me, and despite being bigger than me, he wasn't heavy, just warm and nice.

"I'll take responsibility for turning you into a normal person, Ide. Because despite the fact that you drive me a little crazy, or maybe because of it, I've rather foolishly fallen in love with you." He whispered into the crook of my neck, "Mmm? I love you, is that all right?"

Shitting hell. It almost hurt: the feelings in my chest and the urgent, too-fast beating of my heart, and the way my blood felt too big for my veins. It was verging on agony. But I didn't want it to stop.

I wanted this feeling, and I wanted the man who made me feel it. I wanted to keep him all for myself, and I desperately wanted to accept the warm wash of certainty that maybe it wasn't just me that was different. This crazy man who had dominated my life and thoughts and bed, who had trusted me with such nonchalance in that smug smirk of his, as if it were only natural that I would only want him—maybe he was different.

"Ye probably shouldn't," I murmured back as I let my arms slip around his back, hugging him against me.

"I know, but I do."

"Well I guess it's okay," I said so softly the words almost didn't leave my lips, but he was pressed so tightly against me he could hear anyway. "Because I probably love ye too."

"I'm glad you're not making me bribe it out of you this time." He tried to sound amused, but there was a breathlessness to his words that made me think more of relief.

I twisted my head slightly so I could press a kiss into the small sliver of his face that wasn't buried against my neck.

"Hey, ye were the idiot that decided t' fall in love with a head case like me," I replied.

"Indeed. What kind of guy falls in love with his childhood tormenter?"

"Messed-up ones," I replied with a grin. "Unless the childhood tormentor turns into a sexy, open-minded Adonis."

He chuckled lightly against me and then finally rolled his head to one side, meeting my gaze with his. He was smiling, and it was definitely still a smirk, but it was so warm and somehow tender as he reached forward to catch my lips with his, kissing me softly and deeply while his hand tangled possessively through my hair.

Then he was groaning and rolling himself off me.

"Oh God, how long am I going to hurt for?"

I couldn't help but laugh.

"A few days. Could be longer 'cause I ended up being a bit rough, but ye've no one but yerself t' blame for that," I finished archly as his face dropped into a scowl.

Then he grinned, his face curling into a dangerous smirk. "Oh really? Well, given that you're 'used to it' and were rough, I guess that means that I can just stop holding back with you as well, then?"

"Hmm?" I rolled on top of him. "That was ye holding back? I'd like t' see ye *try* and break me, straight guy."

Despite the fact that he was clearly in pain and was now pinned beneath me, he looked just as smug as always as he met my eyes with his. He scooped my chin up in his hand, reaching up to press a coy kiss to my lips.

"Just remember you said that when I'm done with you, eh?" His voice was low and full of delicious promise.

I gave a dark shiver of delight and returned the kiss. I rolled off him and tucked my body tightly up against his as I used his shoulder as a pillow. We probably looked like a ridiculous couple, but it didn't really matter right then.

"I guess my list is getting shorter."

"Hmm?" Trystan was half-asleep as I pulled the covers over us.

"My list of reasons why I hate summer so much," I explained. He broke open one eyelid and stared at me curiously. And I counted off the reasons on the fingers of one hand.

"My birthday being in the summer holidays, but that doesn't matter now because I can do what I like. Living in the middle of nowhere and having nothing to do in the summer holidays: also kind of a moot point since I moved to York. Constant suncream application: I guess that one isn't ever going anywhere. And lastly: hating going on holiday with ye, but I guess going on holiday with ye might not be so bad these days."

His laugh was low and gruff. "Except for having to keep your hands off me for ten days."

"Oh God, I didn't think of that. Ah well, back to a list of two, then."

On my bedside table Trystan's phone buzzed, and I reached over to get it for him.

"Josh?" I asked as he gave another low chuckle.

"Looks like me and my brother might be in the same boat for this weekend."

Actually, I imagined Josh would be in considerably better shape than Trystan. But I planned on keeping that quiet for as long as possible.

"He all right?" I asked instead.

"Seems so. He wants me to tell you thanks."

I gave a long sigh of relief and tucked myself back in against Trystan's side. He was warm and slightly damp and solid, and his breathing deepened as he fell asleep. I listened to it as I lay awake thinking about what I had done to end up here. There was a voice at the back of my head trying to tell me all the things that could go wrong. But I ignored it, because Trystan trusted me, and for now, that was all I wanted.

HT PANTU is from the countryside in the north of England but has lived in a lot of places because she's not too good at staying put. In her case the stereotypes are true: she loves tea a little too much, drinks beer in the local pub, and talks about the incessant rain (or the lack of it depending on the time of year and state of the hosepipe ban). Her favorite term of endearment is Pumpkin and she doesn't swear unless she's really angry, because she finds it funny watching people's reaction to her primary school cursing. She started writing at fifteen when the stories in her head got too complicated to keep track of. Since then she has only stopped when publications of a less fictional nature were required of her.

See the inside of her head at http://ht-pantu.tumblr.com/.

http://www.dreamspinnerpress.com

PRIDE
AND MODERN
PREJUDICE

AJ MICHAELS

http://www.dreamspinnerpress.com

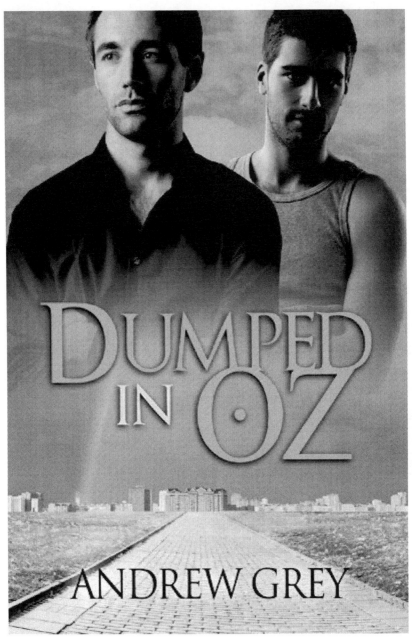

DUMPED IN OZ

ANDREW GREY

http://www.dreamspinnerpress.com

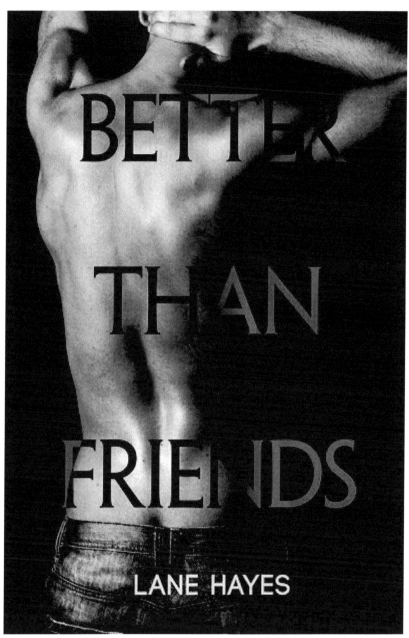

BETTER THAN FRIENDS

LANE HAYES

http://www.dreamspinnerpress.com

Printed in Poland
by Amazon Fulfillment
Poland Sp. z o.o., Wrocław